Battlenaut Crucible

By Robert Jeschonek

FIRST PIE PRESS EDITION, APRIL 2014

www.piepresspublishing.com

The text was set in Minion Pro and Garamond.
Book design by Robert T. Jeschonek

ISBN-10: 0692023356
ISBN-13: 978-0692023358

No one can see the Red Battlenauts except Corporal Scott...

As soon as the two Red Battlenauts hit the ground, the forward cannons on their chests surged to life, glowing with bright golden energy.

"Incoming!" Corporal Scott's pulse quickened. "Chest-mounted energy cannons about to fire!" Everyone was on their feet now--including Khalil and García--and they were all blasting away with slugs and lasers. Half the squad fired at the ten o'clock target, while the other half focused on two o'clock...though they all maintained a loose formation around Scott. Protecting him was more crucial than ever, now that the A.I.s were blind.

Not that Scott planned to hold back any. As the squad pounded away at the Reds, he was right in there, cranking off rounds at both enemy war machines--firing with his left arm gun at ten o'clock while his right arm fired at two.

Suddenly, the Reds' cannons flared and fired. Each Battlenaut unleashed two streams of searing golden energy, sending them blazing over the silver ground toward the Diamondbacks.

Scott sucked in a breath and held it. One of the beams was coming in from two o'clock at an angle that would lead right to him. Even if his squadmates or their A.I.s could have seen it, they wouldn't have been able to do anything to stop it in time.

Scott was about to find out the hard way if CORE armor measured up to Red weapons technology. The same kind of beam that had blown his armor to bits on Chelong III was streaking straight for him and would make contact in a heartbeat...

DEDICATION

To Gordon R. Dickson,
Robert A. Heinlein,
and George Lucas,
for rallying the troops
out among the stars.

CHAPTER 1

Corporal Solomon Scott held his gray-plated Mark VI Battlenaut armor perfectly still in the thick white mist. Around him lay the broken armor of two opponents, dead pilots who'd fought to the last for the cause of the Rightful rebels. Scott had killed them both just moments ago in a firefight that had left his own armor damaged.

Unfortunately, the larger battle going on around him was nowhere near finished. According to comm traffic and the telemetry displayed on the visor of his helmet, dozens of Battlenauts were still smashing the hell out of each other in all directions. The battle for the Commonwealth outpost on planetoid Chelong III was still raging, the outcome up in the air.

But the big picture wasn't the main thing on Scott's mind at the moment. He was more concerned about where the next attack on his own armor would come from and how he'd survive it with a breach in his belly plating.

Tapping buttons on the left armrest keypad, he switched views on the visor, superimposing the telemetry data over feeds from the onboard cameras. As far as he could tell, there was nothing nearby...but the mists of Chelong swirled with crystalline particles that played tricks on sensors as well as eyes.

As he stared at the feed from his aft cameras, the smell of sweat and metal in the cockpit grew sharper, and the hairs on his neck stood up straight. He thought he glimpsed a flicker of movement and gripped the stick tight, ready to fire his rear-mounted guns.

But nothing bounded out of the mist back there, and he didn't shoot. No problem; he was good at keeping a cool head.

Not that anything else in the cockpit of his Mark VI was cool at that point. One of the topside cooling vents had taken a hit, and the whole rig was overheating like crazy. Sweat ran down his sides and soaked every part of him. At least the padded halo mount inside his helmet kept the sweat from running into his eyes and burning the crap out of them.

He was flipping between camera views again when Captain Rollins got on the horn. "Echo Charlie Bravo!" The man's gravelly voice burst from the comm speaker. "Stop standing around, Scott! Dewar and Shen need backup! I just flashed you the stats!"

As promised, Dewar and Shen's telemetry appeared on the visor. They were thirty meters to the right, both taking heavy hits...but from what? It didn't look like there was anyone else in their immediate vicinity. Was the mist screwing with their sensors?

"Damnit, Scott," snapped Rollins. "Get your ass moving!"

Suddenly, something caught his eye on the feed from the rightside camera. He played the armrest keypad, clearing the telemetry data from the visor screen and punching the rightside feed to maximum magnification. "Stand by, sir." He saw nothing...nothing...

Then *something.* A glint, a spark, a flicker in the fog.

"The hell with stand by!" Rollins' voice became a roar. "Shen just went down!"

Scott brought the telemetry back up and saw Shen's specs crashing hard. She was alive, but her armor was fried.

And whatever had fried it was out there somewhere in a rightside direction, exactly where Scott had seen the glint.

Rollins was still roaring over the comm, but Scott blocked him out. His neck hairs were still up, his gut was twisting; telemetry said nothing was out there, but his instincts told him otherwise.

Jaws clenched, he ran spectral overlays on the feed, scanning the full range of infrared and ultraviolet frequencies. Still nothing.

He cut his audio mic so he could talk to himself. "Come on, you piece of *oosh.* I know you're out there."

Scott threw all five feeds on-visor at once--rightside, leftside, frontside, backside, topside--and hit them all with the spectral overlays. Still, he saw no telltale signs of an enemy Battlenaut in any direction.

His instincts were usually good, but maybe they were off this one time. He'd been in battle before; even without actual fog, things could get confusing in the thick of it.

Just then, something Rollins was shouting broke through. "Dewar is down! Get over there *now*, you son of a..."

Grabbing the stick, Scott brought his Battlenaut back

to life. He was just about to turn it toward Shen and Dewar when he spotted a blip on the radar. It only lasted a split-second, but it was enough to jolt him into action.

The monitors tracking his vital signs pinged faster across the board. The radar blip had appeared not to the right of him, but the *left.*

Whatever was coming, whatever had taken out Shen and Dewar, it had managed to circle around him.

Instead of turning right, Scott swung his Battlenaut left. At the same time, he played the armrest keypad, jumping all weapons out of standby mode.

That was when he saw the Red Battlenaut for the first time.

It burst out of the mist with guns blazing, marching straight toward him. It was bigger than his own Battlenaut armor--twelve meters tall compared to ten for the Mark VI--with skin that gleamed bright red from tip to toe. And there wasn't a mark on it that Scott could see.

Without thought or hesitation, Scott opened fire with his main guns. At the same time, he threw a half-dozen missiles at the Red. He needed to hit it hard and fast, not give it a chance to get at his damaged belly plating.

Slugs from the Red's guns peppered the Mark VI, pocking the shielding over the cockpit. His own missiles hit the Red's chest in a cluster, exploding with shuddering force.

But they didn't slow it down or leave a scratch.

"What the *flux*?" Scott opened up with his lasers and sonics at the same time, focusing on what he hoped was a weak spot--the backward-flexing knee joint of one leg. The armor narrowed there and lacked any visible shield plating.

Unfortunately, that didn't mean it was any weaker. The searing crimson beam from Scott's laser tagged the joint, accompanied by waves of oscillating vibratory force...but the Red didn't slow down a bit.

Scott clenched his teeth and stepped his Battlenaut back, then leaped forward, propelling his armor's shoulder toward the Red.

He was met by a shower of heavy slugs thudding into his plating, but they didn't stop him. His Mark VI covered the distance in seconds and slammed into the Red with its full weight and momentum.

Collision alarms wailed, and damage reports flashed on his visor. His vital signs spiked, and his head swam from the powerful impact. It had been a hell of a hit.

And apparently, it hadn't done any damage. The Red stood firmly in place; according to Scott's sensors, its armor hadn't buckled or ruptured in the slightest.

But that wasn't the worst of it. As Scott tried to push his Battlenaut back, he quickly realized it was stuck. He couldn't break away from the Red.

Cursing, he summoned new sensor data on the Red Battlenaut. According to the numbers, the Red's skin had become highly magnetized; its grip was more than strong enough to resist the full torque of Scott's armor's fusion-powered servos.

Seconds after he realized this, two panels popped open on the Red's chest, and twin circular blades mounted on extensible arms spun toward him. A heartbeat later, they were biting into the armor plating over Scott's cockpit, sending up showers of sparks.

Scott flipped on the mic and shouted over the grinding screech of the blades. "Mayday! Echo Charlie Bravo! Mayday!"

The blades cut fast, shearing their way through the

super-hardened metal of Scott's armor like it was cardboard. Sensors showed the cockpit would be breached in less than a minute.

Scott jabbed the keypad, prepping all weapons to fire at once. It was a desperate move, but he couldn't think of anything else.

Not at first, anyway.

What would Bern do? The question flashed through his mind like a flame running down a trail of lit fuel. Bern was an inspiration to him, the reason he'd become a Commonwealth Marine in the first place. She was his grandmother, and she'd been a hero in an earlier war.

What would Bern do?

Suddenly, an idea flared to life. He would barely have time to try it; the blades were about to penetrate the shell of the cockpit.

Scott's fingers flew over both armrest keypads as he hastily shot commands into the armor's control network. Twice, he had to override fail-safes with pass codes and retinal scans.

"Yeah, I know," he said after jumping the last hurdle. "The armor wasn't built for this. Safety specs exceeded. Blah blah blah."

Just then, the Red's dual blades screamed through the armor, whirling mere inches away from his face. His flesh, skull, and brain were seconds from splattering all over the cockpit.

"Let's see how *you* like it." Scott sneered as he punched the last button. His heart was hammering, adrenaline searing through his bloodstream...and now he'd made his last play.

The lights and displays in the cockpit flickered and went out. The fusion power plant in the bowels of the Mark VI roared, and the armor rumbled violently. All around him, he heard a loud, sizzling crackle and hum.

Suddenly, the Red's blades stopped spinning and shot back toward the slits they'd cut. One popped right out, while the other twisted and caught on the edge of the slit. It pulled hard, working its way free--then snapped off the stem on which it was mounted and clattered down into the bowels of Scott's armor.

"*Now* we're talkin'." Scott braced himself against the cockpit couch and waited for what was coming. He'd fought fire with fire, charging his armor with streams of electrical current from the power plant, turning his Battlenaut into an electromagnet. An electromagnet with the same polarity as the Red Battlenaut.

Since two magnets with the same polarity repel each other, the two Battlenauts could no longer stay locked together. With a loud clang, Scott's armor shot away from the Red and crashed to the dusty ground.

"Yeah!" Scott scrambled in the cockpit, redirecting power from his Battlenaut's skin to the rest of its parts. The lights quickly came back up, and the control system rebooted. His helmet visor flickered back to life in a matter of seconds.

Just in time for him to see the Red stomping toward him.

Scott pounded the keypads and worked the stick, fighting to get his armor back on its feet. Servos hummed as he got the Mark VI to sit up, then roll to one side and brace itself with both gauntlets on the ground.

Meanwhile, the Red kept coming. Scott saw it march closer on his visor's video feed, even as he rolled his own armor onto its knees.

"Come on!" His Battlenaut lurched its upper body

erect. Scott hammered buttons, and it drew up one knee, planting its right foot firmly under it.

He felt the ground shake as the Red stormed closer. Why it hadn't already opened fire, he couldn't guess.

Wrenching the stick, he focused the armor's power on the right leg, trying to push up and bring the other foot forward. Once he had both feet flat under him, he'd have the leverage to get the whole unit standing again.

But would he have time to finish the maneuver? The Red's footsteps were getting closer, its image growing larger in the visor video feed.

Scott smelled burning metal and plastic. Servos whined, the armor wobbled...and the legs locked up. The right leg got stuck halfway up, leaving the left foot jammed toe-first in the dirt, unable to flatten and fully extend the leg above it.

Cursing a blue streak, he fought the controls...and then it was too late. Proximity alarms squealed, and the Red Battlenaut suddenly towered over him.

Scott ground his teeth and scowled. Looking past the visor, he saw gleaming red metal fill the blast-tempered glass of the forward viewport.

It wasn't about getting on his feet anymore. The best he thought he could hope for was to take advantage of the Red's close range and unload everything he had.

Is that what Bern would do? Scott took a deep breath, then released it through his teeth. *Hell, yes.*

He counted to three, then played the keypads, quickly bringing every onboard weapon to bear on the Red looming over him. Without pausing, he keyed the system-wide fire command, letting everything loose at once.

Slugs poured up from his guns, bracketed by crimson streams of laser energy. Sonic blasts rippled out of his emitters, and the full complement of missiles leaped from their racks.

The Red took every bit of it without flinching. When the smoke cleared, it was still standing over him, shiny and unmarred as ever.

"Flux *me*." Scott's voice was soft in the cockpit. Sensor data scrolled on the visor before him, displaying the lack of damage in columns of figures that left him stunned.

It didn't seem possible. How could a Battlenaut take that much firepower at close range and not suffer the slightest damage?

No Battlenaut he'd ever seen or fought or heard of could do it, that was for sure. The Red was something new, something completely outside his experience. It was the kind of thing that could win the civil war between the Commonwealth and the Rightfuls.

It was also the kind of thing that could kill him with ease.

Switching to the image from his topside camera, he saw the Red lean down and aim its forward cannons at him. Yellow and red plasma danced in the heart of both barrels as the guns powered up and made ready to fire.

This is it. Even as the words burned in his mind, Scott recalibrated his own lasers, guns, and sonics, bringing them to bear on the Red. He also tripped the self-destruct and started the 60-second countdown; maybe his exploding fusion power plant would finally put a scratch in the Red Battlenaut's hide.

He felt zero fear as the glowing red digits on his visor ticked from 60 seconds to 50 to 40. He wasn't a fearless man, but death itself didn't scare him; it hadn't frightened him since the time he'd died at the age of thirteen. He'd come back a different person...a Marine in the making even then.

The digits read 30...then 20. *Come and get me*, he thought as he opened up hard with all weapons, frying circuits and emptying out his remaining ammo.

Nothing he did seemed to faze the Red Battlenaut at all. When the Red suddenly straightened, it did so with no sign of strain, as if the barrage had nothing to do with its choice of movement.

That's okay, thought Scott. "You'll notice *this*." He grinned wickedly as he watched the countdown on the visor tick from 20 to 15.

And then to 10.

Scott hooted and howled and kept pouring on the punishment. The timer changed to nine, then eight, then seven, then six...

And that was when the Red Battlenaut abruptly charged away from him.

"*Scudge*!" With the timer at four seconds, Scott put the self-destruct on hold. He threw all camera feeds on the visor at once, looking for the Red that had gotten away.

But it was already gone, vanished into the dense mist.

Suddenly, the voice of Captain Rollins burst out of the speaker. "Echo Charlie Bravo! This is Kilo Papa Zulu, responding to your Mayday!"

"About time," said Scott, and then he flipped on the mic. "Watch your six, Kilo! There's some kind of souped-up Red Battlenaut on the loose!"

"I've got eyes on you, Scott." As Rollins said it, Scott spotted him on his leftside camera. "Looks like you've taken a beating."

No kidding. "Recommend you call additional backup,

Kilo Papa." Scott's eyes roamed the feeds, watching for signs of his red-hulled foe. "I threw everything I had at that thing, and it didn't even chip the paint."

"I didn't see it on radar or telemetry," said Rollins as he walked his sand brown Battlenaut toward Scott. "How long ago was it here?"

"Thirty seconds before you arrived," said Scott. "At the most."

"Well, it's gone now," said Rollins. "And no reports of a Red Battlenaut elsewhere, either."

"Trust me, it's out there," said Scott. "And I'm telling you, the damn thing's a *colossus*."

Searchlights flared to life on Rollins' armor, combing the mist around him on all sides. "Must be fast, too, if it ran out of sensor range just before I got here."

"Must be." Even as Scott said it, he didn't think it rang true. If the Red had been a speedster, wouldn't it have beaten him a lot faster? Wouldn't it have crushed him before he could get in any shots?

"Wish I could get my hands on this thing." Rollins kept combing the mist with his searchlights. "Sounds like the kind of tech we could put to good use."

Just then, Scott glimpsed a flicker of movement on his frontside feed, in the mist behind Rollins. "Bogie on your six!"

Rollins spun and focused his forward light on the mist. "You sure about that? Sensors read all clear."

There it was again. "Bogie confirmed!"

Rollins aimed his guns at the area in question. "I don't see it, Corporal."

Suddenly, there it was--the same Red Battlenaut, stalking out of the mist...heading straight for Rollins.

"Incoming!" Playing the stick, Scott rocked his armor back and forth, trying to get it unstuck. "Repeat, incoming!"

"What are you talking about? There's nothing out there." As Rollins said it, his forward light shone directly on the red behemoth marching toward him.

"Can't you *see* it?" Scott's heart hammered. Servos whined, then whirred as he regained control of his Battlenaut's right leg. He straightened it, then pulled the left foot up from where it was wedged and flexed it forward, planting it solidly on the ground. Finally, he was back on his feet.

But he was too late to help his C.O. "All I see is fog," said Rollins, even though the Red Battlenaut was storming toward him in the beam of his own searchlight. "Nothing's there."

It was that exact moment when the Red came to a stop, standing fewer than two meters away. Its forward cannons glowed with roiling energy about to be unleashed.

And then it was unleashed. Twin beams of concentrated golden energy blasted point blank at Rollins' armor.

"No!" Scott couldn't shoot from where he stood for fear of hitting Rollins. He rushed his Battlenaut forward and around until he had an open line of sight.

Rollins' screams over the comm filled his ears...but not for long. Just as Scott started firing, Rollins' Battlenaut exploded. There were no more screams after that.

Then, the Red charged toward Scott with cannons blazing.

The same beams of golden energy that had obliterated Rollins crashed into Scott's armor, stopping him dead in his tracks. The lights in the cockpit flickered, and he knew what he had to do next.

Eject or die.

His armor shrieked as the Red's energy beams blasted it. Sucking in a deep breath, Scott swung his left hand out and smacked the big red button on the cockpit wall.

For a second, nothing happened. The lights dipped, the control systems shut down, and the ejection sequence was interrupted.

Then, everything flashed back to life. The top of the Mark VI blew off, and the cockpit couch launched upward.

As the couch gained altitude, Scott saw his Battlenaut blow to pieces under the Red's assault far below. If the colossus knew the armor's occupant had escaped, it gave no sign--just stormed through the flames and debris and disappeared into the mist.

Then, Scott went higher and lost sight of the whole scene. As the couch leveled off, following its programmed autopilot coordinates to get him to safety, he found himself staring up at the pale gray sky.

Fighter craft zigged and zagged far above him, firing lasers and missiles at each other. A massive carrier ship hung in the distance, a Commonwealth vessel dispatching fresh fighters and Battlenaut reinforcements. A Rightful destroyer cruised toward it, unleashing a fusillade of missiles.

It would all be over soon. If the Rightfuls had an army of Red Battlenauts at their disposal, they would make short work of the Commonwealth forces on every front. They would tear down the Commonwealth government in nothing flat and institute their own form of domination.

Because nothing he knew could oppose the Red Battlenaut. His own Captain hadn't even been able to *see* it when it had been right in front of him.

Which left Solomon Scott with just one question to

consider as the cockpit couch whisked him through the raging battle: why had *he* been able to see it when Rollins hadn't?

CHAPTER 2

A week later, Scott sat at a table in the canteen at the Commonwealth base on Ovid VI, sipping lousy coffee from a chipped black mug. The canteen--a no-frills shed with colorful flags of Commonwealth worlds slapped on the drab metal walls--was packed with Marines, all eating and drinking and talking and laughing.

But none of them were talking to Scott. None were anywhere near him.

Ever since the battle of Chelong III, people had kept their distance. There were too many questions about the deaths of Shen, Dewar, and Captain Rollins, and not enough concrete answers.

Scott had stood by his story, but there wasn't much proof to support it. Apparently, the Red Battlenaut had left behind zero trace of itself--no spent shells or debris or even tracks. As for telemetry, the only recorded trace was the unidentifiable split-second blip from Scott's radar. The rest of the sensor data and video, flashed to remote backup servers when Scott's armor exploded, showed nothing. The same video feeds on which he'd watched the Red Battlenaut in action now showed nothing but misty backdrops from the planet's surface...and, eventually, Captain Rollins' Battlenaut exploding.

In the end, the only traces of Battlenaut activity from the site belonged to Scott, Rollins, and the two Rightfuls whom Scott had taken down before the Red's arrival. The only spent ammo found at the scene belonged to Scott and the dead Rightfuls. So, naturally, there was a shadow over Scott regarding the death of Rollins. Naturally, people weren't going out of their way to get next to him.

That was why he was so surprised when someone finally tapped him on the shoulder.

Looking back, he saw a tall officer towering over him, gazing down with a stony stare. He had three visible scars: one on his left cheek; one stretching from his left temple along the right side of his nose to his jaw; and one winding around his throat, starting at his right earlobe and disappearing into his collar over his left clavicle.

But the scars weren't the most striking things about him. His uniform made the strongest impression; it was black as deep space from collar to boots, with the triple triangular emblem of a major on each sleeve and a single silver insignia pinned to the chest: the stylized gaping maw and fangs of a striking serpent.

The man belonged to CORE--the Covert Operations Response Elite. He was part of the most elite special forces unit in the Commonwealth military--or any military in the known galaxy, for that matter.

This couldn't be good.

Scott rose from his chair and snapped off a salute. "Sir." Even standing, he still found himself looking up. The CORE officer was a full head taller than he was.

The major returned his salute. "At ease, Corporal." He nodded once and pulled a chair out from the table. "Take a load off."

As Scott settled back into his seat, he scanned the room. Almost everyone in the canteen was looking his way or pretending not to. It wasn't every day that one of the gods from CORE deigned to grace them with his presence.

"I'm Major Perseid." The CORE man leaned forward and folded his hands on the dented steel surface of the table. "Major Jack Perseid." He didn't add that he was with CORE; he didn't have to. "I need a moment of your time."

Scott shrugged and tried not to show how nervous he was. "Yes, sir." Perseid didn't look much older than Scott was, but the fact that he was CORE--and seeking out Scott in spite of the cloud over his fate--instantly put Scott on the defensive.

It didn't help when Perseid locked a piercing stare on him. "Let's talk about what happened on Chelong III." His brown eyes were so dark, they were like two black holes. "Let's talk about the Red Battlenaut."

Scott's curiosity was piqued. "Okay." The Marine Investigative Service--the MIS--was already handling his case. Why the hell would a CORE officer have anything to do with it? As far as Scott knew, CORE hadn't even been deployed on Chelong III.

"I've read the report," said Perseid. "It's a pretty amazing story, if it's true."

Scott bristled. "It's true." He matched Perseid's stare with unblinking intensity. "Every word of it."

Perseid nodded slowly. "You're saying this thing was invisible to the naked eye of a seasoned Marine Captain equipped with the latest optical viewing technology."

"Yes, sir," said Scott.

"Yet *you* were able to see it."

Scott nodded. "Yes, sir."

Perseid stared silently for a moment. "You're also saying it left absolutely no trace of itself. No spent ammo, no tracks, no video or data record."

"Except for a blip on the radar, yes, sir."

Perseid nodded and looked around as if to make sure no one was listening. When he turned his head left, Scott realized a fourth scar was visible--a bare strip amid the dark stubble on the back of his scalp, a semicircle running from the crown of his skull to the nape of his neck.

"Well, guess what?" Perseid leaned closer and dropped his voice. "You're wrong."

Scott couldn't help glaring. "Negative, sir." He was sick and tired of people acting like he was somehow to blame for what had happened to Rollins. "I have never been more *right* about anything in my *life*. My memory is *crystal* clear."

"I'm not questioning your memory, Corporal," said Perseid. "I'm talking about the *evidence*."

"The evidence supports my story," snapped Scott. "The wreckage of Captain Rollins' Battlenaut shows scoring from lasers with significantly higher power than those mounted in my armor. I may have been firing weapons when the Captain died, but nothing in my arsenal could have blown apart a Battlenaut like that."

Suddenly, Perseid slapped his hand down hard on the table. Scott had been about to say something else, but he clamped his mouth shut instead.

"You might have *been* there, Corporal," said Perseid, "but you don't know everything about the *evidence*." He raised his eyebrows, and then he got up from his chair. "Would you like me to *show* you what you don't know?"

Scott stared at Perseid but couldn't get a good read on him. If Perseid meant to do him harm--if he was trying to entrap him somehow--Scott couldn't tell. The only thing he knew for sure was that he had to play along. He couldn't say no to a CORE officer...and even if that was an option, he wouldn't do it. He couldn't walk away without finding out what Perseid knew about evidence related to his case. If there was more to the story of what had happened on Chelong III, he had to know what it was.

"All right." Scott downed the last of his cold coffee, plunked the mug on the table, and got up from his chair. "If you've got something to show me, then show me."

For the first time, Perseid managed a slight smile. It looked like it took an effort. "As long as you don't have anywhere better to be right now."

"No, sir," said Scott. "Not at the moment."

Perseid started for the door. "Then let's get this show on the road, Corporal."

CHAPTER 3

Perseid led Scott to a wheeled transport in front of the canteen--a sleek black car, low to the ground, with tinted windows. It looked more like it belonged on a race track than a military base at the edge of a war zone.

Perseid hopped in without a word, and Scott followed. He thought briefly about saying how cool the car was, then decided not to. Why stroke the god's ego? It was probably big enough already.

Perseid started the engine and pulled out of his parking spot. "So you're from Tack." It wasn't a question. "In my experience, Tackers are the biggest pains in the ass in the galaxy."

Scott kept staring straight ahead and shrugged.

"That's been my experience," said Perseid, "as a native-born Tacker myself." Then, he jammed the accelerator pedal to the floor, and the car took off at a high rate of speed.

For a long moment, Scott remained silent. "What part

of Tack are you from?" He thought he should watch what he said, but he also didn't think it would help to keep his mouth shut and say nothing at all.

"Gratus." Perseid swerved left, nearly hitting an oncoming truck head-on. "I was raised on a farm near Yole, in the Scadlands. And you?"

Scott figured Perseid already knew everything about him, but what the heck. "Tisserie, near Vast."

"So you're a Vastie." Perseid spun the steering wheel, and the car shot right, barreling between sheds down a passage that looked too narrow to let it through. "Plus, all that Marine blood in your family. That explains a few things."

"What things does it explain, exactly?" Scott wasn't sure what Perseid was getting at, but he thought he might be on bumpy ground. Grandma Bern's heroic reputation and rank as Commandant of the entire Marine Corps had stirred up a lot of resentment toward him over the years.

"Your outstanding record," said Perseid. "Your extensive commendations. Your clear commitment to excellence." He bolted the car out of the narrow passage and whipped down a wider road lined with Battlenaut armor undergoing repair and maintenance. "You've had to work harder to prove yourself. You've had to fight harder every step of the way, because of who you are--because you're *her* grandson." He said it like a simple fact, like he'd known Scott all his life and was just stating the obvious.

Scott blinked. Perseid's insight had probably come from a psych profile--but still. It had been right on the money.

"That's a *good* thing," said Perseid. "It gives you credibility. It gives you strength of character." Even as he raced around a super-tight left turn, he looked at Scott and smirked. "It makes you exactly what we're looking for."

Scott frowned. What was Perseid talking about? And what did it have to do with the evidence he was supposedly going to show him?

"Almost there." Perseid went even faster, heading for a row of half-cylindrical buildings up ahead. "Better buckle up."

Scott looked at his seat belt. "I'm already buckled up."

"No." Perseid smirked and pointed at his forehead. "I mean *in here*."

On the outside, the building looked nondescript, one of many identical prefab metal structures on base. Guards stood on either side of the front door; otherwise, there were no signs of life.

But the inside of the place was another matter. It was sheer chaos in there.

As Scott followed Perseid through the front door, he heard the sound of breaking glass and shouting. Looking past Perseid, he saw a brawny woman with spiky blonde hair haul off and shove a short dark-skinned man with a white crew cut. Both of them wore all-black CORE uniforms like Perseid.

"What the *hell*, Abby!" the man shouted. "So I dropped a damn *beaker*."

"And corrupted the *sample*, Trane!" Abby's feet crunched broken glass as she shoved him again. "We don't have much to *work* with, remember?"

Trane stumbled back a step and bumped into some kind of multi-pronged silver instrument mounted on a black tripod, nearly knocking it over. The whole place was jammed with high tech scientific gear of every conceivable type, piled on the floor, hanging from the ceiling, overflowing from benches and cases and crates.

In the middle of it all, floating in midair over a glowing neon blue dais, Scott saw something familiar. Its image appeared on computer screens all over the room, altered one way or another by different analytical techniques, superimposed with charts and graphs and streams of data... but instantly recognizable.

After all, he could never forget something that had almost killed him a week ago.

He couldn't take his eyes off it. "Where did you get that?" he asked Perseid.

"We found it in what was left of your armor." Perseid smirked and elbowed him in the side. "I *told* you you didn't know everything about the evidence."

"But they said..." Scott scowled and shook his head. "They told me there was *nothing.* They said there was no *trace* of the Red Battlenaut."

"Do the words 'top secret' ring a bell?" said Perseid.

Just then, Abby finally seemed to notice they were there. "Hey!" She stomped a step toward them and planted her fists on her hips. "Who the *scudge* is *this*? What's the big *idea,* Major?"

"Whoa." Trane stepped up beside her and grinned a lopsided grin at Scott. "Is this *him*? Is this the *guy*?"

"Roger that." Perseid nodded and smacked Scott on the back. "This is the guy."

"Corporal Solomon Scott." Abby narrowed her eyes and cocked her head to one side. "The man who sees Red Battlenauts."

"Red Battlenaut *singular,*" said Scott. "I only saw the one."

Trane chuckled. "That's one more than *most* people have ever seen."

"He's also the only person to bring back a piece of one." Perseid walked over to gaze down at the object floating in the glow of the neon blue dais. "It was jammed in a chunk of housing among the debris from his exploded Battlenaut armor."

Scott stared at the object's image on one of the screens. It was a small silver disk with a gleaming, sharpened edge, a circular blade mounted on a broken stem of polished red metal. The last time he'd seen it, it had cut a slit through his armor and almost sliced its way through his face.

"It broke off when I magnetized the armor plating," he said. "Fell down into the guts somewhere."

"So your after action report wasn't complete hoozehock." Perseid tapped the floating blade with a fingertip, making it spin in the levitational field. "This proves the existence of the Red Battlenaut and exonerates you of all possible charges."

"Yes, sir." Scott suppressed the urge to smile. "I guess it does."

"Guess again." Perseid spun the blade once more. "'Top secret,' remember?"

Scott frowned. "Excuse me?"

"This is top secret." Perseid pointed at the blade. "MIS doesn't know it exists. Therefore, your case remains open. You are still a person of interest in the death of Captain Rollins."

Scott gaped at the blade floating over the dais. It was right there in the open, within reach. "But the evidence..."

Perseid stood in front of the floating blade and folded his arms over his chest. "The evidence has more important things to do than get you off the hook, Corporal."

Scott stood for a moment, glaring at Perseid. "Why did you bring me here? Why did you show me this..." He gestured in the direction of the blade. "...if you aren't going to use it to clear my name?"

Abby leaned forward and sneered at him. "Just to *screw* with you, flux-head."

"To savor your *anguish* when we snatch away your last *hope*," said Trane, bugging his eyes wide and unleashing a burst of demented laughter that Abby quickly joined in on.

Scott was about to storm out when Perseid raised his hands, and the laughter stopped. "Because we need you, Solomon." He looked dead serious as he met Scott's gaze. "We need you to help us stop the Red Battlenaut."

"Do I have a choice?" said Scott.

"Do you even *need* one?" said Perseid. "This is the outcome of the *war* we're talking about here."

Scott shook his head. "I've already been reassigned, haven't I?"

Perseid straightened and headed for the door. "Come with me, Corporal. Your briefing awaits."

CHAPTER 4

Scott didn't say a word as Perseid led him out of the lab building. He was too busy trying to wrap his head around what was happening.

Not to mention, he was irritated. After all the interrogation, all the worrying, and all the crap he'd taken since Rollins' death, CORE had had hard evidence that proved his story all along. Not only had they held it back during the investigation so far, but they had no intention of releasing it anytime soon.

As far as the Marines were concerned, there was still a cloud over him. He might even be found guilty of an infraction or worse. And now, he was being pulled into some other cluster-flux all together.

Things felt like they were flying out of control fast.

"This way, Corporal." Perseid marched over the gray, dusty ground toward the next building over, another half-cylindrical metal structure, completely nondescript. How many times had Scott been past here since Chelong III without realizing what lay inside?

This time, when Perseid led him through the front door, Scott found himself in a sparsely-furnished conference room instead of a cluttered lab. A long green plastic table dominated the space, surrounded by a dozen folding metal chairs.

Only one of those chairs was occupied, and not for long. A woman in a black CORE uniform jumped to her feet instantly and saluted. Her appearance was striking: she had short red hair, a blazing bright smile, and emerald eyes that sparkled and flashed from all the way across the room.

Scott's heart beat faster as she walked toward them.

"Major Perseid." Her voice was high-pitched and strong, with a firm and friendly tone. "All ready for you, sir."

"Thank you, Captain." He nodded at Scott. "This is the guy."

When she looked at him, Scott was sure her smile got bigger. "Good to meet you, Corporal Scott. I'm Captain Cyan Rexis." She extended her hand.

Scott smiled and shook it. "Good to meet you, too, Captain." For the first time since Perseid had approached him in the canteen, he felt completely at ease...almost. The feel of her soft hand in his rattled him in other ways, all of them good.

"Shall we begin?" Rexis looked to Perseid, and he nodded. "Fantastic." Releasing Scott's hand, she crossed the room and grabbed a rectangular remote control from the table. When she pressed a spot on its control surface, the room lights dimmed and the far wall brightened, becoming a screen. "Please, take a seat."

Perseid sat near the middle of the table on one side, and

Scott sat across from him. Rexis watched with a smile as they settled in, then turned to the screen.

"The Red Battlenaut." She worked the remote, and a computer-generated image of a Red Battlenaut appeared on the wall-screen. It didn't look much like the one Scott had fought, other than the fact that it was a Battlenaut and it was colored red. "You're the first to report having seen one, Corporal Scott. But we don't think you're the first to encounter one."

Intrigued, Scott leaned forward and folded his arms on the table.

"We think Red Battlenauts have been very active in the current conflict," said Rexis.

"Active but unseen," added Perseid. "An unknown third party intervening in the course of the war."

Rexis pressed a button, and the screen changed to show graphs and columns of data. "During the past month, reports of unexplained damage and loss of life among Commonwealth forces under battlefield conditions have increased significantly. Even accounting for inaccurate reporting and statistical error, our algorithmic analyses reveal a sharp upward trend." She pointed the remote at the screen, and a plotted line on a graph lit up yellow, highlighting a sudden rise. "In some cases, no one was left alive to testify about what happened. In other cases, surviving witnesses reported inexplicable assaults conducted by what could only have been an invisible opponent."

"Invisible to telemetry as well as the naked eye," said Perseid.

Rexis pressed another button, and the screen showed a photo of metallic debris on a background of red dirt. "Examination of remains in all cases was inconclusive.

Investigators found evidence of scoring by ultra-high energy lasers...and nothing more." She flashed a look in Scott's direction. "Just like in your case."

Scott nodded. "So I'm not the first."

A map of the space sector appeared on-screen, with the systems of the Commonwealth on the right side, colored bright blue, and the Rightful systems--far fewer in number--in yellow on the left. Between them ran a jagged red border, the front line of the civil war. Blinking red dots were scattered along the length of the line, and in some cases well over the line in Commonwealth or Rightful space.

"All these are the locations of suspect incidents." Rexis waved the remote at the screen, and the red dots blinked brighter. There were *dozens* of them. "As you can see, we have identified quite a few."

"Wow." Scott stared at the screen and shook his head. "All that in one month?"

"There have to be more than one of them," said Rexis. "There's no other possible way they could make this much activity happen over these distances in this time frame."

"Though, until now, we had no idea what 'they' were," said Perseid. "You're the first to provide an actual description of the weapon."

"*And* survive an attack by one," said Rexis.

"And bring back a *piece* of one," added Perseid. "You've given us a description and physical evidence in one fell swoop. Now if we could just figure out how the hell you *did* it when no one *else* could."

Scott shrugged. "You haven't figured it out?"

Rexis changed the image on the screen to a set of graphs and tables and medical data. "We've gone over the results of the physical exam you were given after the battle, compared them to your baseline, and compared all that to the data from other personnel involved in Red Battlenaut non-sightings. We've gone over it all a hundred times, from every conceivable approach, and we've got nothing." She spread her arms wide. "Whatever it is that lets you see the Red Battlenaut, we haven't found it yet."

"And that's our priority," said Perseid. "Finding your secret and putting it to use so we can fight these things." He cleared his throat and looked at Rexis. "Though we have another priority, too."

"Tracking the source of the evidence you've obtained." Rexis pressed a button on the remote, and the screen switched back to the map of the sector with the blinking red dots along the front line. "We want to locate the source of the Red Battlenauts."

"And destroy them before they fulfill their agenda," said Perseid. "Whatever that might be."

Scott looked at Perseid, then Rexis, then Perseid again. "Isn't it obvious? The Reds are the Rightfuls' secret weapon. They want to defeat the Commonwealth, right?"

"Negative." Perseid got up and walked to the screen. "According to intelligence, the Reds may be attacking Rightful troops as well as Commonwealth forces. At least seventy percent of these incidents involve unexplained losses on both sides." He ran his finger down along the jagged front line on the map. "Whoever's controlling the Red Battlenauts, it isn't the Commonwealth *or* the Rightfuls."

Scott sat back in his chair, stunned by what he'd heard. If the Red Battlenauts weren't working for either side in the civil war, who *were* they working for? And what did their controllers *want*?

"So now you're seeing the big picture, aren't you?"

Perseid stepped away from the screen and sat on the corner of the table. "You understand why we kept the evidence under wraps, even though it could have cleared your name."

Scott nodded. "You didn't want the word to get out that you have a piece of a Red Battlenaut."

"Whoever's behind this, we don't want to tip them off that we're coming," said Perseid. "Though we assume they're more than ready for us. Who knows how many invisible and undetectable Reds they have at their disposal?" He shook his head at Rexis. "It's a suicide mission, isn't it, Captain?"

Rexis smiled at Scott. "Not if we have someone along who can *see* the bastards."

"So now you know why you've been detailed to our CORE unit," said Perseid. "Because you're indispensable to the success of this mission. Because we need to figure out *why* you're able to see the Red Battlenauts, and we need you to see them *for* us when we *fight* them."

"We can't do it without you," said Rexis.

"Welcome to the team." Perseid walked over and extended a hand.

Scott stared at it for a moment. He'd been given his orders; he was going on the mission. The handshake was only a friendly gesture.

But he still hesitated. He'd never minded taking difficult roads in his life, but this one had so many unknowns, he wondered if he could survive it.

The odds seemed to be against him. He'd had a hard enough time fighting one Red Battlenaut; how could he handle more?

But the fact remained: he seemed to be the only one who could make a difference in this fight.

Even with the odds as steep as they were, he knew one

thing with absolute confidence in his heart: if he hadn't been ordered to join the mission, he would have volunteered.

"Thank you, sir." Scott rose from his seat and shook Perseid's hand firmly. "Thanks for having me."

"Good." Perseid smiled and nodded. "Round up your gear and report to Hangar C-17 by oh-three hundred hours tonight. We leave promptly at oh-six hundred."

CHAPTER 5

Scott arrived at Hangar C-17 fifteen minutes early and flashed his I.D. badge at the side door. He toted everything he owned behind him, packed in an olive drab duffel bag on wheels.

Two Marines manned the door, faces stony until they viewed his badge. Then, when they realized who he was, their eyes instantly changed, filling with disapproval. He'd seen it happen dozens of times since Chelong III; as far as they were concerned, he was under suspicion, his reliability and even his loyalty suspect.

The difference was, this time, their disapproval didn't give Scott the slightest twinge of doubt or worry. He knew there was evidence that backed him up, and people believed him. The hell with everyone else.

When the guards stepped aside, Scott threw the door open and marched into the hangar with his duffel. As soon as he stepped inside, he saw his next ride--a black transport shuttle squatting in the center of the huge space. It looked like a big crab with an ebony shell, its disklike body perched between four spindly struts. The shuttle's body bristled with weapons and instruments, and dual engine pods jutted from the rear, their flared cylinders ending in open silver cones.

Engineering personnel in red jumpsuits hurried around the ship, disconnecting hoses and conduits and running status checks with tablet computers. Other personnel in navy blue security uniforms stood close watch, rifles at the ready.

As Scott approached, a black-uniformed man with a tablet computer in one hand rushed out of the hatch in the belly of the shuttle and down the steps leading to the hangar floor. He spotted Scott immediately and jogged right over to him.

"Corporal Scott?" The man looked to be of Chinese descent, with broad, flat features and a thick black crew cut. He was muscular, like all CORE personnel, and tall--a few centimeters taller than Scott. "I'm Sergeant Vic Fong. Good to meet you." He reached for a handshake.

Scott liked him right away. "Likewise." He returned the handshake. "Reporting as ordered by Major Perseid."

Fong took a look at Scott's ID badge and nodded. "Roger that. Welcome to the Diamondbacks, Corporal."

It was the CORE unit's nickname. "Thanks." Scott glanced at the stylized snake jaws on the chest of Fong's uniform, the symbol that matched the nickname and called to mind a striking serpent. "I understand we're leaving at oh-six hundred?"

"From orbit, yes." Fong hiked a thumb toward the shuttle. "But we're launching from here to the mothership any minute now. Just waiting on a few more people." Suddenly, his eyes flicked away from Scott, looking over his shoulder. "There they are now."

As Fong jogged past, Scott spun to see who had gotten his attention. Seven people in black uniforms had just entered the hangar, loaded down with packs and ruggedized black plastic cases.

Scott knew four of them: Perseid and Rexis were up front, followed by Trane and Abby. The other three were strangers: a short, dark-haired man bulging with muscles; a woman with brown hair pulled back in a tight bun; and a tall woman with a long black ponytail and a lithe, swaying walk.

Fong met the group and accompanied them across the hangar, talking fast to Perseid, who listened and nodded. When Fong showed him something on the tablet screen, Perseid frowned and made a comment; Fong's fingers darted over the touch-screen, changing something, and Perseid nodded with satisfaction.

When the group reached Scott, Perseid stopped. "Glad you could make it."

Scott snapped off a crisp salute. "Corporal Scott reporting for duty, sir."

Perseid nodded. "You've already met Captain Rexis and Lieutenants Trane and Catharsis." He turned and gestured at the three newcomers bringing up the rear. "This is Gunnery Sergeant Joe Balko..."

The man with the bulging muscles nodded at Scott.

"...Lieutenant Masada Feinberg...," continued Perseid.

The woman with brown hair in a tight bun looked at Scott and blinked.

"...and Doctor Monique Beauchamp," finished Perseid.

The tall woman with the ponytail solemnly inclined her head.

Perseid ran his finger along the scar on his left cheek.

"All present and accounted for?"

Fong nodded. "Everyone else is shipside, Major." He tapped the tablet screen three times, and the shuttle's engines whined to life, activated remotely. "Ready for departure, sir."

"Then let's get the hell rolling." Perseid stormed past him. "We've got work to do."

The rest of Perseid's group followed in his wake, leaving Fong and Scott standing alone. Fong tapped the screen a few more times, making the engines run louder, then leaned closer to Scott. "I've got a trivia question for you, Corporal."

"What is it?" said Scott.

"Do you know how many non-CORE personnel have returned in one piece from CORE Diamondback missions?"

Scott shook his head. "How many?"

"None." Fong raised his eyebrows and fixed Scott in a piercing gaze. "In other words, watch your back. This is some hardcore *plang* you've stepped in."

"Roger that," said Scott.

"The Diamondbacks are a family, and you're not one of them," said Fong. "Just something to keep in mind."

"Got it," said Scott, and then he turned and headed for the shuttle. He'd already understood what Fong had told him before Fong had said a damn word. He wasn't operating under any illusions when it came to the Diamondbacks.

As important as he was to the mission, he knew he'd still have to prove himself. And he knew he couldn't take anything for granted when the plang hit the fan.

When everyone was aboard and strapped in, Fong closed the gangway and jumped into the pilot seat. As his fingers danced over the control boards, thrusters on the shuttle's underside hummed. The transport rose, and the four struts that had cradled it folded in snug against the hull.

Through the forward viewport, Scott could see the hangar doors slide apart, opening onto a short, floodlit runway. Then, the engines roared, and the shuttle surged forward, bolting out of the hangar. It raced along the runway a few dozen meters, then suddenly swooped upward, charging into the starlit night sky.

As the shuttle climbed, the Diamondbacks talked quietly among themselves, but Scott wasn't paying attention. His eyes were locked on the viewport, literally staring into space, his mind swirling as he contemplated the adventure that lay ahead.

He'd seen a lot of action since the start of the war, had fought on battlefields from Yolanda to Antimony. He'd fought some formidable enemies, had some life-changing experiences. He wasn't even close to being a wet-behind-the-ears rookie anymore. But he was out of his element, and the weight on his shoulders was enormous. The stakes, if he should fail, were unimaginably high. In so many ways, he was heading off into the unknown, moving in a direction he would not have thought possible just a few days ago.

He wondered what Bern would think of all this--and the answer came to him instantly. She would tell him to quit obsessing and go do his damn job. She wouldn't even wish him luck because he wouldn't need it, because he was a Commonwealth Marine.

After a few minutes, Fong gestured at the viewport. "There it is." He glanced back at Scott and smiled. "What do you think?"

Scott didn't see a thing except stars and darkness. "Not sure." He leaned forward and narrowed his eyes, but nothing changed. "Where is it?"

"You'll see." Fong chuckled and touched controls on the board in front of him. "Let me just switch the lights on."

Suddenly, the outline of a huge, streamlined vessel appeared in the viewport, traced in bright white lights. The hull showed nothing but space and stars, a perfect continuation of its surroundings--but the lights shone on its contours, making it stand out. Without them, Scott was sure it would have still blended in with the starscape around it, completely invisible to his eyes.

"Presenting the CSS *Sun Tzu*." Fong chuckled and looked back at him again. "How about now?"

"Not bad." Scott smiled and nodded. "Nice stealth mode, by the way."

"It's all done with mirrors." Fong winked and turned back to his controls.

Scott was more impressed than he let on. He'd heard of such ships before but had never seen one. "Ghost ship, huh? You guys really are the elite." According to the rumor mill, the technology was very new and its use highly restricted due to its extreme energy consumption curve.

"It's no Red Battlenaut," said Trane, "but it gets the job done."

"Wasn't there an energy consumption issue?" said Scott.

"Not anymore," said Rexis. "Thanks to our new negative mass drive."

"Our *ultra-top secret* negative mass drive," added Perseid.

"Isn't *everything* ultra-top secret?" said Trane. "Including our *bowel movements*?"

As the Diamondbacks laughed, Scott took in the sleek lines of the *Sun Tzu*. It reminded him of an arrow, but with rounded, swooping curves instead of sharp angles and edges.

Instead of a spiky arrowhead, it had a smoothly curving, conical tip dotted with windows. At the other end of its long shaft, it had a cluster of bulging engine pods instead of feathers. Each segment turned slowly--the nose, shaft, and engine block each rotating in opposite directions.

It looked graceful and delicate as it hung in the firmament ahead, though Scott didn't doubt its killing capabilities. It would have to be a lethal vessel to serve CORE's deadly purposes. It would have to live up to its namesake--the Old Earth author of *The Art of War*.

"She's a hell of a ship," said Fong.

"They say they christened her with the blood of a hundred Rightful fighters." Abby said it with the usual dark edge in her voice.

"That's a lie," snapped Perseid. "But she's done well by us so far. She's *more* than a ship." He looked at Scott and nodded. "You'll see."

Scott was already convinced. When he turned his gaze back to the viewport and saw the *Sun Tzu*'s nose glint with strokes of reflected sunlight, a chill ran up his spine.

He hadn't even been aboard yet. How could he feel so much like he was coming home?

CHAPTER 6

Moments after the shuttle landed in the docking bay of the *Sun Tzu*, the hatch dropped open, and the passengers filed out.

Scott was the last one down the stairs, pulling his wheeled duffel along behind him. When he got clear of the shuttle and took a look around, he was surprised; the docking bay, which was located in the fore section of the central shaft, was bigger than he'd guessed on approach. The ceiling was easily eighty meters away, more than high enough to house the two destroyers parked at one end and the small fleet of fighters stacked on racks at the other.

Men and women in red jumpsuits rushed in all directions, hurrying on foot or aboard motorized carts. Everyone seemed to be shouting or dropping gear or banging on things at the same time, filling the place with echoing clamor.

As on any wartime ship or base, there was a feeling of barely controlled chaos in the air--but there was something else, too. Scott felt sharper somehow, his mind clearer, his senses keener. He'd been on the tired side when he'd boarded the shuttle back on Ovid; now he felt completely energized and alert, as if someone had dosed him with stimulants.

Was it his imagination? Was he just charged up because of the excitement of starting the new mission? Or was there another explanation?

"Well now." Perseid, who'd marched over to talk to a female corporal, returned to Scott. "Here you are on my ship. What do you have to say for yourself, Corporal?"

Scott snapped to attention and saluted. "Permission to come aboard, sir."

Perseid returned the salute. "Permission granted. Welcome aboard."

"Thank you, sir." Scott lowered his arm.

"Let's get you situated." Perseid waved at the female non-com he'd been talking to, and she hurried over. "Corporal Solomon Scott, this is Corporal Donna Perihelion. She'll show you to your billet."

Donna was a petite young blonde with a bright, friendly smile. "Good to meet you, Corporal. Welcome to the *Sun Tzu*."

"Good to meet you, too," said Scott.

"After you get him settled, bring him to the Command Deck," said Perseid.

Donna saluted. "Yes, sir."

"We're still launching at oh-four hundred as scheduled," said Perseid, and then he marched off across the vast deck of the docking bay.

"This way." Donna smiled again and gestured for Scott to come with her. Then she started across the deck in the opposite direction from the one Perseid had taken.

Scott followed along beside her, taking in the hectic surroundings. "How long have you been with the Diamondbacks?" he asked, feeling at ease enough to make small talk.

She flashed her smile in his direction. "This is my fifth tour."

Five tours was a long time with a high-pressure group like CORE. "Are you re-upping for more?" said Scott. "Or do you have other plans?"

Donna stopped and gave him a look like she thought he was crazy. "I've never wanted to be anything other than CORE. I still don't." She spread her arms to encompass the bay. "Everyone here will tell you the same thing."

With that, she dropped her arms back to her sides and resumed walking, heading straight for a transport tube along a wall to her right.

Scott decided to change the subject. "So where are you from?"

"Archibald," said Donna. "Quillid City in District Seven."

The CORE Academy was on Archibald, but Scott didn't bring it up. "I've been to Archibald a few times, but never Quillid City. Pretty place, from what I saw."

"It is, isn't it?" The transport tube doors slid open when Donna held up her I.D. "What about you, Solomon? Where do you call home?"

Scott entered the passenger cabin in the tube after her. "Tack. The town of Tisserie, near Vast, to be exact."

Donna pressed a button, and the cabin launched upward through the tube. "Never been there. What's it like?"

"Beautiful." Scott's stomach lurched, then calmed as the cabin reached the limit of its climb and shot into a perpendicular tube, moving horizontally. "Jeweled mountains, lavender skies, illuminated forests, and golden seas. Fields of coppery glow-grain stretching as far as the eye can see."

"Sounds nice." Donna smiled again. "Sounds like you love it there."

Scott shrugged. "I guess I do."

"You'll love it here more." Donna nodded. "You'll see."

"You think so?" said Scott.

The cabin stopped moving, and the doors slid open. Donna paused and gave him a meaningful look before stepping out. "CORE gets in your blood like nothing else, Solomon. It'll change you."

Scott followed her out into a metal-walled corridor. "The Marines already did that," he said.

"You only *think* so because you've never been CORE before," said Donna.

"I'm not CORE now, either."

Suddenly, she spun and pointed an index finger at him. "Not *yet*." Then, she gave him a wink and spun away again, zipping off down the corridor. "Billet's this way!" she shouted over her shoulder. "How about getting a move on?"

Scott stowed his gear in the billet and followed Donna across the *Sun Tzu* to the Command Deck. When the big double blast doors swept open before them, Scott started forward... then froze, instantly disoriented.

The chamber in front of him looked like it was open to space. Instead of walls, floor, and ceiling, he saw stars and darkness all around. Instead of floor-mounted chairs in front of wall-mounted consoles, black-uniformed crew members floated in antigravity harnesses, surrounded by holographic controls in all the colors of the rainbow. He knew only one person in the room--Vic Fong, who seemed to have more control holos around him than anyone else.

As Scott took it all in, he had chills; he'd never seen anything like it. The command decks he'd been on in the past had all been crowded, cramped, and packed with equipment. This one, on the other hand, looked like something a hyper-advanced alien civilization might have installed on an intergalactic vessel.

Donna bumped his shoulder, snapping him out of his reverie. "Pretty cool, huh?"

"That's putting it mildly," said Scott.

"CORE gets all the best toys." Donna giggled. "And we put 'em to good use."

"This is *way* beyond anything else I've seen in the fleet." Scott shook his head. "What if the Rightfuls got hold of it?"

"Not a prob," said Donna. "We've got self-destruct systems you wouldn't *believe*. Not that we'd ever *need* them, the way *this* baby handles."

Just then, the blast doors shot open behind them, and Scott heard footsteps and a familiar voice.

It was Perseid. "It's time, people!" He brushed past Scott and Donna without acknowledging them and headed for the center of the Command Deck. When he stopped walking, a circle of white light pulsed to life under his feet. "Launch in five minutes!"

Without being asked, the crew members floating in their mid-air harnesses shouted out status updates in quick succession. Some of the updates were familiar to Scott, but others were new, referring to things he'd never heard of before.

Finally, Vic Fong spoke up. "Negative mass drive ready. Maneuvering thrusters ready."

"Engage thrusters." Perseid waved a hand in front of him, and several holos appeared. From where Scott stood, they looked like an assortment of readouts and monitors. "Take us out to launch distance."

"Aye, sir." As Fong said it, the starscape started sliding past all around. The ship was moving forward, away from planet Ovid, in preparation for full-blown launch.

"Hey, Solomon." Donna leaned close to Scott and kept her voice low. "Ever watch a star-jump from up front like this?"

Scott looked around at the scene drifting past, as if the prow of the ship were transparent. "Not like this."

She elbowed him in the side. "Then you're in for a treat."

"Coming up on one minute," said Fong. "And *mark*."

A red digital countdown appeared in midair at the front of the room. It was already whipping through seconds, racing toward zero.

As the countdown continued, Scott heard a low hum building. The decking beneath his feet--solid enough though it showed an image of the starry space outside the ship--began to vibrate with quickly increasing strength.

"Thirty seconds!" said Fong.

"You'd better hold on to something," whispered Donna, and then she took Scott's hand. "Trust me on this."

"Ten seconds!" said Fong. "Nine...eight...seven..."

"Charge the grid," said Perseid. "Position masses."

"Grid charged," shouted one crew member.

"Optimum mass positioning achieved," shouted another.

Meanwhile, Fong kept counting. "Four...three...two... one..."

"Launch!" said Perseid.

Suddenly, the starscape seemed to explode. The darkness of space bloomed with millions of streaks of light, the distended tracks of stars surging past the hurtling ship. Each streak was a spectrum unto itself, running from nearby blue to distant red.

The view was beautiful, something Scott had never seen in quite the same way before. His heart pounded, and chills dashed up his spine; he felt as if there were no ship around him at all, as if he were sailing through the cosmos under his own power, drinking in the magnificence of the universe.

Just then, Donna squeezed his hand, reminding him she was there. "See?" Her breath was warm in his ear. "Didn't I tell you it was better to hold on to something?"

Scott smiled at her, watching as the multicolored light of the passing stars played over her face. He had to admit, she was cute...and the hand-holding had been a good sign. But he knew he should get his footing among the Diamondbacks before jumping into anything.

"What a view." As he said it, he let go of her hand. "It really takes your breath away."

"People say they get used to it," said Donna. "But I never do. I bet you'll feel the same way." She smiled, and her eyes drifted up to meet his.

Scott swallowed. He thought he should look away, but her gaze held his in place as if with magnets.

Fortunately, Fong's voice broke the mood. "We are now underway, sir. Shall we maintain the heading you requested earlier?"

"Affirmative," said Perseid. "Best possible speed to

Shard, in the Veda system."

"Aye, sir." Fong's fingers flew over the holo controls glowing and blinking around him. He spun around in his antigrav harness, worked a bank of holos behind him, then spun back around to face forward again. "Estimated time of arrival is 72 hours from now."

"Excellent." Perseid stepped off his glowing disk, and the light at his feet went out. "That gives us more than enough time to get our Marine friend fit to fight." He turned and smirked in Scott's direction.

Scott frowned. Since when was he not fit to fight? He'd been fighting the civil war for the past nine months, ever since the first shots were fired.

Perseid strolled over and stood stiffly in front of him. "What do you say, Corporal? Ready to give one of *our* Battlenauts a try? We're sure as *flux* not putting you in the middle of a *hotzone* without *armor*."

Scott nodded. "I'm fully rated on all combat armor, sir."

"No you're not." Perseid smirked and shook his head. "Believe me, you're not."

Donna laughed, and so did half the Command Deck crew. Scott got a sinking feeling in his belly as he wondered what the hell was so funny.

"Driving a tin can is one thing." Perseid put a hand on Scott's shoulder and led him toward the doors. "Driving a high performance piece of bleeding edge super-tech equipment is something else entirely."

Scott was annoyed and trying not to show it. "Is that so?"

The doors opened, and Perseid guided him through. "You know how to *crawl*, Corporal. Now it's time to get your scudge together and learn how to *run*."

CHAPTER 7

The Training Center was a huge chamber in the central shaft of the *Sun Tzu*, adjacent to the cargo bay. It was a giant, open space, completely empty when Scott and Perseid entered except for a pair of big black armored figures facing each other in the middle of the room.

Battlenauts. Even at a distance, Scott recognized them instantly--realizing, at the same time, how different they were from any Battlenauts he'd seen.

The details became clear as he got closer. These Battlenauts were much sleeker than any he'd piloted or faced on the battlefield. They looked more like giant, heavily muscled humans than blocky mechanical constructs. They were all curves and contours instead of right angles and sharp edges.

"There it is." Perseid stopped ten meters from the Battlenauts and gestured at the one on the right. "Your assigned armor for the duration of this mission."

Scott narrowed his eyes as he scanned the gleaming black hardware. Something jumped out at him right away... something that was missing. "No weapons?" He didn't see a single gun barrel or missile chute anywhere on the armor. "Is this strictly a defensive unit?"

"Don't worry." Perseid chuckled and walked the rest of the way to Scott's Battlenaut. "It has everything you'll need."

Scott scowled as he followed. What kind of Battlenauts were these? Their hulls looked perfectly smooth and seamless. Was neither one equipped with weapons systems?

"Put your hand here." Perseid pointed at a spot on Scott's Battlenaut's left leg, just above the knee. "Press it flat against the surface."

Scott stepped forward and did as he was told. The spot was just above eye level, the hull warm to the touch. In fact, it didn't feel much like metal at all...more like some kind of hard plastic.

"The plating is molded from enhanced superhard carbon nanotubes overlaying a morphic film," said Perseid, as if he'd been reading Scott's mind. "The next best thing to indestructible."

Scott looked at his hand on the Battlenaut's leg. "What's this supposed to do?"

"Tune the armor to your DNA," said Perseid.

"Which does what?"

"Puts you perfectly in synch," said Perseid. "You can move your hand now."

Scott tried to pull his hand away but couldn't at first. It was stuck, as if the armor didn't want to let it go. "What the hell?" But when he pulled harder, his hand popped free.

Perseid laughed. "You're bonded now. It's like you're part of it."

Scott's hand had a mild case of pins and needles, and he tried to shake it off. "What kind of Battlenaut *is* this?"

"The blow-every-other-Battlenaut-out-of-the-water kind," said Perseid. "The kind you never want to come face to face with if you're driving one of those other Commonwealth jalopies."

Scott shook his head. The new unit was so different from anything he'd piloted, he wasn't convinced. "Now what?"

"Now you put it on." Perseid clapped his hands and raised his voice, aiming it up at the Battlenaut. "Authorization Perseid one-one-three, kilo bravo victor papa seven-nine-zero-zero-two. Provide ingress!"

With only the faintest whirring sound, the Battlenaut lowered itself to its knees. Its chest and abdomen flowed open as if they were covered by liquid metal, revealing a simple black pilot's couch inside.

"Get in." Perseid gestured at the open armor. "Make yourself comfortable."

Scott hesitated, wondering what he was in for. Then, he clambered into the unit and lay back against the couch. Its padding was much softer than that of the couch in his old standard-issue Commonwealth model and molded itself to the shape of his body.

Meanwhile, Perseid opened the other Battlenaut and climbed inside the same way. "There we go. Now repeat after me, speaking in a firm, clear voice as follows." He cleared his throat. "*Recognize Corporal Scott comma Solomon.*"

Scott repeated the words loud and clear, enunciating each syllable. "*Recognize Corporal Scott comma Solomon.*"

Perseid kept talking. "*Program vocal imprint in three, two, one: Mary had a little lamb. Its fleece was white as snow.*"

Scott held off. He could easily imagine that this was all an initiation prank, and a recording of him reciting the nursery rhyme would haunt him for the rest of his career.

But when he saw Perseid glaring and spinning a finger in the air, he knew he had to go along with it, prank or not. "*Program vocal imprint in three, two, one,*" he said. "*Mary had a little lamb. Its fleece was white as snow.*"

"*The quick brown fox jumps over the lazy dog,*" said Perseid.

Scott sighed, then repeated the line.

"*Systems activate,*" said Perseid. "*Preset Alpha Zero One.*"

"*Systems activate. Preset Alpha Zero One.*" As soon as Scott said it, his Battlenaut popped up from its knees to a standing position. The chest and abdomen flowed shut, sealing him off inside the armor, and the couch sucked up against him. *What the hell?*

For an instant, the interior of the Battlenaut was pitch black. Then, a swath of holographic displays lit up around him, like a glowing, multicolored funnel with his upper body in the middle.

Scott looked around at the holos, which provided numbers, charts, and graphs depicting the status of the unit, its surroundings, and Scott himself. Then, he heard a loud knocking against the hull of the chest--three echoing raps in quick succession.

"Hello in there." Perseid's voice came next, booming all around him. "Corporal Scott, can you hear me?"

"Roger that." Scott wasn't sure his response would get through; he couldn't find a mic to talk into or any related controls.

But Perseid heard him anyway. "Don't just stand there. Take that thing for a spin, Corporal."

"How?" Scott reached up and ran his fingers through

the holos, but nothing happened. He looked down, trying to find armrest keypads, but there weren't even any armrests. He couldn't find a stick, either, or any of the usual buttons, knobs, or switches on the walls. "Where are the damn controls?"

"All you need is your *voice*," said Perseid. "Why do you think I had you *train* the unit to accept your vocal imprint?"

"Total voice control?" said Scott.

"Not total," said Perseid. "The holo displays are eye-movement activated. Two blinks for on or off. Change settings by focusing, dragging, etc."

"What if my voice and eyes go out at the same time?"

"Then we don't need you anymore," said Perseid. "Self-destruct time."

"Right." Scott experimented with the holos as Perseid had said, and they worked. If he blinked twice and focused on a particular readout, it grew larger. Staring at a control for a few seconds made it change setting. Gazing at a display and sliding his eyes one way or another moved it in the direction he chose.

"All right, playtime's over," said Perseid. "Let's put that thing through its paces."

Suddenly, a massive blow struck Scott's Battlenaut. The holo readouts showing the armor's status changed rapidly, spiking across the board.

"Get moving!" Perseid's voice had a taunting edge. "There's plenty more where *that* came from."

Instantly, Scott shifted into battle mode. His senses sharpened, his head cleared, and his thoughts raced, presenting him with options.

As unfamiliar as the CORE Battlenaut was, he was determined to put it to work for him. "Frontside viewer on." He wasn't sure how to frame voice control commands, so he tried to keep them simple...and it worked. The holo readouts slid away to either side, and a viewer window appeared in front of him, showing a video feed from the frontside cameras.

The feed came up just in time to show Perseid's Battlenaut unleashing a punch with one ebony fist. Scott's armor shook under the onslaught but stood its ground.

"Aren't you going to *do* anything?" Perseid shouted over the comm. "Maybe I was wrong, thinking a Marine like you could handle top-of-the-line equipment like that."

"Microphone off," said Scott. "Punch enemy's torso with right fist."

Suddenly, a new voice spoke in the armor...a male voice, smooth and serene. "The command 'Right punch to gut' will be sufficient, along with a requested level of force."

Scott grinned. Apparently, his new armor came equipped with an onboard artificial intelligence, an A.I. smart enough to suggest a more concise command.

Might as well put it to use. "Right punch to gut!" said Scott. "Maximum level of force!"

The armor obeyed instantly. He felt the weight of its right arm swing back, then forward, carrying the rest of the unit's bulk along with it. At the same time, he watched a wireframe holo of his Battlenaut projected in midair to the left of the viewer window, going through the same motions. On the viewer itself, he saw his armor's gleaming right fist plowing into the belly of Perseid's Battlenaut.

"That's more like it!" said Perseid. "Now let's see what else you can do!"

"Left punch to head," said Scott.

"What level of force?" said the armor's A.I., still

prompting him.

"Maximum!" snapped Scott, and his Battlenaut launched a blow as ordered, aimed straight at the head of Perseid's armor. On the viewer, Scott saw his Battlenaut's left arm whip back and lash out--only to be deflected when Perseid lashed up his own right arm to block the strike.

"Nice try," said Perseid. "Are you *sure* you've seen action in the war?"

"Right knee to gut!" said Scott. "Maximum force!"

He felt the Battlenaut's mass shift suddenly back as its right knee lunged up and forward. Checking the viewer, he saw the top of the knee connect with the belly of Perseid's armor, making it double over from the impact.

"Lucky shot," said Perseid. "But you'll have to do better than that."

"Left shoulder to chest! Maximum force!" said Scott.

His Battlenaut crouched and plowed its left shoulder into the chest of Perseid's unit. A resounding *clang* rang out at the impact, followed by the clatter of armor plating as Perseid struggled to stay on his feet.

Scott knew he needed to follow up fast to keep his advantage. "Right uppercut punch to chin." His Battlenaut did as he ordered; on the viewer, he saw his giant black fist swing up and crash into Perseid's chin. "Left hook punch to face." Again, he watched one of his fists blast into Perseid's armor like a runaway wrecking ball.

Scott got in two more big hits before Perseid spoke again. "Barely satisfactory." Another blow was coming, and Perseid caught it with one armored hand. "You need some training, Marine."

"Flux that," hissed Scott, and then he gave another order. "Weapons online."

Just then, Perseid let loose a barrage of rapid-fire blows to Scott's upper body, pounding the hell out of his head and chest. Scott counted five, six, seven blows; each new one knocked his armor back, to the right, or to the left, depending on the angle of impact.

"Step back," he told his Battlenaut, hoping for some breathing room. But as the armor took a backward step, Perseid caught it in the knee with a stomping kick, making it stumble.

"Stabilize! Stay on your feet!" said Scott, but he didn't need to say it. Servos whirred as the Battlenaut automatically compensated and regained its balance, planting both feet solidly on the floor.

Even as the unit kept itself upright, the A.I. piped up again. "Weapons are online."

Scott grinned. What a machine! It even reminded him, without being asked, that the onboard weapons were ready. Why hadn't Commonwealth Command installed the same system in every Battlenaut in the fleet by now?

On the other hand, he had no idea what weapons were available. He hadn't seen a single gun, sonic projector, or missile launcher on the unit's exterior.

Meanwhile, Perseid was taking advantage of his brief hesitation. Lunging forward, he grabbed hold of Scott's Battlenaut, wrapping his arms around its torso. He pitched Scott one way, then another, trying to throw him off his feet.

"You're going down!" said Perseid. "Shortest armor orientation session of all time!"

Sweat ran down Scott's back and sides, and his heart hammered like a fighter's fist in his chest. He knew it was only a practice session, and the stakes weren't life and death... but they might as well be. If he made a fool of himself during his first ride in a CORE Battlenaut, he'd never live it down. The Diamondbacks might never fully trust him on the battlefield.

Again, Perseid wrenched him hard to one side. Servos whined in protest, but Scott's armor stayed on its feet.

"What weapons are available?" Scott asked the A.I.

"Projectile guns with dummy rounds. Lasers at one-half power. Sonics limited to close-range." The A.I. paused as Perseid gave the armor an especially strong heave. "Drone pods fully powered."

With the other weapons in training mode, the words "fully powered" sounded promising. "Deploy drone pods," said Scott. "Target opponent unit."

"Deploy *all* drones?" asked the A.I.

"Yes!" said Scott as the Battlenaut rocked again. "Don't make me tell you again, Frank!" He surprised himself, calling the A.I. by a name like that. He'd done the same with his old Battlenaut, the one that had been blown to pieces on Chelong III. It had helped him, in the thick of a fight, to think of the big, lumbering machine as a person. Not that the reason for the name mattered, as long as New Frank launched those drones...whatever their capabilities were supposed to be.

As if Frank had anticipated his uncertainty, additional feeds appeared on the viewer, showing topside, rightside, leftside, and backside views along with the frontside feed. In each one, Scott saw sections of the Battlenaut's smooth hull...only it wasn't so smooth anymore. Each section was studded with rounded lumps the size of softballs.

As Scott watched, the lumps pushed outward and broke free of the armor, then leaped into the air under their own power. They went straight for Perseid's Battlenaut, all thirty or forty of them swarming his head and shoulders at once.

Perseid only got in one more good heave before the drones made contact with his armor. They slammed into it and bounced off like bowling balls, pounding it again and again with enough force to make him release his hold on Scott.

"Cool," said Scott as he backed his Battlenaut away from the carnage. "I wonder what else this baby can do."

"Beanstalk demo is available upon request," Frank said instantly. "Would you like to activate the demo?"

"Do it," said Scott.

Suddenly, the cockpit filled with a high-pitched electrical whine mixed with a loud clacking sound. The Battlenaut shuddered; then, its legs started to grow, lifting the armored torso into the air and Scott's couch along with it.

As Scott's armor grew taller, Perseid's drone-besieged Battlenaut fell away from the frontside camera. The other feeds showed the floor of the Training Deck getting farther away on all sides.

Then, the armor stopped expanding. "Maximum safe height for current clearance achieved," said Frank. "Beanstalk demo completed."

Scott grinned. *I can't believe how great this armor is.* "Right kick to chest," he said. "Maximum force."

Just as Scott's Battlenaut hauled back its right leg, Perseid's armor started Beanstalking, too. But the kick still landed before Perseid reached maximum height, sending his half-grown Battlenaut toppling backward, hitting the floor with a loud crunch.

"*Yes*!" cheered Scott. "He is *down*!"

No sooner had the words left his mouth than an alarm klaxon whooped in the cockpit. "Alert!" said Frank. "Catastrophic strike imminent!"

"What are you talking about?" Scott watched the viewer and saw no sign of danger--just Perseid's Battlenaut lying on its back on the floor of the Training Deck.

"Incoming!" said Frank.

"*What* incoming?" said Scott. "Where are you *seeing* this?"

"It has not yet occurred," said Frank. "My prognostication software predicts, based on current conditions, that incoming fire will arrive in 35 seconds...34...33..."

Prognostication software? "If you know it's coming, *neutralize* it!" Scott's eyes flashed over the viewer and holo readouts, looking for a clue to the source of the predicted fire--finding nothing.

Meanwhile, Frank continued the countdown. "Twenty seconds...19...18...17..."

"Damnit!" said Scott.

Just then, there was movement on the viewer. The chest and abdomen of Perseid's armor expanded, swelling upward. It looked like a balloon inflating, stretching as air pressure pushed out in all directions from inside it.

"Ten," said Frank. "Seven...six...five..."

"Back away!" Whatever Perseid's armor was doing, Scott knew he needed to move fast to escape it. "Best possible speed!"

"Three," said Frank. "Two...one..."

Scott's Battlenaut had only taken half a step back when the front of Perseid's Battlenaut exploded. Shrapnel from the blast pounded Scott's armor, blowing it off its feet and punching a multitude of dents in the once-smooth hull.

"Mother-fluxer!" shouted Scott as his Battlenaut slammed to the floor. The couch protected him from most of the shock of impact, but the fall still jarred him. Going down in defeat while sparring with Perseid was the last thing he'd wanted to do.

But it was a done deal now. After the crash, Scott's frontside video feed showed only the ceiling of the Training Deck. His Battlenaut was on its back, looking up.

"End of exercise," Perseid said over the comm. "Consider that the kill shot."

At the sound of that voice, Scott came to a boil. "Frank! Use the same weapon *he* just did!"

Frank didn't answer. After that, the holos disappeared, and Scott's Battlenaut slumped. When the lights in the cockpit went out, Scott was left in darkness again.

"Don't bother trying to fight back," said Perseid. "I've implemented remote power override. Like I said, the exercise is over."

With that, the chest and abdomen of Scott's Battlenaut flowed open, and the couch released its grip. For a moment, he lay there, grinding his teeth, wanting only to have another shot at Perseid's Battlenaut to prove what he could do.

Then, he sighed deeply and climbed up out of the unit.

Perseid was just hopping out of his own armor at that moment. "What do you think, Corporal?"

Scott sat on the edge of the chest cavity and glared. "I think I'd like to spar another round, Major. Power me up."

Perseid laughed. "Some other time. What I want to know is, what did you think of the CORE Battlenaut? Did it measure up to your old Marine model?"

Scott was in a bad mood but could see no advantage in lying. "It far exceeded it across the board," he said. "It's an amazing piece of equipment."

"You haven't even maxed the specs yet," said Perseid. "You didn't come close to fully exploiting its capabilities."

Scott nodded. "We sure could've used these on the front lines. Why doesn't *everybody* have them?"

"You'll have to ask Command," said Perseid. "*If* you survive this mission. And after what I saw here just now, you're going to need lots more training hours to do that."

"Because you beat me?" said Scott. "Let's go best two out of three and see what happens."

"I'll have Captain Rexis schedule you for heavy drills for the rest of the trip to Shard," said Perseid. "In between classes and shipboard duties."

"Classes?" Scott couldn't keep the surprise out of his voice.

"That's right," said Perseid. "Consider this an intensive training cruise. We need you *sharp* by the time we see action."

"Duties?" said Scott.

Perseid smirked. "For the duration, you're a member of this crew. As such, you will fulfill the shipboard duties of any Diamondback."

Scott stared at him. "What duties are those?"

"Report to Captain Rexis," said Perseid. "She'll lay it all out for you." With that, he turned on his heel and headed for the door, leaving Scott behind him wondering what the hell kind of mission he'd signed on for.

Since when did a seasoned Commonwealth Marine have to go through training and classes while detailed to a CORE unit? Since when did he have to perform shipboard duties? He was helping track down the Red Battlenauts; wasn't that duty enough?

Swinging his legs up out of the cockpit, he slid down the side of the Battlenaut and landed on the floor. He was sweated from the exercise, irritated with Perseid, and worn down by lack of sleep. His whole life had changed dramatically in just a few hours--not an uncommon thing for a Commonwealth Marine, but uncommonly dramatic this time around. Uncommonly crazy.

And he had a feeling things were only going to get crazier.

CHAPTER 8

Captain Rexis cut Scott a break. When he reported to her as ordered, she did indeed lay it all out for him--a busy duty and training schedule that wouldn't leave him much time for anything else. But she also gave him six hours' rack time commencing immediately, which was just what he needed. He could have kept going, he was trained to function under conditions of extreme sleep deprivation, but the rest would work wonders on his alertness and performance.

Back at his billet, he collapsed on the lower bunk he'd been assigned and finally let himself relax. Memories of the events of the day washed over him like a warm tide, lulling him ever closer to the brink of sleep.

At some point, he left it all behind and drifted off into a state of unconsciousness. This was part of his training, too--falling asleep quickly, grabbing rest when he got the chance. Often, in the field, he was lucky just to catch a couple winks between engagements.

As Scott slept, he had a lucid dream that mixed up elements of his life. First, he was back on Chelong III, riding his old gray Battlenaut through the mist. Then, he was in his CORE armor on the Training Deck of the *Sun Tzu*, looking for the Red Battlenaut. When he heard the sound of giant, stomping footsteps, he looked at the backside video feed--and saw two enormous human legs. Leaning back, he turned his gaze upward, only to see that the figure looming over him wasn't the Red Battlenaut after all, but his grandmother, Bern. He tried to run, but she scooped him off the floor and lifted him up, laughing wickedly.

Grandma Bern clenched her fist around him, cracking his armor like an eggshell. As Scott wailed and writhed within it, Bern hurled him across the Training Deck, which became the Iridess Chasm on Tack. He was thirteen years old and about to die all over again.

Suddenly, instead of flying through the air, he was running through the chasm under cover of darkness. Another boy--blond, half his age--ran alongside him, legs scrambling to keep up. The boy's name was Cairn, and he'd been a prisoner much longer than Scott, held captive by the man who was chasing them.

The heaving breath of that man drove Scott and Cairn to run as fast as they could. He was an evil man, a monster who'd haunted Scott's nightmares again and again since that night.

Scott felt the man's fingertips brush his sleeve, and he ran harder. He had to get away, no matter the cost, no matter what he knew was about to happen.

Then there was a sound like a roaring beast, like a monster, and something lifted him off the ground. His feet pedaled helplessly in the air, searching for purchase, searching for anything solid...finding nothing. He spun in circles, head over feet, picking up speed as he whipped through the chasm, leaving poor Cairn far behind him.

That was when he saw it--Penitent Peak, racing toward him with all the speed and purpose of inexorable destiny. He screamed as loud as he could, louder than he'd ever screamed before or since. With that, the towering crag became the Red Battlenaut, towering implacably in the moonlight. Spinning blades emerged from its chest, pushing toward him.

Which was when he heard the terrible rumbling noise booming across the landscape. It exploded like thunder or a chain of cluster bombs bursting in rapid succession, throwing off blasts that echoed from the walls of the chasm. With each echo, the crashing booms grew louder instead of fading, until they filled his head with an unbearable torrent. Then, the loudest boom of all struck with deafening force, throwing him right out of his sleep.

Heart hammering, Scott sat up suddenly on his bunk. It was only then he realized the noise had not originated in his dream.

It was coming from the bunk above him. Someone up there was snoring like a buzz saw blaring through a megaphone on maximum amplification.

Cursing, Scott swung his legs off the bed and planted his feet on the cold metal deck. Just then, between the trumpeting snores from above, he heard the sound of nearby snickering laughter.

Looking around the dark room, he saw Trane lying on his belly on an upper bunk, grinning down at him. His white crewcut and teeth stood out in the darkness. "Welcome to your new billet, rookie." He didn't bother lowering his voice. "Looks like you landed the best spot in the place."

As Trane snickered some more, the snoring got even louder. Wondering who was responsible, Scott stood up for a look above him--and saw Abby Catharsis sprawled over the mattress, head tipped back and mouth gaping.

"All that noise from one woman." Trane snickered again. "Doesn't seem humanly possible, does it?"

Scott sat back down on his own bunk. Sleep was looking farther and farther away with each honking blast from above.

"It's like this every night," said Trane. "She's as dependable at snoring as she is in a firefight."

"Huh." Scott shrugged. "So what do I have to do to get a different rack?" He knew the answer before he asked the question, but he asked it anyway.

"Not be the new guy." Trane laughed.

Scott pointed at the empty bunk under Trane's. "What about that one?"

"It's taken." With that, Trane rolled over on his side to face the wall. "But don't worry, you'll be okay. You'll get used to the noise sooner or later."

The snoring jumped up another notch, hitting its loudest level yet. Scott lay back and stared at the bottom of Abby's bunk for a while, wishing he had earplugs--and thinking about his dream.

He hadn't thought about Iridess Chasm in ages. The most traumatic events of his life had happened there, the dark struggles that had almost ended him forever. There had been days when those terrible times had dominated his mind like never-passing storm clouds...but he'd chosen long ago not to dwell on them. It was better, always better, to keep moving forward.

Why then had those memories come back to him now? Was it the stress of the new mission? The cloud hanging over him since Chelong III?

Or was there another reason altogether, something deeper? Some kind of warning that he didn't dare ignore?

"Sweet dreams, rookie," Trane said with a final snicker.

Without a word, Scott rolled over on his side and pulled the pillow over his head, trying to block out the noise from above.

CHAPTER 9

By the time Scott rolled out of his rack, he'd slept maybe three hours--but the sleep had been broken, so it was hard to be sure. It had been impossible to sleep soundly with all the ruckus going on around him. Not only had Abby's snoring never let up, but Trane had joined in with snoring of his own, just as loud. The two had snored in counterpoint, each one letting out a loud blare whenever the other breathed in.

They were still going at it when Scott left the room to shave and shower. They weren't even done when he came back, got dressed, and left. Even through the closed door of the bunkroom, the sounds of their bullhorn duet carried into the corridor behind him.

Scott yawned and rubbed his eyes on his way down the hall. He actually felt more tired now than before he'd gone to bed. How the flux was he going to get through the day?

Yawning again as he rounded a corner, he walked right into someone who was charging toward him--Donna, who ended up stumbling into his arms.

She looked flustered at first, her face bright red, then broke into a bright smile. "Solomon!" She lingered for a moment in his embrace, holding on to his upper arms. "How's it going?"

"I need coffee, bad." Scott's voice was hoarse from lack of sleep. "Strong, strong coffee, with a side order of stims."

Donna frowned as she did the mental math. "Abby's snoring got to you?"

Scott nodded. "Trane's just as bad."

"That's the worst billet on the ship." Donna looked apologetic. "Nobody wants it, so the newbie gets it."

"No worries." Scott managed a smirk. "I just won't sleep for the rest of the trip."

"There's another option." Donna eased herself against him. "You could bunk with me. My billet's in another room, you know."

Scott's temperature rose a few degrees. It was a tempting offer--but he had a feeling he should steer clear for now. "I'll keep that in mind, thanks." He smiled and let go of her.

She stayed close, gazing up into his eyes. "The offer stands, Solomon." Popping forward on her toes, she kissed him on the cheek. "You're always welcome."

"Thanks." Scott felt himself blushing and looked away. "Now which way to the coffee?"

Donna hiked a thumb over her shoulder. "Straight, then left, then right, then right again." Next, she pointed an index finger down the hall behind Scott. "As for my billet, it's back that way, across from yours."

"Got it." Scott smiled and started to move away from her.

But Donna grabbed him by the wrist and held him there

a moment more. "And in case you're wondering, no, I do not extend this invitation to just anyone."

"Right." Scott nodded seriously.

"There's just something about you I like." Donna squeezed his wrist. "Something special, you know?"

Scott nodded again. "Thanks, Donna. I appreciate that."

"Any time." She gave him a flirty look and let go of his wrist. "See you at the briefing, Solomon."

Scott frowned. "Briefing?"

"They just called one for nineteen hundred hours in the auditorium," said Donna. "CORE officers only, but you're invited, too. Be there or be square."

With that, she jabbed his chest with the tip of her finger and darted away from him, zipping down the hall.

Scott stood there for a long moment, staring after her, wondering if she'd told the truth about not inviting just anyone to her rack. Then, he yawned again and continued down the corridor, determined to gulp as much coffee as he could in the next fifteen minutes before the briefing.

"We have confirmed our destination." Captain Rexis stood stiffly at a podium in the well of the auditorium, addressing the two dozen personnel gazing down at her. "There is no longer any doubt that the mystery metal originated on the planet Shard."

Scott listened and sipped coffee from his vantage point in the top row of seats. From where he sat, he had a great view of the backs of the CORE officers' heads. They were fanned out below him along a curved bowl-like slope, some spread out, some clustered together. No one was sitting near him, but that was by design; Scott had slipped through the doors at the last possible second to avoid having company. He wasn't in the mood and didn't want any distractions that might make him miss something.

Down in the well, Rexis clapped her hands, and a holographic control panel rippled into view. Her fingers played over rows of glowing buttons and dials, making them change color from red to blue, green to yellow, purple to pink. Then, the lights in the room dimmed, and a gigantic holo projection flared to life in midair behind her, filling the space from floor to ceiling with a familiar image expanded to towering size.

It was the circular blade from the Red Battlenaut, the one that had broken off in Scott's armor. Seeing it again, blown up to such an enormous scale, brought back memories of the way it had almost killed him on Chelong III.

"Our science team confirms that this artifact is composed of a biometallic substance found only on Shard," said Rexis. "Specifically, its makeup is identical to that of the titanium alloy claws and teeth of certain metal-based lifeforms native to the Shard biosphere."

The holo behind her changed to an image of a creature with gleaming bluish-silver skin. It reminded Scott of a big jungle cat from Earth, but with two heads, six triple-jointed legs, and spiny armor plating.

Rexis looked up at the image, then turned back to the audience. "What is not clear to us at this time is how the fabricators of the blade managed to subdue the unstable nature of the alloy." She played the holo controls again, and the image changed to what looked like a blob of molten, silvery metal. "Until now, all reported attempts to process Shard biometals into usable components have resulted in the breakdown of the biometals' molecular structure.

"Once separated from the body of a living creature, these materials lose cohesion and cannot be molded into other forms. The special properties that make them unique--extraordinary tensile strength, impenetrability, and superconductivity--cease to exist upon separation from a viable metallic-organic host.

"At least until now." Rexis ran her fingers over the controls, changing the image to another view of the mysterious blade. "Somehow, whoever built and deployed the Red Battlenaut has figured out a way to work with Shard biometal--to reshape it without causing it to shed its desirable properties and lose cohesion." She changed the image to a computer-generated interpretation of the Red Battlenaut from Chelong III.

Just then, a hand shot up in one of the lower tiers. "This biometal." It was Trane, sounding rested and refreshed though he'd helped deprive Scott of needed sleep. "Could it be responsible for the Red Battlenaut's stealth capabilities?"

Instead of Rexis, someone in the next row down from Scott answered the question. "Unlikely," he said in a clipped British accent. "The biometal's recorded properties do not lend themselves to such capabilities."

"As far as we *know*," said Trane. "But we've never even been able to isolate the metal from its host organism and work with it in a *lab*, have we, Khalil?"

"True." Khalil sounded irritated. "But we *have* studied it while it was still attached to organic systems."

"Which could mean nothing," said Trane. "The material's properties while part of a living system could vary dramatically from those that manifest after separation from that system."

"But we have the current *artifact* to study, don't we?" snapped Khalil. "What story has it told us so far?"

"A *short* one," said Rexis. "No clue to the stealth capabilities. But maybe they're only evident in other components or the Red Battlenaut armor as a whole. We just don't know."

"We don't know *much*, do we?" said Joe Balko, the heavily muscled guy who'd been aboard Scott's shuttle to the *Sun Tzu*. "Nothin' like goin' in *blind*."

"Since when does that matter to the Diamondbacks?" spoke up Perseid from the front row. Jumping to his feet, he pumped his fist against the serpent insignia on his chest. "Boo-rah!"

Everyone in the room did the same thing, except Scott. Then, they all sat back down.

Rexis cleared her throat in the well. She touched a holo control, and the big projection changed to an image of a rotating planet striated with gradations of silver and gray. "Balko's right," she said. "In many ways, we *are* going in blind. We can read sensor scans of pieces like the circular blade, but scans of operational Red Battlenaut units are invisible to all but one of us...the same person who was able to see a Red Battlenaut when no one else could."

When she said it, most of the people in the room turned and looked at Scott, who was in the middle of sipping his coffee. He returned their gazes impassively and slowly lowered his cup.

"Which is why we've called this meeting," continued Rexis. "We need to develop strategies for the Shard task force. We need to figure out ways of fighting an enemy who is invisible to sensors and all but one of our personnel."

"And we need to do it behind enemy lines," added

Perseid. "On a world with a *very* hostile biometallic-based ecosystem. Even in the best of times, it's a nasty little hellhole."

"Imagine a planet inhabited by living knives of every shape and size," said Rexis. "Without armor, you'd be slashed to pieces within seconds. Even *with* armor, you'll be in danger every step of the way. There are creatures on Shard that can hack right through carbon nanotube plating."

"Sounds like a real day at the beach," said Balko.

"What exactly is our objective, anyway?" said Masada Feinberg, the brown-haired woman who'd also shared Scott's shuttle to the *Sun Tzu*.

"Our primary objective is to locate and shut down any biometal processing facility that might be present on Shard," said Rexis. "Our secondary objective is to gather intel on the Red Battlenauts and their controllers."

Perseid stood and faced the audience. "We plan to conduct a thorough reconnaissance from orbit, including automated A.I. probes of the surface. We'll gather as much data as we can and refine our objectives prior to insertion of the task force."

Trane blew his breath out loudly. "Looks like we've got our work cut out for us."

"When *don't* we?" Balko laughed, and so did everyone else.

"As always, preparation is critical," said Perseid. "Which is why we're putting together working groups to plan strategies. Each group will focus on a different aspect of the mission and hone solutions via gaming and simulations."

"Then we'll pull everything together in one global simulation," said Rexis. "See how it all works when the moving pieces bang up against each other."

"When do we start?" asked Feinberg.

"We're going into breakout sessions immediately," said Rexis. "Except Corporal Scott."

Scott sat straighter and clenched his jaw as everyone turned to stare at him.

"You'll be reporting to Engineering for your daily work detail," said Rexis. "Then the Training Deck for Battlenaut drills. After that, at eleven hundred hours, you'll join the Surface Warfare Group headed by Lieutenant Trane."

Scott didn't like being singled out and treated like a rookie, but he nodded and got to his feet. "Yes, ma'am." As usual, he didn't have any choice in the matter.

"See you later, Corporal." Trane said it with a wiseass edge to his voice. "And bring your A-game."

Scott bristled but kept it to himself. "I will, sir." With that, he marched up the aisle and out of the auditorium, leaving the others to continue the meeting.

He thought it was ridiculous to be sent off for menial duty when he had more experience with the Red Battlenauts than anyone in the room, but he did as he was told. Not that he was afraid of challenging superior officers when the situation called for it...but clearly, this wasn't such a situation.

Better to go swab the deck or whatever he needed to do to get through the next few hours without pissing anyone off. He could have his say later at the Surface Warfare working group.

If that plang-hole Trane would *let* him, that is. Meanwhile, maybe Engineering duty wouldn't be all that bad after all.

CHAPTER 10

"Look what the *cat* just puked up!" Chief Engineer Lieutenant Torus Azimuth roared the words from the upper catwalk of the vast Engineering Deck. "Some kind of rancid hoozehock, it looks like! I swear, I can *smell* it all the way up *here*!"

Scott stood on the floor below and looked up at him, thinking dark thoughts. "Corporal Solomon Scott reporting for duty, sir."

"I know who you are!" said Azimuth. "We *all* do, don't we?"

It seemed like every man and woman in Engineering was watching the scene unfold. Scott saw them leaning over the catwalks, standing on the floor, poking their heads out of nooks and accessways in between. They all wore red jumpsuits with black Diamondback emblems, and every one of them seemed to be grinning and nodding at the same time, agreeing with their Chief.

Azimuth spread his arms wide. "You're a celebrity!" Though he was a short, squat man--a full head shorter than the two men flanking him on the catwalk--he looked and sounded intimidating. His face, with its dark, arched eyebrows, crooked nose, and beady eyes, had a satanic quality that added to the impression. Even his hair looked devilish, the shaved black bristle drawing to a sharp point in the middle of his broad forehead. "You're a real four alarm big shot, aren't you? Your fame precedes you!"

Scott said nothing. In his years as a Marine, he'd been baited by the best. He wasn't about to let Azimuth get his goat.

"The only one to ever see a supposed Red Battlenaut! The only one to bring back a piece of one!" Azimuth pulled a big wrench out of his overloaded tool belt and thrust it overhead. "Let's give Corporal Scott the welcome he deserves!"

With that, Azimuth started whacking his wrench against the catwalk railing, and the rest of his crew followed suit, banging tools against the nearest metal structures or surfaces. The cavernous Engineering Deck filled with a cacophony of metal crashing against metal, clanging like an orchestra of out-of-tune broken bells.

Scott stood patiently and waited for it to die down. He'd expected some ball-breaking, it came with the territory when stepping into a tight-knit, ultra-elite group like CORE. But he had to admit, it was starting to get old.

When the clanging stopped, Azimuth tossed his wrench over the railing. It hit the floor less than three meters from Scott and bounced twice, landing just a few centimeters from his left boot.

Scott glanced down at it, then calmly returned his gaze

to Azimuth. The less he reacted, the sooner Azimuth would get bored with riding him.

Probably. "So how's your *grandma*, Corporal?" Azimuth sneered when he said it. "*Commandant* grandma, I should say."

"Commandant Chalice is just fine, sir," said Scott. "I'll tell her you asked."

"You do that!" Azimuth raised his satanic eyebrows. "You tell her I won't give you any special treatment, too!"

"None expected, sir." Scott clenched his jaws and kept up eye contact with Azimuth. He might have to take the Chief Engineer's plang, but he didn't have to bow his head like a whipped dog when he did.

"What a woman, that granny of yours," said Azimuth. "A real *hellcat* in the sack."

Everyone howled with laughter except Scott, who was inwardly seething. Azimuth had just crossed the line.

"I'll be sure to tell her you said *that*, too," snapped Scott, though he knew it was the absolute worst thing he could have said.

"Ha! I *knew* it!" Azimuth pulled a screwdriver from his belt and chucked it down. It bounced once and hit Scott in the knee. "You're a *rat*! You're gonna report us to *Grandma Hellcat* every chance you get!"

Scott glared at him. "No, sir! As a Marine, I am required to observe the chain of command at all times." He paused, took a breath, then let it out slowly. "I'm here to do my duty and follow orders, plain and simple."

"Is that so?" Azimuth stroked his chin and widened his eyes in a fiendish expression. "Then I have an order for you, Corporal. Get your ass in the primary grid chamber and polish the contacts on the negative mass manipulators."

Scott was stunned. "While we're in flight?" Had he heard correctly?

"Are you making me *repeat* my order?" bellowed Azimuth.

"But it's *suicide*," said Scott. "The energy flow will *fry* me as soon as I walk in the room."

Azimuth pulled a hammer from his belt and cracked the railing with it. "So you're *refusing* to obey my orders?"

"Did you mean you want me to polish the manipulator contacts in the *secondary* grid chamber, perhaps?" said Scott.

"Enough!" Azimuth banged the hammer three more times, then shook it at Scott. "Report to Dr. Beauchamp for an immediate psych evaluation."

Scott started to say something, then caught himself. At least a psych eval would get him away from Azimuth for a while. "Sir, yes sir." With that, he spun on his heel and marched off past the leering, chortling engineering crew.

On his way out, he heard Azimuth's hammer clatter to the floor behind him, hopping across the hard metal deck plates.

"Get the flux out of here, you insubordinate piece of oosh!" shouted Azimuth. "Don't come back until you've got your jar-head *head* on straight!"

Scott just kept walking. As the door slid open before him, he heard the crew jeering and more objects hitting the floor, but he didn't look back.

Dr. Monique Beauchamp pursed her lips and nodded when Scott described what had happened in Engineering. "I see." She sat in a high-backed black leather swivel chair in her office, making notes on a tablet computer in her lap. "Chief

Engineer Azimuth told you to kill yourself, and you did not comply."

"Correct." Scott sat across from her on a metal folding chair, feeling nervous--partly because he was worried about the outcome of the psych eval and partly because Dr. Beauchamp was so attractive.

Her face was long, with high cheekbones and aquiline features. Soft black hair flowed down over her shoulders, gleaming in the muted light of the office. Even the loose-fitting Diamondback uniform she wore couldn't hide the voluptuous curves of her body.

What kept Scott on edge the most, though, was the sensuous vibe that she gave off. When she looked his way, her gaze lingered on him, her deep brown eyes half-lidded behind stylish holographic lenswear. Her movements were languorous, graceful and catlike, even simple ones like crossing her legs or tapping the screen of her tablet. And her voice was throaty, with a light French accent.

Though she'd been on the shuttle with him the day before, this was the first they'd been alone together in such close proximity...the first he'd gotten the full effect of her charms. It was making it damn hard for him to concentrate, to say the least.

"So." Beauchamp tossed her head from side to side, shifting her hair back from her face. "You've followed orders in the past that could have led to your death, have you not?"

"Yes." Scott's eyes drifted downward, skimmed the curves of her ample chest, then shot back up to meet her gaze. "But this was different. This made no sense."

Beauchamp sighed. "In a world without court martial, disobeying a direct order might not be such a serious matter. Sadly, in *this* world, we must consider different possibilities."

"So I should have followed the order and entered the active grid chamber? Is that what you're saying?"

"Not at all." Beauchamp tapped her tablet three times, then aimed a grave stare at Scott. "I am saying it's possible that Azimuth's order could have been given for a different reason."

Scott frowned. "Such as?"

Beauchamp set aside her tablet and leaned forward, clasping her long-fingered hands over her knee. "You are familiar with the term 'hazing,' yes?"

Scott leaned back and folded his arms over his chest. For a moment, he just sat there and scowled. "Hazing," he said finally. "I know the term."

"Chief Azimuth is notorious for it," said Beauchamp. "I hope you won't take it personally. He does it to everyone when they first arrive."

"Okay then." Scott blew out his breath and nodded slowly. "So they're all laughing their asses off in Engineering right now."

"All over the ship, actually." Beauchamp shrugged. "In fact, I saw the video feed before you got here."

"Great." Scott looked away and clenched his jaw. "Just great."

"But it's not a bad thing, is it? Not really." She tipped her head, and the hair on that side fell away from her neck and shoulder. "As far as the people on this ship are concerned, you are unproven. That means you are potentially dangerous in the field...and just as dangerous off the field because your grandmother is the Marine Commandant. If you look a little foolish now and can be a good sport about it, it will make them feel more comfortable around you, yes?"

"I understand how hazing works," growled Scott. "Are

we done here?"

Beauchamp narrowed her eyes and stared at him for a moment, then settled back in her chair. "Hmm." She retrieved her tablet from the side table and tapped the screen a few times. "I'm curious. Did you have many friends in your last unit?"

"Of course I had friends," said Scott.

"But did you have *good* friends? And *many* of them?" Beauchamp read something on her tablet. "I see you contacted no one from your last unit before debarking from Ovid VI with the Diamondbacks."

"So what?" said Scott.

"And you've contacted no one since," said Beauchamp.

"Been a little busy."

Beauchamp flipped through data on the tablet. "So would you say you *do* have many good friends from your last unit? And the ones before that?"

Scott checked his wrist chronometer. "I have armor drills in five minutes, Doctor. I better get going."

"Drills can wait. Answer my question." Beauchamp shifted, uncrossing her legs. "Have you made many good friends in your previous units?"

Scott shook his head. "No." He hated that she was right. "I haven't."

Beauchamp nodded. "Is it safe to say you're a loner then?"

Scott knew she knew it was true. She just wanted to hear him say it. "Yes. It's safe to say." He started getting out of his chair.

"Then you are doomed." Beauchamp turned her gaze to the tablet. "You cannot be a loner among the Diamondbacks and expect to survive."

Scott sat back down. "I know how to survive. I know damn well how to work with a team."

"There is the flaw in your thinking." She raised an index finger and wagged it back and forth. "This is not a *team*. This is not some group of interchangeable, easily replaceable strangers. It is a *family*."

"Family?" said Scott. "Already got one, thanks."

"Do you?" Beauchamp held up the tablet. "Your file hardly mentions them, except for your grandmother."

Scott checked his chronometer again. "Listen." He popped up out of his chair and straightened his uniform. "I'm already late for my drills. Gotta go."

Beauchamp rose and blocked his path to the door. "At least let me leave you with one last question."

"What?" said Scott.

Beauchamp leaned toward him. "Why are you so alone, Corporal Scott?" She held his gaze for moment, letting the words hang in the air between them. Then, she stepped to one side, clearing the way.

Scott nodded and marched past her. The door slid open as he approached it, then swooshed shut behind him as he rushed into the hallway.

Hurrying toward the Training Deck, he thought about what Beauchamp had said. He wanted to put it right out of his mind, banish it to make room for his many more pressing concerns.

But he couldn't. In a few short minutes, she'd managed to get under his skin. Was it just because she was so good at it, or because he was so tired and having a crappy day? Or was there another reason, perhaps?

What if the question made him uncomfortable because it hit a little too close to home?

CHAPTER 11

Scott felt better once he got inside the cockpit of his Battlenaut on the Training Deck. The armor was still new to him, but he felt more at home there than anywhere else on the ship. He felt more at ease piloting the war machine than dealing with unpredictable, pain-in-the-ass human beings.

And the more time he spent inside it, the better he got at handling it. Alone on the Training Deck, he focused on weapons configuration, target practice and basic maneuvers, working to master the voice control interface and eye-movement holo displays. After two hours of putting the Battlenaut through its paces, his confidence level was much higher, his grasp of the armor's capabilities and limitations more complete. It was finally starting to feel like an extension of him, just as his old non-CORE armor had before its destruction.

During the hours of solo practice, his troubles from earlier in the day were forgotten. All that mattered was the Battlenaut around him, the way it responded to his commands with increasing speed and grace...walking, then running, then leaping over obstacles...missing targets, then hitting their edges, then making bull's-eyes with every shot. He was getting the hang of it and feeling better than he had all day.

That was when the other three Battlenauts stomped into the room.

Scott saw them storming toward him from gates in three corners of the Training Deck--three CORE Battlenauts like his own. As they marched in his direction, their morphic hulls transformed, reshaping smooth black carbon nanotube skin into the barrels of projectile guns, laser emitters, and sonic weapons. "Frank, identify the approaching pilots."

"Unable to comply," said Frank the A.I. "Identification data unavailable. Comm blackout protocols in force at this time."

Scott's heart pounded. This was either a surprise exercise or a surprise attack. Without inter-armor comms, he had no way of knowing which one.

His only option was to fight back first and ask questions later.

"Form and charge guns, lasers, and sonics!" As he called out the commands, he ran his eyes over the holo displays, enlarging the video feeds showing the three Battlenauts. With practiced flicks of his eyes, he dragged the feeds side-by-side and pulled in streams of sensor data for each Battlenaut directly beneath them.

Meanwhile, a computer-generated wireframe diagram of his own armor showed weapons growing from the hull as ordered. A tubular laser emitter sprouted from each shoulder, and projectile guns grew from each hip. At the same time, sonic blasters emerged from his forearms, each one a row of concave amplifier dishes mounted along the length of a silver rod.

"Weapons formed and charged," said Frank, sounding as calm and self-assured as ever. "Lasers at three-quarters power. Long-range sonics available. Guns armed with live ammo."

"Did you say *live*?" Scott didn't think he'd heard correctly. During his last visit to the Training Deck, he'd only had access to dummy rounds.

"Correct," said Frank. "Live ammo is now available for immediate deployment."

"What about the other Battlenauts? Are they armed with live ammo, too?" Even as Scott asked the question, he saw all three enemy units open fire on the video feeds. Slugs clattered against his armor from three directions, slamming into it with the explosive force that could only come from live ammunition. "Scratch that, Frank. They just answered my question."

As Scott's Battlenaut rocked under the onslaught, he saw two of the attackers stop in their tracks, while the third kept stomping toward him. It changed shape as it walked, pushing out a round, broad shape from the center of its chest, like the stump of a tree trunk.

"Fire all weapons at approaching unit," ordered Scott. "Maximum power."

His armor unleashed a barrage of slugs, laser beams, and sonics all at once, slamming into the oncoming Battlenaut. The full fury of all that weapons fire slowed the armor's approach but didn't stop it or knock it down.

Scott kept up the bombardment but could see it wasn't working. His opponent just kept plowing forward, the stump on its chest getting longer with each step. "It's growing a damn battering ram!"

"An *electrically charged* battering ram," said Frank. "I can do the same thing if you like."

Scott almost gave the go-ahead, then changed his mind. "Negative! Hit him with the drone pods!"

"How many?" said Frank. "Given this armor's current configuration, six pods are now available."

"All six then! Form and fire immediately! Cease fire from all other weapons!"

As soon as he gave the order, his Battlenaut stopped firing slugs, lasers, and sonics. The wireframe diagram showed six spherical drones bubbling up from the armor's back and shoulders, then bursting free and racing away toward the enemy with the battering ram.

"Drones away," announced Frank.

"Now bring us around," said Scott. "Run full speed for the Battlenaut at five o'clock."

Watching the video feed of the battering ram unit, he saw the drone pods swarm around it and attack, pounding its head, back, and lower abdomen with a flurry of blows. One of the pods swooped down and tagged the Battlenaut's left knee, making it stumble in mid-stomp. Then another blew into its right ankle, knocking it off-balance.

While the walking battering ram floundered, Scott's armor caught heavy fire from the other two Battlenauts, positioned at five o'clock and one o'clock--a mix of slugs, lasers, and sonics. The fire intensified as Frank followed Scott's order and ran full speed toward the Battlenaut at five o'clock.

"What's my current chance of success?" Scott had to yell to make himself heard over the thunder of weapons fire.

"Prognostication software predicts forty-seven percent chance of success," said Frank, "if you maintain your current course."

"What if I change course and go after the unit at one o'clock?"

"Eighty-three percent chance of success," said Frank. "Change course?"

Scott grinned. "What do *you* think?"

Without answering, Frank changed course, veering from the Battlenaut at five o'clock to the one at one o'clock.

"Rotate lasers to rearward firing position," said Scott. "Keep up full power barrage on unit at five o'clock."

"Done." As Frank said it, the wireframe showed Scott's armor's shoulder-mounted lasers flip over to face the Battlenaut at five o'clock. On the rightside video feed, Scott saw beams from the lasers lash out at the five o'clock Battlenaut, slashing over its gleaming black hull.

But the flow of slugs from back there continued, slamming Scott from behind even as the Battlenaut at one o'clock plastered him with fire from dead ahead.

Scott thought fast as he continued his full-tilt charge. If only he had another edge to use when he got in close. "Major Perseid said I didn't max your specs," he told Frank. "That I didn't come close to exploiting your full capabilities. What other capability could you deploy right now?"

For a few seconds, Frank didn't answer. "May I suggest Missile Mode?"

Scott was less than thirty meters from his opponent now. "Do it!"

Suddenly, in mid-stride, his Battlenaut changed configuration drastically, shifting from bipedal form to something else altogether. Scott saw it visualized on the wireframe diagram--the Battlenaut's humanoid body compressing, its arms and head melting with the trunk and legs into one smooth bullet-like shape.

Scott's Battlenaut's feet left the ground and flowed together with all the rest into a big, black missile with Scott packed inside. There was a roar as the power plant belched out a burst of thrust, and then the full package rocketed toward the one o'clock Battlenaut at a high rate of speed.

The slugs, laser beams, and sonics kept coming, but Scott's newborn missile, with its streamlined profile, punched through the wave of resistance without slowing.

"Five seconds till impact," said Frank. "Four seconds. Three seconds."

Scott clenched his jaws and held his breath. The video feed showed the one o'clock Battlenaut racing toward him--faster, ever faster.

"Two seconds," said Frank. "Brace for impact."

Just then, Scott's missile-formed armor collided with its target, striking the enemy's chest dead center and knocking it off its feet, driving it backward.

Scott's armor and the one o'clock Battlenaut plowed across the room for fifty meters until they crashed into the Training Deck's wall. When they hit, the force of the impact jolted Scott, but the cockpit couch held him tightly and prevented any injuries.

His opponent twitched and sparked under him, then went limp. As Scott converted his armor back to humanoid form, the impacts of a fresh flurry of slugs battered him from behind. He pushed away from his downed enemy to face whoever was back there.

Just as he turned, another salvo hammered him from another direction. The first Battlenaut, the one he'd hobbled with a swarm of drone pods, had regained its footing and somehow neutralized the pods, which were nowhere to be seen. Together with the Battlenaut that had formerly held a five o'clock position, it was laying down a steady stream of slugs directed at Scott.

"Rotate lasers to forward firing position," he said. "As soon as they've turned, fire one at each incoming Battlenaut."

The wireframe showed his shoulder-mounted lasers spinning around and recalibrating to aim at the two opponents. "Done," said Frank.

"Target each Battlenaut with a projectile gun, too," said Scott, "and open fire."

"Roger that," said Frank.

Scott could see from the wireframe that Frank had followed his orders. "So what other surprise capabilities do you have up your sleeve?"

"I can generate a radar-resistant smokescreen," said Frank. "Nano-bead particulates in the smoke scatter and confuse enemy radar signals."

Even as the A.I. said it, Scott saw one of the other Battlenauts pump out clouds of smoke on a video feed. "Negative! Give me something else!"

"We haven't deployed biofilm yet," said Frank.

The smoke had already obscured one Battlenaut from view and was rolling in to block the other. Meanwhile, Scott's armor was rocking from the double bombardment of the two Battlenauts' firepower. According to the status displays, potentially ruinous microfractures were developing in his own Battlenaut's carbon nanotube hull. "Then do it! Do it now, Frank!"

"Targeting the unit in visual range," said Frank. "Forming biofilm cannon."

The wireframe diagram showed one of Scott's shoulder lasers melting into the hull, which then grew a different kind of weapon with a big, gaping barrel. The barrel, which had a diameter bigger than the Battlenaut's head, stretched out and angled upward, then fired a spherical bundle into the air. The bundle seemed to disappear after it launched, as it exceeded the span of the wireframe holo.

But Scott saw where its flight took it on the video feeds. Before the smokescreen could obscure his view completely, he saw the bundle strike the Battlenaut that was still visible, striking it right on the chest. As soon as it hit, the bundle splattered, covering the front of the Battlenaut's armor with a lumpy green slime.

As Scott watched, the slime crawled over the armor, spreading in all directions. Within seconds, the Battlenaut was coated and stuck; it tried to move, but the slime locked it in place like a glistening, bright green statue.

At that point, two of the three enemy Battlenauts were out of the picture. Before Scott could celebrate, however, the third Battlenaut, the one that hadn't gotten the biofilm treatment, leaped out of its smokescreen and streaked toward him.

"Alert! Incoming!" Red light and a fast, high-pitched pinging filled the cockpit as Frank sounded the alarm. "Initiating evasive maneuver." Scott didn't even have to order him to evade; automatic fail-safes took care of that.

But his Battlenaut just couldn't move fast enough. It lunged left, bolting out of the way--and its opponent still hit it with a crushing impact, slamming it down to the floor.

The crash knocked the breath out of Scott. The couch held him, but his head still whipped hard to one side, giving his neck a nasty twist.

Just like that, his unit was on its belly, trapped under the weight of the Battlenaut. He saw it on the backside video feed, sitting on top of him. As for the frontside feed, it showed only a view of the floor.

"Frank! Get up!" Scott glared at the feed of the Battlenaut weighing him down. Triggering the eye movement-based controls, the concentrated focus made the image enlarge and push aside the other feeds, staring him in the face. "Get out from under that thing!"

Just then, the red light in the cockpit winked out, and the rapid pinging stopped. "Unable to comply," said Frank. "I have received notification that this exercise has concluded."

Scott pumped his elbows back angrily, plunging them deeper into the couch's padding. "Son of a bitch!"

"I will now proceed with pilot extrusion as ordered," said Frank. "I look forward to our next activity together, Corporal Scott."

With that, the couch slowly rotated, turning over to face upward. As the hull of the unit's back flowed open, Scott could see that the Battlenaut that had defeated him was no longer sitting on it. He blinked as the bright light of the Training Deck poured into the dark cockpit and washed over him.

The couch released him, and he climbed out of the armor. As he emerged from its back and shoulders and took a look around, he finally saw who'd been piloting the three opponent units in the live-fire exercise.

"Hey there!" Donna Perihelion walked toward him, grinning. "Great sparring, Solomon! Three against one, and you still put up a hell of a fight."

Scott wanted to be angry because he'd lost, but he couldn't do it. "So that was you in there?" He gestured at the Battlenaut on its knees behind her. "Why wouldn't you I.D. yourself?"

"So you wouldn't bring any preconceived notions to the bout." Donna stood, face flushed, and planted her hands on her hips. "So you could come as close as possible to a battlefield experience, from live ammo to unknown pilots with unknown capabilities."

Scott heard two sets of footsteps behind him and turned to see the other two pilots approaching. One was a tall black man who looked to be in his early-to-mid twenties. The other was half a head shorter and years older, a man with dark hair and bronze skin.

"Meet the rest of the squad." Donna walked over and stood beside the taller man, who smiled. "This is Roy Taggart, our top sharpshooter. And this..." She walked over to the other man. "...is Everisto García."

Scott nodded at both men, but only Taggart nodded back. García flashed a cold gaze in his general direction, then looked away without emotion or acknowledgement. *Hardcore.* Scott recognized the attitude.

But he wasn't going to act that way himself, as bugged as he was after the surprise bout and defeat. "Good to meet you." He stepped forward and reached for García, who grudgingly returned the handshake without making eye contact. Then, he shook Taggart's hand, too. "Thanks for the fight."

Taggart grinned. "Any time." He seemed like a friendly guy.

"You posted some solid scores today," said Donna. "You seem to be getting the hang of that CORE Battlenaut just fine."

Scott hadn't known that she'd been scoring him.

"Thanks." She hadn't mentioned that she was some kind of training instructor.

"I have no doubt that you'll be fully rated on that armor in no time. Which is a good thing, since we'll be at Shard in three days." Donna walked over and punched him in the arm. "Now get your ass to Engineering. Chief Azimuth has been screaming for you."

Scott's stomach twisted. "I thought he was done with me for the day."

"Apparently not." Donna shrugged and punched him again. "He said something about polishing the manipulator contacts in the secondary grid chamber."

Secondary...not *primary*. So maybe Azimuth wasn't going to order him to kill himself again. "All right." Scott blew out his breath. "Thanks for passing that along."

"No problem," said Donna. "So maybe I'll see you later, then."

In the brig, probably, thought Scott, *after I break down and murder Chief Azimuth.* But what he said was, "Maybe you will."

"Great." She flashed him a huge smile before he headed for the door. Maybe it would have made him feel good if he hadn't been going back to the hellhole known as Engineering. Maybe he would have been in better spirits if the crappy day he'd been having had finally been over.

CHAPTER 12

By the time Scott finally headed for his billet that night, he felt like the walking dead. His exhaustion was overwhelming, his head full of static, his eyes glazed over. He was still moving, but only on autopilot; his every last reserve of energy had been totally depleted, leaving him just enough juice to shuffle off to bed.

It had been a hell of a day. After the surprise sparring on the Training Deck, he'd gone to Engineering and taken a different kind of beating. Chief Azimuth hadn't thrown tools at him like before, and he hadn't done anything like ordering Scott to kill himself, but he'd worked him like a rented mule.

It seemed like Scott had scrubbed every centimeter of Engineering...then gone back over it all a second time...and a third. Not only had he polished the manipulator contacts in the secondary grid chamber, but he'd hand-cleaned the entire chamber from floor to ceiling. Sanitizing every catwalk, niche, and accessway hadn't been enough; he'd also had to clean, lubricate, and recalibrate every tool, spare part, and piece of equipment in the department.

And the whole time, Azimuth had trailed after him, watching his progress and insulting him. How many times had he called Scott a piece of hoozehock or a mother-fluxing plang-licker? It had all blurred together after a while and faded into the background of his haze of exhaustion.

After six hours of hard labor, Azimuth had finally released him. By then, Scott had been two hours late for the Surface Warfare Group meeting, but he'd shown up anyway, secretly hoping it was already over so he could just go get some rest. But his hopes had been in vain; the meeting had still been in full swing.

Trane, the head of the group, had torn Scott a new one for being so late--and then the meeting had kept going. It had run for another three hours, then four more after a five-minute break. Scott had to hand it to the Diamondbacks: they were determined to be ready for the Red Battlenauts when they made landfall at Shard.

It had been a real marathon session, and Scott had been called on often to weigh in on the group's strategies. Just when his brain had felt at its fuzziest, he'd been tapped again and again for insights and opinions, then challenged just as often over both. Toward the end, he'd started to fade, and Trane had caught him drifting off three times. More than once, he'd said things that hadn't entirely made sense, and he'd had to backtrack and correct himself.

When the meeting had finally ended, he'd gratefully trudged off toward his billet--only to be cornered by Donna. She'd talked his ear off for fifteen minutes (or was it an hour?), before he'd managed to disengage and resume his march toward oblivion.

Just then, when he'd been only half a corridor away from bed, a burst of alarms and flashing lights had signaled a shipwide drill. Surging with adrenaline, he'd run to his most recent post--Engineering--and worked with the team there to follow emergency procedures under simulated battle conditions.

By the time the drill had run its course, two more hours had passed. He'd stayed in Engineering an hour more before he'd finally been able to get the hell out of there and call it a day.

Now, finally, his billet was dead ahead. He shuffled along the last few meters to the door, made his way inside the darkened room, and found his rack as the door slid shut behind him.

Unfortunately, he wasn't alone. Just like the night before, Trane and Abby were in their own racks, snoring with abandon.

For a moment, Scott stood by his bed and listened to the thunderous duet. He hadn't thought it could get any louder than the night before, but it had. Even being as tired as he was, he couldn't imagine sleeping through that racket.

But if he went another night with little or no sleep, he was going to have a problem. He knew his sleep deprivation limits, and he knew he was hitting the wall right now.

So his choice was clear. He had to get out of that room. He had to take Donna up on her invitation.

Yawning, Scott trudged out of the room to a door down the hall and across from his assigned rack room. The door slid open when he approached, revealing another darkened space--thankfully, one without a pair of champion snorers going at it inside.

When Scott stepped in, the door slid shut. It took a moment for his eyes to adjust to the darkness, and then he had a look around.

There were twelve bunk beds in the room, six along each wall, and half the racks were full. Slowly, he walked between them, peering at their contents, searching for Donna.

He found her at the end of the row, on the top bunk. She was sleeping on her side, facing out, her mouth open slightly.

Trying not to wake Masada Feinberg, who was sleeping in the rack below her, he slowly climbed two rungs up the ladder at the foot of the bed. Reaching for Donna, he tapped her lightly on the shoulder.

It took a few tries to get her attention. When she finally opened her eyes and saw him, she instantly broke into a wide, sleepy grin. "Hey," she whispered, reaching over to stroke the top of his hand. "You came!"

"Trane and Abby are off the charts again," said Scott. "I can sleep through a lot, but those two are ridiculous."

"Well, there's plenty of room up here." Donna gave his hand a tug.

"Are you sure about that?" Scott frowned. Her rack didn't look roomy at all; it hadn't been made for two people.

"Absolutely." Donna slid over, opening up a little space. "We'll make it work."

Scott hesitated, wondering what he was getting in for. But then he climbed the rest of the way up and rolled into the rack beside her. It was against his better judgment, he wasn't sure he wanted to get involved with anyone on any level...but he needed sleep so badly, he felt like he was ready to pass out.

"There, see?" Donna snuggled up tight against him and

laid her arm across his chest. "Plenty of room."

Scott nodded and let out a long, exhausted sigh. "Thank you." He looked over at her and smiled. "I'm so tired, I can't see straight."

"No worries." She let her hand drift slowly over his chest. "I can empathize. I used to have a rack in the same room as those two, and it was like trying to sleep in a Battlenaut factory."

"It was a tough day," said Scott. "One damn thing after another."

"Including that crazy surprise armor drill on the Training Deck, right?" Donna laughed softly and batted his chest with her hand.

"That wasn't so bad." Scott shook his head. "It might even have been the best part of the day, actually."

"Except this part," said Donna.

"Exactly." Scott met her gaze and held it for a moment. It was then he knew, without a doubt, that she would do whatever he liked if he chose to make a move. Her body was against him, her hand touching his chest, her face just centimeters away from his--and she was willing. She was ready for anything and waiting to see what he would do next.

He considered the possibilities. He was a red-blooded man, and she was attractive...but he was also exhausted. As tempted as he was, as much as he might hate himself later for missing out, he just didn't have it in him.

Yawning, he slid his arm around her shoulders. "Thanks again," he told her. "I really owe you for this."

Donna picked up on his signals and relaxed against him. "That's right, you do." She ran her fingers down over his abdomen and kept them there a moment. "And I intend to collect."

Scott didn't address her comment. He could already feel himself drifting off as the possibilities that had been circling the two of them slowly faded away.

"Good night," he said, and then he gave her shoulders a squeeze, feeling truly grateful to be there with her after his lousy day. "Get me up when you get up, okay?"

"I'll do that," said Donna. "You can depend on me."

Scott smiled. His eyes were closed, but he could tell from the sound of her voice that she was smiling when she said it.

CHAPTER 13

Less than two days later, when the *Sun Tzu* slowed its near-faster-than-light travel at the edge of the Veda system, Scott was a changed man--fully rested and ready for anything. Sleeping in Donna's rack that first time and once afterward had really done the trick; without Trane and Abby's nonstop snoring, he'd been able to catch up on some of his much-needed lost sleep. That had made him better equipped to muscle through the hassles of shipboard life and prepare for the mission to Shard.

Which was good, because things hadn't gotten any easier for him. His schedule had stayed just as intense, packed with duty (in different departments, thankfully, not just Engineering), CORE Battlenaut training, shipwide drills, and meetings of the Surface Warfare Group. The Diamondbacks had run him ragged, pushing him to the limit in every possible way; without the rest he'd gotten with Donna, he wondered if he would've made it through as well as he had.

As for any other developments with Donna, Scott managed to keep them on hold. It was a situation that couldn't last forever, but at least for now, it seemed to be working out okay. There'd be time enough to reconsider after Shard, he figured. Assuming they all made it back from the mission, of course.

The *Sun Tzu* was less than three hours from Shard when Perseid called Scott to the Command Deck. Scott was annoyed, in the middle of prepping his Battlenaut for landfall, but he also wondered what Perseid might want.

When the door to the Command Deck opened, Scott had to take a moment to get used to the place again. He hadn't been there since his first day aboard the ship, and the illusion of standing unprotected in open space made him feel a little dizzy.

On the other hand, the sight of the gray and silver planet up ahead was familiar to him by now. Shard had been on his mind a lot lately; he'd been studying it for days, memorizing landmarks, flora, and fauna that could help him survive its hostile environment. He'd been helping to plot strategies for battle on its surface, ways to defeat Red Battlenauts or anyone else the Diamondbacks encountered. He knew that planet well, though he also knew he'd never truly understand it until he got down there.

After adjusting to the see-through environs of the Command Deck, Scott stepped up to Perseid, who was standing on a circle of white light in the middle of the deck with his hands clasped behind his back.

"Corporal Scott reporting, sir." Scott snapped off a

crisp salute.

Perseid spoke over his shoulder. “At ease, Corporal.”

Scott relaxed.

“We’re almost there,” said Perseid. “Should be an interesting experience.”

“Yes, sir,” said Scott.

“I’m willing to bet it’ll be full of surprises.” Perseid glanced over his shoulder. “But you’re ready for all that, am I right?”

“Absolutely,” said Scott.

Perseid nodded. “You’ll be our eyes and ears on Shard. Assuming the Reds haven’t figured out a way to hide from you, too.”

“It’ll be a damn short mission if they have,” said Scott.

“It’ll be a damn short *war*,” said Perseid. “*Or*, best case scenario, we come out of this with more than just *you* able to see the bastards.” He turned to Scott. “That’s why Dr. Beauchamp will be watching your telemetry like a hawk, looking for irregularities. We need to know what makes you special when it comes to spotting the Reds.”

“Okay.” Scott couldn’t say he hadn’t seen this coming. Perseid had said from the start that he wanted to figure out Scott’s secret power and put it to work for the Commonwealth.

“She’ll do the same with the other pilots, too. We hope the data will lead to a breakthrough in seeing Red Battlenauts.” Perseid leaner closer, meeting Scott’s gaze. “That won’t be a problem for you, will it?”

“No, sir.” Scott shook his head firmly. “Not a problem.”

“Because we absolutely need to spread your capability around.” Perseid tipped his head to one side. “Because what if something happens to you?”

“I understand,” said Scott.

"We've got one guy who can see the Reds. One guy with the fate of maybe the entire quadrant on his shoulders." Perseid narrowed his eyes. "Now what happens if we lose that one guy?"

"The quadrant is fluxed," said Scott.

"Totally fluxed." Perseid reached out for a handshake. "Which is why I called you up here. I wanted to personally wish you luck."

Scott shook his hand. "Thank you, sir."

"I realize this is a hell of a lot to put on one guy's shoulders," said Perseid.

"I can take it," said Scott.

"I know you can." Perseid tightened his grip. "Why do you think we've been putting the screws to you since you came aboard?"

Scott stopped shaking Perseid's hand. Suddenly, the grueling regimen of his life on the *Sun Tzu* made sense.

"It was a test?" Scott frowned. "And I passed?"

"What do you think?" Perseid let go of his hand. "Now go get ready for planetfall and show us what you're *really* made of. Show the whole *quadrant*."

"Yes, sir." Scott saluted.

"We've got twelve hours of orbital reconnaissance," said Perseid. "Then you'll get your chance."

"I'll be ready."

"You better be." Perseid waved him off and turned to face the view of the approaching planet. "Of all of us, you damn well *better* be."

After leaving the Command Deck, Scott went back to prepping his Battlenaut...but not for long. An hour later, he was summoned to a conference room by Captain Rexis.

When Scott entered, Rexis and seven other Diamondback officers were staring at a holo projection cube hovering over the big ebony conference table in the middle of the room. Right away, Scott identified what they were watching as video of the surface of Shard--a recognizable landscape of gray and silver shapes gleaming in the cold light of a pale yellow sun.

"Corporal Scott." Rexis gestured at the screen. "These are some of the first images from the A.I. probes sent to Shard."

Scott nodded and moved closer, watching the hovering cube as the video continued to play within its boundaries. It was like gazing into a cube-shaped window, following a scene near the planet's surface thousands of kilometers below.

"Take a good look," Rexis told him. "Let me know if anything jumps out at you."

Scott watched closely but didn't see anything unusual. The A.I. probe was shooting video from what seemed like a few hundred feet up, zipping along over fairly nondescript land undisturbed by artificial structures.

"What do you see?" said Khalil, who was sitting at the end of the table nearest to Scott. "An army of Red Battlenauts on the march?"

"Just metal," said Scott. "Lots and lots of metal."

"That's what we're seeing on telemetry, too," said Rexis. "Not that that means anything, when it comes to the Reds' stealth capabilities."

Just then, Masada Feinberg spoke up from the middle section of the table. "Second feed's coming in." She was playing a tablet computer, flicking her delicate, spindly fingers over the screen.

"Put it up," said Rexis.

A second holo cube appeared alongside the first, displaying video from a different location. In this feed, instead of a flat, relatively featureless landscape, Scott saw rolling hills covered with the Shard equivalent of forests--stands of treelike biometallic organisms, shiny and conical as evergreens dipped in platinum. There were ponds and lakes, too, filled with gleaming liquid metal like mercury or molten silver.

"That's a thousand kilometers due West from the first feed," said Feinberg. "For reasons we don't understand at this time, it's a region with a much higher concentration of lifeforms."

Scott could see she wasn't exaggerating. When the probe passed over clearings in the forest, he saw they were crowded with herds of big, gleaming beasts, the local versions of cows or rhinos. The ponds and lakes were life-filled, too; triangular fins and V-shaped tails broke their surfaces as the probe hurtled overhead. Even the air was populated. Flying creatures swirled in the distance, sunlight glinting off their light aluminum-like bodies as they darted out of the probe's way like tiny fighter craft.

"Well, Corporal?" said Rexis. "Do you see anything out of the ordinary?"

"Other than an unprecedented ecosystem based entirely on biometallic lifeforms, that is," said Trane with a snicker.

Scott stared intently at the second feed, looking for anything non-native...but came up empty. The probe banked around a mountainside, then followed a mercury river through a valley lined with low-growing metallic scrub--and still, nothing unusual revealed itself.

"No sign of the Reds?" said Rexis.

"Nothing yet." Scott checked the first feed, too, and saw more of the same as he'd seen there before. The probe just kept sailing along over drab, rolling plains with no flora or fauna in sight.

"Maybe there's nothing to see," said Abby. "Maybe whoever built the Reds got what they came for and left."

"That would suggest a limited effort," said Taggart. "Maybe they only built a few units instead of a whole army."

"Which wouldn't be a bad thing at all," said Abby.

"But is highly unlikely," said Khalil, "given the number of incidents which we suspect are the result of Red intervention."

"I hate to say it, but I agree with Khalil." Trane scowled and shook his head. "The Reds did more than drop by here for a cup of biometallic ore."

Just then, Scott lunged closer to the table, running into its edge, and everyone looked in his direction. Something had caught his eye on the second feed.

Then it was gone, as the probe kept whizzing along above the planet's surface. "Can we play back the last fifteen seconds of feed two?" His heart was pounding when he said it.

"Yes." Feinberg's fingers danced over her tablet, and a copy of the second feed cube appeared beside the original. Within the new cube, the video from the feed spun backward, making it look as if the probe had suddenly changed direction and started zipping back the way it had come.

"Right there!" said Scott, and the feed froze. "Now start it forward again, but slowly."

All eyes in the room were locked on the video as it crawled forward again.

"What exactly did you see?" asked Khalil.

Scott didn't answer. His attention was totally focused on the left side of the cube, where a huge tangle of what looked like copper wire slipped into view.

As he watched, the tangle of wire seemed to ripple, as if waves of heat were flowing over it. The rippling stopped, then started again--and the tangle changed shape.

"Stop!" said Scott. "That's it!"

Feinberg paused the video, but Scott wasn't happy with the freeze-frame. The new shape was severely blurred. The most he could make out was the corner of a square shape angled into the upper left quadrant of the shot. Whatever the thing was, the rest of it protruded outside the camera's field of vision.

"What do you see?" said Trane.

"Not sure. Move another frame forward," said Scott.

The video flicked forward another frame, and the unknown object was still there, just as blurry. What the hell *was* it?

"Another frame," said Scott. Still, there was no change. "One more." The image stayed the same.

"What are you looking at?" said Rexis. "Where is it located?"

"Upper left corner of the shot." As Scott said it, he looked at Feinberg and twirled his index finger. Feinberg picked up the hint and moved the video forward another frame.

Rexis pulled out a holographic pointer and directed its bright red beam at the general area where Scott saw the blurred shape. "So what does it look like to you?"

"I don't know. A blur." Squinting, Scott leaned further forward. "Can we roll the video ahead in very slow motion?"

Seconds after he asked, the video crept forward, a frame

at a time. At five frames in, maybe seven, the blurred object started looking like a silver cube. Then, as the probe veered right, even the cube slid out of the shot.

"Now it's gone." Scott shook his head and leaned back. "I don't know what it was."

"Take another look," said Rexis, and he did. In fact, he went back over the video a dozen times, rechecking the same segment. Always, the results were the same: he saw the blurred object turn into a silver cube, then disappear. There was no clarity to be found whatsoever.

But there was guidance nonetheless.

"All right." Rexis let out a heavy sigh after the twelfth review of the video. "At least we know where we're going."

"We do?" Trane sounded like he thought she was crazy.

"Corporal Scott saw something," said Rexis. "He doesn't know what it was, but it was *something*. And that's good enough for me. That tells us exactly where we need to be."

"But the feeds are still coming in," said Khalil. "What if there's something else he should see? Something that's more important?"

"That's why he's going to stay glued to the feeds." Rexis nodded at Scott when she said it. "He's going to watch as much as he can and let us know of anything else that catches his eye. Right?"

Scott nodded. "Yes, ma'am."

"And if he doesn't find anything else, we'll stick with Plan A." Rexis pointed at the freeze-frame of the planet's surface hovering over the conference table. "We'll move in on that location and light the place up."

"Assuming our onboard A.I.s can target the Reds effectively," said Abby.

"They should do the trick," said Rexis. "We know our sensors and cameras can detect Red equipment, though the resulting data and video are invisible to everyone except Scott. If the Reds can't hide from our equipment, the computer-driven A.I.s should zero right in on them when we take humans out of the equation."

"And if the A.I.s fail?" said Khalil.

"That's where Scott comes in," said Rexis. "He'll tell us *exactly* where to shoot...won't you, Corporal?"

"You can count on me." Scott tried to sound confident, though he had his doubts. "If there's one thing I'm good at, it's seeing Red."

CHAPTER 14

Scott's Battlenaut marched down the drop ship's rear gangway, just a few steps from the surface of Shard. The planet's mysteries and dangers were closer than ever now, waiting to challenge him.

Not that they'd have an easy time getting to him when they tried. Scott was surrounded on all sides by armored Diamondbacks committed to protecting him. As a secret weapon, the only one who could see the enemy, he had to be shielded at all times. If things went south in a big way, the Diamondbacks had orders to get him back to the *Sun Tzu* at any cost.

Protect the Red-detector: that was the heart of the team's surface warfare strategy for this mission. Scott knew it was the right strategy, he had no doubt in his mind...but he still hated the thought of it. His instinct was to take the point and drive hard at all times, not hang back while someone else drew fire on his behalf.

"Here we go." Abby's sharp tone came through crystal clear over the comm. She was on point, in command of the squad. "Keep it tight, people."

"Roger that," said Trane, who was stomping down the gangway on Scott's left. "Locked and loaded, good to go."

No one else said anything right away. They were about to step out into an inhospitable environment, with unknown enemies in the wind and high stakes on their shoulders. Lack of focus in the first moments on the surface could lead to early casualties and premature mission failure.

On his frontside feed, Scott watched Abby's Battlenaut cover the last few meters of ramp directly ahead. Without hesitation, she stomped right out onto the planet's surface--in this place, a deep bronze flat with a pebbled texture.

The squad held up behind her as she stood for a moment, surveying the area. Projectile guns had formed on both her forearms, and she swept them back and forth as she looked for trouble.

"All clear." She kept the guns raised as she moved forward again. "For now."

The rest of the squad took that as their cue and followed her out.

With Trane on his left and García on his right, Scott took his first steps on Shard. He was letting Frank the A.I. do the driving, with overrides for course correction and sudden stops or starts as needed. Minor adjustments were handled just fine by Frank, whose autopilot capabilities had been demonstrated as outstanding during every drill and exercise on the *Sun Tzu*'s Training Deck.

That was a good thing, because Scott had other minute-by-minute mission critical tasks on his plate. Chief among them, he had to eyeball his video feeds constantly, watching for any signs of Red activity in case Frank and the other A.I.s missed it.

As good as the A.I. systems were, Scott didn't trust them entirely. The Reds were so adept as concealment, he couldn't imagine they hadn't planned for A.I. involvement.

As Scott walked across the pebbled bronze ground, he brought up every feed and used eye control to arrange them side by side in front of him. He locked them in place, then flicked his eyes from one to the other along the line, checking for aberrations, finding nothing...yet.

Then, on his frontside feed, he saw something lunge out of a hole in the ground at eleven o'clock, a golden blur streaking toward the ebony bulk of Abby's Battlenaut. For an instant, Scott thought it might be a Red threat, blurred by masking technology--but the blur was just the product of fast movement. As soon as the thing landed in front of Abby, its image clarified.

It was some kind of biometallic creature, like a gold-skinned serpent with the head of a wolf. As it reared up in front of Abby, it bared its golden fangs and unfurled rows of gleaming blades like cleavers running along the sides of its body. Pulling back, it looked like it was ready to strike.

Which was exactly when Abby's armor grew a large-bore shoulder cannon and blasted five rounds right through the creature's skull in short order. Headless, its body flopped to the ground at Abby's feet.

"Avoid contact with native fauna whenever possible," said Abby, quoting the pre-mission briefing they'd attended aboard the *Sun Tzu*.

"That was native fauna?" said Trane. "Looked more like García after a bender."

García said nothing in reply. His armor looked as

implacable as ever when Scott stole a glimpse at his rightside feed.

"That was a documented species, actually," said Khalil, who was stationed at Scott's seven o'clock behind Trane. "It could have tunneled right into her armor and devoured her down to the bone in less than a minute."

"You sure about that?" said Trane. "She's pretty stringy."

"And there are nastier creatures than that down here," said Khalil. "*Much* nastier."

"Not counting the Reds," said Donna.

"Move out!" Abby marched her Battlenaut over the creature's carcass as she said it. "We're still three klicks out from our target."

The squad fell in behind her. The drop ship had put them down some distance from the location Scott had spotted on the probe feed. They had some ground to cover, but it was better than landing too close and getting blown to pieces right off the bat. This way, even if the Reds had detected the drop ship's approach, the squad still made landfall and had a chance of reaching the target in one piece.

For a while, the seven Diamondback Battlenauts continued their march in relative silence--no chatter over the comms, no gunfire, no surprises. They looped around a dark gray slope that kept them out of eyeshot of the target, letting them close to within half a klick of it before they'd have to emerge from cover.

The whole time, Frank did the driving while Scott scanned the feeds. He saw some amazing sights--bizarre plantlike lifeforms and creatures close by or at a distance, bodies grown from biometallic materials. There were beasts like pygmy unicorns plated in glossy blue titanium armor... trails of dull gray-green powder flowing in intricate patterns over silvery flatlands...galvanized pods like pitcher plants the size of full-grown men, spewing showers of ball bearings into the air. He was struck by how strange and beautiful Shard was, even as he recognized how deadly it could be. For every butterfly of lacy aluminum fluttering by, he saw a giant lizard-thing studded with silver spikes or an elephantine leviathan covered in whirling razor-sharp blades and spring-loaded jaws with hundreds of serrated teeth.

But he didn't see any Reds. He didn't see any mysterious blurs or incongruous visuals that might suggest a cloaked presence.

At least until the squad finished rounding the slope.

"Approaching target coordinates," said Abby. "Safeties off, people."

Scott followed her around the last curve of the slope, gazing intently at his frontside feed. Then, as the leading edge of the target slid into view, Abby stopped, and Scott did the same.

"So this is it? A bunch of empty space?" Abby pointed one of her projectile guns toward the coordinates. "Is that what you see, Scott?"

"No, ma'am." Scott's eyes were wide as he gaped at the feed. "It most certainly is not."

What he saw was anything but empty space. "Holy flux." It was an enormous structure, a huge, cube-shaped building sprawling across the valley. "It's some kind of facility. A *big* one."

"Amazing." Trane stepped forward, angling for a better view. "My A.I. sees it, too...but I don't see a damn thing."

The rest of the squad pushed forward, too, breaking formation.

"I don't see it, either," said Khalil. "But yes, my A.I. tells me it's there."

"Are you *sure* it's there?" said Balko.

Even García joined in. "Maybe the A.I.s are wrong."

"It's there, all right." Scott saw the image clearly in his frontside feed, rock-solid stable and free of distortion. "But who knows what it's there *for*." From a distance, the walls of the structure looked completely smooth and seamless, reflecting the sky and landscape without giving any clues to what lay within. "It just looks like a big silver box."

"A factory, maybe?" said Donna.

"A processing plant for biometals, I'll bet," said Trane. "It's what we expected."

"No one coming and going, according to my A.I.," said Abby.

"We need to get closer," said Khalil.

"To the giant, unidentifiable building on the planet of living knives." Trane's voice oozed sarcasm. "I can hardly wait."

"It's why we're here." Abby grew a laser out of each shoulder and added barrels to the projectile guns on her forearms. "We're going in."

"As one big cluster of Battlenauts stomping up to the front door." Trane snorted. "Awesome plan."

"We don't even know where the front door *is*," said Abby. "We need to draw them out."

"I wish we could just surround the place and blow it to kingdom come." said Balko. "Just bring it down."

"But we want *prisoners*, remember?" Abby's voice was getting sharper. "Otherwise, the *Sun Tzu* could've bombed the scudge out of these coordinates from *orbit*." She blew out her breath loudly. "We've already *gone over* all this. Now quit yapping and *move out*."

With that, she started forward, marching in the direction of the cube-shaped structure. The squad fell into formation and followed--Scott in the middle, with the others arranged around him.

Whatever was waiting for them in that mirror-walled edifice, they were heading straight for it, taking the fight to the Reds. Six Diamondbacks and one Marine were going up against unknown odds, buttressed only by mechanical armor, determination, raw courage, and A.I.s who could see what they could not.

CHAPTER 15

As the squad crossed the silver terrain, there were no signs of movement from the structure. That only heightened the tension as the Diamondbacks marched and waited for something to happen. The closer they got, the more tense they became.

They were sitting ducks, and they knew it. Abby was leading them along the curve of the slope, approaching what might be the back side of the building--the side facing away from the heart of the valley--but they were still out in the open, with no cover or camouflage. They would be visible to anyone inside the structure, easily detectable by surveillance equipment. And because they were bunched close together to protect Scott, they provided a tighter target for any weapons fire from behind those mirrored walls.

The pressure was on. It was cool inside the cockpit of Scott's Battlenaut, but sweat still ran down his sides and back. He'd been in tough situations before, but none quite like this.

As his eyes flicked back and forth over the video feeds, he spoke to his A.I. "Frank. Form additional large-bore swivel-mounted guns on upper arms and hips. Add a dorsal laser turret between shoulders."

"This configuration will limit the use of certain capabilities requiring high mass utilization," said Frank. "Drone pods and biofilm ejectors will be offline. Beanstalk function will be unavailable. Proceed?"

"Do it." Scott wanted as much straight-up firepower at his command as possible.

"See anything, Corporal?" said Abby.

"Nothing new," said Scott. "The place is still buttoned up tight."

"Maybe it's abandoned," said Donna. "Or maybe it's only periodically manned and operational."

"Makes sense," said Balko.

"Maybe," said Trane. "Unless you consider what a high-value target this is. *I* wouldn't leave it unprotected."

"Agreed," said Khalil. "At the very least, they've left a garrison to defend it."

"But it's *invisible*," said García.

"Not to our A.I.s, it isn't," said Khalil. "Not to Scott, it isn't."

Just then, Scott saw something twitch at two o'clock. He threw his rightside feed on maximum mag--only to realize it was just an armadillo-like creature, scampering across the terrain. No danger there.

No *nothing*, in fact, as the squad drew closer. Not a peep out of the Reds--so *were* they inside, and if so, what were they up to? Were they waiting for the right moment to pounce, or were they all just asleep at the wheel, lulled to complacency by the facility's cloak of virtual invisibility?

After a while, Abby spoke. "We're a hundred meters from the structure. Still no movement."

"Come out, come out, wherever you are." Trane snickered.

"Get your A.I.s looking for a door," said Abby. "We need a way in."

Scott maxed the magnification on his frontside camera and scanned the side of the building. Still, he could see no seam or break in the gleaming skin of the wall looming overhead. "I've got nothing. The outer surface appears to be uninterrupted."

"Damn," said Abby. "Looks like we might have to blast our way in."

"If we *can*," said Khalil. "Maybe that's the *real* reason it's unprotected--because it's *impenetrable*."

"Impenetrable my ass," said García. "We'll find a way in."

The squad went further, covering another twenty-five meters. Scott kept watching the feeds for signs of trouble and saw nothing alarming. Meanwhile, his heart rate rose in direct proportion to the amount of visible danger. The more nothing he saw, the more tense he became.

"My A.I. says there's a wall up ahead," said Donna.

"That's right," said Scott. "An enormous wall, eighty meters high, with a mirrored surface. I can see us reflected in it as we get closer."

Another twenty-five meters passed...then ten more. Abby's Battlenaut continued to stride forward, its broad feet crossing the silver ground.

Then, suddenly, she stopped. "What the flux? Thing's putting out some kind of radio signal."

"My A.I. picked it up, too," said Khalil. "It's moving out in all directions from the structure."

"Why?" said Donna. "What's it doing?"

"I'll tell you what it's doing," said Trane. "It's disappearing! It's blocking our A.I.s!"

"He's right!" said Abby. "My A.I. just went blind!"

"Mine, too," said García.

Everyone said the same thing, and Scott confirmed it. Flicking off the comm channel, he spoke directly to his A.I. "Frank, describe your current visual input."

"There is none," said Frank. "All visual input has ceased."

Looking around the cockpit, Scott saw that wasn't quite accurate. All the video feeds were still coming in clear, and all sensors were still providing data. "You're telling me you have no visuals? What about sensors?"

"No visuals," said Frank. "No sensor readings, either. I am quite literally in the dark, Solomon."

Scott switched the comm back on. "My A.I. is blind, too," he told the others. "But video and sensor feeds are working fine."

"Same here," said Abby. "But without the damn A.I., I can't see the Red structure."

The rest of the squad agreed. Video and sensor feeds weren't much good if the human pilot couldn't see anything Red-related.

"Impressive," said Trane. "That radio signal carried a computer virus that reprogrammed the visual signal processing subroutine in the A.I.s. Video's still coming in, but they can't *see* it."

"And *we* can see *video*, but not the *Reds*," said Khalil.

"Good thing we brought a secret weapon," said Abby.

"Corporal Scott, you're going to have to walk us through this, after all."

"Roger that." Even as he said it, Scott caught a glimpse of something hurtling down in front of the squad. "Incoming!" he cried, as loud as he could.

The hurtling object plunged into the ground less than a meter from Abby, barely missing her armor.

"Damn!" said Trane. "Those Reds don't waste any time, do they?"

"What is it?" snapped Abby. "My A.I.'s blind, and all I see on video is empty ground!"

Scott rushed up and got a look at what had just crashed down. It was a slim, triangular fin, three meters long and painted flat black, with a sharp nose driven into the metallic ground. A cylindrical housing hugged the central shaft several centimeters behind the nose. As he watched, the housing turned clockwise and started sliding forward.

"Everybody move!" hollered Scott. "Go go go!"

As one, the Diamondbacks lurched away from the landing site. Scott's armor lumbered after them; Frank couldn't see, so Scott had to pick a direction and tell him to run.

"*Warhead*!" said Scott. "It's gonna' *blow*!"

Just as he said it, the missile exploded behind him, swamping him with a shockwave of shuddering force.

CHAPTER 16

The explosion rocked Scott's Battlenaut but didn't knock it down. Frank, ahead of the game even though he was blind, managed to keep the armor on its feet.

The others weren't all so lucky. Checking the feeds, Scott saw Donna's Battlenaut go down on its belly, while Balko's hit the ground on its side.

"Form up!" Abby was shouting urgently over the comm. "Scott, what *was* that?"

"Some kind of missile!" Scott's eyes locked on the topside feed, looking for more incoming fire--and quickly finding it. Two objects launched from the roof of the structure, flashing toward the squad on arcing vapor trails. "Two more on the way!"

Scott's mind raced. He had split-seconds until the second volley found its mark--not enough time to figure firing solutions and flash them to his squad-mates.

Better and faster to take action himself. "Frank! Retract

all projectile weapons! Form and fire shoulder-mount anti-missile missiles at these coordinates!" Using eye control, he reconfigured the topside feed, superimposing a numbered grid over the view. Watching the incoming missiles, judging their trajectories against the numbers on the grid, he barked out two sets of coordinates. He just had to hope that Frank, though sightless, still had enough geospatial awareness to program the missiles to get where they needed to be.

Even as Scott fed Frank the coordinates, he could see from the holographic wireframe of his armor that Frank had already pulled in the guns and grown missile launchers from his shoulders.

The A.I. didn't waste time talking. Scott felt the shock of the two launches, and holo readouts showed the missiles' trajectories as they climbed.

It was going to be touch and go. Scott was good at quickly calculating firing solutions on the fly, but the incoming missiles were moving fast, and his A.I. wasn't a hundred percent.

He did pretty well, considering. Topside showed one of his anti-missile missiles colliding dead-on with an enemy rocket, blowing it apart in midair.

Unfortunately, his second shot missed. The other enemy missile streaked toward the squad, then hit the ground in the middle of the group and exploded on impact, bowling over everyone who was still standing.

Just like that, a squad of elite Diamondbacks and one Marine were thrown in total disarray. Naturally, that was when the next wave descended on them...but it wasn't a wave of missiles.

Seconds after landing on his back, Scott saw them: three figures leaping, not launching, off the roof. Even from a distance, they looked familiar.

When he sat up and threw the feed on maximum mag, any doubt of what they were went out the window. "Enemy sighted!"

"What enemy?" said Abby.

The feed was very clear at max mag. Scott could see pale sunlight glinting off one of the leaping figures, revealing armor of a certain color he knew too well.

"Reds!" Scott's heart hammered when he said it. "Red Battlenauts, three of them, heading straight for us!"

"Everyone up!" shouted Abby. "Prepare to fire!"

Scott was already in motion. "Stand up, Frank!" Glancing at the wireframe, he saw his Battlenaut roll to one side, plant its hands on the ground, and boost itself up on its knees. "Ready anti-missile launchers!"

"Firing coordinates?" Frank's voice was calm, as if this were just another exercise on the Training Deck.

Watching the topside feed, Scott saw the Red Battlenauts dropping fast. They were spread out in a spearhead formation--one on point, the other two fanned out on his rear flanks. They were too far apart for him to take them with one or two shots--not that he really thought it would ever be that easy with juggernauts like those.

"Coordinates, please," said Frank.

"Talk to us, Scott!" said Abby. "Tell us where to shoot!"

Scott took a breath and closed his eyes for a split-second. When he opened them again, he slid smoothly into action. He'd prepared for this situation back onboard the *Sun Tzu*; now, it was just a matter of letting it happen.

"Bearing two-two-niner, angle forty-five degrees," he said, giving the squad a rough direction as he watched the numbered grid. Tracing the Reds' descent on the feed, he picked likely coordinates, typed them on a hovering holo keypad, and flashed them to the rest of the squad. "I'm sending coordinates now!"

"Received!" said Abby. "Fire!"

Everyone who was back on their feet cut loose at the same time, filling the sky around the Reds with slugs, missiles, and laser beams. Only Khalil and García's guns remained silent, as they continued to work their way back to upright positions.

"Keep firing!" said Abby. "Don't let up!"

Scott released his missiles, too, and watched them cruise toward the Reds on the feed. One went wide, sweeping off to the left of the point Battlenaut--but the other slammed into the chest of the right-flanking Red. The missile blew on impact, sending the Red spinning off course--but otherwise unscathed, as far as Scott could see.

As for the other two Reds, they just kept coming, passing through the curtain of slugs, missiles, and lasers as if it were no more than a holographic sky show, intangible and harmless. They quickly dropped out of the field of fire and touched down thirty meters away.

"One direct hit! He's deflected but undamaged," Scott said over the comm. "The other two have touched down. Targets at ten and two o'clock."

"Let's get this party started!" said Trane.

"Fire at will!" said Abby.

Scott clenched his jaw and glared at the frontside feed. Things were about to get interesting.

Back on Chelong III, the Red's superior energy weapons had chewed through Rollins' and Scott's armor like a chain saw through tissue paper. But CORE armor was an entirely different animal with much higher tensile strength and energy dispersal capabilities per square centimeter. The big brains--Rexis, Trane, and Khalil--were confident that the Diamondback Battlenauts would hold up against Red firepower...but there was only one way to know for sure.

And here it came. As soon as the two Reds hit the ground, the forward cannons on their chests surged to life, glowing with bright golden energy. They were about to fire the same weapons that had destroyed Scott's old Battlenaut and killed poor Captain Rollins.

"Incoming!" Scott's pulse quickened. "Chest-mounted energy cannons about to fire!" Everyone was on their feet now--including Khalil and García--and they were all blasting away with slugs and lasers. Half the squad fired at the ten o'clock target, while the other half focused on two o'clock... though they all maintained a loose formation around Scott. Protecting him was more crucial than ever, now that the A.I.s were blind.

Not that Scott planned to hold back any. As the squad pounded away at the Reds, he was right in there, cranking off rounds at both enemy war machines--firing with his left arm gun at ten o'clock while his right arm fired at two.

Suddenly, the Reds' cannons flared and fired. Each Battlenaut unleashed two streams of searing golden energy, sending them blazing over the silver ground toward the Diamondbacks.

Scott sucked in a breath and held it. One of the beams was coming in from two o'clock at an angle that would lead right to him. Even if his squadmates or their A.I.s could have seen it, they wouldn't have been able to do anything to stop it in time.

Scott was about to find out the hard way if CORE armor measured up to Red weapons technology. The same kind of beam that had blown his armor to bits on Chelong III was streaking straight for him and would make contact in a heartbeat.

CHAPTER 17

The beam from the Red's cannon slammed into the upper body of Scott's Battlenaut with shuddering force. Bright light drowned out all the camera feeds at once except the backside view. The comm went dead, and the cockpit filled with a high-pitched, piercing whine.

But the armor didn't blow apart. A moment passed, and the CORE Battlenaut held together against the searing assault. It was still standing, ready to fight back, long past the point at which Scott had ejected from his old armor during a similar attack.

"Now that's more like it." Scott smirked and checked his holo readouts, which showed that all systems remained nominal. His Battlenaut wasn't anywhere near being ready to explode. "You're not getting off easy *this* time."

"Excuse me," said Frank. "Could you provide me with a firing solution for one of the Red Battlenauts? I am unable to see or detect either one."

Suddenly, Scott's Battlenaut lurched back a step, shoved off balance by an increase in the beam's power. Frank quickly restabilized, but Scott realized the armor had its limits.

Time to switch off the weapon at its source. "Red Battlenaut at two o'clock, Frank. Height 12 meters. Form and fire biofilm cannon."

"What size payload?" said Frank.

"Maximum possible."

"The requested strike will severely limit additional use of biofilm and other mass-hungry applications," said Frank.

Scott already knew that. In a live fire situation, resource hogs like biofilm should be used sparingly, when other means had failed...but the Reds were coming on strong. Maybe some up-front shock and awe could take the wind out of their sails. "Fire ASAP!"

The wireframe figure showed a shoulder-mounted cannon forming and firing a bundle. The cockpit wrenched back as the payload launched, propelled toward a target only Scott could see.

The biofilm pod leaped the distance and burst against the Red's head. Watching the topside feed, Scott saw the lumpy green slime spread fast, expanding over the gleaming red skin of the monstrous enemy Battlenaut.

Seconds later, the energy weapons on the Red's chest cut out, taking the pressure off Scott. That was when he finally had a moment to survey the status of the rest of the squad.

The camera feeds told the story. Scott's six teammates were still standing, but they were taking a pounding and firing blind. A single Red Battlenaut was holding them all at bay, beating them up with blasts from his forward energy weapons. Apparently, the Diamondbacks couldn't even see the actual fire and use its path to determine firing trajectories of their own.

As Scott took it all in, the comm suddenly reconnected, filling the cockpit with the sound of shouting Diamondbacks. Abby was louder than anyone, cursing up a storm when she wasn't bellowing Scott's name.

"I said *come in*, Scott!" She cursed some more. "Wake up, you *mother-fluxer*!"

"I copy, Lieutenant!" said Scott. "My comm was down, but now it's back up!"

"Who gives a scudge!" snapped Abby. "Tell us where to *shoot*!"

Scott double-checked the numbered grid overlaid on the image of the attacking Red on the feed. "Ten o'clock, thirty meters out, twelve meters high."

Abby didn't bother discussing it any further. "Everyone fire on those coordinates *now*!"

All six Diamondbacks--and Scott--swung their weapons around at once and took aim where he'd said. Without hesitation, they all cut loose, filling the air with a stream of projectiles, laser beams, sonics, and missiles.

Though six of them were shooting at what appeared to them to be thin air, plenty of ordnance connected with its target. Scott saw a high percentage of slugs, lasers, and missiles slam home, mostly in the Red's head and upper torso region.

The concentrated fire seemed to have an effect. The Red Battlenaut jerked back, and its energy weapons disengaged. Something sparked on its abdomen, then sparked again, brighter. A puff of smoke filtered from one of the cooling vents on its back, curling up toward the sky.

Scott felt a surge of hope. As blind as the rest of the

squad had become, it was actually doing some damage. Maybe the Red bastards weren't unbeatable after all.

"How're we *doing?*" said Abby.

"Making a dent!" said Scott. "Recommend we keep pouring it on!"

"You heard the man!" said Abby. "Give it all you've got!"

As the besieged Red staggered, Scott stole a glance at the one he'd tagged with the biofilm. As expected, the green slime had enveloped the armor, coating it from tip to toe. The Battlenaut twitched underneath the film as it tried to break free--then emitted flashes of light from its chest cannons as it tried shooting its way out.

As Scott watched, there was another flash, and a patch of slime burst free. The hole it left was small, but it was a start; it would only be a matter of time until the Red worked itself all the way out of its cocoon. "Can we fire more biofilm, Frank?"

"Not recommended," said Frank. "The first shot consumed a high percentage of usable mass on hand."

"All right then." Scott would wait till the other Red was down, then shift the squad's fire to the one in the biofilm before it could break loose and join the fight. "Not a problem."

Scanning back over the feeds, he saw that the focused fire was continuing to have an impact. The Red taking the brunt of the squad's attack stumbled back and almost fell. The smoke coming out of its cooling vent had gone from a puff to a cloud, and it showed no sign of letting up. The sparks on its abdomen had turned into a constant, flickering blaze, which was spreading.

All it took was a missile to the chest, fired by Trane, to

knock it down. The Red collapsed, its backward-bending knees folding up under its falling body. It hit hard, sending a tremor through the silver ground under Scott's armor's feet.

"He's down!" said Scott. "Hold your fire!" Time to turn to the other Battlenaut and let him have it with all barrels. "Redirect fire to target at two o'clock, thirty-two meters out, height twelve meters."

"Squad redirect!" said Abby, though she didn't have to. Everyone except Trane was already turning their weapons to the second target. "Fire at will!"

In a few short moments, the Red had cleared away a large section of biofilm, exposing its forward cannons. As Abby ordered the squad to fire, the Red charged its cannons with crackling golden energy, ready to let loose.

The squad opened up with a vengeance, hammering the Red with every kind of ordnance at hand. The latest bombardment was better focused than the first one had been, as most everything came to bear on a single area--but that area was the cockpit cowling, which Scott guessed would be the best-protected part of the Red's armor.

Better to drop the crosshairs, he thought. "Recommend aiming ten degrees lower!" he said.

"Aim ten degrees lower!" said Abby.

Everyone followed the order, and the stream of weapons fire shifted downward. Before it could strike the chest, though, the Red's forward cannons blew out twin blasts of golden energy.

This time, the blasts were much brighter than before. Instead of running parallel and picking out different targets, they coalesced, forming a single beam that was zeroed in on a single target.

"Incoming!" shouted Scott. It was all he could do as

the blazing beam slashed toward the squad. It was moving too fast to avoid--too fast for him even to call out a more detailed warning. Whatever was going to happen when it hit, it was well beyond his control.

Not that that would make it any easier later, when he remembered this moment. When he remembered the sight of the beam colliding with the armor of one of his squadmates, sending it hurtling over the metal plain like a broken toy. When he remembered the sound of Donna's scream before her comm cut out.

"Donna!" he howled, even as he knew it was too late. "Donna!"

"Scott!" said Abby. "What the hell's our status?"

Scott hesitated. One of the holo readouts fanned out in front of him listed vital signs for the rest of the squad. Donna's were blinking red, the numbers dropping as he watched. "Our status is, that thing's firing some kind of high-powered beam merging the output of two cannons. We need to...we need to..." The numbers were still falling. "We need to take out those cannons. Fire right into them."

"Then call it!" said Abby. "We need firing solutions."

Again, Scott hesitated. Donna's numbers paused in their free-fall, holding steady, giving him hope. "Okay." His eyes swung back to the camera feeds. Staring at the image of the Red and the numbered grid superimposed over it, he thought fast, calculating possible solutions. "Bearing one-six-three, angle forty-eight degrees!"

"Balko, Khalil, García," said Abby. "Fire on those coordinates!"

Scott worked another instant, then rattled off a second solution. "Bearing one-six-eight, angle forty-eight degrees."

"That's us, Trane," said Abby. "You, too, Scott!"

Everyone locked on the coordinates he'd given and blasted away. On the feed, Scott saw the squad's slugs and lasers pump into both big forward cannons on the Red's chest, zooming dead-on into the gun's broad muzzles.

Suddenly, there were two thunderous booms as the cannons exploded. The Red Battlenaut collapsed to the ground, chest blown apart and pouring out billows of black smoke.

Scott didn't pause to celebrate. His eyes shot to the holo readouts, going straight to Donna's vitals. When he saw them, his spirit sank like a stone.

Most of them were dark. Heart rate, pulse ox, respiratory rate, blood pressure...none were registering. As for body temp, it was dropping fast.

Scott swallowed hard. He couldn't take his eyes off the readouts. He couldn't stop thinking about what they meant.

Her body had shut down. None of the signs of life were showing up at nominal levels on the sensors installed in her cockpit.

According to the readouts, Donna Perihelion was dead.

CHAPTER 18

"Scott!" Abby was hollering over the comm. "I said *get moving*. Lead us to the Reds!"

Scott was still in a daze, still staring at Donna's zeroed-out vital signs. She'd been his best friend since he'd joined up with the Diamondbacks; he still couldn't believe she was gone.

"Come on, Scott!" said Abby. "We still can't *see* these damn things, and we need to extricate the pilots and salvage what we can!"

Scott shook his head to try to clear it. He'd lost friends in battle many times before; he damn well knew he needed to shrug it off and act like a professional.

Still, the thought of Donna's lifeless body wedged in the cockpit of her crumpled Battlenaut kept him frozen in place. "What about..." Back on the *Sun Tzu*, he hadn't wanted to get involved with her, but now... "What about Donna?"

Just as he said it, he heard a soft beeping sound. His

eyes flew back to the holo readouts, and he saw something he'd thought he might never see again.

Donna's vitals were back on the board and slowly rising.

"Scratch that!" he said. "She's still alive!"

"I've already called for an evac," said Abby. "Now let's stay on task! Where are the Reds we took down? Are they still armed and mobile?"

Switching back to all-business mode, Scott peered at the feeds. Both Reds were still down and smoking. "No movement at all, but I can't tell if their weapons are still active."

"What about the pilots?" said Abby.

"Unknown," said Scott. "I see no one emerging from the wreckage."

"Then let's get going," said Abby. "Quit pissing around here."

"Yes, ma'am." Scott headed for the nearest Red, the one at two o'clock. Meanwhile, he kept one eye on Donna's vitals, watching as they slowly crept upward.

When he got close to the Red, he moved more cautiously. He knew the armor could still be deadly; even if the pilot were incapacitated, booby traps and self-destructs could still lurk within...especially given the high level of secrecy demonstrated by the Reds' creators so far.

As Scott prowled alongside the toppled armor, Abby and Trane stayed close, with the rest of the squad not far behind. Everyone seemed subdued, though they'd just defeated two Red Battlenauts, as if Donna's takedown had knocked the wind out of their sails.

"So it's right here?" said Abby.

"Yes," said Scott.

"Can we retrieve the pilot?" said Abby.

"I don't know." Scott made his way to the Red's upper body, trying to get a look at the cockpit, but his Battlenaut wasn't tall enough. Fortunately, he had a way to change that. "Frank. Activate beanstalk function."

"Beanstalk function is available in armor's current configuration," said Frank. "Height?"

"Keep going until I say stop," said Scott.

With that, his Battlenaut's legs started growing, lifting the torso into the air. Within seconds, Scott was high enough to look down at the Red's cockpit with his cameras. "Stop," he said, at which point Frank made the legs stop growing. "Cockpit's still sealed. The cowling's damaged, but unbroken." In other words, the pilot was still inside.

"Pilot must be unconscious," said Trane. "Otherwise, he'd have ejected by now."

"You'll have to cut him out of there, Scott," said Abby.

Just as she said it, Scott heard the muffled pops of explosive bolts blowing, and the cockpit zoomed up out of its socket in the Red Battlenaut's head. It flew skyward before he could do a thing to stop it, disappearing into the clouds far above.

"Mother-fluxer!" shouted Scott. "He just ejected! The cockpit's already gone sub-orbital."

"Damnit," said Abby.

"Should we contact the *Sun Tzu*?" said Balko. "Tell them to intercept?"

"Negative," said Scott. "They won't be able to see it any better than you can."

"All right then." Abby drew and released a deep breath. "We'd better get the other one before *he* gets away, too!"

Scott was disappointed at losing the pilot, but not for long. Watching the feeds at over twice his normal height, he spotted something in the distance--something that demanded his attention.

He saw light glinting off metal...the manufactured metal of something not native to Shard. And it was moving toward them fast, storming across the silver floor of the valley.

"I see the third Red Battlenaut," he said. "The one that didn't land with the others. It's on its feet and coming this way."

"Right," said Abby. "Then you need to *move*. Get your ass over to the other wreckage and cut out the pilot before he ejects."

"But what about the incoming Red?" said Scott.

"Call coordinates as soon as you can!" said Abby. "Now *go*!"

"Deactivate beanstalk!" Scott ordered Frank.

"Deactivating," said Frank, as the Battlenaut's legs shortened and its torso dropped.

"Now I want you to *run*," said Scott. "Maximum speed. Bearing one three niner--the location of the other cloaked target we were shooting at."

"If you say so," said Frank.

Scott stole a glance at Donna's vital signs and smiled tightly. They were low as hell but steady; she was hanging on. Now if she could just make it a little longer.

Scott's Battlenaut broke into a run, charging toward the other smoking wreckage. Its long strides carried it quickly across the valley, even as the third Red continued its approach.

If the Red kept going at its current speed, Scott guessed it would arrive in two or three minutes, max...so time was of the essence. Before the Red got within shooting range, Scott needed to extract and lock down the crashed pilot, then turn his full attention to the rest of the squad. Since none of the others could see the Red, he was their only chance at fighting it effectively.

"Status!" said Abby.

"Coming up on the wreckage." At the most, Scott was three strides from the downed Battlenaut--close enough to see that the cockpit was still sealed and in place. "Incoming Red is half a klick out, coming in at bearing..." He checked the grid overlay on the rightside feed. "...one seven six." He checked readouts and did some quick mental math. "ETA two point five minutes."

"You heard the man," Abby told the squad. "Form on me and take aim at bearing one seven six."

"Roger that," said Trane. "Proceeding to aim at thin air, as usual."

As the squad moved into formation, Scott reached the downed Red. Fortunately, it lay on its side, with the cockpit wedged against the ground so the pilot wouldn't be able to eject if he tried. That was good news, unless he had orders to self-destruct to avoid capture...in which case, Scott would lose his prisoner and maybe get blown to smithereens himself.

In other words, he still needed to move fast. "I need a cutter," he said. "Form a power saw, Frank."

"Already in process." Frank's prognostication software was amazing. The A.I. had anticipated Scott's need and moved to fulfill it before he could even voice a request.

The wireframe figure showed one of his Battlenaut's arms turning into a huge chain saw. On the frontside feed, Scott could see the saw spin into action.

"Frank, I need you to cut the cockpit free," said Scott, "and disable any explosive bolts."

"Further guidance will be necessary," said Frank. "I am unable to see the cockpit you are referring to...or anything else, for that matter."

"Understood." Scott stared at the frontside feed, judging the position of the cockpit. "Extend chain saw at a 320 degree angle. Maximum extension 1.5 meters from torso."

"Affirmative," said Frank.

Watching the frontside feed, Scott saw the chainsaw align just as he'd instructed at the corner of the cockpit cowling. "Move the saw forward approximately 30 centimeters and begin cutting."

"Yes, Solomon."

The feed showed the chainsaw pushing forward and biting into the socket around the cockpit. "Move the saw forward another 30 centimeters. Cut from right to left, moving along a 45-degree inclination."

The saw chewed through the metal linkages holding the cockpit in place on one side, spitting out showers of sparks.

"Solomon," said Frank. "I am still functionally blind, and I have no access to my sensors...but I seem to have a rudimentary awareness of touch. I can feel the metal as I cut it--just barely."

"That's great, Frank!" said Scott. "Use it to guide you! Make sure you cut the explosive bolts before they can blow."

"Yes, Solomon." Frank's cutting speeded up. At the rate he was going, it would only take another moment to free the enclosed pod.

Meanwhile, the third Red continued its approach, stomping toward the squad with its forward cannons charged and ready. It was maybe a minute and a half away.

Scott ground his teeth as he looked from one feed to the other, dividing his attention between the cockpit cutting and the approaching Red. It was going to be damn close.

"Scott!" said Abby. "Status!"

"Cockpit's almost out," said Scott. "Red's almost here. About a minute away."

"Same bearing?"

He double-checked. "Affirmative. Bearing one seven six."

"Stand by, people!" said Abby. "Prepare to fire on Scott's mark!"

Sweat trickled down Scott's back as Frank finished cutting, freeing most of the cockpit and severing the explosive bolts. The cockpit tipped toward him out of the socket--but the lower edge, which was partly wedged against the ground, remained attached. It would have to be pried the rest of the way out.

"Frank," said Scott. "Reconfigure chainsaw into a standard arm. Use both arms to break the cockpit out of its socket."

"Describe the cockpit's location, Solomon," said Frank.

"Same as before, but the top edge is leaning sixty centimeters out of the socket."

Frank reached out with both hands but missed the cockpit rim. His fingers closed--but Scott saw they had closed around nothing.

"Five centimeters lower," said Scott. "Hurry!"

This time, Frank's hands clamped around the edge of the cockpit. "Did I get it?"

"Yes!" said Scott. "Pull it out of there!"

The cockpit was wedged against the ground, stuck in place by the weight of the Red Battlenaut pressing down on it.

"Status!" said Abby.

Scott checked the feed. "Thirty seconds!" It was a

guess, but not far off. The incoming Red was almost upon them.

Meanwhile, Frank gave the cockpit a hard tug, and it came free in his hands. "I have succeeded, haven't I, Solomon?"

"You got it!" said Scott. "Now just don't let go! And get back to the rest of the squad *right now*."

His Battlenaut started running, clutching the cockpit pod against its chest with both hands. "Are we heading for another firefight? If so, which weapons would you like me to prep?"

"Surprise me! Aim at bearing one seven six!" said Scott, and then he shouted over the comm at the squad. "Diamondbacks, fire! It's right on top of you!"

The squad opened fire on the bearing he'd called, filling the air with a wave of slugs, lasers, drone pods, and sonics. It was enough to make the Red stop forty meters out and return fire. Blasts of golden energy leaped from its forward cannons, blazing toward the squad.

"Incoming!" shouted Scott as his Battlenaut quickly closed the distance. "Energy beams at eleven and one o'clock!"

As he said it, the Red's twin blasts flashed down and made contact--one with the ground, barely missing Khalil as he took a step forward, and the other with Balko. If it had been a combined beam, Balko might have suffered the same fate as Donna--but the single stream of power wasn't enough to blow him off the battlefield. Catching the force of the strike on his chest, he staggered back two steps but didn't go down. If anything, he fought harder, growing new guns on his shoulders and doubling the volume of ordnance he put in the air.

It looked like the Diamondbacks were holding their own. They still couldn't see a visible trace of the Red, but they were standing their ground against it.

At that point, Scott reached the action. His Battlenaut roared up, carrying the captured cockpit against its chest, and opened fire with the latest weapon grown by Frank--a belly-mounted flamethrower.

"Dragon's Breath." That's what Frank called it when Scott asked what the hell it was. "A stream of nuclear fire produced by the armor's fusion power plant. In effect, a miniature solar flare."

Scott watched the forward feed as tongues of tightly focused nuclear flame lashed out at the Red. They didn't interrupt the flow of golden beams from its forward energy cannons--but they did leave scorch marks that Scott could see between blasts. Maybe, if he kept up the bombardment, the Dragon's Breath would do more than scorch the Red's paint job.

"Are we having an impact?" said Frank. "Is the Dragon's Breath meeting your expectations?"

"Just keep it up," said Scott. "Keep firing at those exact coordinates."

"I will do so," said Frank, "but keep in mind, prolonged use of this weapon will affect power consumption required for other functions."

More fiery tongues lashed from the flamethrower, further singeing the Red's hull. At the same time, the Diamondbacks kept up their barrage, blasting away with slugs, lasers, missiles, and sonics. The Red responded by continuing to comb its energy beams through the squad, jarring the CORE Battlenauts without knocking any down.

"Dragon's Breath is scorching the Red's armor," Scott

reported over the comm. "Suggest everyone switch from current ordnance."

"What the hell," said Abby. "Let's do it."

The Diamondbacks stopped shooting as they reconfigured their Battlenauts to fire Dragon's Breath instead of conventional ammo, missiles, lasers, or sonics. It was then, during that brief letup when Scott's flamethrower was the only CORE weapon still firing, that the Red suddenly stopped shooting and turned away from the squad. Instead of facing the Diamondbacks, it seemed to zero in on Scott's Battlenaut.

Which didn't make a damn bit of difference to Scott. He kept pouring on the Dragon's Breath, pumping superheated nuclear fire against the Red's chest--and he started seeing results. A patch of the enemy's armor began to melt under the bombardment, oozing down slowly in bright crimson globs.

Just then, the rest of the squad finished reconfiguring and unleashed their own Dragon's Breath onslaught. Five new streams of blistering flame exploded against the Red, washing over its upper body in a blinding torrent.

But the Red stayed focused on Scott. It took a step toward him, bucking the tide of his own Dragon's Breath, and then it took another.

Then, it took three more, and stopped. Scott's flamethrower was still slamming it, but the other five were splashing into the empty air behind it. The Red had moved beyond the bearing they'd been targeting, and they couldn't see what its new location was.

Scott knew he needed to fix that. "New bearing on the Red!" He checked the forward feed and its grid overlay. "Change to one-eight-one!"

"Roger that!" said Abby. "New bearing one-eight-one!"

The squad shifted left, and its combined barrage of flames caught the Red once more.

"Contact!" said Scott. "Keep pouring it on!"

As the fiery fusillade lapped at its armor, the Red rotated its upper body to face the squad. Bathed in flame, it stared at the Diamondbacks for a moment, as if from the depths of Hell. Then, it rotated its torso again and faced Scott.

After which, it took three long strides, again walking out of range of the squad's flamethrowers.

Scott's eyes widened as he realized what was happening. The Red Battlenaut's pilot was figuring something out--something crucial.

"Change bearing again!" Scott called out over the comm. "One-eight-niner!"

Again, the squad shifted its fire...and again, the Red stepped out of it toward Scott.

"Oh, no." Suddenly, Scott could feel his advantage slipping away. Victory was becoming much less likely for him and the Diamondbacks.

Because the Red's pilot had figured out that Scott was the only one who could see him. When he changed position, Scott was the only one whose weapon never stopped hitting him.

Therefore, Scott had just become the most important target on the battlefield.

"Scudge!" shouted Scott. "He knows I can *see* him!"

"What's...-ott?" All of a sudden, Abby's voice over the comm was crackling and breaking up. "Can't...you..."

"Captain!" said Scott. "New bearing!"

"I can't...what..."

"I said *new bearing*," said Scott.

But this time, no answer, not even a broken one, came back to him. He called out the names of other Diamondbacks, and they didn't answer him, either.

The comm was down. The squad couldn't see the Red, and now Scott couldn't tell them where it was.

And the Red was stomping toward him, charging up its energy cannons.

"Frank!" said Scott. "Can you fix the comm?"

Frank paused. "Are you sure they are down? I have an incoming message."

Scott scowled. "A message? From who?"

"From the Red Battlenaut," said Frank. "Connecting now."

CHAPTER 19

Scott's blood ran cold as he stared at the forward feed. The Red Battlenaut, which had been storming toward him, suddenly stopped in its tracks.

A voice filtered from the speaker in the cockpit, electronically altered beyond any hope of recognition. "Hello, Corporal Scott."

Scott glared at the image of the Red on the feed and said nothing. He wasn't about to acknowledge that the Red pilot had correctly identified him.

"That's right, Sol. I've been tapping your comm," said the pilot. "But I didn't need to do that to figure out your secret."

Again, Scott didn't respond. Instead, he glanced at Donna's vitals, which were still low and steady, then checked the squad's status via the topside feed. All five Diamondbacks were still shooting their Dragon's Breath flamethrowers at the patch of thin air where the Red had been a moment ago.

If only Scott could send them a message about where the Red was *now*.

"You're an *anomaly*. A *loophole*," said the Red's pilot. "You can *see* us. You shouldn't be able to, but you *can*."

Scott wasn't about to comment on that one, though he did finally break his silence. "I am prepared to accept your surrender," he said, "in the name of the Commonwealth of Worlds."

The pilot's laughter, electronically distorted as it was, sounded strange...not much like laughter at all. "*My* surrender?"

"I am also empowered to offer you asylum," said Scott, "in exchange for cooperation."

"You've got it all wrong." The pilot laughed again. "You're not on the *winning* side *this* time."

Go ahead, thought Scott. *Keep laughing*. While the Red pilot was yukking it up, Scott was busy watching the Diamondbacks on the feed. One of them--Abby--stopped shooting and turned in his direction. So did the other four.

They'd figured it out, hadn't they? Scott's comm was cut off, and they'd figured out he was in trouble. Now, if he could just get them to give him the help he needed.

"Form projectile weapons on both shoulders," he told Frank. "Target bearing one-nine-five, elevation ten meters."

"That configuration will not leave sufficient energy for full-power Dragon's Breath utilization," said Frank.

"Just do it." As Scott said it, the rightside and leftside feeds showed newly grown guns appearing on his Battlenaut's shoulders, then swinging up to aim at the Red's cockpit.

"What's this?" said the Red's pilot. "A last-ditch effort to fight your way to freedom? Don't bother!"

Scott had no intention of firing the new guns. He just

wanted to point as clearly as possible at the Red for the Diamondbacks' benefit. "I repeat, I am prepared to accept your surrender," he said.

The pilot laughed again. "And *I* am prepared to accept that *cockpit* you've been lugging around." Just then, his energy cannons fired a warning shot at Scott's Battlenaut's feet. "Then we can talk about whether I bring you back alive, so we can dissect you and find out what makes you tick, or if I should just kill you right here and close the loophole."

Watching the feeds, Scott saw the Diamondbacks moving toward the Red. To their credit, they were aiming their flamethrowers at just about the right place. Abby must have ordered them to get closer to be sure they hadn't misjudged the situation.

Scott helped them by moving to the right, getting the Red to turn further away from them. The whole time, Scott kept his arm-mounted guns pointed up at the Red, indicating the coordinates the Diamondbacks should target.

"So what will it be?" said the Red's pilot. "Surrender or death? I don't care either way."

"Death," said Scott, "for *you*. Air support's on the way."

"No it isn't," said the pilot. "Your ship can't *see* me."

Scott took another few steps to the right, teeing up the Red for the Diamondbacks' assault. "They can *hit* you if they *nuke* the area. Which they *will*."

"I've been jamming your comm," said the pilot. "You couldn't get a signal *out* to call for air support."

"*That's* the *signal*," said Scott. "Loss of comms. So you're right--*I* didn't send a signal, *you* did."

The pilot hesitated. "You're bluffing, not that it matters. As long as we take *you* off the board, it's mission accomplished."

The Diamondbacks were getting closer. Scott stood his ground and braced himself for what was about to happen. "Well, I'm sorry to disappoint you," he said, "but I'm not the one leaving the board at this point."

"Technically, you're right," said the pilot. "Your *friends* are the ones leaving *first.*"

With that, the Red whirled and ran toward the Diamondbacks.

Scott was stunned; the pilot must have been watching his backside camera feeds more closely than he'd let on. "Run, Frank! Bearing one-four-seven, maximum speed!"

As Scott's Battlenaut charged, the Red raced in a circle around the squad, blasting away with his energy cannons. Missiles pumped from launchers on his shoulders, streaking toward the Diamondbacks, who were firing blindly at the coordinates Scott had pointed them to moments ago.

It was one direct hit after another--Abby, Trane, Balko, Khalil, García. The air filled with flashes of fire and puffs of smoke, none of them coming from the Red. Things were going south in a hurry.

Just then, Frank spoke up. "The cockpit pod I am carrying is heating up quickly. The skin of the pod is now one thousand degrees Celsius and rising. A few more seconds, and it will be hot enough to damage your armor."

Scott thought fast. "Stop running! Turn around and throw the cockpit as far as you can!" Checking his backside feed, he saw where he wanted the cockpit to go and scoped a new set of coordinates. "Bearing three-four-three, Frank!"

"I will do that," said Frank, and then he did as he'd been told. On the feed, Scott saw the Red cockpit hurtle in an arc through the sky and land on the metallic ground in front of the big silver cube.

The other Red must have been tracking the cockpit closely, because he gave up circling the squad and bolted after it in a heartbeat. The pressure on the Diamondbacks was gone.

Now all Scott had to do was disable the Red. "Frank! Reconfigure in Missile Mode! Launch at bearing three-four-five, maximum thrust. Adjust for moving target, approximate speed thirty-five miles an hour traveling west by southwest!"

"Yes, Corporal Scott," said Frank, and then the Battlenaut wrenched and twisted into a new shape, becoming a missile ready for launch. "Three, two, one."

With that, the reshaped armor leaped off the ground and rocketed toward the running Red. Its flight path, though Frank couldn't actually see the target--or anything else, for that matter--was a perfect beeline for the Red.

"Brace for impact." Seconds after Frank said it, the missile-shaped Battlenaut slammed into the Red's left leg, blowing it apart from hip to knee.

The Red crashed down on that side, collapsing to the ground in a shuddering fall like a chopped-down tree. Parts and pieces shattered and splintered in the impact, littering the silver plain with mechanical debris.

As for Scott, his missile-mode armor went down in the crash, caught under the Red's fallen bulk. "Reconfigure to standard mode," he told Frank. "Get us the hell out from under here and extract the enemy cockpit."

With all the hums, whines, and *clackety-clacks* of metal, plastic, and carbon nanotube transformation, the missile changed itself back into a Battlenaut.

That was when the Red's pilot spoke over the comm. "Nice move, Sol." His voice sounded strained through the distortion. "But I've still got checkmate, you loser."

"How do you figure?" said Scott as his Battlenaut heaved its way out from under the Red.

"Because *you* get *nothing*." The pilot chuckled. "I've got master self-destructs for my whole squad implanted in my brain. All I have to do is *think* an activation code to *trigger* them."

As he said it, Scott heard a muffled blast not far away. "Move faster!" he told Frank. "Hurry!"

"That was the cockpit you just retrieved," said the pilot. "All gone now. Guess what's next?"

Scott muted the comm and spoke urgently to his A.I. "Frank! I need you to climb on top of the downed Red and cut out its cockpit. Turn around, it's right behind you."

"Yes, Solomon." As ordered, Frank turned to face the Red. Reaching out, he touched the Red's armor with one hand. "I can feel it. I continue to have an awareness of touch."

Without further delay, Frank clambered on top of the downed Battlenaut. Feeling around, he quickly found the cockpit, then went to work on it.

Pressing his arms together, he merged them into a single giant chainsaw, then drove the saw down into the top edge of the cockpit and started cutting.

As Frank drew the whirling blade down the middle of the cowling, Scott heard another explosion--this one massive enough to rock his armor with shockwaves. The first blast was followed by a chain of subsequent blasts putting out shockwaves of their own.

Even before Scott checked the feeds, he knew what the pilot was blowing up this time...something big enough to send out those kinds of shockwaves...something that might contain enough ordnance and equipment to trigger those secondary blasts.

"So much for the mystery facility you came to investigate. So much for the silver cube," said the Red's pilot. "Now you'll never know what was inside it. You'll never be able to plunder its secrets."

Checking the forward feed, Scott saw that his Battlenaut's saw had cut a gash down the full length of the cockpit.

"Pry it open, Frank!" shouted Scott. "And let me the hell out of here!"

"Guess what I'm going to destroy *this* time." The pilot laughed. "Us! You and me! That's what!"

Scott had a chance, but it was going to be close; the enemy pilot would only need seconds to set off the next self-destruct.

Scott needed to slow him down. "Frank! Broadcast interference over the comm channel! Maximum volume!"

"Yes, Solomon," said Frank.

As ear-splitting interference began shrieking over the speakers, the back of Scott's Battlenaut flowed open, and his cockpit flipped back and up. The couch let go of him, and he scrambled out of the interior cavity and over his armor's shoulders.

He leaped from the shoulders and landed on the Red's hull just as Frank finished tearing the two halves of the Red's cockpit cowling apart. Frank had reconfigured his giant chainsaw into a pair of huge claws, and he was using them to peel the cowling open as if it were made of aluminum foil.

Without hesitation, Scott dove into the gap Frank had opened. He plunged toward a young blond-haired man stretched out on a pilot's couch of his own inside the Red Battlenaut.

Frank's audio interference screamed from the cockpit's

speakers. The pilot was wincing with agony, holding his hands over his ears to try to block out the noise...and then, suddenly, the weight of Scott's body slammed down on top of him.

Before the pilot could form a thought that might blow the two of them to kingdom come, Scott hauled back his right fist and punched his lights out. He slugged the pilot as hard as he could in the face, driving his head to one side--hoping he'd knocked him unconscious with that one blow.

He had. The pilot slumped, eyes closed, against the couch.

"Cut the audio, Frank!" Scott shouted over the blasting interference. He repeated himself twice, louder each time, until Frank finally heard him over the open comm and shut down the cacophony.

Breathing hard, Scott got up from the pilot and looked around. There were holographic video feeds, as in his own Battlenaut cockpit, projecting images of devastation from outside--fire and smoke and rubble, all that was left of the Red facility.

But Scott and the Diamondbacks would not return to the *Sun Tzu* empty-handed. They had the wreckage of three downed Red Battlenauts to take back with them--one complete with functional cockpit. And they had a Red prisoner to interrogate...once Dr. Beauchamp determined he was free of booby traps. (If she could *see* him, that is.)

As Scott looked around the cockpit, a shadow fell from above, drawing his attention. It was a welcome sight--the drop ship from the *Sun Tzu*, gliding overhead.

Scott boosted himself up out of the cockpit, taking care not to cut himself on the sliced-open cowling. His first thought was to run to Donna and make sure she got the care she needed immediately...but he glanced back into the cockpit and hesitated. What if he stepped away, and the Red pilot awoke and escaped? What if the pilot came around just enough to trigger self-destructs in the wreckage of the three Red Battlenauts?

It was a straight-up no-brainer, and he knew it. Getting the prisoner into secure custody was the absolute top priority--the key to the success of the overall mission and the survival of the Commonwealth and Rightfuls alike.

Clenching his jaw, Scott took another look around. As the drop ship descended a hundred meters away, two Diamondbacks marched to meet it. The other three ran to the wreckage of Donna's unit; Scott wished he were going with them.

But for now, he would just have to hang back, do his job, and hope for the best.

"Please let her be okay," he said quietly, offering up a prayer...and then he climbed back inside the Red Battlenaut's cockpit and unstrapped the pilot.

CHAPTER 20

As long as the morning had been, the rest of the day turned out to be much longer for Scott. He wasn't getting shot at anymore, but he was in high demand for one simple reason: he was the only one who could see all the Red wreckage.

Even powered down, disabled, and blown apart, the Red Battlenauts remained mostly concealed from everyone else. Larger pieces were just as invisible to the naked eye and high tech equipment as they had been while part of a greater whole. Tiny pieces, for some reason, became visible, but the big stuff remained unseen and undetectable.

The prisoner stayed in stealth mode, too. Diamondback personnel couldn't see him at all; it was up to Scott to secure, transport, and lock him away in the *Sun Tzu*'s brig.

On top of all that, it was up to Scott to direct every phase of the salvage effort. He had to locate and point out every bit of debris, then personally supervise as work crews gathered it up (which, in most cases, was like gathering up make-believe wreckage, since they could only see tiny bits of it). He had to closely monitor how much was loaded onto the cargo ship--which arrived soon after the drop ship--to ensure the load fit in the hold and did not exceed the ship's tolerances. At the same time, he had to watch for anything potentially hazardous, like active power plants and unexploded ordnance, and assign them to protected storage.

Most of it was up to him, the one person who could see every bit of wreckage that the Reds had left behind. He was sore, tired, and worried sick about Donna, but he had to keep going till the last of it was cleaned up and hauled back to the *Sun Tzu*. Any piece could turn out to be an all-important clue leading to the next stage of the search for the source of the Reds.

"You're *sure* this tub's full of Red junk?" Chief Azimuth stood in the open hatch of the cargo ship and scowled at its contents. "Looks to me like there are just a few pieces scattered around."

"It's there, all right." Scott walked along the fringe of the massive pile of Red Battlenaut pieces, ticking off items on a tablet computer checklist. "I see it plain as day."

He felt like he knew the contents of the hold by heart at that point. He'd spent over twelve hours locating each and every piece and supervising its removal, so the details were ingrained in his mind. Now that he was back onboard the *Sun Tzu*, he would get to know them even better; it was up to him, as the only one with "Red-vision," to oversee the unloading process and study the pieces that remained invisible to everyone else.

Azimuth had a gleaming silver wrench in his hand, and

he waved it at the unseen salvage. "Well, I've been told to assist you with this..." He let the words hang to convey his disapproval. "...but I think an *imaginary friend* might be more along the lines of what *you* need for this imaginary *load*." He chuckled at his joke and glanced around as if he expected his ever-present Engineering crew to laugh along with him.

If there was ever a time when Scott might be in the mood to deal with Azimuth, this wasn't it. He had one goal in the forefront of his thoughts: getting to the medicenter to spend time at Donna's side. He'd heard she was in a coma, but he hadn't made it back to the *Sun Tzu* to see her until now. If only he could finish the checklist and get past Azimuth...

"Well, I'm done here for now." Scott double-tapped the tablet screen and lowered it to his side. "Though you're welcome to keep working." Grinning, he gestured at the largely invisible heap of equipment and debris.

"Ha, ha." Azimuth said it sarcastically. "Very funny, Mr. Celebrity." Taking a step forward, he poked his wrench at the space in front of him. "So what happens if I just walk in that direction? Will I bump into this invisible wreckage, or will I magically pass right through it?"

"Why don't you try it and find out?" said Scott.

Azimuth took another step forward. "If it's all really here, and not some hoozehock figment of your imagination, I'd like to know how the flux they did it. How could they make it undetectable by any equipment and unseen by anyone except *you*?"

"If I knew, I'd make it visible to *everyone*," said Scott. "Too much work for *me* this way."

"What you're saying is, there's nothing I can do to assist." Azimuth sounded relieved.

That made Scott think harder to come up with something

for him to do. "Actually, if you could increase the shielding around this bay, that would be great. Just in case some kind of external signal is causing this cloaking effect."

Azimuth shrugged. "I suppose that's possible. Maybe some kind of neutrino pulse that blends in with the cosmic background radiation."

"Exactly." Scott headed for the door. "Block out every kind of signal you can think of. Maybe all this will finally come into view." He swept his arm in a wide arc to indicate the room's contents.

"Okay." Azimuth scratched his head. "Whatever you say, Mr. Celebrity. You're the big expert here."

Scott didn't have the time, energy, or desire to have it out with him, so he just kept walking. Anyway, it wouldn't matter; Azimuth would probably keep baiting and haranguing him till the day he died.

"Get back here as soon as you can," said Azimuth just as Scott stepped through the doorway. "Apparently, I need your supervision so I don't do anything wrong."

Scott didn't turn back. "Don't worry," he said over his shoulder. "I'm sure someone will clean up after you like always."

Then, before Azimuth could lob another crack his way, he shut the door behind him and raced off toward the medicenter.

Donna did not look good. Her face and shoulders were covered with cuts and bruises. Her left arm and right leg were immobilized in green organic crystal casts, suspended in midair by antigrav nodes.

But at least she was alive. According to the holographic

readouts floating above her, she was in stable condition. She was stuck in a coma, but at least she was out of immediate danger.

Scott stood beside her bed and stared down at her, eyes burning. He felt guilty for not doing more to keep her from getting hurt. Maybe, if he'd kept her closer or followed a different course, she wouldn't have ended up like this.

He wanted to reach down and touch her, but she was so banged up, he was afraid to try. It was then that he realized just how much he was going to miss her. Even with all the work he had ahead of him, it was going to bother him not to have her around.

Just then, Dr. Beauchamp drifted over and checked the holo readouts. "Talk to her if you like. Remember, she can hear what you say."

Scott nodded. He knew from first-hand experience how right she was. Back on Tack, after his escape from the Iridess Chasm and his terrible fall at Penitent Peak, he'd actually died...then spent months in a deep coma after being revived. He still remembered things that people had said by his bedside when they'd thought he couldn't hear them--everything from whispered prayers to secret revelations.

"It will help stimulate her mind if you talk to her," said Beauchamp. "It will have a therapeutic effect, especially coming from you, as close as you two have gotten. As much as you mean to her."

Scott frowned. He and Donna hadn't tried to hide their friendship, but hearing Beauchamp mention it had surprised him. It had made him feel strange.

In the short time that he and Donna had known each other, they'd indeed gotten close. She was his best friend on the ship; they'd even shared a bed. Seeing her injured filled him with sadness and regret.

So why had he felt a twinge of doubt when Beauchamp had talked about their relationship?

"Fine. This is fine." Beauchamp worked her way through the holo readouts, then smiled at Scott. "Her numbers look good."

"That's great," said Scott. "She took a hell of a hit."

"You can have all the padding and restraints in the world," said Beauchamp. "They will only protect you from so much in those big tin cans."

Scott rubbed his eyes and nodded. Suddenly, he felt completely exhausted. "When do you think she'll come out of it?"

"Hard to say at this stage." Beauchamp glided to the foot of the bed, where a holographic chart appeared at her approach. "Once the swelling in her brain goes down, I'll have a better idea."

Scott felt himself about to yawn and stifled it. He thought about catching some Z's, but that just depressed him. Even if he slept in Donna's bed to get away from Trane and Abby's snoring, he doubted he'd get much rest.

"As soon as there is a change, we will reevaluate." Beauchamp finished with the chart and flicked it away with a sweep of her hand. "Meanwhile, I can devote my full attention to *you*." She tipped her head to one side and beamed a warm and knowing smile in his direction.

Scott felt his cheeks flush.

Beauchamp raised her eyebrows and pointed an index finger at him. "To be exact, I need to devote my attention to examining your telemetry records from Shard."

Scott relaxed and smiled back at her as if he'd understood all along. "Right."

"I've already downloaded everything from your armor's internal drives," said Beauchamp. "It's just a matter of comparing all that--the complete record of all your body's responses to stimuli on Shard--to the baseline record we set during your pre-mission physical. Then, we see how that compares to telemetry and camera feeds from other members of the squad at key points. When you were all looking at a Red, for example, but only *you* actually *saw* it, what physiological differences were there?"

"I hope you figure it out," said Scott. "Being the only one who can see everything Red-related is running me ragged."

Even as he said those words, the voice of Major Perseid broke in over the shipwide intercom. "Corporal Scott, report to the brig. Corporal Scott, report to the brig immediately."

Scott sighed at the speaker set into the wall above the door. "See what I mean?"

Beauchamp nodded. "You're under a great deal of stress." She tipped her head to the other side. "So why is it that you don't seem particularly stressed out to me?"

Scott frowned. "That's funny, because I *feel* stressed out."

"I don't know," said Beauchamp. "You've been subjected to a lot of pressure since you first came aboard the *Sun Tzu*. If anything, I'd say you've *thrived* on it."

Scott shrugged. "If you say so." It was true, he was good at keeping a cool head under pressure. Nevertheless, he didn't think he'd been *thriving*, exactly. If he'd been at the top of his game, would Donna have ended up in a medicenter bed?

"So, tell me." Beauchamp stared at him through slitted eyes. "What happens when the stress finally lets up?"

The truth was, it never did. But Scott wasn't going to tell her that. "I'll be thrilled. Good luck examining those telemetry records from Shard, because the sooner the heat's off me, the better."

Beauchamp folded her arms over her chest with her usual languorous grace. "During our first session, I asked why you were so alone. Now, I would like to leave you with another question." She stepped closer to him and lowered her voice. "What will you do if you lose the only person you've reached out to on this ship? The only one you can depend on?" She cast a meaningful gaze at Donna on the bed. "What will you have left to keep you going?"

Scott wasn't in any kind of mood to be psychoanalyzed. He actually felt the urge to tell her to keep her shrink hoozehock to herself at a time like this.

But something she'd said--which part, he wasn't sure--had touched a nerve. Did it have something to do with the strange way he'd felt when she'd mentioned how much he meant to Donna and how close he and Donna had become?

All he knew for sure was that he couldn't stop and think about it right now. "I have to go," he said, pointing at the intercom speaker. "They need me in the brig."

"They do, don't they?" Beauchamp gestured toward the door. "I guess you'd better get going."

Scott nodded in Donna's direction. "Would you let me know if she takes a turn for the worse?"

"Or if she wakes up, yes," said Beauchamp.

"Thank you." Scott hurried to the door, which slid open in front of him.

"And Scott?" Beauchamp's voice held him at the threshold. "Donna is not the only one you can depend on."

Instantly, Scott thought of Grandma Bern. "You're

right," he said over his shoulder. "Maybe I need to call home."

"Yes," said Beauchamp. "Or you can always come and talk to me again." She clasped her hands behind her and made a little bow. "At your service, Corporal."

Scott smiled and nodded. "Thanks." Not that he would likely have time in his crazy schedule to talk over his feelings. Not that that could take precedence over stopping the Reds and saving the Commonwealth.

And not that he really needed it. He'd done just fine without it so far, even after all that had happened.

If dying hadn't stopped him, was there anything he couldn't handle on his own?

CHAPTER 21

"We've noticed changes in the prisoner's cell," said Major Perseid when Scott entered the anteroom of the brig. "Objects have been moved around. Bedclothes. That leads us to think the prisoner might be awake."

Scott frowned, very aware of all the eyes trained on him at that moment. Perseid, Rexis, Trane, Abby, and Khalil were all standing in a semi-circle, staring at him with dark intensity. The way they looked at him, he felt like he'd done something wrong by being singled out, like it was something he should have prevented.

"Since you're the only one who can see and hear him, you'll have to perform the interrogation," said Perseid. "Plus which, you've said he seems to think there's some kind of connection between you."

"You two get all buddy-buddy down there on Shard?" Trane said with a sneer. "Or was it something more meaningful?"

Scott ignored him. "He knew my name and rank from monitoring our comms."

"If he was monitoring comms, he must have heard other names, too," said Rexis.

"He also figured out that I was the only one in the squad who could see him," said Scott.

Perseid and Rexis were looking at Scott with disapproval. He wished he'd had time for a mission debrief before now; it wasn't good, the way the information was coming to light.

He knew he needed to clarify quickly. "As I said, he figured it out. When he moved out of the line of fire, there was a delay in targeting as I called his new coordinates. That suggested I was the only one who actually had eyes on him."

Perseid folded his arms over his chest and nodded grimly. "I wonder if he was able to transmit that information to anyone?"

"We'll never know," said Rexis. "Red transmissions seem to be as undetectable to us as everything else about them."

"If he did contact someone, he didn't have much to tell them," said Scott. "I didn't verbally confirm his conclusions, and I was careful not to give him any useful information during our exchange."

"You'll have to do the same when you interrogate him," said Rexis. "Expect that he'll be seeking information as much as you are."

"Not that he can get the information *out*." Khalil gestured at the sealed, windowless door of the brig cell behind him. "We've triple-reinforced that room every way we know how. Assuming he possesses some hidden transmission capability, we will block any signal he tries to send."

"Fortunately, the Reds don't possess any technology we

aren't prepared for." Trane smacked himself in the forehead. "Oh, wait, they do!"

"Which would only matter if Corporal Scott were inclined to reveal any secrets to the prisoner." Perseid raised his eyebrows as he looked at Scott. "*Are* you so inclined, Corporal?"

Scott shook his head. "Absolutely not, sir."

"Then you're going in." Perseid stepped aside, clearing a path to the cell door. "And you're going to get as much as you can out of him while giving away as little as possible about us. Is that correct, Corporal?"

"Sir, yes sir." Scott cracked off a sharp salute and headed for the cell door.

"Here." Rexis shoved a tablet computer at him. "Remember to take notes. The rest of us won't hear a word he says until we crack the Reds' stealth technology."

Scott took the tablet. "Understood."

"We'll be recording video and audio the whole time, though." Rexis smiled. "For future reference. For when we can see and hear everything."

"*If*," said Trane.

"*When*." Rexis gave Scott's upper arm a squeeze. "Now get in there and *good luck*."

"Thanks." Scott summoned up a grin and reached for the passcode keypad mounted beside the door.

When Scott entered the cell, the Red pilot was lying on a bare cot with his knees drawn up, staring at the ceiling. The pillow, bedsheets, and blanket were strewn over the floor.

"Doesn't anybody knock around here?" The pilot said it without looking at Scott. "Now what if I'd been in the middle of something?"

"Then I guess you'd be S.O.L.," said Scott.

At the sound of Scott's voice, the pilot's head rolled over to train his cobalt blue eyes in his direction. "Why, if it isn't Corporal Scott!" His voice was laced with sarcasm. "Finally! Someone who can actually *see* me!"

Scott shrugged. "Trust me, it's not that exciting."

The pilot laughed. "You *love* being special...being the only one who see me. Admit it."

"Honestly? I could do without it." Scott pulled up the only chair in the cell, an antigrav float with a cushioned black seat and back, and sat down three meters from the bed. "So how's it going? How's your visit so far?"

"Are you kidding?" The pilot swung his legs off the bed and sat up, grinning. "I'm on a CORE ship with a secret Diamondback task force! Could it *get* any cooler than *this*?"

Scott kept his poker face in place as he tapped the tablet, making a note. *Aware of CORE and Diamondbacks.* "You're from Tack, aren't you?" He looked up from the tablet. "Goyo, maybe? Or Syssop?" Now that he could hear the pilot's voice without electronic distortion, he recognized his accent.

"Spoken like a true Tackie," said the pilot. "I know *exactly* where *you're* from. Tisserie, near Vast."

Scott was surprised but tried not to show it. The pilot had done a little *too* well pinpointing his native region...not that he was about to admit it. "So, what should I call you?"

"Chrysanthemonium aspergillus," said the pilot. "Either that, or no-name gobbledygook flippersnapper."

"Cut me some slack," said Scott. "You already know *my* name. Why not tell me yours, and we'll call it even."

The pilot lowered his head and gave Scott a sinister,

leering look. "Guess."

Scott sighed. "Come on. At least tell me your *first* name."

"Guess." The pilot's voice was a hiss.

"Forget it," said Scott. "I'll just call you flux-face or something."

"I'll give you a clue." The pilot leaned forward and slowly raised an index finger to point at Scott. "You already *know* what it is."

Scott shook his head. He wasn't going to play games with the pilot. "So why did you ask to see me? What's on your mind?"

"You, actually." The pilot slid back, drew up one knee, and leaned against the wall. "I can't stop thinking about you."

Scott winced. "Like you've got a *crush* on me or something?"

The pilot tipped his head back and gazed at Scott through narrowed eyes. "It's just interesting how things work out sometimes. Who could have imagined we'd be brought together like this?"

"Not me." Scott rubbed his chin, wondering how he might get information out of the guy. The pilot was so alert and cagey, he felt like a dead end...but maybe Scott could exploit the weird personal interest he seemed to have. "I guess it was meant to be."

"Destiny?" The pilot smirked. "I'll buy that."

"Maybe it happened for a reason," said Scott. "Maybe we're meant to help each other."

"Hm." The pilot looked up at the ceiling. "Wouldn't that be something?" He didn't sound very sincere. "Helping each other bring peace to the galaxy?" He snickered.

"I'm just saying." Scott clasped his hands behind his

head and tipped his antigrav chair back. "Anything's possible, isn't it?"

"You're right about that," said the pilot. "You don't *know* how right you are."

"So." Scott cleared his throat. "Where do we start?"

The pilot leaned forward and stared at him, then got to his feet. "That's easy." He crossed the room, approaching Scott.

Instantly, Scott's heart beat harder. Every muscle in his body tensed, getting ready to spring into action.

But the pilot stopped short of him by half a meter. "We start with you," he said, his icy gaze locking with Scott's. "We start with you guessing my name."

Scott unclasped his hands and lowered them from behind his head. "Why bother? Even if I guessed it correctly, you wouldn't tell me."

"I won't *have* to tell you," said the pilot. "You'll *know*." Blue eyes glittering, he leaned toward Scott and lowered his voice. "I told you before, you *already* know."

"And *I* told *you*, I *don't* know." Scott's guard was up, his mind racing with hand-to-hand combat scenarios. The pilot didn't stand a chance against him. "So let's talk about something that *matters*."

"My *name* matters." The pilot leaned closer. "Our *past* matters."

Scott frowned, taking his closest look yet at the pilot's face--still seeing no trace of familiarity. "We don't *have* a past. And I don't appreciate you wasting my *time* like this."

"We *do* have a past." The pilot sneered and nodded. "We *have* met before, and I *know* you remember."

"Then you're wrong," said Scott, "because I don't."

"There's no way you could forget," said the pilot. "No

way in hell." He held Scott's gaze another moment, then slowly withdrew and went back to his cot. "Think about it. Search your mind. I guarantee the memories are in there."

"Right." Scott thought for a moment, hunting for an angle. "So if I remember meeting you, we can talk about the people you're working for?"

"If you remember how we met," said the pilot, "the people I work for will be the *last* thing you'll want to talk about."

"So let's talk about them *now*," said Scott.

The pilot shook his head and lay down on the cot. "I'm done talking for now. I need you to leave, Sol."

Scott's eyes widened. How did the pilot know his first name? He was sure no one had said it over the comm.

"Don't you know the meaning of the words 'get out?'" snapped the pilot.

Scott got up from the chair and started for the door. Was it possible? *Had* he met the Red pilot somewhere before?

"And Scott?" said the pilot. "If you're lying about remembering me to protect your reputation, you'll get nothing out of me."

Scott looked back over his shoulder at him but didn't reply.

"Believe it." The pilot rolled over to face the wall. "I won't let you screw me again, Scott. Not like before."

Scott scowled and kept walking. He'd had enough of the pilot's shtick.

"This time, *I'm* doing the screwing," said the pilot. "And you're the one paying the price!"

CHAPTER 22

"Hey! Watch it!" said Trane. "You almost knocked over the hydrochloric acid!"

"Sorry." Scott snapped his attention back to the chemicals and equipment in the lab around him. He knew he needed to focus one hundred percent on the task at hand, testing pieces of the Red Battlenauts retrieved from the surface of Shard.

But he also knew it wouldn't be long until his attention wandered again. The fact was, he couldn't stop thinking about the Red pilot.

Since their meeting in the brig a day ago, Scott had become obsessed. He kept playing back his memories of what the guy had said and how he'd looked, hunting for some clue that would remind him of where and how they'd met before.

If, indeed, he did have memories of a past meeting, and the pilot wasn't just making it up to get inside his head.

"You're distracted as hell," said Trane. "Tell me again why you need to be here?"

"Because I'm the only one who can see all the pieces of the Reds' armor and extract samples," said Scott. "You can't run your tests without me."

Trane sighed. "I keep hoping the answer will change." He reached for a purple-stained slide and placed it under the lens of the electron microscope. "Since you're here anyway, take a look at this." He stepped aside and gestured for Scott to take over.

Scott stepped in and looked into the viewer on the device. He saw the same thing he'd seen in every other magnified sample so far: tiny crystalline shapes arranged in a spider-web pattern around a central diamond-like particle.

"Same result, right?" said Trane.

"Yes." Scott turned knobs on the microscope, sharpening the focus. "Another viral web in the exact same pattern."

"Which confirms it." Trane clapped his hands together. "All three Red Battlenauts and the rubble from the building were coated with identical viral particles arranged in identical matrices at the microscopic level."

Scott looked up from the device. "And that coating might be what's creating the stealth capability?"

Trane scowled and shook his head. "There's no trace of it in the samples from the prisoner. Unless there's a different process at work when it comes to cloaking a living organism."

"Hm." Scott rubbed his chin. "And it's definitely not something the Reds picked up on Shard. You said it's not native to the planet."

"Not a chance," said Trane. "The genetic structure of the virus shares no markers with any known Shard lifeforms.

Plus which, none of *our* armor came back with a trace of the stuff on it. It's not from *around* here." Hands on hips, he walked off across the lab, frowning in thought.

Instantly, Scott's mind returned to the pilot. Maybe he was starting to seem a little familiar after all--or was that just because Scott kept thinking about him?

The only thing Scott knew they had in common for sure was their homeworld, Tack. That did make it more possible that their lives had intersected. Could they have gone to school together or met at a summer camp? Maybe they'd gone to the same church...or, more likely, crossed paths at boot camp or the Academy. Scott certainly couldn't remember everyone he'd ever met back home or in the military.

Why, then, did the pilot claim to remember him so well? And not in a *good* way? Had Scott burned him at some point and moved on, not realizing the guy would come back to bite him in the ass someday? It was possible, wasn't it? Scott thought of himself as a good guy, but he'd never claimed to be perfect.

So who *was* that pilot?

Scott's thoughts returned to the business at hand as Trane strolled back over, scrubbing his knuckles through his bright white crewcut. "So far, the virus hasn't exhibited any cloaking-related properties. That raises the question of what it *can* do." He stopped at the microscope and took another look at the slide mounted there. "Or maybe that's not important. Maybe that's beside the point."

"How so?" said Scott. "Isn't cracking the virus' capabilities our top priority, if it might be connected to the stealth technology?"

"But our *other* priority is *finding* the Reds." Trane looked up from the microscope. "Perhaps we can trace the virus' genetic structure to a biosphere on record."

Scott nodded. "Good plan."

"We'll start now." Trane tapped the countertop, summoning holographic controls to float in midair in front of him. "While we keep testing the virus' capabilities and tolerances, of course. Moving forward on parallel tracks is the way to go, don't you agree?"

"Absolutely." Even as he said it, Scott was drifting off on his own personal parallel track again, ransacking his mind for the umpteenth time for some clue to the pilot's identity. Just like every other time, he was coming up empty.

"I'm bringing in Abby, Khalil, and Feinberg," said Trane as he manipulated the glowing holo-controls. "With that much brainpower at work, I guarantee we'll solve this mystery."

Maybe teamwork would be the answer to Scott's mystery, too. Other people were working on it already; maybe one of them would come up with something before it finally drove him crazy.

All he needed was a hint. Just a nudge, and the tumblers would fall into place, the vault would unlock, and he would remember.

Maybe then he could get some real answers, the kind that would help the Diamondbacks stop the Reds before it was too late.

"As far as we can tell, the man in the brig does not exist." Captain Rexis spread her arms and shook her head. "He's a nobody in every sense of the word."

A wave of disappointment rolled through Scott. As he stood there stiffly in Rexis' office and took in the verdict, his spirit fell like an anchor tossed overboard from a seagoing vessel, heading straight for the bottom.

"We've run searches based on what you've told us about him." Rexis swung her arms in and plopped them on the desk in front of her. She looked more angry than disappointed. "And we've come up empty."

Scott scowled. He hadn't given them much to work with, but he'd hoped *something* would turn up.

"Based on your description, we came up with a computer-generated image of the pilot." She picked up an 8" by 10" printed photo from her desk and handed it over to Scott. "We circulated that to all military and law enforcement sources...but no one could I.D. him."

Scott nodded as he gazed at the image. "This is a good likeness of him. I can't believe it wouldn't generate any leads...especially since we know he's from Tack, a Commonwealth world. There *must* be some kind of evidence in the Commonwealth records."

"Not that *we* can find." Rexis leaned back in her chair. "He's a *ghost*."

"Damn." Scott glared at the computer rendering of the prisoner. What *was* it about that guy? "Is there anywhere else you can look?"

"Believe me, we've tapped every resource at our disposal." Rexis shook her head. "It's *critical* that we I.D. this Red. But it's like he never existed. Either that, or..." She turned her head and stared into space, looking deep in thought.

"Either that or what?"

Rexis returned her gaze to him. "Either that, or he's being protected."

Scott frowned and took a seat, dropping onto the

antigrav chair floating in front of the desk. "You think so?"

"Actually, it's the only explanation that makes sense to me." Rexis folded her arms over her chest. "It explains a lot of other things, too."

She was right. The more Scott thought about it, the more he agreed with her. Protection and guidance from inside the Commonwealth would have greatly enabled the Reds' secrecy, access to information, and freedom of movement through Commonwealth space.

"You think someone in the Commonwealth is backing the Reds?" said Scott.

Rexis propped her elbows on the armrests of her chair and steepled her fingers in front of her face. "If they are, they'd have to be in the upper echelons to pull off what they've done. *And...*" She raised her eyebrows. "...they'd be willing to do *anything* to protect their secrets."

Her meaning wasn't lost on Scott. "So we might be up against our own people," he said.

"It's possible." Rexis unsteepled her fingers and used them to rub her temples. "In which case, we've already tipped them off, and the ice we're on is getting thinner by the minute."

"Wow." The implications were pretty ugly. They would transform the mission from a risky hunt for a secret force upsetting the balance of power to a paranoid struggle in which no one could truly be trusted.

"Enough to give you a migraine, isn't it?" Rexis kept rubbing her temples. "Or keep it permanently cranked up to maximum intensity."

"So what do we do next?" said Scott.

"Carry on with the mission, I suppose. Remain aware of the possibilities." Rexis shrugged. "I still think you're our best weapon. The personal interest the Red has in you--I think you can use it to our advantage."

"I'm not so sure," said Scott. "He won't even tell me when and how we supposedly met."

"Keep trying," said Rexis. "Maybe it'll come to you."

Scott took another look at the computer rendering of the pilot, fighting for recognition...but he drew another blank. Whatever secrets might be locked away inside his own mind, he couldn't touch them. "Still nothing."

"Don't give up." Rexis tapped her lower lip with a forefinger as she stared at him. "You know what else you could try? Ask a family member. Someone you can trust without reservation."

Was she talking about Grandma Bern? "If you mean Commandant Chalice, I'm not sure she'd remember the pilot any better than I do."

"I'm more interested in her resources than her memory." Rexis raised an eyebrow. "You might be surprised what the Commandant of the Marine Corps can come up with when she puts her mind to it."

Scott thought about what she was saying. Getting in touch with Grandma Bern was not a simple matter. He'd spent his adult life making it a point not to play that card--but maybe, given the stakes, it was time. Maybe Bern could turn over rocks that no one else could, especially if Rexis was right about a possible conspiracy in the Commonwealth's hierarchy.

"I'll see what I can do," said Scott. "But I can't promise anything. The Commandant doesn't always take my calls."

Rexis tapped the obsidian desktop in front of her, summoning a cluster of holo-controls. "I'll schedule radio time for you on the top-security encrypted channel...as much as you need. Twenty hundred hours tonight sound good?"

"Sure." Scott got up from his chair. "I'll let you know how it goes. Just don't expect any miracles."

"Don't worry," said Rexis. "We're working *all* the angles. Sooner or later, something's got to give."

"Commandant Chalice is not able to take your call at this time," said the holographic projection of the pretty redhead in the Marine uniform. "She will contact you at her earliest convenience, Corporal Scott."

"Thanks." Scott saluted and closed the comm channel. The redhead--Lori, one of Bern's personal assistants--vanished from the chair across the round black table from Scott, which was where her image had been projected.

With a sigh, Scott got up and left the comm booth. It hadn't surprised him that Bern wasn't available; as Marine Commandant, she was busy beyond belief. But he'd been looking forward to seeing and talking to her. It had been at least eight months since the last time they'd spoken, and he missed her. He'd had the time set aside, approved by Captain Rexis, and now he'd just have to wait until Bern called back.

Not that he was going to let that time go to waste. He hadn't seen Donna all day, so now was the perfect opportunity.

When he got to the medicenter, Doctor Beauchamp was away. A male nurse named Golah Tourmal was in charge until she got back.

Tourmal ran the stats for Scott, which wasn't exactly an uplifting experience. Donna's vital signs had been irregular throughout the day; she was finally stable, but Beauchamp was worried that she might be losing ground.

"We'll see how she holds up tonight," said Tourmal.

"Maybe having you around for a while will give her the boost she needs."

As Tourmal walked off to do paperwork, Scott pulled a chair up beside the bed and sat down. Taking Donna's hand, he caressed it, watching the motion of her chest as she inhaled and exhaled medicenter air.

"Can you hear me, Donna?" he said softly. "I know you've been through a lot, but you need to get better fast. We need your help." He stopped caressing her hand and held it tightly. "*I* need your help."

As always, Donna showed no sign that she had heard him. Her chest rose and fell, rose and fell as breath passed through her.

"The Red prisoner claims to know me, but I don't remember him," said Scott. "I feel like everything's riding on this, and I can't figure it out."

Donna just lay there, still and silent as ever. She had no answers or encouragement to offer from the depths of her coma.

"Maybe, if you were awake, you could talk me through this," said Scott. "Or at least make me feel better. You've been great at that since Day One."

Again, she had nothing to offer. Just another dead end.

Scott sighed and sat back, holding on to her hand. It was warm and pulsing with blood, with all the heat and force of life--but none of the animation. Without movement or voice to interact with, she might as well have been another piece of furniture.

Disheartened, Scott slumped in his chair. A wave of hopelessness rolled through him, dragging him down. The future of the quadrant rested squarely on his shoulders, and he felt like the weight was crushing him. He was tired of thinking about it, tired of trying so hard to stop it from coming down around him.

He was just plain tired. Before long, his eyes flickered shut, and he started to drift off. His brain disconnected from consciousness, and dreamlike images passed before his mind's eye.

At first, the images focused on Donna, but she wasn't in bed in the medicenter. She was down on Shard, sharing the cockpit of Scott's Battlenaut, squeezed next to him on the pilot's couch. She and Scott were laughing and kissing as they unleashed one volley after another from the Battlenaut's guns, firing again and again at an unidentified target.

Then, suddenly, Scott was outside the Battlenaut, standing directly in its line of fire. As laser blasts and barrages of slugs poured toward him, he ran, barely getting out of the way in time.

Somehow, as he ran, he knew Donna was still doing the shooting. He couldn't see inside the cockpit or hear her voice over the comm, but he knew she was trying to kill him.

He also knew he wasn't on Shard anymore. The planet's surface had changed from silver metal to dirt and rock in all shades of brown. When the Battlenaut's guns churned up clouds from the ground around him, the dust was dark brown, and the chips of rock were pale tan.

Panting for breath, Scott raced across the plain as fast as he could, running serpentine patterns to evade the Battlenaut's fire. As fast as he ran, though, the long strides of Donna's Battlenaut were closing the gap between them.

Scott ran harder. A missile flashed past, barely missing him, and he bolted left--right into the path of another missile. This time, the hurtling object clipped his head, sending him spinning to the ground.

Scott tumbled head over heels three times before he came to a stop. Dazed, he sat up and looked around, poised to leap into action. He stuck his right arm behind him to prop himself up--and the arm kept going, passing through thin air.

Crying out, he caught himself with his left hand, holding on to a rocky ledge. It was then he saw that he was on the brink of a sheer drop. He'd barely saved himself from a fall of thousands of meters straight down.

Gasping, he scrambled away from the ledge, but he didn't get far. The Battlenaut with Donna inside was standing ten meters away, pointing an array of weapons right at him.

With the ledge behind him and the Battlenaut in front, Scott had nowhere to run. As the weapons aimed at him started to hum in preparation for firing, he took a deep breath and clenched his fists, getting ready to die.

That was when a mysterious figure leaped down out of nowhere, grabbed him under his arms, and vaulted away with him in its grip. As Scott's feet left the ground, Donna's Battlenaut's weapons pounded the spot he'd just occupied, chewing it into smoking rubble.

"Who are you?" Scott craned his head for a glimpse of his rescuer's face but couldn't make it out in the shadows of the hooded cloak he was wearing. "Tell me your name."

The rescuer said nothing. He just went on soaring through the sky, dodging weapons fire cast up from behind by Donna's Battlenaut.

Unable to see the face of whoever was carrying him, Scott turned his attention to the scenery sliding by far below. Only then did he realize he was somewhere different.

The vast brown plain had become a gigantic canyon, sprawling to the horizon and beyond. It was like a gaping maw carved into the ground, deep and broad enough to contain multitudes and swallow up the world in its entirety. A skyscraping crag towered at its heart, jabbing upward like a slender, jagged thorn.

Scott felt dizzy as his savior flew him over the hungry vastness. He was terrified of it for some reason, though he'd never been afraid of heights. It was as if all the darkness in his life had gathered down there like a thick black fog, clutching at his soul to drag it down and hold it fast forever.

"I want to go," he told his rescuer. "I want to get away from here."

It was then that they froze in midflight, hovering high above the canyon. The rescuer said something as he lifted him up, and his voice sounded like the voice of a little boy.

Then, he dropped him.

Scott plummeted face-first toward the mammoth canyon below, but he didn't scream. He just watched as the dark depths raced up toward him, looking more and more familiar the closer they got.

Until, finally, he recognized them. All at once, he knew exactly where he was and why he'd felt dizzy and afraid.

It was all because he was plunging into the Iridess Chasm on Tack, where he'd suffered and died. The towering crag flashing by in the heart of it was Penitent Peak.

Suddenly, something flipped him around to face upward, and the man in the cloak was there above him. With a sound like a little boy laughing, he pulled back his hood, exposing his features for Scott to see.

At first, the man's face was that of the Red pilot, with his cobalt blue eyes, blonde hair, and angular nose and cheekbones. But as Scott watched, the face compressed, becoming rounder and softer. The eyes grew larger, the hair thicker, the head smaller. He still had the body of a grown man, but his face became that of a child.

A child glaring at him with blistering, naked rage.

It was then that Scott was struck by the shock of full recognition. His heart hammered in his chest as he realized who the child was, who he'd become...and where they'd met.

The sky was lit with bursts of lightning all around. The wind whooshed past as Scott plunged downward, rocketing toward the floor of the chasm. The boy in the cloak said something, but he couldn't hear it.

Then, the boy lashed out with his fist, which was the size of a man's, and plowed it into Scott's face. Scott's head whipped to one side; he felt bones break and teeth break free from the impact.

The boy hit him again, flinging his head to the other side. Scott lost more teeth and felt hot blood fill his mouth.

Before the boy hit him again, he said something else, and Scott heard him this time. It was a single word, a name--and Scott didn't have to search his mind to connect with it. He knew it all too well.

Vore.

He said it aloud himself, through shattered teeth and bloody lips--a word that had haunted his every bad dream for years--but he said it as a question.

And when the boy heard it, he howled with rage and hit him again. Not that the pain much mattered, because both of them were about to hit the chasm floor at a high rate of speed. Scott sensed it racing up to meet them like a battering ram, as if propelled by rocket engines from below. Any second now, it would turn them into pulp.

Any second now, it would finish the job it had started thirteen years ago.

In the face of impending oblivion, Scott screamed his lungs out, screamed for all he was worth. He thrashed and kicked like a lunatic, as if somehow that would gain him purchase against the fall.

Then, at the height of his screaming and thrashing, he felt someone squeeze his hand...squeeze it so hard, it felt like it might break.

Spurred by the pain of that squeeze, he snapped out of the nightmare. He stopped screaming, and his eyes shot open, revealing the medicenter around him.

Panting and soaked with sweat, Scott slumped against the chair. He looked around to see who'd awakened him--and it was then he realized he was alone.

Except for Donna.

Just then, the medicenter door swept open, and Nurse Tourmal entered the room. "What the hell?" He frowned at Scott. "Are you all right?"

Scott sat up and nodded. "She squeezed my hand." He looked at Donna. "She squeezed it *hard*."

Tourmal checked the holographic readouts hovering over her, then marched to the foot of the bed, where her chart appeared. "I don't see any change."

"But it's still a good sign, right?"

"Absolutely." The way Tourmal said it made Scott think it wasn't such a good sign after all.

The truth was, Donna didn't look any different than before Scott had dozed off. She lay there in a state of near total stillness, eyes closed, chest rising and falling gently. When Scott squeezed her hand, she didn't squeeze back.

But he knew what he'd felt. He knew she's pulled him out of his nightmare before he could crash to the chasm floor.

He knew she was coming back.

For now, though, he couldn't stay by her side. Now, with the face and name from his dream still echoing in his head, he had business elsewhere. He had the information he'd been searching for; now, he had to put it to use.

"I have to go." He leaped out of his chair and ran for the door.

"Are you sure?" said Tourmal. "You're flushed and soaking wet. You might have a fever."

"Let me know if her condition changes," said Scott as the door slid open before him. "I want to know *immediately*."

"At least let me do a quick exam," said Tourmal. "It'll only take a minute."

Scott paused at the threshold and shook his head grimly. "I don't have a minute."

"Well, you should take one." Tourmal scowled. "At least tell me where I can reach you."

"The brig," said Scott, and then he bolted out the door and down the corridor.

CHAPTER 23

There were three armed and body-armored guards in the brig when Scott charged through the door. Instantly, all their rifles swung around to point in his direction.

Scott stopped and raised his hands in front of him. "Stand down," he said. "I need to meet with the prisoner."

The middle guard tapped the side of his helmet, and glowing text flowed down the faceplate in a long column. "You're not on the schedule."

"Doesn't matter." Scott lowered his hands. "This is a crucial matter of Commonwealth security."

"You'll need authorization from Major Perseid or Captain Rexis," said the middle guard. "Our orders are clear."

"I can't wait for that," said Scott. "I need to get in there now."

"No can do," said the guard. "Come back with proper authorization."

Scott took a deep breath and let it out slowly. "Okay,

listen up." He stepped forward until the barrels of all three rifles were centimeters from his chest and shoulders. "After days of banging my head against the wall, I finally have a lead on this prisoner's identity. Do you really think it would be wise *not* to act on this lead *immediately*? Do *you* want to be the one to tell Major Perseid that you kept me *waiting* while the entire *Commonwealth* remains at risk from that man's *allies*?"

The middle guard thought about it for a long moment. "We have our orders. If something happens to the prisoner, we'll be on the..."

"*Nothing's* going to happen to him," said Scott. "I'm the one who *captured* him. I'm the only one who can *see* one hundred *percent* of him all the time! He's *my* responsibility."

Jaws clenched, the guard stared him in the eye from behind his faceplate...then lowered his rifle. "I'm personally calling Captain Rexis the minute you step in there."

"Good enough." Scott nodded. "Knock yourself out."

The other two guards lowered their rifles and stepped aside, clearing the way to the cell door. Scott walked toward it without hesitation, rushing into a confrontation which for thirteen years he'd never imagined would be possible.

"Again with the not knocking," said the pilot when Scott entered the darkened cell. "Didn't anyone *ever* teach you manners?"

"Lights on full." As soon as Scott said it, the overhead lights flashed up to full strength. It was then he saw the pilot lying on his cot across the room, shielding his eyes with his arm. The bedclothes were no longer scattered on the floor; he had put them back on the mattress and was lying on them.

"Thanks a lot!" snapped the pilot. "You could at least

have left them at half-strength!"

Scott ignored his complaint. "I thought you were dead."

"Because my *eyes* were closed?" said the pilot. "It's called *sleeping*."

"For the past thirteen years, I thought you were *dead*," said Scott. "I thought you *died* at Iridess Chasm."

"Ah." The pilot sat up and rolled his legs off the side of the cot. "You've guessed, haven't you?"

"Cairn," said Scott. "Your name is Cairn."

"Finally." Cairn grinned. "It took you long enough." He got to his feet. "I was starting to think you'd *never* figure it out."

Scott was torn between shock, confusion, and anger. "But how? How is it you're still alive?"

"Good question," said Cairn. "I might ask the same of *you*." He pointed an index finger at Scott. "But I already know, don't I? Vore told me all about your death and resurrection."

"Vore?" Scott frowned. "But I thought..."

"That he fell to his death when I pushed him off Penitent Peak?" Cairn shook his head slowly. "Guess again, Sol."

Scott was slammed by a fresh wave of shock. It was hard enough believing that Cairn had survived that terrible day. Hearing that Vore--the man who'd kidnapped them both back on Tack--had also survived was almost too much to take.

"He was wearing an antigrav vest," said Cairn. "Doesn't it figure, as prepared as he was?"

Scott just stared at him. The story of the single worst day in his life was changing by the minute--if Cairn was to be believed.

"When I pushed him, he dragged me down with him," said Cairn. "What you didn't see--because you were bleeding out on the ledge at the time--was how he activated his antigrav vest fifty meters from the chasm floor and pulled us up at the last minute."

Scott kept staring. "But I never knew. Nobody did. Neither of you was ever found."

"Because we went off the grid," said Cairn. "Just like before, when you were with us, when he first took you. We went underground."

"Oh my God." The implications sank in quickly, leaving Scott even more stunned.

"Not that you ever *looked* real hard for me," said Cairn.

"How could I?" said Scott. "I didn't know you were alive!"

Cairn narrowed his eyes. "But you knew what that monster was like. You knew how tricky he could be." His voice rose with building anger. "You can't *tell* me you never thought we might have survived. You can't *say* you never thought I might still be out there somewhere."

Scott knew he had no reason to be ashamed...but he still felt that way. Cairn was getting to him. "How long were you with Vore after that?"

Cairn laughed bitterly. "Does it matter? Does it really matter?" He laughed again. "*Forever*."

Years of servitude to a psychopathic predator. Scott had only been with him a few *days*, and it had been bad enough. "I always thought...if you were dead, at least you were free of him."

"Yeah, Sol." Cairn sneered. "That was something you promised to *help* me with, remember? Getting free? As long as I helped *you*?"

Scott nodded. He and Cairn had made a pact on that long-ago night in the Iridess Chasm. They had pledged to join forces to escape--and at first, it had worked. Scott had hit Vore over the head with a rock, then run for his life with Cairn by his side. Unfortunately, Vore had not stayed down for long; he'd chased them for miles through the winding arroyos and tunnels of the chasm, then followed them up the steep slopes of Penitent Peak. When Vore had caught up with them, he'd beaten Scott brutally, stopping only when Cairn charged across the ledge and knocked him over the brink.

Scott had thought of that moment often in the years since, and it had given him many nightmares. Again and again, the sight of Cairn tackling Vore over the edge had come back to him, clear as day...but he'd never imagined for even an instant that Cairn was still alive. He'd never truly thought he was still suffering at the hands of Vore or some other human monster, desperately in need of rescue.

But there he was. And he wasn't happy.

"You *did* help me," said Scott. "And I can never thank you enough. But you've got to believe me--I thought you were dead."

"You *wanted* to think that," snapped Cairn. "You wanted to *move on* and forget what you'd *been* through. You didn't want to think about the *abduction* or *Vore* or *me* or *any* of it. And it worked out pretty *well* for you, didn't it? *Until now.*"

Scott shook his head, but he knew Cairn was right about some of it. *Of course* Scott had wanted to forget and move on; it was either that, or dwell on what had happened and let it ruin his life.

But Cairn was dead wrong about the rest. "It *didn't* work out well for me. My life has been a *constant struggle.*"

Churning with emotion, Scott raised his voice and lurched a step closer to Cairn. "Not a day goes by that I don't think about what *happened*--or remember that scared seven-year-old *kid* who went over the cliff to *save* me."

Cairn waved him off with disgust. "You're full of scudge, you know that? You'll say *anything* to dig yourself out from under."

Scott took another step toward him. "Don't you *ever* presume to tell me how *I* feel or what *my* life has been like."

"Flux you," said Cairn, but he backed down a little. Whipping around, he stomped over to a corner of the cell and punched the wall.

Meanwhile, Scott took a deep breath and tried to calm down. He wasn't going to get anywhere by having a screaming match with Cairn. Better to stay in control, to be the one pushing Cairn's buttons instead of vice versa. "So how did you get away?"

Cairn kept facing the wall while he spoke. "From where?"

"From Vore," said Scott. "How did you get away?"

"Who said I ever did?" Cairn braced himself against the corner, shoulders rising and falling. After a long moment, he turned back to face Scott. "Hey, remember what he used to say? About the monster saying hello?"

"'How does a monster say hello?'"

"*Raarrhh!*" Cairn clawed the air when he said it. "Remember how it pissed him off that we never *laughed* at that? Like we were in the mood to laugh at *anything*?"

Scott nodded grimly.

"Know what else he said? He kept saying he was going to come get you again."

Scott frowned. "Who's that?"

"Vore." Cairn's grin had a nasty edge. "He used to say that all the time. He always said you were his favorite."

The thought of it made Scott's guts twist, but he tried not to show it. "Now here we are. Together again."

"That's right." Cairn sauntered over and stood in front of him. "Two old friends, reunited after all these years. Only this time, instead of trying to *save* each other, we're trying to *kill* each other."

"Speak for yourself," said Scott.

Cairn laughed. "So you *weren't* trying to kill me down on Shard then?"

"That's right," said Scott. "I didn't know it was you."

"Ah," said Cairn. "If you *had* known, you wouldn't have tried to stop me from attacking your squad?"

"Stopping you and killing you are two different things," said Scott. "Anyway, that's not how it happened. Neither of us died on Shard, and now we're reunited after all those years."

"It must be destiny." Cairn's voice oozed sarcasm.

"Why not?" Scott shrugged. "Otherwise, it's an awfully big coincidence, don't you think? That after all this time, in all the vastness of space, we ended up in the same place, shooting at each other?"

Cairn laughed. "You're forgetting the third possibility. What if it's not destiny, and it's not a coincidence, either?"

Scott scowled. "What do you mean?"

Cairn laughed again, turned on his heel, and marched back to his cot. "That's not the question you came here to ask, though, is it?" He threw himself down on the cot and crossed one leg over the other. "So what's the *big* question, Sol? The one that determines your next move?"

"You already seem to have an idea what it is," said Scott.

"Why don't you just go ahead and save me the trouble of asking?"

"Okay, but I'm warning you," said Cairn. "You won't like it."

Scott spread his arms wide. "Try me."

"All right." Cairn turned his head to look at Scott. "The people I work for...the ones who control what you call the Red Battlenauts. Your next best chance at finding them will be Oberon, in the Sigma Zeta Gamma system."

"Oberon." Scott narrowed his eyes. "Why are you telling me this?" He wanted to believe Cairn's cooperation was genuine, but the way Cairn had been acting made him think it probably wasn't.

"For old times' sake." Cairn grinned and winked.

"So what else can you tell me about this information?" said Scott. "What did you mean when you said I wouldn't like it?"

Cairn raised his eyebrows. "That part's a surprise." With a laugh, he rolled his head on the pillow to look at the ceiling instead of at Scott.

"It doesn't have to be," said Scott. "Come on, tell me."

"If I were you," said Cairn, "I'd take what you have and get the hell out. You don't want to kill the golden goose, do you?"

Scott sighed. He needed to know more, but Cairn was shutting down on him. Maybe it would be smart to continue the questioning another day. "All right," he said. "If that's how you want to play it."

"Very glad we're on the same page," said Cairn. "Now how about letting me catch some shuteye?"

"After you answer one more question," said Scott. "How do I even know there's any truth in what you've told me?"

Cairn looked at him with a darkly glittering gaze. "Because I know you can't *stop* what's going to happen. If anything, I want you to *see* it happen. So it's in my interest to tell you the truth."

Scott stared at him for a long moment. "I wouldn't be too sure that we can't stop it."

"Whatever you say." Cairn winked and returned his gaze to the ceiling. "But you need to remember, I won't be pulling your ass to safety this time. We're not on the same side anymore, Sol."

"But we *could* be," said Scott.

"Oh, sure," said Cairn. "Anytime you're ready to join up with my people, let me know. I'll be happy to put in a good word for you."

"Thanks, I'll keep that in mind," Scott said sarcastically, and then he left the cell.

"Oberon." Scott snapped out the word as soon as the cell door closed behind him. "We need to go to Oberon."

Perseid and Rexis were waiting for him in the outer room of the brig, both looking grim with arms crossed over their chests. They also looked slightly bleary--no surprise, since it was the middle of the night. The guards must have called them, as promised, when Scott entered the cell...though where the guards were at that moment, Scott didn't know.

"He just decided to tell you that?" Perseid nodded in the direction of the cell door.

"I finally figured out who he is," said Scott. "Then he told me."

"Just like that," said Perseid.

"Pretty much."

"And we know the information's reliable how?" said Rexis.

Scott pointed at the cell. "He claims it's in his interest to tell us. He says it doesn't matter if we know, because we can't stop what's going to happen there. He wants us to see it happen, whatever it is."

Perseid rubbed his eyes hard. "And that's all he gave you? That's all you got out of him?"

"His identity, too. I got that." Scott shrugged.

Rexis frowned and tipped her head to one side. "So who is he?"

"Name's Cairn Barrie," said Scott. "He and I...we were both abducted when we were kids by a man named Larvis Vore. Vore murdered our parents and took us to a secret bunker in the wilderness.

"I was thirteen, and Cairn was seven. We escaped and fled through the Iridess Chasm, but Vore caught up with us. In the process of saving me, Cairn sacrificed his own life...I thought. But it turns out he survived."

"Now here he is," said Perseid. "Awfully big coincidence."

Scott nodded. "That's what *I* said."

"He didn't say anything else about what's supposed to happen at Oberon?" asked Rexis.

"No," said Scott. "Maybe I can get it out of him next time we talk."

"Or maybe not," said Perseid. "I wouldn't give up the intel that easily. Would you?"

Scott shook his head and rubbed the back of his neck. "I keep hoping I might be able to get through to him because of what we went through as kids. But I don't know. He seems pretty angry at the way things worked out."

"I agree it's worth playing that card, though," said Rexis. "Just don't get your hopes up."

"Damnit." Perseid paced across the room and stopped at the door of Cairn's cell. "We're being led around by the nose here. We don't have a choice."

"We have to go to Oberon," said Rexis. "We have to try to stop what might be about to happen there."

"Or fight our way clear of whatever trap the Reds have waiting for us." Perseid snorted and turned from the door. "If there's even a trap at all and not just a patch of empty space that's on the opposite side of the quadrant from where the *real* action's happening."

Rexis nodded in agreement. "Oberon's our only shot."

"At least until we come up with better intel," said Scott. "We'll keep examining the Red debris from Shard, won't we?"

"Absolutely," said Perseid. "Trane seems to be closing in on a breakthrough as we speak. He's been working day and night on it."

"Then maybe we'll find another lead before we go too far in the wrong direction," said Rexis.

Scott looked from Rexis to Perseid and back. "*If* it's the wrong direction."

"You know what I'm thinking?" Perseid ran a finger along the scar on his left cheek. "This is all too perfect. It might have been a setup from the start, meant to flush us out. Meant to flush *you* out in particular, Corporal--the one man who could see through their cloaking technology."

"Why else would Cairn turn up like this?" said Rexis. "At just the right time in just the right place?"

Scott scowled. "But how would they know to send him? How would they know I was the one who could see through their cloaking tech?"

"It must have gotten back to them from our own people." Rexis raised her eyebrows. "The same Commonwealth conspiracy that must have been protecting Cairn's identity all this time."

Scott thought about it. "Maybe you're right." Planting his hands on his hips, he stared at the floor. "But if that's the case, if traitors within the Commonwealth armed forces know our every move, do we even have a chance of beating the Reds?"

"Do you intend to back out if we don't?" said Perseid.

Scott straightened. "Hell no."

"Ask anyone on this ship, and they'll give you the same answer," said Perseid. "But you already knew that, didn't you?"

"Hell yes," said Scott.

"Then let's quit pissing around." Perseid marched toward the door. "I'll be on the Command Deck if you need me, ordering the crew to set course for Oberon."

"Aye, sir," said Scott.

Perseid paused as the door slid open in front of him. "Debrief at oh-seven hundred, Corporal."

"I'll be there," said Scott.

With that, Perseid stormed through the open door and disappeared into the corridor beyond.

CHAPTER 24

Scott lay in bed--his own, assigned bunk, not Donna's--and tried to force himself to sleep. The bunkroom was quiet for once, no Trane or Abby present to snore up a storm...but he still couldn't manage to doze off.

He couldn't stop thinking about Cairn Barrie and the conversation they'd had. It seemed unreal, like something out of a dream--something he couldn't seem to wrap his head around.

The dead boy had returned...just as Scott himself had come back to life so many years ago. The two of them had a deep connection, forged in Iridess Chasm and strengthened by sacrifice on Penitent Peak. But now they were working against each other in a time of war, battling for the highest stakes imaginable.

How exactly had it come to this? How had Cairn ended up with the Reds? What did he know that he wasn't telling? Scott wished he knew.

Cairn seemed committed to the Red cause, whatever that was. So why had he given up Oberon? What was his plan?

Even as Scott lay in his bunk, the *Sun Tzu* was racing toward Oberon at top speed. What would the Diamondbacks find when they arrived? What were their odds of success when they still hadn't managed to penetrate the Reds' cloaking technology?

There were too many questions. They whirled through his mind like spinning plates, keeping him awake even though he was physically exhausted.

The only comforting thoughts he had were about Donna and the way she'd squeezed his hand. Finally, he had genuine hope for her recovery; though her condition hadn't changed since the squeeze, he believed in his heart that it was only a matter of time until she awoke.

What would happen after that, he couldn't say. He'd had some doubts earlier about where they might be headed, but none of that would matter unless Donna recovered.

Meanwhile, he had to help the team get ready for Oberon. There was so much work to do, he felt guilty about being in his rack at all.

So what the flux? Why keep wasting time if the chances of falling asleep were next to nil?

Rolling over, Scott swung his feet off the bunk and dropped them to the cold floor. Rising from his rack, he yawned and stretched, then gathered his razor and towel and headed off to the showers. Perseid had said the debrief was set for oh-seven hundred, which was two and a half hours away. Plenty of time to get ready and get coffee.

At least he wouldn't be late.

*****

"You appear to be one of a kind, Corporal Scott," said Doctor Beauchamp, kicking off the debriefing. "Among the crew of this ship, that is."

Scott, who was seated at the long table in the conference room, lowered the coffee cup from which he'd been about to drink. All seven people in the room were staring at him with keen interest at that moment.

"When faced with a Red Battlenaut or Red personnel, you exhibit a unique response." Beauchamp touched the edge of the table, and holographic images sprang to life--a chart on either side of her, each with a jagged line plotted from left to right. "This is one example. Here we see the response of a member of the squad to the appearance of a Red Battlenaut on the surface of Shard." She gestured at the chart to the left of her. "The response is mapped as a combination of EEG, EKG, galvanic skin response, microbiome fluctuations, and other measurements." She gestured at the chart on the right. "And *this* is Corporal Scott's response."

Scott stared. The jagged line on his chart was clearly elevated, running much higher than the line on the chart of the other squad member.

"Holy plang," said Abby. "Big difference."

Beauchamp turned and traced the line on the anonymous squad member's chart. "As you can see, the response remains depressed throughout the encounter. All indicators are low, suggesting diminished stress to the subject's systems." Turning to Scott's chart, she traced the line there, lingering at the apex. "Meanwhile, Corporal Scott underwent considerable stress, reaching a peak far above the high point of the other subject."

"Which tells us what, exactly?" said Khalil.

"I'm getting to that." Beauchamp touched the table's edge, and the charts were replaced. "Here we have Corporal Scott's response at a different moment." She gestured at the chart on her right. "And this is the aggregate response of the rest of the squad." She traced the plotted line on the chart on her left. "Again, the squad's response suggests a lack of sensory stimulation. Corporal Scott's response, however, is consistently elevated." She ran her finger along the line on Scott's chart and nodded. "This definitively shows that there is a difference in how sensory information is received and processed between Corporal Scott and the others."

"And you've figured out what caused this difference?" said Major Perseid.

Beauchamp touched the table, and the charts went away. "We performed a multiphasic analysis of Corporal Scott, mapping all levels of his physiology from anatomical to subatomic to quantum." She touched the table, and a 3-D wireframe figure of a man appeared on her right, surrounded by text and data. "We did the same for all other members of the expedition to Shard." This time, six wireframe figures appeared on her left--four male, two female.

"But you did a full workup on Corporal Scott before the mission," said Rexis. "And you compared it to the rest of the crew at that time."

"Correct." Beauchamp smiled. "But we did not have the same data at our disposal. We did not have hard numbers on physiological states during Red encounters." Beauchamp nodded. "This time, we did. Charted responses suggested directions for deeper analysis--specifically, the nervous and immune systems. Eventually, we found a concrete difference that manifested only during Red intervention--an immune reaction blocking chemical receptors in neurons associated with sensory input. Essentially, whenever the subject sees Red artifacts or personnel, a firewall in his or her brain blocks the image, effectively rendering it invisible."

"That's a pretty damn sophisticated immune response," said Feinberg.

"But what mechanism triggers it?" said Khalil. "The sight of a Red is the cue, but what reacts to that cue and switches on the firewall?"

"This." Beauchamp touched the table, and the image of a bumpy, thorny sphere appeared in front of her, big as a fist, tinted red. "A virus."

"That's impossible," said Feinberg. "Are you trying to tell us that a *virus* detects and blocks all sensory input related to the Reds?"

"Viruses *plural*." Beauchamp gestured at Trane, who sat just around the corner of the table from her. "And that is where *he* comes in."

"*Merci*, Doctor." Trane got to his feet and straightened his uniform. "Indeed, there is more than one virus at work here. The Red Battlenaut armor retrieved from Shard is coated with matrices of viral particles. After intense study, we realized that this virus becomes active in proximity to the firewall virus. It serves as a catalyst, signaling the firewall virus to trigger the immune response that blocks Red sensory input."

"Wait a minute." Khalil frowned. "That's impossible, isn't it? One virus can't signal another over a distance."

Trane thumped his fist on the table and grinned. "It can if they're *quantum entangled*."

"Seriously?" said Feinberg. "Quantum entangled

viruses?"

"It works for molecules." Trane shrugged. "Why not viruses?"

Rexis narrowed her eyes and leaned forward to stare at the image of the virus. "So what you're saying is, thanks to quantum entanglement, the catalyst virus can affect the firewall virus over great distances."

"Causing the firewall virus to reconfigure itself and initiate an immune response," said Trane. "Until then, the firewall virus disguises itself as a dormant rhinovirus variant within the host."

"Rhinovirus," said Rexis. "The common cold, you mean."

Trane nodded. "Which is why it went undetected until we were able to observe its reconfigured state during Red exposure."

"So this firewall virus," said Scott. "I don't have it?"

"Correct," said Beauchamp. "But you're the only one in the squad who doesn't. Perhaps you have a natural immunity."

Scott frowned. "Then how did everyone else get it? How did the Reds manage to spread it?"

"We don't know." Beauchamp sighed. "We've just started to understand it."

"We don't know how to stop it yet, either," said Trane. "We're working to engineer a viral or nanotech-based countermeasure, but that research is still in its early stages."

Perseid got up from his chair and paced along the length of the table to where Beauchamp and Trane were standing. "I guess I don't have to tell you how soon we need a solution. We're due to arrive at Oberon in two days."

"We're aware the clock is ticking," said Beauchamp.

"God only knows what situation we're flying into," said Perseid. "Having more than one person able to see the Reds would vastly improve our odds."

"We're also continuing to work another angle that could enhance our intel," said Trane. "The DNA and RNA of the Red viral forms aren't native to Shard. We've been comparing the virus' genomes to available genetic databases to determine a likely planet of origin."

"Which could also be the Reds' planet of origin," added Beauchamp. "Or at least a scientific research hub."

Perseid nodded. "Status of that effort?"

"We've covered about 75 percent of the databases," said Trane, "with no success so far. But the A.I. is continuing to cross-check as we speak. I estimate completion in a day and a half."

"All right then," said Perseid, "but devising Red virus countermeasures is still top priority. That and extracting more intel from Cairn Barrie." He turned his gaze on Scott. "You're going back in soon, right?"

For what it's worth, Scott wanted to say, but he just nodded. "I'll keep talking to him."

"Great," said Perseid. "Keep milking your history together, and keep him guessing. He's been throwing you off balance; now it's your turn."

"Any information could be vital," said Rexis. "Even the smallest throwaway line could turn the tide in our favor."

"Understood," said Scott.

"Okay then." Perseid clapped his hands together. "Everybody get back to work. Dismissed."

CHAPTER 25

Scott spent an hour with Donna in the medicenter, then put his CORE Battlenaut through its paces on the Training Deck to let off some steam. By the time he was done, he'd gone through five hundred rounds of dummy ammo and racked up perfect scores against every solid and holographic target generated for the exercise.

Unfortunately, he didn't feel much better when it was all over. Having memories of Iridess Chasm and Penitent Peak brought so strongly to the surface made him feel lousy. Knowing Cairn Barrie was back from the dead and holed up in a cell a few decks away stuck a black hole dead center in his belly. It was one thing to have nightmares about his experience; it was something else altogether to have the past brought to life and shoved in his face in the middle of a crisis.

He just wanted to stop thinking about it for a while, but the Training Deck exercise didn't clear his mind for long.

As he climbed out of the cockpit and down the hull of his Battlenaut, the full force of memory surged back to him, rushing into every chink in the mental armor he'd tried to construct. He remembered the screams of his mother and father, the terror he'd felt as black-lipped Vore killed them with knives and dragged him away. He remembered the pain and shock of being murdered himself, beaten to death by Vore on that ledge on Penitent Peak. The sight of little Cairn tumbling off the cliff blazed in front of his inner eye as if it were happening all over again at that very moment.

He'd spent years dealing with what had happened, breaking it into manageable pieces and pushing them into boxes in his brain. Now that every box had been thrown wide open, he felt like he was teetering on the cliff again, facing a drop of epic proportions.

With a sigh, he headed for the exit, bound for another session in the lab with Trane and the others. He'd be busy enough to distract himself a little, at least until his next visit to Cairn. He just wished there'd be more to take his mind off Iridess Chasm.

As if on cue, one of the big gates leading out of the Battlenaut bays shot open in front of him, revealing a towering mass of metal.

At first, Scott thought it was one of the CORE Battlenauts...but as the armored giant stomped out of the shadows of the bay, he saw that wasn't the case at all. It was a Battlenaut, all right, but not a CORE model.

In fact, it was almost identical to his Marine Corps Mark VI Battlenaut, the one he'd lost to the Reds on Chelong III. The only major difference he could see was the color; instead of gray plating, this Battlenaut was armored in blue and silver.

Scott couldn't help smiling. The CORE Battlenauts were more advanced across the board and handled like a dream in combat--but he still had a soft spot for his Marine Corps armor. It was comparatively primitive, but it had saved his skin too many times to count and helped him dispatch a legion of enemies.

Not to mention, there was something about the lines of it. The CORE units looked sleeker and more humanoid, but this one--it was somehow more exciting. More of a classic, like a boxy old automobile compared to a modern-day no-frills personal transport.

"I'll be damned." Scott walked up to the Mark VI and ran his fingers over the side of its left ankle. "Now that's a sight for sore eyes."

The Mark VI raised the gun on its right arm and cranked off three rounds, firing slugs at a floor-mounted solid target clear across the Training Deck. All three slugs punched through the bull's eye in close formation.

"Nice shooting!" Scott raised his voice so the pilot inside the Battlenaut could hear him. "Who *needs* A.I. guided targeting with *those* guns!"

Just then, a rack of hexagonal plates in the Battlenaut's chest and abdomen folded downward, exposing the cockpit and the pilot within--none other than the ship's helmsman, Vic Fong. "That's one of the things I love about this model. It's totally hands-on."

Scott stepped back to take in the full height of the Mark VI. "There's something to be said for hands-on. You don't have to worry about your A.I. going rogue, for one thing."

"And it leaves more room for you to act on instinct, doesn't it?" said Fong. "Your reactions aren't muffled by layers of verbal commands and A.I. subroutines."

"Plus you only have to worry about trusting yourself, not a computer." Scott nodded and folded his arms over his chest. "I'd ride one into battle again in a heartbeat."

"Me, too." Fong played the armrest keypads, and the upper body of the Mark VI swiveled from side to side. "But this one's just for show, I'm afraid."

"That's too bad," said Scott.

"I'm a hobbyist." Fong played the keypads again, making the guns tilt up and down while the torso kept swiveling. "Instead of restoring antique furniture or classic automobiles, I restore classic Battlenauts."

"Great hobby." Scott grinned. "How many do you have?"

"This is the only one aboard ship," said Fong. "But I've got three more back home, including a Mark I in mint condition."

"How'd you manage that?" said Scott. "The Mark I was decommissioned twelve years ago."

"I won it." Fong's grin widened. "In a poker game."

"You're kidding!" said Scott. "A poker game with *who*? The Commonwealth Secretary of Defense?"

Fong shook his head. "Just a factory foreman from the plant where they manufactured the Mark I. He ran one last unit through the line before they retooled. Socked it away for a rainy day."

"And then he *lost* it playing *poker*?"

"What can I say? Drinking made him stupid." Fong shrugged. "And I'm a hell of a poker player. Care for a game sometime?"

"Only if you bet the Mark VI," said Scott.

"Not going to happen," said Fong.

"Can I at least take her for a spin?"

Fong thought it over. "Sure. What the hell? Just remember, you break it, you bought it." His fingers played the keypads, and the Battlenaut shifted to its knees so he could get out of the cockpit.

Before Fong could turn over the Mark VI to Scott, though, Trane's voice blared over the Training Deck PA system. "Corporal Scott, report to Lab Five. Corporal Scott, report to Lab Five immediately."

Scott clenched his jaws as the stress he'd briefly forgotten rushed back in on him. "Damnit." Seeing the Mark VI and talking to Fong had chased it away, but Trane had brought it all right back. "I have to go."

"No worries," said Fong. "I'm giving you a rain check. You'll get plenty of time behind the wheel of the Mark VI."

"Thanks." Scott smiled and headed for the door. "I just hope we won't have to wait for the end of the war to *find* that time."

"Call your grandma!" shouted Trane as soon as Scott walked into Lab Five. "You need to *call her* right now!"

Scott frowned. "What the hell are you talking about?" Looking around the lab, he saw Abby, Khalil, and Feinberg staring back at him. They were all sitting around a holographic projection of a red letter "X" in a red circle, spinning on its Y-axis like a penny on edge.

"We've just been *data-blocked*." Trane stalked back and forth like a tiger in its cage, eyes wide and wild. "Just as we were finally making *progress* tracking the viral DNA, someone threw a *data-block* on us. Now we can't go any further down that trail!"

"Wait," said Scott. "What trail, exactly?"

"The Red firewall virus," said Khalil. "We couldn't match its full genome to anything on file, so we tried *pieces* of it. Ultimately, we matched a piece of its DNA to an engineered virus from an old military medical R&D project."

"What kind of R&D project?" said Scott.

"Something to do with post-traumatic stress disorder," said Feinberg. "*Prevention* of PTSD, not *treatment*."

"It was called Project Lethe," said Khalil. "It started 25 years ago on the Commonwealth capitol world, Archibald. Part of the firewall virus matches part of a virus created for Lethe, though other parts don't match at all."

"And that's all we know," said Feinberg. "Because just as we reached deeper, somebody data-blocked us. We were locked out of the channel. No matter where we search, Project Lethe never shows up."

"That's why we need you to call your *granny*!" shouted Trane. "We need Commandant Chalice to get us past the block!"

"From what we can gather, it was put there by Military Intelligence," said Khalil. "One of their A.I. drones, anyway. Project Lethe must be on a watch list of some kind."

"And you can't get past the block on your own?" said Scott.

Suddenly, Trane shot forward and snapped out his words in Scott's face. "If we could do that, we wouldn't be begging *you* to call *Grandma*, would we?"

Scott wanted to force Trane to back away from him, but he didn't. Instead, he squared his shoulders and matched his gaze with an icy stare. "I've already got a call in to her," he said stiffly.

"Perfect!" said Trane. "Then you'll ask her about removing the block?"

"I'll see what I can do," said Scott. "No promises."

"She *has* to help us." Trane lurched away from Scott and paced across the lab. "This is a bona fide *lead* on the Reds. I can *feel* it."

"The fact that we've been data-blocked just confirms it," said Abby. "We were getting close to something important. Otherwise, our search wouldn't have been shut down."

"The block also suggests high-level involvement," said Feinberg. "It takes someone with serious pull to order an A.I. drone that throws blocks like that."

Trane stopped pacing. "All I know is, this could be the key to everything. This could lead us straight to the Reds, reveal their plans, and end their stealth tactics. It could literally save the Commonwealth."

"I understand." Scott nodded. "I'll try to reach the Commandant again and let you know what happens."

"When?" said Trane. "Right after you leave here?"

"Yes," said Scott. "Right after that."

"I'll go with you." Trane marched over and stopped in front of him. "I can explain the technical fine points."

"That's all right." Scott turned and headed for the door. "I think I can manage."

As promised, Scott tried again to contact Grandma Bern... but the result was the same. According to Bern's assistant, Lori, the Commandant was not available.

"Can you tell me when Commandant Chalice might return my call?" asked Scott.

"I'm so sorry, but no." Lori, whose holographic form was seated across the round black table from Scott, smiled sadly and shook her head. "That information is classified, actually."

Scott frowned, wondering what his grandmother was up to this time. The fact that she'd been unreachable for days, and her whereabouts were classified, told him she was involved in something far from routine.

Even so, his own business was pretty important. "Is there any way you can get a message to her? It regards an urgent security matter."

Lori winced. "Unlikely, Solomon." Her expression changed to a smile. "But for you, I can try."

Scott grinned. "I can't thank you enough. I wouldn't ask if it wasn't critically important."

"I know that," Lori said brightly. "So what's the message?"

"Actually," said Scott, "I'd prefer to send it to you under encryption."

"You do realize this entire communication is encrypted, don't you?" said Lori.

"Trust me," said Scott. "It's not enough."

There in the comm booth, he recorded his message for Bern, telling her what they'd found out about the firewall virus and Project Lethe. He told her about the data-block and the need to dig deeper as only she could. He begged her to do anything she could to help get to the bottom of the Reds' secrets and give the Diamondbacks the edge they needed to save the Commonwealth from whatever the Reds had in store.

He also told her about the theory that a conspiracy in the upper echelons of the Commonwealth might be the driving force behind the Reds. He asked her to investigate as best she could and let him know what she found.

And then he told her about Cairn Barrie. If anyone could fully appreciate the significance of reconnecting with Cairn, it was Bern. Back during Scott's recovery from the events in Iridess Chasm, not a day had gone by without Bern at his side, helping him through the struggle to regain the future he'd almost lost. Without hesitation, she had stepped into the role of his murdered parents, getting him through the crisis and going on to raise him in the years that followed.

Though she wasn't at his side now, he still felt like he was unburdening himself to her. It felt good to get things off his chest; he was tempted to tell her much more--about Donna, about the battle on Shard, about how tough it was being the only one who could see and sense everything related to the Reds. But he knew his time on the comm channel was limited, so he wrapped up his message.

"Call me as soon as you can," he said. "And remember, I love you."

With that, he closed the channel. He left the booth just in time, as it turned out; Dr. Beauchamp paged him over the P.A. just as he walked out into the hall.

CHAPTER 26

"Testing," said Beauchamp, speaking into the glowing red holographic microphone floating in front of her mouth. "Testing, testing, one, two, three."

Scott gave her a thumbs-up from across the anteroom of the brig. Her voice was coming in with crystal clarity through the earpiece he was wearing. "Got it." He nodded and adjusted the way the earpiece was seated in his ear. "Loud and clear, Doctor." He walked over to join her by the cell door.

"Very good." Beauchamp handed him a thin silver wand, twenty centimeters long, with a spherical crystal on the end no bigger than the tip of his little finger. "Use this to scan him. It is already set to take the readings we need. However..." She handed over a tablet computer. "...you must use this to record your findings. Remember to type all data into the form, since the actual data from the wand will not likely be visible to anyone but you."

Scott nodded. This was why Beauchamp had paged him after he'd made his call to Bern--to gather medical data from Cairn. To anyone other than Scott, every sensor scan of Cairn looked perfectly blank, as if the cell in which he was imprisoned was empty.

"Take your time and capture all the data you can," said Beauchamp. "Remember, it is just as crucial that we study Cairn's physiology as the Red Battlenaut wreckage. We must confirm Trane's two-virus theory--or reject it and develop another."

"Right," said Scott. "There's just one thing I don't understand." He held up the diagnostic wand in one hand and the tablet in the other. "How am I supposed to type up the data if I don't have both hands free?"

Beauchamp's thick red lips curved upward in a smile that seemed tinged with pure pleasure. All her expressions had that same sensuous flavor. "Use your nose?" Though her voice was throaty, her laugh was a girlish giggle.

Scott raised the tablet and pretended to try to type with his nose--then shook his head. "That won't work."

"Here." She took the wand and tablet from him. "*Allez oop.*" Still smiling, she plugged the skinny end of the wand into a jack on the top edge of the tablet, then handed it all back to him.

"Ah." Scott nodded. "Now *this* makes sense."

"Just point this at the subject and switch on the tablet." Beauchamp tapped the crystal on the tip of the wand. "The tablet is already programmed to run the desired tests in sequence. You will view the results in one window." She tapped the screen of the tablet with one glossy red nail. "You will retype the data in another window alongside it."

"Okay, fine," said Scott. "No problem."

Beauchamp's eyes glittered when she looked at him. "If there is a problem, simply excuse yourself, and you and I will iron it out."

"The only problem I can think of right now is the person on the other side of this door." He bobbed his head toward the cell. "I doubt he'll cooperate."

"Perhaps you could try a different approach." Beauchamp tipped her head to one side and narrowed her eyes. "Instead of trying to access sensitive information, see if you can engage him in small talk. Ask him about things that have nothing to do with the Reds--his life before he met them, his family, his home. Ignore his efforts to bait you. Just try to open a dialogue."

Scott shrugged. "I'll give it a try. But he really hates me."

Beauchamp clasped her hands behind her back and leaned forward with a smile and one raised eyebrow. "Perhaps his *true* feelings are more complex than that. Give him a chance to come around, Corporal Scott. He might surprise you."

When Scott entered the cell, Cairn was on the floor doing push-ups. He wasn't breathing hard; maybe he'd just gotten started.

"Sol!" He barked out the word between reps. "Funny meeting...*you* here."

Scott sat down on the antigrav chair and placed the tablet on his lap. "What can I say?" He switched on the tablet and pointed the wand at Cairn. "I missed you."

"Plus you need to...run a medical exam...on me." Cairn smirked up at him. "Hence the...diagnostic wand."

"Nah," said Scott as the first test procedure booted up on the tablet. "This is our new Red Deprogrammer device. Guaranteed to change a Red into a Commonwealther at the press of a button."

"I'm starting to feel...more corrupt...and more boring... already." Cairn laughed as he continued his push-ups.

"So what've you been doing?" As Scott spoke, he watched a set of numbers appear on the tablet screen--Cairn's vital signs. Meanwhile, a form slid onto the screen beside the list of vitals, and a holographic keyboard popped up under the tablet when he squeezed the side. Using the keyboard, he tabbed through the form and typed in the numbers from the other side of the screen.

"I've been working out mostly." Cairn did two more pushups, then stopped and lowered his knees to the floor. "That and dreaming."

"About what?" said Scott.

"About you." Cairn snorted. "I've been dreaming about the look you'll have on your face when you get to Oberon and realize just how *bad* things have gotten and how there's nothing you can *do* about it."

"Thank God," said Scott. "I was afraid you might say you were dreaming about me in a *dirty* way."

"Nope." Cairn chuckled. "I never fantasize about jerk-offs who leave me for dead after I save their lives and everything."

"Good to hear." Scott finished typing up the vitals and tapped the screen, moving to the next test in the preprogrammed sequence. "Because the other thing would've been just too awkward."

Cairn lay back on the floor and started doing sit-ups. "So how far are we from Oberon now? A day and a half?

A day?"

"Something like that." The new test analyzed the composition and condition of Cairn's microbiome--the cloud of microbes surrounding his body. A new customized form appeared, and Scott continued entering data as before. "Sounds like you can't wait to get there."

"Like I said...seeing the look on your face...will be sweet." Cairn sneered. "I've been waiting for *years*...for that. For seeing your spirit...utterly *crushed*...beyond repair."

"So you'll feel better when you get your payback?" Scott didn't look up from the tablet. "Will that finally fix things between us?

"How *could* it?" said Cairn. "I'll hate you for the rest of my *life*."

"Right." Scott kept typing. "For not coming to get you even though I thought you were dead."

Cairn sat up and stopped. "You knew." He gave Scott a look of absolute contempt. "Deep down, you knew. And you still did nothing."

"I saw you *fall*. And then *I* died." Scott met his gaze. "I was *dead* when they found me, remember? They used an experimental procedure to revive me, but I was still a *mess*. It took me over a *year* to recover." What a nightmare it had been. Bern had pulled strings to make the procedure happen and bring him back...but sometimes, he'd wished she hadn't. The word "agonizing" didn't begin to describe what he'd gone through.

But surviving it had toughened him. It had made him the man he was today.

Not that that held any water with Cairn. "Poor baby." He spit on the floor at Scott's feet and went back to doing sit-ups. "At least you weren't still...the captive of a sick bastard...

who got off on *torturing* and *abusing* you."

"Well, if I'd known you were out there, I would have done everything I could to save you." Scott returned his attention to the tablet, where he typed the last of the microbiome data. As the next test started, he decided the conversation had gotten too volatile and tried reshaping it as Beauchamp had suggested. "So tell me, do you still have family on Tack?"

"Who the hell knows?" Cairn's voice was thick with anger. "I haven't had much...of a chance...to go look for them."

The new test, a subatomic scan, chugged along as Scott copied over the results. "Do you have any brothers or sisters? If you told me, I forget."

Cairn kept doing sit-ups. "Two brothers...and three sisters. I haven't seen them...since I was taken by Vore...back when I was six."

"I could look them up for you," said Scott. "Let you know where they are, at least."

Cairn paused. "Don't even try to *tell* me you haven't looked them up already. As soon as you realized who I was, you must've run a complete background check."

"Not me. Been a little busy." Scott raised his eyes from the tablet. "You're not the only thing on my to-do list, you know."

Cairn stared at him for a moment before resuming his exercise. "Don't bother with the family reunion. Those people won't even know who I am anymore."

"I don't know about that," said Scott. "What if they still love you after all? What if they want you back?"

"I'm nothing but a ghost," said Cairn. "Leave it alone, Sol."

"Whatever." Scott shrugged and finished the subatomic scan. "Believe it or not, I'm trying to help."

"Trying to *play* me...is more like it." Cairn did three more sit-ups and got to his feet. "Well, the palsy-walsy routine won't *work* with *me*. I'll *never* open up to you, *plang-hole*."

"Just making conversation," said Scott. "Plus, I'm curious. You and I never really got to know each other back in Iridess Chasm."

"No loss there." Cairn started doing jumping jacks.

Scott ran the next test and typed up the results as Cairn continued his workout. When he'd finished, he proceeded to test number five--a quantum scan designed to detect infiltration of dangerous bodies from parallel universes. "I don't know, Cairn. I think we could have been friends."

"Then you must have...suffered brain damage...when you died."

Scott ignored the remark. "You know what I remember?" He stopped typing. "I remember you breaking down in tears out in the Chasm, and me comforting you."

"You have a...vivid imagination," said Cairn.

"I also remember helping you climb Penitent Peak," said Scott. "I remember you holding on to my hand for dear life."

Suddenly, Cairn stopped doing jumping jacks and turned away from him. "Flux you." He grabbed a gray towel from the cot and wiped his face with it. "I was seven years old, and I'd been held captive for over a year. I'd have held on to *anyone* if I'd thought they could help me."

Scott opened his mouth to say something, then noticed a blinking readout on the tablet. The wand had picked up an abnormal quantum signature coming from Cairn.

Tapping a few controls on the tablet, Scott zeroed in on the signature. It was located in Cairn's head, around the middle of his brain.

Using the comm function on the tablet, Scott flashed a text message to Beauchamp, describing the finding. She texted him right back: SWITCH TO HOLOGRAPHIC TOMOGRAPHY SCAN OF THE BRAIN, TEST SEVEN IN THE SEQUENCE.

Scott jumped ahead two tests to the holographic tomography scan and switched it on. As he pointed the wand at the back of Cairn's head, the crystal on the tip of the wand glowed blue.

A moment later, an image of a human brain appeared on the tablet. Scott touched the screen, requesting a view of a midsagittal section; immediately, the brain split in half along the midline and the left side faded away, leaving the right.

There, in the center of the right midsagittal section of Cairn's brain, Scott saw a jagged, ruby red object with crystalline spines like the rays of a star.

"What the hell?" he said, frowning at the screen. As he watched, the object flared with light and vanished...then reappeared. It went on pulsating like that--brightening, vanishing, and reappearing--in a continuous cycle.

Cairn turned to look at him. "What is it?"

Scott wondered if he should keep it to himself--then decided full disclosure probably wouldn't make any difference. "There's something in your brain. Some kind of spiky red object."

"Does it keep fading in and out?" asked Cairn.

"Yes." Even as he said it, Scott could see the pulsation continue on the screen of the tablet.

"Congratulations," said Cairn. "You found my personal self-destruct mechanism." He tapped the side of his head and laughed. "Maybe you can tell me why it hasn't blown us all to kingdom come yet."

"Good question." Scott didn't mention that the cell had been triple-reinforced to block all known types of transmissions (except the security camera feed and the comm channel allowing him to text Beauchamp). "Tell me how it works, and maybe I can figure it out."

"It's a quantum bomb," said Cairn. "Powerful enough to destroy this entire ship. That's all you need to know."

Scott zoomed in on the midsagittal plane and tried using holographic tomography to pop up a view of the inside of the bomb. For some reason, all he could see under the bomb's jagged shell was a featureless blotch of gray. "How do you trigger this thing, did you say?"

"Wish upon a star." Cairn bugged his eyes and chuckled.

"Seriously," said Scott.

"I'll tell you this much." Cairn nodded and winked. "If I could get the damn thing to work, we wouldn't be standing here right now. I've been trying to trigger it since I got here."

"Well, thanks for giving it a shot," said Scott. "I appreciate the effort."

Cairn's expression darkened. "Any time."

Scott fired Beauchamp a text describing the bomb, and she wrote back immediately: RUN A COMPLETE BRAIN SCAN, TEST NUMBER 12. RECORD ELECTROMAGNETIC FREQUENCY AND FLUCTUATIONS.

Scott followed her instructions and put the new test in motion. A wave pattern appeared on the screen of the tablet, bordered by rows of statistics.

"Careful." Cairn stepped closer and folded his arms over his chest. "Don't want to accidentally set off the bomb now, do you?"

Scott shrugged and kept working. "I've been dead before. It's no big thing."

"No fear, huh?" Cairn nodded. "Maybe you'd make a great Red after all."

"Wow." Scott's tone was sarcastic. "You make me want to sign up on the spot."

"Why the hell not?" Cairn grinned. "You ought to consider it before the scudge starts hitting the fan."

Scott kept typing up data from the brain scan. "All I have to do is betray my comrades and commit treason against the Commonwealth I've sworn allegiance to, right?" He snorted. "Sounds appealing."

"You'd be on the winning side," said Cairn. "Plus which, you and I would be working together again. We'd be *friends* again."

"No kidding." Scott glanced up at him. "So you'd give up your vendetta just like that? No payback needed?"

"That's right." Cairn nodded. "If you switch sides, I'll let it all go. We'll have a fresh start, you and I."

Scott watched him a moment more before returning his eyes to the tablet. "I like the idea of us being friends again. Can't we do that without my betraying everything I stand for and care about?"

Cairn shook his head. "I've told you the terms. You have until we get to Oberon to accept them."

"Well, thanks for your generosity," said Scott. "I'll take it under advisement."

"You do that, Sol," said Cairn. "I'll be waiting."

CHAPTER 27

A day later, as the *Sun Tzu* approached Oberon's home system, Scott found himself back in the conference room with the Diamondback senior officers--Perseid, Rexis, Abby, Trane, Feinberg, Khalil, Beauchamp, Fong, García, and Azimuth. Perseid had called one last briefing to update the team on the latest developments before everyone launched into final preps for the mission ahead.

"We are thirteen hours out from Oberon," said Perseid, "and we have no idea what to expect." Standing at the head of the long table beside Rexis, he looked grim. "Sensors have not picked up any signs of unusual activity."

"What about Cairn Barrie?" said Khalil. "Has he given us any insight?" He looked across the table at Scott when he said it.

"Negative," said Scott. "Cairn refuses to cooperate."

"So our blindness continues," said García.

"Not quite," said Rexis. "Trane and his team have

had some success opening our eyes for this mission." She gestured at Trane, who sat at the opposite end of the table.

"That's right." Trane stood. "We've developed an inoculation that kills the firewall virus." Reaching into a hip pocket of his black uniform, he drew out a hypodermic filled with bright green liquid. "It should enable us to see Red materiel and personnel."

"It was quite a challenge," said Beauchamp. "We had to draw the firewall virus out of its dormant state by exposing subjects to the catalyst virus from pieces of Red wreckage. Once we had samples of the activated firewall virus, it took a while to analyze its structure and develop an antiviral countermeasure."

"It's a tremendous advantage," said Perseid. "Assuming we encounter Reds at Oberon, they won't expect us to be able to see them."

"Great work," said Fong. "I guess this means Commandant Chalice got the data blocks lifted?"

"Negative," said Trane. "Corporal Scott didn't come through for us."

"Not yet, anyway," said Scott. "I'm still waiting to hear back from the Commandant. She's been off the grid the past few days."

"Doesn't much matter at this point," said Trane. "She isn't part of the equation anymore."

Scott bristled. "Don't write her off. She'll come through for us, wait and see."

"Sure she will." Trane sneered. "Clearly, we're not at the top of Granny's list of fish to fry."

Perseid cleared his throat loudly. "Moving on..." He gave Trane a meaningful stare. "We've got another surprise in store for the Reds."

"If there *are* any Reds at Oberon," added Rexis.

"Exactly." Perseid gestured at Beauchamp. "Doctor, if you will?"

Beauchamp nodded and stood. When she touched the edge of the table, a hologram appeared before her--the computer-rendered image of Cairn based on Scott's descriptions. "Meet our Trojan Horse."

Scott frowned. He knew what a Trojan Horse was but didn't understand how the reference applied to Cairn.

"Mr. Barrie has a quantum bomb in his head." Beauchamp touched the table again, and a midsagittal view of a human brain appeared beside the image of Cairn. A spiky red crystalline object pulsated along the midline. "This is a computer rendering of Cairn's brain with the bomb inside, based on the data reported by Corporal Scott. The explosive is actually quite powerful, in spite of its small size. Mr. Barrie claims it can destroy this entire ship, but we estimate it can destroy much more than that. A *fleet* of ships, perhaps."

"And this walking bomb is still aboard *this* ship *why?*" said García.

"Because we might be able to use him," interjected Perseid. "We could hand him over to the Reds, then trigger the bomb remotely."

"How are we going to do that?" asked Fong. "Surely, we can't control the bomb trigger mechanism."

"Surely we *can*." Beauchamp put up a third image above the first two--a series of overlapping jagged lines plotted on a chart. "Since Corporal Scott could find no trigger device anywhere on Mr. Barrie's person, we concluded that the device must respond to his thoughts. After Corporal Scott mapped Mr. Barrie's brain activity, we were able to construct a device that will block his neural impulses and substitute our own commands, broadcast at the same frequency. In short, we can make the bomb do what we want, using a signal disguised as Mr. Barrie's own thoughts."

"And you say this thing could knock out a *fleet*?" said García.

"That's just a guess on our part," said Rexis. "We haven't been able to view the bomb's interior with holo tomography, so we can't determine its capacity that way."

"And there's no record of Commonwealth forces encountering a quantum bomb this small before," said Perseid. "Larger versions have been extraordinarily destructive, but this one might be more advanced and just as powerful."

Scott frowned. "So you'll just hand him over and blow him up?"

Beauchamp held up her left wrist and pointed at the oblong device strapped around it like a chronometer. "This remote control will trigger the bomb." She tapped the surface of the gleaming silver oval mounted on the strap, and it swirled. "Press it three times, and the final signal will be sent."

"And Cairn will be blown to smithereens," said Scott.

"He would've done the same to us," said Trane. "He *tried*, didn't he?"

Scott didn't answer. He didn't like the direction the briefing was taking. It was true Cairn had said he'd tried to blow up the *Sun Tzu*, but did that make it right to detonate Cairn by remote control?

"Anyway, we'll only use the quantum bomb as a last resort," said Perseid. "It's just another weapon in our arsenal."

Scott still didn't like what he was hearing...but why? Had Cairn succeeded in making him feel guilty about what had happened at Iridess Chasm? Or was something else affecting him? Was it possible he felt some connection to Cairn, though the man clearly hated him and wanted to see him suffer?

Scott would have to think about it later. Perseid was wrapping up the briefing.

"That brings us all up to speed for now." Perseid clapped his hands together. "Until we know more, let's get ready for our arrival at Oberon. Prepare all Battlenauts for planetfall, though armored deployment is not a certainty at this time."

Everyone at the table nodded.

"We know so little, we need to be ready for anything," said Perseid. "Not that we aren't *always* ready for anything."

Everyone in the room jumped out of their chairs and shouted "Hoo-aah!" as one.

"Dismissed!" said Perseid, and the Diamondbacks charged toward the door.

Seven hours later, when Scott had finished prepping his Battlenaut, he headed to the medicenter for one last visit with Donna before Oberon.

Unfortunately, the medicenter was crazier than usual when he arrived. There were dozens of Diamondbacks standing in a line that snaked down the corridor, all waiting to get their inoculations of the firewall virus counteragent.

Marching past the waiting Diamondbacks, Scott zipped into the medicenter and made a beeline for Donna's bed. Beauchamp and Tourmal, who were giving the crew their shots, looked up when he passed...then returned their full attention to the bare biceps they were injecting.

At least they'd pulled a curtain around Donna's bed. The

room was still noisy, but Scott had a modicum of privacy for his visit.

Standing beside Donna's bed, he took her hand. "Looks like it's time for another mission," he told her. "So how much longer are you going to lie there and keep slacking?"

Donna gave no response. If anything, her body seemed more still than ever.

"Well, you better get up off your lazy ass soon," said Scott. "The squad needs you. *I* need you." He squeezed her hand. "So get a move on."

Just then, Beauchamp pushed through the curtain. "Her condition has not changed, Corporal. No improvement."

"But she's not getting worse?" said Scott.

Beauchamp shook her head sadly. "I do wish we would see more responsiveness, though. I wish she would squeeze someone's hand again soon. The longer she remains comatose..."

"I understand." Scott gently touched Donna's forehead. "At least you don't need to inoculate her."

Suddenly, Beauchamp frowned thoughtfully. "Maybe I do." Reaching up, she stroked her lower lip with one fingertip. "Maybe that is not such a bad idea, actually. She could awaken at any time, in which case she should be prepared to identify the enemy." Without another word, she flowed back through the curtain and was gone.

Scott bent down and kissed Donna's cheek. "Take care of yourself, okay? I'll see you as soon as I can." He kissed her other cheek, too. "Who knows? Maybe next time I see you, you'll be up and around. Maybe you'll dance your way right out of here."

Scott walked out through the curtain just in time to see Perseid getting his shot, which surprised him.

"Hello, Corporal." Perseid smiled as Tourmal held up a loaded hypodermic.

Scott frowned. "You weren't in line, were you?" He wondered if he'd walked past Perseid in the corridor without noticing him.

Perseid shook his head. "I *cut* line. One of the perks of command." Just then, the hypo hit his bicep, and he winced. "But medicine is still the great equalizer, isn't it?"

"Yes, sir." Scott managed a smile.

"How is she?" Perseid bobbed his head toward Donna. "Any improvement?"

"Negative," said Scott. "But at least she hasn't taken a turn for the worse."

"Damn." Perseid rolled his sleeve down and stepped away from Tourmal, making room for the next man in line. "I know Beauchamp's doing everything she can for her."

"I think she might have just gotten an idea," said Scott. "She said something about giving Donna the antiviral inoculation."

"But how would that..."

Perseid was interrupted by Rexis' voice over the P.A. "Major Perseid, report to the Command Deck. Major Perseid, report to the Command Deck *immediately*."

Perseid's manner changed instantly from easygoing to intense. He stiffened, standing straighter, and his friendly smile became a grim stare. "Corporal Scott, you're with me." Spinning on his heel, he headed for the door.

Scott did as he was told, falling in step behind Perseid. When they reached the corridor, they both broke into a run.

En route, Perseid didn't say a word--and didn't have to. The way he'd been summoned suggested that something serious had happened. Speculating about what it might be would be a waste of time.

There was also no need for Perseid to explain to Scott why he needed him along. Scott was still the only person aboard the *Sun Tzu* who could see one hundred percent of Red materiel and personnel all of the time. If the Reds had made a move, of course Perseid would need his only certified Red spotter at his side.

There was nothing to say until they reached the Command Deck and saw what awaited them. It was that simple.

The door to the Command Deck swept open, and Perseid ran right through. "Report!" he snapped in mid-stride, before his feet had stopped moving.

Scott ran in next and stopped sooner, hanging back to assess the situation. In the view ahead, visible through the transparent prow of the ship, he saw the orange and yellow sphere of Oberon, poised between the binary stars that kept it bathed in perpetual daylight. The planet was still small, in the distance, hours away.

"Sir!" Rexis, who was standing up front with hands clasped behind her back, looked tenser than Scott had ever seen her. "We've detected a vessel in orbit around Oberon." She paused. "A *Commonwealth* vessel."

Perseid came to a stop in the middle of the deck and planted his hands on his hips. "*Which* Commonwealth vessel?"

"The *Samuel Nicholas*," said Rexis.

Scott was surprised. The *Samuel Nicholas*--named for the ancient founder of the United States Marine Corps--was the flagship of the Commonwealth Marines.

Perseid scowled. "What the hell is the *Sam Nicholas* doing here? It wasn't mentioned in any of the fleet movement bulletins."

"Unknown." Rexis' voice tightened. "But it shows signs of having taken heavy fire. So does the Rightful ship orbiting nearby."

"Holy flux." Perseid blew out his breath and ran a hand over the black bristle on his scalp. "Have we hailed the *Sam Nicholas*?"

"Yes, sir," said Rexis. "No reply. No transmissions of any kind."

"You said she shows signs of taking heavy fire," said Perseid.

Rexis raised her voice to be heard clearly by the Command Deck control A.I. "Maximum magnification on the *Samuel Nicholas*."

As soon as she called out the order, the view zoomed in on a wedge of Oberon. The massive bulk of the *Samuel Nicholas* drifted at the edge of the atmosphere, listing precariously to one side and spilling black clouds into space from gashes in her hull.

Without thinking, Scott stepped forward, mesmerized by the sight. The flagship was the mightiest vessel in the Commonwealth fleet; it must have taken extraordinary firepower to wreck it like that.

One thing was clear to him: the Rightful ship had not done the damage. It was smaller than the flagship and looked like it was in far worse shape. Something had snapped it in two down the middle, leaving splintered halves open to the vacuum of space, barely held together on one side.

"They didn't do that to each other," said Rexis. "Damage patterns aren't consistent with Commonwealth or Rightful weaponry. The sheer scope of the destruction suggests an overwhelming ambush by superior forces."

"What the hell are we flying into?" said Perseid. "These ships shouldn't *be* here, and they *sure* as hell shouldn't be blown apart like that."

"Looks like Cairn gave us accurate information." Rexis looked at Scott when she said it.

Scott nodded.

"Smashing up the *Sam Nicholas* like that would be next to impossible," said Perseid, "unless the attackers were undetectable."

"Like the Reds," said Rexis.

"Which still doesn't explain why these ships were here at all." Perseid frowned and rubbed his chin. "Why would the flagship of the Commonwealth Marines be in the same place as a Rightful vessel if they weren't shooting at each other?"

"I wish I knew," said Rexis. "Marine H.Q. has no comment."

"I guess we'll find out soon enough." Perseid clapped his hands together and spoke loud enough for everyone on the Command Deck to hear. "Has everyone been inoculated against the firewall virus?"

His question was greeted by a chorus of affirmatives. Scott was the only one who didn't join in, since he had no need for the antivirus countermeasure.

"That's good, because we're going in." He turned in a circle, surveying his crew in their antigrav harnesses, surrounded by holographic controls. "Be alert to *any* sign of Red activity, no matter how small. Don't hesitate to issue an *instantaneous* warning. If the bastards come at us like they did the *Sam Nicholas*, every second will mean the difference between life and death." He stopped turning when he got to Scott. "In fact, I want *you* on the Command Deck from this moment on, Corporal, just in case the viral countermeasure takes a while to kick in. You're the only one aboard guaranteed to spot Reds without delay or distortion whether you've had an inoculation or not."

"Aye, sir," said Scott.

"Set him up with full access to visual feeds and sensor data," Perseid told Rexis.

"Yes, sir," said Rexis.

"Now then." Perseid flung out an arm and pointed at Fong the helmsman. "How fast can you get us to Oberon?"

Fong manipulated holo controls and checked readouts. "Just under five hours, if I step on it."

"Then do it," said Perseid. "Direct heading for the *Sam Nicholas*."

"So we're going straight in?" said Fong. "No roundabout approach in case the Reds are waiting?"

"Absolutely not," said Perseid. "I've got a feeling time is of the essence. There might be survivors in need of help." He glared at the view of the devastated ships in orbit. "If the damned Reds want us, let them come and get us. We're ready for them this time."

CHAPTER 28

For the next five hours, Scott watched carefully for any sign of the Reds in the vicinity of Oberon...and saw none. The planet drew closer, the *Samuel Nicholas* and Rightful ship drifted brokenly, but no Red vessels appeared nearby. If the Reds were still around, they were so well hidden that even Scott with his Red spotting abilities could see no trace of them.

He had a feeling that could change very soon, though. The *Sun Tzu* was only a few thousand meters away from the wrecks and closing fast. When she got in good and close, the time would be perfect for a Red sneak attack.

"Take us in on thrusters, Lieutenant," said Perseid. "One quarter speed, nice and easy."

"Aye, sir," said Fong, playing his bank of holo controls like a virtuoso on a grand piano. "One quarter thrust."

"All hands to battle stations," added Perseid. "Condition Red."

"All hands to battle stations," repeated Rexis, announcing it over the shipwide P.A. "Condition Red."

The *Sun Tzu*'s approach slowed. The wrecked ships, framed against the orange-yellow backdrop of Oberon, grew larger at a slower rate.

"Red activity?" Perseid asked the question without taking his eyes off the forward view.

"Nothing at this time," said Scott.

"They could be hiding behind one of the derelicts," said Fong. "Or behind the planet, for that matter."

"Very true," said Perseid. "Keep monitoring all likely avenues of approach."

As the drifting ships expanded, the tension on the Command Deck ratcheted up like a reactor building toward critical. There wasn't any of the usual chatter or noise--just silence as everyone watched and waited. Scott imagined the whole ship was probably the same way, though he hadn't left the bridge in over five hours.

"Life signs?" said Perseid.

Khalil was manning the science station from an antigrav harness hovering near Scott. "One life sign in proximity to the *Sam Nicholas*." He worked the holo controls some more and nodded. "It's coming from a lifepod, sir."

"What about the Rightful ship?" said Perseid.

Khalil worked for a moment. "No life signs," he said finally.

Perseid cleared his throat. "And what's the standard crew complement of the *Sam Nicholas*?"

"Two hundred and eighty-five," said Rexis.

Everyone was quiet as the implications settled in. Then, in a hushed voice, Khalil spoke for all of them. "One survivor out of two hundred and eighty-five."

"Unless some of them got away," said Perseid. "Scan for life signs on the planet's surface."

"Scanning," said Khalil.

"Meanwhile, let's bring in that lifepod," said Perseid. "Get a retrieval team out there ASAP."

"Already on the way," said Rexis.

"Still no sign of the Reds," offered Scott.

"Other than the demolished warships in orbit." Perseid folded his arms over his chest and shook his head slowly. "The bastards must have some kind of *firepower*."

"Retrieval team has eyes on the lifepod," said Rexis. "They report minor damage to the exterior, but life support does not seem to have been compromised."

"Good news from the planet's surface, too," said Khalil. "Multiple life signs detected. Fifty-nine signals, all told."

Scott's heart beat faster. Maybe Bern had survived after all and escaped to the planet's surface.

"I'm picking up weapons fire down there, too," said Khalil. "Looks like a firefight in progress."

Perseid nodded and unfolded his arms. He paused a moment, gazing at the view of the shattered ships and the planet's giant disk...and then he spoke. "Prepare drop ships for launch. Alpha and Beta Squads, report to launch bay for immediate departure. That includes you, Corporal." He looked at Scott.

Scott nodded. "Aye, sir."

"We're going down," said Perseid. "In force."

"'We?'" said Rexis.

"'We' but not you," said Perseid. "You're in command of the *Sun Tzu* until I get back."

Rexis frowned. "Do you really think that's a good..."

"No argument." Perseid chopped his hand through the

air, cutting her off. "If what I suspect is true, there's no way I'm *not* leading this expedition." He headed for the door, waving for Scott to follow. "But first, we're going to talk to that survivor."

By the time Scott and Perseid reached the landing bay, the retrieval team's skiff had returned. The lifepod they'd recovered lay on the deck in front of their boxy little craft, encircled by crewmen in red jumpsuits.

As the crewmen parted to let Perseid through, Scott saw Chief Azimuth and Doctor Beauchamp working on the pod. Azimuth was prying with his big silver wrench at a clamp bolt near the base of the pod, while Beauchamp was busy running a diagnostic wand over the hull.

"His vitals are strong," Beauchamp said when Perseid approached. "Elevated, but you would expect that after the kind of stress he must have been through."

Perseid touched the skin of the pod. "How long until we get this thing open?"

"Ask Mr. Celebrity!" Azimuth pulled hard on his wrench, grunting and scowling with the effort. When he let up the pressure, the bolt hadn't moved a centimeter. "The longer he stands over there like a lazy *ass* instead of *helping* me, the longer this stays sealed!"

Scott wanted to punch him in the face, but instead he went over and took hold of the wrench. Together, the two of them cranked the wrench back harder than ever...and the bolt moved half a turn before locking up again.

"Come on!" snapped Azimuth. "Put your *back* into it! Grandma Hellcat can't help you with *this* one!"

Scott's temper flared, and he poured it into his effort.

This time, the bolt turned all the way, and the clamp came loose with a loud *crack*.

"There!" said Azimuth. "See what you can accomplish when you stop waiting for *Granny* to come to your rescue?"

Resisting the temptation to take a swing at him, Scott pulled the clamp free, releasing the lid. As the lid swung upward, the man inside the pod shot to a sitting position.

Breathing hard, gripping the sides of the pod, he gaped at Scott--his uniform, specifically. "Semper fi!" Relief flooded his face. "Thank God!"

"That's right." Scott saw the survivor was wearing a Commonwealth Marine uniform, too. "Semper fi."

"What's your name, Marine?" said Perseid.

The man in the pod looked like he was in his early-to-mid twenties. His round face was smudged with grease and blood, and the brown stubble on his scalp had been singed black on one side. "Sergeant Pylo Brahma of the *Samuel Nicholas*, sir." Brahma saluted as Beauchamp pushed in and waved her diagnostic wand over him. "May I ask what ship this is?"

"The *Sun Tzu*." Perseid stepped closer and bent down to fix Brahma in an urgent stare. "Now tell me, what was the *Sam Nicholas* doing out here with a Rightful warship?"

"That's top secret, sir." Brahma squared his jaw, then frowned and slumped. "Though I guess it doesn't matter much now."

Perseid looked at Beauchamp, who finished checking the readings from her wand, then nodded and stepped away. "Get to it, Sergeant," said Perseid. "We don't have much time."

"Secret peace talks with the Rightfuls," said Brahma. "That's why we were here. High-level talks to end the Civil

War."

"I had a hunch." Perseid glanced at Scott, then returned his gaze to Brahma. "Who was aboard, Sergeant? What Commonwealth dignitaries were present?"

"The Undersecretary of State, Trellor Gulack," said Brahma. "Defense Minister Byron Clay. And the Marine Corps Commandant." Brahma lowered his eyes. "Commandant Bernice Chalice."

Suddenly, time crashed to a halt for Scott. His stomach twisted in a painful knot, and his heart seemed to stop beating.

He understood why Bern hadn't been taking his calls. He knew where she'd been all this time when he'd been trying in vain to reach her. It made perfect sense, now.

There was just one thing he didn't know, and the thought of it froze his blood. There was one question he needed to ask, and he was afraid to hear the answer.

Maybe it was just as well that Perseid did the asking. "Where are they, Sergeant? What happened to the dignitaries?"

"Gulack and Clay died in the ambush," said Brahma. "The ambush by *invisible* ships."

Though Scott dreaded hearing the rest of the story, he couldn't help jumping in. "What about the Commandant?"

"I don't know." Brahma shook his head wearily. "I don't know if she's alive or dead."

Time continued to stand still for Scott as Brahma's words echoed through his head. He felt the pressure of eyes on him and looked around--saw stoic grimness from Perseid, supportive concern from Beauchamp, and mortified guilt from Azimuth, who moments ago had referred to Bern as "Grandma Hellcat" and made fun of Scott for waiting for

"Granny" to come to his rescue.

Meanwhile, Brahma kept talking. "These *ghosts* who attacked us, they ripped through our defenses like a chain saw through *tissue paper* and boarded the *Sam Nicholas*. The Rightful ship, the *Augustus*, didn't fare any better. None of us could *see* or *detect* them. It was a *bloodbath*."

"What do you mean you don't know?" Scott said it a little too harshly. "What happened to Commandant Chalice?"

"A squad of Marines put her in a drop ship and got the hell off the *Sam Nicholas*. I was part of the rear guard action that helped them get away." Brahma shrugged. "I don't know what happened to them after that."

"They must be on the planet's surface," said Perseid. "That explains the lifeforms."

"And the weapons fire," said Scott. "We need to get down there *now*."

"You'll be flying into a *death trap*," said Brahma. "The *ghosts* will tear you to *shreds*! I'm *telling* you, they're completely *undetectable*!"

"Not anymore," said Perseid. "We're ready for them."

"You mean you *know* about these things?" Brahma's eyes flew wide open. "What the hell *are* they?"

"The enemy," said Perseid. "The *real* enemy. The reason we're out here."

"*Enough*." Scott's moment of stopped time ended with a roar of blood in his ears. Adrenaline blazed through his body in a fiery surge, and his heart hammered like a hypercharged solo by an out-of-control drummer in a band. He was seized by the overwhelming urge to race to the surface of Oberon and open fire on the Reds, blasting away indiscriminately until every last one of them lay dead and smoking in the sun. "We need to *go*. We need to get *down* there."

Perseid clapped him on the shoulder. "Agreed." When their eyes met, it was crystal clear that they were on the same page.

Without another word, Perseid marched clear of the crowd around the lifepod and broke into a run. Scott did the same, propelled by the continued flow of adrenaline in his bloodstream...and visions of Bern in his mind.

He could see her as he ran, under fire by the Reds, firing back but hopelessly outnumbered and pinned down. It was only a matter of time until they pressed all the way in and trapped her in a crossfire of slugs, lasers, and missiles.

It was only a matter of time until she died, with her grandson so close yet so terribly far away.

Galvanized, Scott ran faster down the corridor, passing Perseid on his way.

The drop ships were loaded, fueled, and ready by the time Scott and Perseid charged into the launch bay. Crew members ran and shouted in all directions, making final preparations for departure.

It was all just static to Scott. He was focused only on getting to the surface of Oberon, leaping into his armor, and saving Bern.

Storming through the chaos, he stopped a running crewman in red coveralls and asked where they'd loaded his Battlenaut. The crewman pointed at one of the drop ships and darted away, intent on his duties.

Scott was just about to bolt toward the ship that held his gear when a hand on his shoulder stopped him. Whirling, he expected to see Perseid--and found himself staring down at Azimuth instead.

As always, the blustering engineer looked like a devil, complete with arched eyebrows, crooked nose, and dark hair drawn to a point on his forehead. But for once, he also managed to look half contrite. "Sorry for what I said about your grandma," he said. "I was just trying to goad you into cranking that bolt."

Scott looked around nervously. "I have to go..."

"She's a wonderful woman, that Bern." Azimuth nodded sincerely and squeezed Scott's shoulder. "Good luck bringin' her back."

"Thanks." Scott broke free of Azimuth and headed for the drop ship. The clock in his head was ticking loudly, counting down the seconds that remained until he could get to his grandmother.

Perseid met him at the base of the gangplank, and they rushed into the drop ship together. As soon as they were inside, the gangplank rose to meet the rest of the hull and clanged shut.

"We'll get her," Perseid told him as they strapped themselves into side-by-side flight couches. "We *have* to. She's the *Commandant*, for flux sake."

Scott cinched his last strap with a hard yank. "Those bastards are dead. Every last one of them. Don't even try to stop me."

"Why would I do that?" Perseid said with a smirk. "We'll kill the sons of bitches *together*."

With that, the engines roared to life, and the drop ship hurtled from the launch bay into open space.

CHAPTER 29

After the drop ship had landed and the squad had donned its armor, Scott ran down the gangway in his Battlenaut, first to leave the ship. He was dying to charge straight into the heart of the action...at least until Perseid's voice blared from the cockpit speaker. "Corporal, wait!"

Scott told Frank the A.I. to stop running, and his Battlenaut came to a halt in the powdery orange sand at the base of the gangway. The whole time, all Scott could think about was Bern, fighting for her life among the desert dunes of Oberon. The clock in his head was ticking louder than ever now, almost loud enough to drown out Perseid's voice.

But not quite. "We are sticking to a tight formation with you in the middle," said Perseid. "Protecting you is still a priority--especially until we see how well the inoculations work in the field." His Battlenaut stormed down the gangway past Scott, then stopped and raised its left arm. "Alpha Squad, form on Scott!"

When Perseid said it, the other five Battlenauts aboard the drop ship stomped down the gangway and surrounded Scott. He only knew two of the pilots--García and Taggart--though he knew more in Beta Squad, which was debarking from the second drop ship fifty meters away.

"Now listen up!" said Perseid. "We're half a klick due east of the battle zone, so we don't have much ground to cover. We'll be in the thick of it in nothing flat, and we don't know what exactly to expect. So *lock and load* and be ready for *anything*."

Almost everyone offered up a "boo-yeah" or a "hoo-rah." Only Scott remained silent. The hell with war cries; he just wanted to get down to the killing.

"We're going in there to get our Commandant," said Perseid. "So let's blow the hell out of anything that looks like a Red and give her a chance to fight her way clear."

Again, everyone but Scott let out a war cry...though he did feel the urge to say something. Specifically, he wanted to tell Perseid to shut up and get moving or else get the hell out of his way so he could go save his grandma.

But it didn't come to that. "Move out!" Perseid barked the words and started marching forward. As he went, his Battlenaut's arms sprouted guns, a laser cannon formed from each shoulder, and a missile launcher grew from his back.

"Fall in, Frank." Scott followed with the rest of the squad, calling up weapons of his own for the fight to come. "While you're walking, form a large-bore gun on the right shoulder and a high-powered laser on the left. Mount them both on turrets."

"Yes, Solomon," said Frank.

Scott thought for a moment, then got an idea. "Frank, are you able to manifest *new* forms that are not yet part of your morphic inventory?"

"Explain further, please," said Frank.

"If I describe a new form to you, can you create it without having done so before?"

"Perhaps." Frank sounded thoughtful. "As long as the specifications don't require me to exceed available mass constraints."

"Good." Scott nodded. "Then let me tell you what I want." He proceeded to describe the new form he had in mind, taking care to be as precise as possible. "So what do you say? Can you do it?"

"Yes," said Frank. "But this new configuration will require me to channel significant mass away from the weapons. I will only be able to maintain a single projectile weapon, sonic projector, or laser emitter. Missiles, biofilm, and drone pods must remain offline."

"What if we go with *none* of them?" Scott thought of something and smiled grimly. "Can you reallocate all weapons mass and energy into a single instrument?"

"What kind of instrument?" said Frank.

Scott told him, and Frank said it could be done. "Would you like me to implement the configuration you've described?"

"Not yet," said Scott. "Wait for my order."

"All right," said Frank. "In the meantime, would you like me to use my prognostication software to calculate the likelihood of success of this new configuration?"

"No thanks," said Scott. "Just be ready. The order's coming any minute now."

Alpha Squad continued forward over the orange dunes,

heading southwest as Beta Squad went northwest. The two squads would converge on the battlefield from the south and north, catching the Reds in a pincer movement. At least that was the plan.

"Stay sharp," Perseid said over the comm. "We're almost there."

He didn't really have to say it, as the sounds of battle were roaring up ahead. Scott heard volleys of slugs chattering against Battlenaut armor, missiles exploding, sonics shrieking, lasers screaming. A cloud of black smoke erupted into the sky, and the torso of a Battlenaut--a Commonwealth model--skidded along the dune's crest, broken and burnt.

Scott switched off the comm with a flick of his eyes and spoke only to his A.I. "Move, Frank! Break ranks and run toward the action!"

Without a word, Frank jolted the Battlenaut into action. Pushing between the Diamondbacks, he lurched out of formation and ran hard toward a nearby dune.

"Scott!" shouted Perseid. "Get back here!"

Scott switched the comm back on. "I'm adding a prong to the pincer," he said. "Coming in from due west."

"Negative, Scott!" said Perseid. "Stick to the plan! That's an order!"

"I can't hear you. You're breaking up." Scott closed the comm channel completely, shutting out all traffic from Alpha Squad. "Keep going, Frank. Manifest the new form I told you about."

"Yes, Solomon." As Frank said it, the holographic wireframe diagram in front of Scott changed shape, becoming bigger and blockier. "Manifestation complete."

Watching the wireframe, Scott nodded with satisfaction. His armor no longer looked like a CORE Battlenaut;

thanks to Frank, it had taken the shape of a *Red* Battlenaut, identical to the computer renderings generated from Scott's descriptions.

"Now bring up that instrument I requested," said Scott. "Reallocate all weapons mass and energy as needed."

"Done," said Frank.

Scott glanced at the wireframe to verify that the job was done, then turned his gaze to the frontside feed and the battle ahead of him.

Through the feed, Scott saw a ring of battered Commonwealth Battlenauts standing back to back, under siege by a pack of towering Reds. The Reds were hammering away while the Commonwealth forces fired blindly, missing most of their shots because they couldn't see the enemy.

The dozen or so Commonwealth Battlenauts didn't look like they could hold out much longer against the Reds. Most of them were heavily damaged, venting smoke, barely standing; less than a third of them seemed to be intact and fit to fight.

But every last one of the Commonwealth Battlenauts was still shooting, determined to protect whoever was tucked away in the center of the ring.

Bern. That was where she had to be--in the middle of the ring of defenders. Scott's heart pounded as he strained for a glimpse of her but came up empty; she was too well shielded.

He would just have to wait until the fighting was over. "Charge, Frank! Run toward the nearest Red Battlenaut!"

Frank complied. Scott's disguised Battlenaut raced across the sand to the closest Red, which was pounding the Commonwealth Battlenauts with hails of slugs.

As Scott approached, the Red stopped shooting

and turned to face him. Scott slowed down, but the Red didn't open fire; apparently, he couldn't quickly tell that the newcomer was not a true Red.

That was exactly the reaction Scott had hoped for. Running straight at the Red, he swept back the instrument he'd specially requested from Frank: an enormous scarlet sword formed from both arms merged together.

"Slash through his midsection!" When Scott got the words out, he saw the wireframe figure swinging its sword... also watched the electrified carbon fiber blade sweeping toward the Red on the frontside feed.

As expected, the sword ripped right through the Red's armor in a shower of sparks and flashed out the other side without slowing. The Red jerked and sputtered, then split along the gash, its top half shunting forward. The top stopped sliding, held in place by struts and cables--but then its weight dragged the whole unit headfirst to the ground.

By then, Scott had already moved on to the next Red. This one didn't even turn or react when he strolled up beside it, just fell toward him as the giant blade cut through its left leg. Frank backed away just in time to avoid being taken down with it.

"Take that, you bastards." Scott spotted his next target. "There's another one at ten o'clock, Frank."

"On my way." Frank sounded as calm as ever. "Also, Major Perseid is calling."

Scott considered ignoring the hail, then gave in and reopened the comm channel so he could hear the incoming transmission.

Perseid's voice exploded in the cockpit. "...-or the last time, is that *you*, Corporal?"

Scott heard a round of slugs rattle off his armor from

behind. "Frank! Who just fired at us?"

"That was friendly fire at minimum intensity," said Frank. "It came from Major Perseid's Battlenaut, which is located thirty-five meters away at six o'clock."

Scott checked his backside feed. Sure enough, Perseid was back there with guns pointed in his direction.

Scott opened his mic over the comm channel. "Hold your fire! Yes, it's me!"

"I thought so," said Perseid. "The fact that you *look* like a Red and you're *killing* Reds kind of gave it away."

"You going to keep *talking* about it?" said Scott. "Or help me slaughter these mother-fluxing *Reds*?"

Perseid's answer was to launch a brace of missiles at an oncoming Red. The missiles kicked the Red through the air when they blew, driving it deep into a nearby sand dune.

As Scott scanned his feeds, he saw that the rest of Alpha Squad was doing its part, too, hitting the Reds hard with missiles, slugs, sonics, and lasers. The attacks seemed to take the Reds by surprise, sending some of them staggering and taking others out of the fight altogether. For once, Commonwealth forces weren't firing blind or dependent on a single Red-spotter to call out enemy coordinates.

At least that was the case with Alpha Squad. On the other hand, the Battlenaut Marines in the heart of the fight were still in dire need of help.

Breaking away from Perseid, Scott stormed toward another Red who was blasting away at the Marines. On Scott's orders, Frank raised the sword overhead and took aim at the Red, preparing to cleave it from head to toe.

Before he could swing, another Red hurtled up from behind and spun Scott around with a bolt of golden energy. The bolt sent Scott's Battlenaut stumbling away from its target, fighting to stay on its feet.

"Damn!" shouted Scott. "Keep your balance, Frank!"

"I will do so," said Frank. "Then what?"

"Then carve up the Red that shot us!" said Scott. "That's what!"

Frank did as he was told. Scott's Battlenaut teetered briefly, then steadied itself. As the Red who'd shot it let loose another energy bolt, Frank dodged left and lunged forward, swinging the sword around. The blade sliced through both cannons mounted on the Red's chest, leaving gaping cavities roiling with golden energy. Seconds later, the unleashed energy blew, throwing the Red back and down in a smoking heap.

With one opponent down, Scott whipped around to go after his original target. It was then he realized the Reds were storming the Marines' defenses; every Red who wasn't already battling a Diamondback converged on the ring of Marine Battlenauts at once. The Marines, who still couldn't see them, went on firing wild as the Reds--who made every shot count--advanced inexorably.

The time for Scott's Red disguise was over. He needed firepower more than camouflage now. "Return to original configuration, Frank! And form every weapon you can, set to maximum intensity!"

"Yes, Solomon," Frank said smoothly.

The Battlenaut clanked and clacked around Scott as it shifted shape. On the wireframe, he saw it change from a Red to a Diamondback model, becoming more compact and adopting more humanoid outlines.

When the conversion was done, Scott saw weapons grow from the skin of his Battlenaut, popping up almost everywhere. When they'd finished forming, the wireframe diagram was studded like a porcupine with projectile guns, laser emitters, and sonic projectors.

Scott's Battlenaut was good to go. "Maximum intensity, Frank!"

"Thank you for the reminder," said Frank, "but you did not even have to tell me the first time."

Scott's heart hammered in his chest. "Then do you know what I'm going to tell you to do *next*, Frank?"

"Yes," said Frank. "Attacking the enemy *now*."

Scott didn't even have to give the order. His Battlenaut broke into a run, charging hard toward the Reds who were assaulting the ring of Commonwealth Battlenauts.

As the Reds kept up their fire, Scott blasted away at them with everything he had. He went after three at once, laying down a triple barrage of slugs, lasers, and sonics. The tactic worked, scoring a flurry of direct hits that left the Reds on their feet but ended their fire against the Commonwealth forces.

Then, one of the three lurched toward Scott, charging its energy cannons...but a missile from Perseid knocked it out of the picture. That left Scott free to focus on the other two.

When both of them unleashed energy blasts in his direction, Frank automatically dodged them. Then, at Scott's order, he formed a biofilm launcher and pumped a load of the stuff at one of the Reds' energy cannons. The green substance quickly clogged the weapon's muzzle, causing it to backfire and blow a hole in the Red's armor. The Red went down hard after that, smoke pouring from its chest.

As that Red dropped, the other opened hidden ports on its torso and launched a surprise of its own--a volley of high-powered arrows. Instead of bouncing off Scott's armor, six of them penetrated and stuck...then emitted some kind of pulse that flashed through every square centimeter of the Battlenaut. Instantly, the cockpit went dark.

"What the hell was that?" said Scott, but Frank didn't answer.

Something crashed against the armor from outside, and Scott felt it teeter backward. He looked around frantically, wishing he had some kind of emergency manual override controls. Diamondback Battlenauts didn't *need* overrides, except for a manual release on the cockpit ejector mechanism; that was what he'd been told, anyway. In the event of primary power loss, the unit would tap its batteries to spark all systems back to life.

Sure enough, after thirty seconds, the lights flickered back to full intensity, the armor stopped teetering, and the control holos reappeared in front of Scott. From what he could see, power levels were quickly climbing, and the weapons would be fully charged in thirty more seconds.

"Frank?" said Scott. "Are you back online yet?"

After a few more seconds, a slow, distorted voice slurred through the cockpit. "Yuuuuuhhh..." It quickly got faster and cleared up, becoming recognizable as the voice of Frank. "Yuhh-yes, Solomon. I am h-h-h-here."

Scott frowned. Frank had never stuttered before. "All right then." There was no time to consider the implications, as the Red who'd fired the arrows was on the move. Scott saw him on the frontside feed, stalking toward him with energy cannons crackling. "Fire all weapons at the incoming Red. Maximum intensity!"

There was a pause before Frank answered. "F-f-firing weapons, S-S-Solomon."

Scott watched the frontside feed but saw no weapons fire from his Battlenaut's guns. "Ready when you are, Frank."

"Cuh-cuh-continuing to f-f-f-fire." Frank's voice fluttered and shot higher on the last syllables. "D-d-directhitsonalltargets S-S-Solomon." His words accelerated and crushed together, sounding like a recording played back at high speed.

Still, Scott saw no outgoing weapons fire on the frontside feed. "Are you sure about that, Frank?"

This time, Frank spoke in his normal, even tone. "Absolutely, Solomon. The target has been heavily damaged."

That wasn't what the feed was showing. Watching the video, Scott saw the Red stomping forward with no damage whatsoever. According to the holo readouts, however, Frank's statements were accurate. The readouts showed that all weapons had been fired, and the Red was losing power and venting smoke.

Scott thought fast. Had the arrow strikes done something to Frank and the sensors? If so, how could Scott regain control over the situation? "Frank, are you all right?"

"Never better, Solomon," Frank said calmly. "What about you?"

The Red on the feed was getting closer, but what could Scott do if Frank wasn't following his orders? "I'm fine, thanks." Maybe reverse psychology would work. "Stop firing weapons and stand down, Frank. Cease fire immediately."

There was a pause. "Done, Solomon."

This time, Solomon's order had an impact...but not the one he'd wanted. Watching the feeds, he saw the view suddenly swing away from the Red and settle on a Diamondback Battlenaut. Then Frank opened fire, aiming at the Diamondback instead of the Red.

Scott tried reverse psychology again. "Keep firing, Frank." But this time, it didn't work at all. Frank just kept pouring it on, hammering the Diamondback unit. "I need you to perform a complete systems shutdown, Frank." Scott didn't expect it to work, but he knew he had to try.

"Shutting d-d-down, Solomon," said Frank, but nothing changed.

Almost nothing. Seconds after Scott gave the order, green biofilm slime started pumping into the cockpit from the air vents.

"Shutdown cuh-cuh-cuh-complete, Solomon-n-n-n," said Frank, his voice turning high-pitched again and emitting a freakish giggle.

CHAPTER 30

In a matter of moments, Scott would be dead. The fast-spreading biofilm would expand to fill the cockpit, locking him in place and choking the life out of him.

The Red arrows must have injected a computer virus into his Battlenaut. Frank the A.I. had become corrupted and was trying to murder his own pilot.

Scott had only one recourse. Reaching down, he slapped the red button installed on the right edge of his couch, the only manual override control in the whole Battlenaut.

Instantly, he heard the magnetic clamps release with four simultaneous *bangs*. Then, an overhead hatch sprang open, and the cockpit leaped up out of the Battlenaut's body.

It didn't fly far, though. The biofilm must have damaged its thrusters or guidance system or both, because the cockpit pod flipped over after emergence and dove into the sand thirty yards from Scott's Battlenaut.

That left Scott upside-down in the ejected pod--but the

biofilm had stopped pumping. At least he wasn't going to smother in a tin can filled with quick-drying green death-slime.

Unbuckling his straps, Scott rolled his legs over and down, turning himself upright in the tight space. Then, bracing his back against the couch, he drew up his legs and unleashed a double kick at the cockpit cowling. When he saw it give a little, he hauled back his legs for another try.

It took five kicks to break open the cowling. As sunlight and the noise of battle poured into the cockpit, Scott clambered out headfirst.

Emerging into the heat and smoke and clamor, he quickly took a look around, assessing the scene. From what he could see, the Diamondbacks had taken some of the pressure off the Commonwealth Marines, but the protective ring was buckling. Though the Reds were no longer invisible to everyone on the battlefield, they were still dominant thanks to their greater numbers.

As for Scott, he was completely unarmed and unprotected in the midst of heavily armed Battlenauts, and his own armor was coming after him. It was a deadly gauntlet, a seemingly unsurvivable situation--but Scott was highly motivated and had been through nightmare scenarios before. Taking advantage of his smaller size and greater agility, plus the fact that most of the Battlenauts would be shooting at each other instead of him, he might just have a shot at eluding Frank and reaching Bern. But he would have to be fast and alert, at the absolute top of his game.

When a flicker of motion caught his eye, he whipped around to see his Battlenaut charging toward him, bristling with weapons. In case there was any doubt about Frank's intentions, the Battlenaut cranked off a series of rounds in

Scott's direction, chewing up the cockpit pod and kicking up tufts of sand.

Propelled by a burst of adrenaline, Scott spun and ran like lightning toward the ring of Commonwealth Battlenauts at the heart of the fight. He might just have a better chance of survival there--and a chance of finding Bern.

Slugs from Frank's guns poured past Scott as he charged across the sand. Agility was his biggest advantage over the less maneuverable metal-clad giant, and he made the most of it. Running in a serpentine pattern, he nimbly dodged laser beams and sonic blasts as Frank kept up the onslaught.

As Scott darted between Red Battlenauts, the wisdom of his chosen route was obvious. Like a mouse among giants, he was able to scamper between the feet of the towering Reds to avoid Frank, who couldn't fit through the same gaps. As Frank kept firing his weapons, he hit the Reds instead of Scott, who zipped right out of range.

Tagged by Frank's stray shots, the Reds spun and turned their guns on him, stopping him in his tracks. That gave Scott a chance to bolt toward the inner circle of the Commonwealth's defenses.

Unfortunately, when Scott ran into the open ground between the Reds and the Commonwealth forces, he found himself in range of other guns. Friendly fire pelted the sand around him, laid down by Commonwealth Battlenauts shooting at the Reds. Scott had to weave more erratically than ever to avoid it--and then a missile hit and exploded ten meters away, knocking him off his feet.

His ears were ringing as he rolled over on his side and looked up, squinting at a Commonwealth Battlenaut with the blazing sun behind its head. The Battlenaut kept its missile launcher pointed in his direction and its optics trained on him, no doubt assessing his threat level. Scott wondered if this was how he would die, without armor, at the hands of friendly forces.

Suddenly, a blast of golden energy struck the Commonwealth Battlenaut in the chest, and it swung its missile launcher around to point in a different direction. Scott saw his chance and took it, scrambling to his feet and sprinting away.

Explosions erupted behind him as he ran hard for the inner circle. He was aiming for a gap in the line when the ground shuddered under his feet, and one of the Commonwealth defenders crashed down in front of him. Scott barely missed getting pinned under it and dashed in a new direction, running along the fallen giant's smoldering length.

Just as he was about to loop around its feet, Scott felt the heat of a laser beam searing past. Looking back as he threw himself behind the fallen Battlenaut's leg, he saw his rampaging Diamondback armor storming toward him, firing lasers and sonics.

Frank's voice boomed over the armor's P.A. system. "Solomon! It is safe to return. The damage to my circuitry has been repaired." Even as he said it, Frank unleashed a flurry of laser fire and slugs. "Come back, Solomon. We will defeat the Reds together."

Scott wasn't about to let himself get pinned down. Leaping up, he bolted away from the fallen Battlenaut and continued heading for the inner circle.

Slugs pounded the sand behind him, just missing his running feet. Lasers flashed past to the right and left, filling the air with the smell of cooked ozone.

Scott kept serpentining, but with all the fire he was

drawing from Frank, he was surprised he hadn't been hit yet. Maybe the same malfunction that had turned Frank rogue had affected his targeting systems.

"You need help, Solomon," said Frank. "I am dispatching my drone pods to assist you."

Scott reached deep and found the strength to run faster. Drone pods could do some serious damage to an armor-plated Battlenaut; Scott hated to think what they could do to his unprotected human body.

"Here they come, Solomon," said Frank. "You won't have to wait long now."

Glancing back over his shoulder, Scott saw a cluster of drone pods hurtling toward him like a swarm of angry bees. Turning his gaze forward again, he continued his life-or-death charge toward the inner circle--though he really hadn't thought through what he'd do when he got there. The pods could weave between the Commonwealth Battlenauts with ease and follow him through, so he wasn't exactly heading for a safe haven. He'd just have to hope an opportunity for survival would present itself.

Arms and legs pumping, Scott raced between two Commonwealth defenders and into the inner circle they'd been protecting. Before he could take a look around, though, one of the pods slammed into his back, pitching him facedown on the sand.

As soon as he hit, another pod clipped his right shoulder, and a third punched his left calf hard enough to send a bolt of sheer agony flashing through his body.

As the fourth blow cracked against his tailbone, he knew he wouldn't be able to take much more. Without some kind of intervention, the black spheres would go on pounding him until his bones and guts liquefied inside his skin.

Another blow clocked his neck and the back of his skull, making him see stars. Forcing his head up, he searched for some kind of weapon--any piece of debris he could use to fend off the pods. But there was nothing in arm's reach.

Just then, he took two more hits in rapid sequence--one to his left side, the other to his right hip. The flare of pain that followed was so strong, he clenched his jaws and shut his eyes against it. When he opened them again, he saw the feet of a Battlenaut running toward him.

Looking up, he saw that the feet belonged to a Commonwealth model with green armor. He didn't get to see much more, though; the Battlenaut reached him in a heartbeat and swung its hand toward him, forcing him to duck.

Scott felt a rush of wind as the Battlenaut's hand swept over him. He heard a clashing, clattering noise, like a pile of scrap metal being dumped from a truck...and right away, he knew what it had to be.

Sure enough, when he lifted his head and looked back over his shoulder, the drone pods were gone. The Battlenaut had batted them away from him.

Whoever was at the controls of that unit, he was a hell of a pilot. A lesser Battlenaut jockey might not have been able to knock the pods away without hitting Scott...but this one had left him without a scratch.

Pushing himself to his knees, Scott stared up at the towering green Battlenaut, wondering who was in the cockpit. For a long moment, the Battlenaut stared back at him, giving no clue to its operator's identity...and then, it did.

A woman's voice called out over the unit's P.A. "Hello, Solly!" It was a voice that Scott recognized instantly, a nickname used by only one person.

"Bern!" He should have known. *No one* was a better Battlenaut pilot than his grandma. "Thank God you're all right!"

"I got your messages," Bern said from inside the armor. "I called and left one for you, too."

"I brought the Diamondbacks, Grandma," shouted Scott. "They're going to get you out of here."

"I hope they're *armored*, at least." Bern laughed loudly. "Unlike *you*. What happened to your *Battlenaut*, Solly?"

"Damn thing went rogue, Grandma." Scott shrugged. "That's where those *drone pods* came from."

"Your own armor turned on you?" Bern laughed again. "You do realize you'll never live that down, don't you?"

"*I* won't tell if *you* won't, Grandma."

Her reply was drowned out by the roar of enormous engines approaching from above. As Scott looked skyward, a massive shadow fell over the inner circle--the shadow of a giant spacecraft sliding into place to block out the sun.

The belly of the ship was red from stem to stern. A circular hatch irised open in the middle, and a cylindrical beam of glittering white energy shot downward.

It shot down into the heart of the inner circle and enveloped Bern's Battlenaut. Instantly, the armor left the ground, slowly rising within the beam as if it were riding an elevator.

They were taking her. She was right there in front of him, and the Reds were taking her.

"Bern!" Adrenaline surged through Scott, and he bolted toward the beam. Just as he was about to enter it, Bern's Battlenaut suddenly accelerated, shooting upward like a guided missile.

Scott never took his eyes off her as he ran into the beam.

He rose slowly at first, as Bern had done, and steeled himself for the sudden acceleration he expected at any second.

Meanwhile, far above him, Bern's green Battlenaut passed through the circular hatch into the ship. As soon as the armor disappeared from view, the beam of glittering white energy switched off.

By then, Scott was about ten meters off the ground. When the beam cut off, he dropped like a stone, landing on his back on the hot sand.

He lay there a moment, helpless, glaring up at the Red leviathan. As the hatch on its belly irised shut, he knew there was nothing he could do to rescue his grandmother. They had her; it was that simple.

Scott was hundreds of meters below, without armor or a ship of his own. He didn't even have a comm device to call for help. He'd be lucky if he made it through the battle without getting stepped on, let alone saving the Commandant of the Commonwealth Marines single-handedly.

The ship's engines roared, and it slid away, exposing the battlefield to the blazing sun once more. Scott squinted against the influx of light, then raised a hand to shade his eyes.

It was up to the *Sun Tzu* now. Surely, the crew had spotted the Red ship on sensors, even if it seemed to phase in and out. Maybe, they'd even seen it snatch Bern's Battlenaut or had picked up a distress signal she'd sent. Rexis wouldn't hesitate to charge to the Commandant's rescue...if she could.

If the *Sun Tzu* didn't already have its hands full. If the Reds hadn't already blown it to bits, which Scott wouldn't even know about since he didn't have a radio.

If the *Sun Tzu* wasn't able to pursue, what then? How could Scott ever find Bern in the vastness of space?

How could he stop the Reds from using her for whatever malevolent plans they had in mind?

He had no idea.

Closing his eyes, he let the sounds of raging battle wash over him. It was almost peaceful. Something exploded nearby, and he didn't even jump.

The battle, like Bern's fate, was out of his control. He could no nothing to change either one.

At least for now.

CHAPTER 31

Less than an hour later, the battle was over. The Commonwealth had won--if losing the Marine Corps Commandant to the Reds could be called "winning." Scott survived, though Frank had made another run at him in missile mode and been barely deflected by Trane and Khalil.

Two hours later, Scott was evacuated from the surface of Oberon aboard one of the drop ships. When the drop ship's gangway opened inside the landing bay of the *Sun Tzu*, he looked out--and found himself face to face with a line of rifles pointed in his direction.

The guns weren't aiming at him, though. When Scott walked down the gangway, the Diamondbacks holding them parted to let him through. They were much more interested in the cluster of twelve shackled Red prisoners debarking behind him.

The Diamondbacks and Commonwealth Marines had rounded them up after winning the battle. The Red leaders had left them behind in their rush to get away with Bern.

As Scott watched the Diamondbacks lead the prisoners off the drop ship at gunpoint, he wanted to beat the truth out of them. He wanted to do anything in his power to make them tell him where Bern had been taken.

Instead, he stood by as they shuffled past him with eyes glazed over and jaws set. He glared at them, sending each a silent message crackling with the raw power of his hatred: *Talk to you soon.*

As the last prisoner moved past, Scott heard Perseid's voice nearby. "Corporal Scott!"

A bolt of pain shot through Scott's back and neck as he turned toward Perseid. Frank's drone pods had really given him a pounding. "Sir?"

"Get to the medicenter." Perseid pointed at the nearest exit. "Do it *now*."

"I'm fine." Scott forced himself not to wince at the latest jolt of pain as he pointed at the Red prisoners. "What about them? When do we start interrogations?"

Perseid ignored the question. "Your own armor went rogue and nearly killed you. I'd say that's reason enough to stop by the medicenter, wouldn't you?"

Scott sighed. "Speaking of my armor, have you *found* it yet?"

"No." Perseid shook his head. "Our last sensor contact was fifty klicks from the battlefield...then nothing. Maybe it went underground or self-destructed. Who knows?"

"So it's down there running wild?" said Scott. "Not good."

"We'll hunt it down later," said Perseid. "If the quadrant's still here then." With that, he headed for the exit. "Now get your ass to the medicenter. I've got to call Command."

Scott watched him go, then left the landing bay himself... only he wasn't heading for the medicenter as ordered. Not this time.

When Scott rushed onto the Command Deck, Rexis called out to him immediately. "Corporal!" Clearly, she was busy as hell--the whole place was--but she still spotted him right away. "Get to the medicenter!"

Scott stopped in his tracks. Perseid must have figured out where he was going and called ahead...not that Scott was going to let it distract him from the question he'd come to ask. "The Red ship. What happened to it?"

"Gone from the system," said Fong, who was floating in his antigrav harness nearby. His hands danced over the holo-controls fanned out around him as he spoke. "Course unknown."

Scott scowled. "What are you talking about? Didn't you *follow* it?"

Fong didn't say a word. Instead, he shook his head and slid his gaze toward Rexis.

Scott took the hint and turned his glare in her direction. "You mean you *didn't*? You let the Red ship get away with the *Commandant*?"

"We didn't know they had her," said Rexis. "*You* were the only *eyewitness*, and you were completely off the *comm*. Everyone else on the surface was in a state of chaos."

"Unbelievable." Scott rubbed his temples. "You didn't think there might be a good reason for going *after* them?"

Rexis stiffened. "For all we knew, they were trying to lead us into an ambush. Or they might have been trying to lure us away from our ground forces. I decided not to take the chance."

"Then you made the wrong call." Scott was on thin ice and he knew it--but he didn't care. Let her court martial him if she wanted; it wouldn't change the fact that she'd lost Bern to the Reds. "You let them *take* her."

Rexis narrowed her eyes. "You *saw* what they did to the *Sam Nicholas* and the *Augustus.* Do you really think the *Sun Tzu* would have done any better?"

"I guess we'll never know, will we?" said Scott.

Rexis stormed over and stopped in front of him, her face centimeters from his own. "There were other considerations, Corporal. All *hell* is breaking loose, in case you didn't notice. *Someone* has to get word back to HQ before the Reds make their next move." She lowered her voice. "Not that I have to *explain* myself to you."

Scott almost pushed it too far. Even with her icy gaze locked on him, and the force of her anger pressing against him like a weight, he opened his mouth to say something that he damn well knew would put him in the brig.

Then, he closed it again. He was deeply upset, so worried about Bern that he almost couldn't stand it--but pissing off his commanding officer wouldn't solve his problems. It wouldn't bring back Bern.

So, instead, he nodded. "Understood."

That seemed to take some of the fire out of Rexis' furnace. "I know how you're feeling." Her expression turned sympathetic. "But she's a tough woman. She'll get through this, and we'll get her back."

"Right." Scott nodded, but he wasn't sure he believed her. The Reds could have taken Bern anywhere. "But we definitely didn't get a bearing on their course out of the system?"

Fong spoke up again. "Sensors tracked them as far as the sixth planet, and then we lost them. The Reds used some kind of reality-distortion drive that turned local space inside-out, and then they were gone."

Scott took in a deep breath and let it out slowly. "So no trail, then?"

"Correct," said Fong. "No trail."

"Okay then." Scott nodded. "Thanks for the update." He wasn't being sarcastic. As disappointing as the news was, they'd told him what he needed to know. They'd made it clear what he'd have to do next.

Seek guidance elsewhere.

Turning, he headed for the door. No one said a word as he left.

When Scott entered Lab Five, Trane was in the process of hugging Beauchamp and letting out a whoop of delight.

"You did it!" Spinning Beauchamp around, Trane caught sight of Scott in the doorway. "She did it!"

With a cool, feline smile, Beauchamp gently freed herself from Trane's hug. "The A.I. trackers did most of the work, actually. But yes, it is true. We have done it."

"Done what?" asked Scott.

"Traced the genomes of the Red viruses," said Beauchamp. "The catalyst virus and the pieces of the firewall virus that did not match the engineered virus from Project Lethe on Archibald."

Scott's heart beat faster. "You've found their source?"

Trane nodded and brushed orange sand from his black uniform. He'd beaten Scott back to the *Sun Tzu* but hadn't cleaned himself up from the battle yet. "Absolutely, unequivocally, yes."

Scott raised his eyebrows. "That's pretty definite." He knew Trane wasn't prone to undue optimism.

"The Project Lethe trail led nowhere, thanks to the data block," said Trane. "But Monique kept the A.I. trackers searching the genetic databases while we were on Oberon. By the time I got back, they'd finally made a positive match."

"The viruses clearly belong to a species found only on Dornick VII," said Beauchamp. "They represent unique strains of a pair of symbiotic, quantum-entangled viruses that attack the parts of the brain that control the senses."

"Dornick VII." Trane laughed and slammed the palm of his hand down on one of the metal counters. "Now we know where the Red bastards are hiding."

Scott frowned. "Or maybe they just manufacture the viruses there."

Trane grinned and shook his head. "But it's the perfect *hiding place*. It's probably *swarming* with the Red-blindness viruses. To anyone infected with the firewall virus, the planet would be practically *invisible*."

"But the strains that cause Red-blindness aren't native, are they?" said Scott. "They had to be engineered to perform that specific task, right?"

"I think it's safe to say that the Reds would let the engineered strains loose," said Trane. "Especially if it meant hiding the whole damn *planet*."

It made sense. Scott looked at Beauchamp, and she nodded in agreement.

As for Trane, he flew over and slapped Scott on the back. "Now we know where to go to get your grandma back. Now we know where to go to smash the damn Reds once and for all!"

"Sounds good to me." Even as Scott said it, his stomach clenched. What if Dornick VII *wasn't* the Reds' center of operations? The evidence was persuasive, and the logic was sound, but something about it still gave him a bad feeling in his gut. Maybe it was intuition, warning him of a possible mistake.

Or maybe he was just worrying too much. The stress kept getting stronger as the clock kept ticking, and Bern--wherever she was headed--was getting farther away.

"Don't worry," said Trane as if he'd been reading Scott's mind. "We'll get her back before you know it." He winked at Scott and gave his shoulder a squeeze.

"Thanks." Scott managed a smile in spite of the bad feeling in his gut. "I hope you're right."

When Scott left Trane and Beauchamp in Lab Five, he headed for the medicenter--then changed his mind when he got halfway there. Swinging around a corner, he aimed for the brig instead. He would just have to wait to check on Donna and get the once-over ordered by Perseid. At the moment, with Bern's time ticking away fast, the twelve Red prisoners were much more important.

As Scott whipped around the last turn before the brig, he saw that the place was under heavy guard. Four Diamondback men in full body armor, complete with helmets, stood outside the door...two on either side, all carrying big rifles.

The two guards closest to the door stepped forward when Scott approached. "Hold it," said the younger of the two. "We're on lockdown here. Nobody gets in or out."

"I'm cleared for that." Scott tried to push past, but the

guard and his partner blocked him.

"Like I said." The younger guard shook his head. "It's a lockdown situation."

"Are they interrogating the prisoners?" Scott tried to push through again and failed. "I'm telling you, I've got ultra-top secret clearance."

"Actually," said the younger guard, "we were ordered specifically not to let *you* through."

Scott stared at him in disbelief. "Ordered by who?"

"Major Perseid," said the guard.

Scott backed away. "Perseid? Where the hell is he?"

The guard bobbed his head toward the door of the brig. "Inside."

"Then tell him to get out here. I want to talk to him." Scott felt a wave of anger rising in his chest. The Reds on the other side of the door knew where Bern was, they *had* to...but he couldn't get to them.

At that point, the older of the two guards spoke up. "Major Perseid left orders not to be interrupted. You'll just have to wait to talk to him."

"Also," said the younger guard, "he left orders for you to go the medicenter."

"Right." Scott glared at the two guards for a moment, then turned and marched off down the corridor. The brig was a dead end, at least for the time being.

The question was, why? Was Perseid afraid Scott would come on too strong in an interrogation? That he'd take it too far because of Bern?

Or maybe it was the other way around. Maybe Perseid was the one going too far, and he wanted to keep the Commandant's grandson out of it.

Whatever the reason, Scott didn't like it. He wanted to

confirm Trane and Beauchamp's findings and beat the drum to race to Dornick VII as soon as possible. He wanted to make the bad feeling in his gut go away.

Or, maybe, find out the reason it was there in the first place.

CHAPTER 32

Finally, Scott went to the medicenter. He had his orders, and he had nowhere else to go. He couldn't get to the Red prisoners, so he might as well get his checkup out of the way.

The door swept open and he crossed the threshold. Looking to his left, he saw the privacy curtain around Donna's bed, pulled all the way around.

On the far side of the room, Nurse Tourmal looked up from a patient and grinned. "Corporal Scott!" He adjusted the antigrav I.V. bag floating alongside the patient and hurried over. "Good to see you. Glad you could make it."

Scott wasn't in the mood for pleasantries. "I didn't have much choice. Major Perseid and Captain Rexis both ordered me down here."

"I'm sure they had a good reason." Tourmal kept grinning and rocked on the balls of his feet. "I think you'll understand soon."

"I already understand," snapped Scott. "They wanted

me out of the way."

"I'll bet it was for your own good," said Tourmal.

Scott was getting annoyed. "You think so?" He cocked his head to one side. "Is that your expert opinion?"

Tourmal caught on and raised his hands in front of him. "Well, it is, but that's not...what I mean is..."

"Forget it." Scott slashed a hand through the air, cutting him off. "I'm done here." He was sick of Tourmal, sick of the medicenter, sick of being there instead of the brig...and he felt his temper rising. If he didn't leave, he might say or do something that he'd regret later.

Whipping around, he headed for the door.

"No, wait!" Tourmal chased after him, landing a hand on his shoulder. "You've got to stay!"

Scott shrugged out of his grip as the door swept open. "Like hell I do."

Then, suddenly, a soft voice called to him from behind the curtain. "Solomon?"

And Scott froze.

"Solomon?" said the voice...a woman's voice, weak but familiar. "Please stay."

Scott's heart pounded in his chest. He turned from the doorway, and his eyes flew to the curtain. He couldn't believe what he'd just heard and what it meant. "Oh my God."

Tourmal grinned and slapped Scott on the back. "See why everyone kept trying to get you to come down here? It *was* for your own good, after all."

Scott pushed past him like he wasn't there. He felt like he was in a daze or a dream, drifting toward something that was wonderful and impossible at the same time.

Stepping forward, he took hold of the end of the curtain at the head of the bed. As he slowly pulled it aside, the metal rings clattered along the antigrav track, clacking together as the curtain bunched up.

And there she was, just as he remembered--except her eyes were open. And she was smiling.

And speaking with that voice he'd once thought he might never hear again. "Hello, Solomon. Long time no see."

Scott stepped through and pulled the curtain shut behind him. Then, without a word, he bent down and kissed her softly on the forehead.

When he pulled back, her eyes were closed, and he felt a twist of panic in his chest...but then they opened again and lighted upon his face. "Did you miss me?" she said.

"Yes." Scott didn't even have to think about it. "I missed you a lot."

Her smile widened. "I already knew that." The cuts and bruises that had littered her face after Shard were all healed now. She still looked fragile, but she had a pale glow and a sparkle in her eyes. "I hear you stopped by a bunch of times while I was out."

Scott shrugged. "I needed to get away from Trane and Abby's snoring."

Donna giggled softly. "I think I heard it in my coma, even."

Impulsively, Scott took her hand and kissed it. "We should've moved them in here from the start. Then maybe you'd've woken up sooner."

"Or just gone down deeper," said Donna. "Though I was pretty deep already."

"So you weren't just pretending to be comatose to get out of duty, then?" Scott kissed her hand again. "Because that's what everyone was saying."

"They were right." Donna winked at him. "That's exactly what I was doing."

"Well, I'm glad you decided to end the fake coma," said Scott. "I'm glad you stopped being so damn lazy."

Donna watched through half-lidded eyes as he kissed her hand once more. "Oh, Solomon." Suddenly, the snarky tone was gone. "I feel like it's been a hundred years."

"I know." Scott held her hand against his lips and breathed the words between her fingers. "Me, too."

"I wish I could...I didn't..." She looked over at the green crystalline cast on her left arm, then the one on her right leg, both suspended from antigrav nodes. "I wish this hadn't happened." When she looked back up at him, her eyes glistened with tears.

Scott felt a shiver along his spine...a shiver not of warning but of strong emotion. Then, though he'd kept her at arm's length for so long, though he'd doubted his feelings and tried so hard to avoid complications, he leaned down over her without a word and did something he'd never done before.

It was something he hadn't done in all the hours they'd spent together or all the nights they'd shared a bed. It was something he'd thought about but not that day, not with everything that had happened.

But as soon as he did it, he knew how utterly right it felt. He wished he'd done it sooner.

Because, as his lips touched hers for the first time, every bit of doubt in his heart and mind was burned away instantly like fog in the light of the sun.

She kissed him back without hesitation or reservation, as if she'd been waiting forever for this outcome. Her lips pressed against his like the petals of a rose, soft and moist and fragrant.

When they parted, she beamed up at him with an expression of pure joy. "Now *that* was nice. *Much* nicer than being in a coma."

"Or fighting my own armor," added Scott.

Donna's expression darkened, becoming sadder. "I heard about what happened on Oberon." Reaching up with her right hand, she touched his cheek. "I'm so sorry they took your grandmother."

Scott nodded. "I'll get her back, don't worry."

Donna frowned. "Do we have any idea where they took her yet?"

Scott shrugged. "Trane and Beauchamp traced the Red viruses to Dornick VII, but I don't know. Just because the viruses' genomes originated there doesn't mean it's Red HQ."

"And that's the only possibility?"

"We have prisoners," said Scott. "Perseid's interrogating them now."

"Good." Donna smiled warmly. "Whatever they know, he'll get it out of them."

Scott looked away. "I hope you're right."

"I *know* I am." Donna pressed his cheek with the palm of her hand, turning him to face her again. "Because now that we're together, everything *has* to work out." With that, she guided him down and kissed him again.

This time was better and more intense than the first. Scott wanted to believe so much in what it meant--that they belonged together, that Bern's rescue and everything else would work out--that he focused every bit of his hope and faith and desire on the touch of her tender lips.

He had waited so long for her to wake up, had wondered so often if it would ever even happen. Now, like a miracle, there she was...like a sign that Bern would come back to him, too.

They parted again, and Donna had more tears in her eyes. "I knew all along." She ran a fingertip along his jawline. "About you and me."

Scott turned his head and kissed her finger. "You were there for me right from the start."

"I never gave up on you, Solomon," said Donna. "And I never will."

A thousand things to say rushed through Scott's mind. There were so many words he could say, so many promises he could make...but the future was uncertain. War was everywhere, chaos reigned. Who knew if they'd survive long enough to live up to a single promise made in that moment.

So, instead of saying anything, he simply kissed her again. He felt the warmth of her love radiate into him, felt the comfort of the connection they shared growing stronger in the midst of all the madness.

And he knew he'd been a given a gift, one that would make it possible to face whatever the Reds had in store for him and so much more besides.

Hours later, Scott left her there, asleep in the medicenter, and went to the mess to get some coffee. Now that his romantic interlude was over, he needed to get back to work. And as far as he was concerned, he had only one job to do.

Find Bern.

When he was done fixing coffee, he turned to leave for the brig...and Perseid's voice spoke over the intercom. "Corporal Scott, report to the brig. Corporal Scott to the brig."

"If you insist." Scott shrugged, sipped his coffee, and started down the corridor.

When he got to the brig, the same four guards were still posted outside--but this time, they didn't stand in his way.

In fact, the younger one grinned as he approached. "Did you finally make it to the medicenter? Did you get your surprise?"

"Yeah." Scott stopped and smiled. "It was the best thing that happened all day." Reaching out, he shook the young guard's hand.

"We were thinking we might have to lead you there at gunpoint," said the older guard on the other side of the door.

"Some guys just can't take a hint," said another guard standing beside the older one.

"Well, thanks for making sure I finally did." Scott stepped forward, and the door slid open. "It really made my day."

"Happy to help," said the young guard. "I like getting some good news for a change."

"You and me both." With that, Scott walked past him into the anteroom of the brig. As the door whisked shut behind him, three men looked in his direction without smiling: Perseid, García, and Balko.

"Corporal." Perseid looked and sounded tired. His black uniform was rumpled, his sleeves rolled up to the elbows. He wiped his hands on a dark cloth as he spoke. "How was the medicenter?"

"Great, thanks." Scott nodded once. The mood in the room was grim; no need to be effusive. "How were the Reds?"

Perseid kept wiping his hands. "Difficult." He looked at García and Balko, who both nodded in agreement.

"Stubborn. At first."

Scott folded his arms over his chest. "And later?"

"Talkative." Perseid didn't sound like he took any joy in saying it, or doing whatever it was that he'd done. He just kept wiping his hands on the cloth like a mechanic who'd just crawled out of a Battlenaut's guts. "One of them, anyway."

"So what did he say?" said Scott. "What do we know?"

Perseid looked him in the eye. "We only got it from the one man. We need you to confirm it with Cairn Barrie."

Scott scowled. "What makes you think he'll give us anything?"

"Your history. Your rapport." Perseid shrugged. "He told you about Oberon, didn't he?"

"I can try." Scott wanted to help instead of sit on the sidelines--but Cairn was a game-player. It was true that he'd told him about Oberon, but only when it had been too late for the Diamondbacks to stop the attack there.

"You'd better do a lot more than try." Perseid stopped cleaning his hands and stuffed the cloth in a hip pocket. "According to the prisoner we broke, a core Commonwealth world is about to be attacked by the Reds."

"Which one?" Scott searched his mind, running through the list of core worlds: *Archibald, Balustrade, Corazon, Tiananmen...*

"Tack." Perseid's voice was icy as he said it. "Our prisoner claims that Tack is the Reds' next target."

Scott stiffened. "Are you sure?"

Perseid ran his thumb along the scar across his throat. "Our Red was convincing. We had to dig deep to get it out of him...deep enough that I doubt he was lying."

Scott was still reeling from the news about Tack. First the Reds had taken his grandma, now they were planning to strike his homeworld. "Why Tack?"

"A beachhead in the heart of the Commonwealth," said Perseid. "A strategic location from which to strike the other core worlds."

Scott thought of all the people he knew on Tack--all the friends and relations, distant and close. He thought of all the places he knew there, from the town of Tisserie where he was born to the Iridess Chasm where he'd died. And the more he thought of the Reds running rampant through those places and slaughtering those people, the angrier he got.

"Bastards." The word was a hiss when he said it. "Have you already notified Command? Are they sending in the fleet?"

Perseid shook his head. "I want confirmation. There's still a chance the intel's bad, planted to draw us away from the real target."

"Cairn's a tough nut," said Scott. "Why not interrogate him like you did the other Reds? Get your confirmation that way?"

"Because that way, things get rough." Perseid looked at Balko and García. "And there's a hell of a bomb in his head."

Scott knew better than to ask for more details. Some things, he just didn't need to know. "All right. I'll talk to Cairn."

Perseid stepped aside and gestured at the door to Cairn's cell. "The sooner the better," he said. "The clock's ticking."

Scott nodded. "Tell me about it." He could hear that very ticking in his own head, louder than ever. And only a twisted enemy who despised his every breath could help him in his race against time.

Scott hesitated at the door, inhaling deeply. Then, committing to his course of action, he clenched his jaw and typed his pass code on the keypad.

"Good luck, Corporal," said Perseid.

Scott didn't answer as the door slid open before him.

When Scott entered the cell, he thought at first that he was under attack. Cairn, who'd been squatting on the cot, leaped off it suddenly and charged across the room.

Scott tensed instantly, ready to fight back...but Cairn stopped less than a meter away. "There." Grinning, he moved his head in a circle, staring at Scott's face. "There it is. Just like I expected."

Scott had no patience for games, but knew he had to play along to get anywhere. "What's that, Cairn?"

"The look on your face." Cairn pointed at him and chuckled. "The one I was *dreaming* about. The one that happened when you realized just how *bad* things are and that there's nothing you can *do* about it."

"I think you're seeing what you *want* to see," said Scott. "I'm feeling just fine."

"You're full of *plang*." Cairn snorted and snapped his fingers a few centimeters from Scott's nose. "I can see right through your lame-ass façade. I know you *too well*, Sol."

"Well, good for you," said Scott.

"By the way," said Cairn. "You're *late*."

Scott frowned. As usual, Cairn was trying to keep him off-balance. "Late for what?"

"You missed the deadline," said Cairn. "The deal's off the table."

"What deal?"

Cairn looked at him as if he were a total moron. "If you'd joined the Reds before we got to Oberon, I was going to stop trying to get payback, remember?" He threw his arms up in a gesture of exasperation. "But you didn't join up before Oberon, so the deal's off. So much for us *working* together and being *friends* again."

"Damn it," said Scott. "I've been so *busy* lately. Can't you give me a little more time to think it over?"

"One last chance to join the winning side?" Cairn sneered and leaned closer. "Why not? You have until you walk back out that door." His eyes flicked to the door of his cell, then back to Scott's face. "After that, you're *cut off*, you dumb son of a bitch."

Scott nodded and tapped a finger against his lower lip. "You know what might help me make my mind up? A gesture of good faith."

Cairn laughed. "What *kind* of gesture?"

Scott locked eyes with him. "Tell me where they took the Marine Commandant."

Cairn met his gaze with a steely glare of his own. "Now why the flux would I do that? So you can be a big *hero*?"

Scott wondered how much he should say--then decided, since they were playing for such high stakes, to go all in. "So I can bring home my *grandma*." This time, he was the one who leaned forward, pushing Cairn back out of his way. "The Commandant's my *grandmother*."

Cairn's eyes widened and his eyebrows rose. Then, his features settled back into a cruel sneer. "Now *that* is rich."

Scott badly wanted to punch him in the face but held himself back. "So what about that good will gesture?"

Cairn turned and strolled back to his cot. "I'll tell you, but it won't have a thing to do with good will. Because I *guarantee* you'll be too late to *help* her, just like you were too late to stop the attack on Oberon."

Scott's heart sank when he heard that, but he knew he had to keep pushing. "Then go ahead. If it's too late anyway, go ahead and tell me."

"I did warn you it would be like this, you know. Back when you first visited me here." Cairn lay down on the cot, drew up his right knee, and crossed his left leg over it. "I *did* say that *I'd* the one doing the screwing this time, and *you'd* be the one paying the price."

"Enough already," said Scott. "If it's too late to help the Commandant, tell me where she is and get it over with. Or don't you want to see me hopeless and defeated?"

"Are you kidding? After the way you left me to Vore and the other wolves?" Cairn looked at him with a glare of pure, perfect hatred. "I can't wait."

In spite of what he'd said, the room was silent for a long moment after that. As Scott waited with the clock ticking ever louder in his head, he wondered if grabbing Cairn by the throat and choking the hell out of him might speed things along.

Finally, Cairn broke the silence with a single word, a single syllable. "Tack."

"That's where they took the Commandant?" asked Scott.

"Wouldn't you?" Cairn laughed. "It's where the first major offensive will be launched against the Commonwealth's core. Correction." He cleared his throat, pretended to check a nonexistent chronometer on his wrist. "*Has been* launched."

Scott's heart was pounding. He had the confirmation that Perseid needed, but he might not have gotten it in time to save Bern, Tack, or the Commonwealth. He needed to get back to Perseid without delay and get the wheels rolling.

Whirling, he started for the door...then paused and looked back over his shoulder. "You're okay with this? Doesn't it matter to you that Tack's your homeworld, too?"

Cairn laughed louder than ever. "Why do you think I *picked* it? I *want* the place to go up in flames!"

Scott shook his head and turned away.

"So what's your decision on my offer to join the winning side?" said Cairn. "Remember, it expires as soon as you walk out that door."

"What the hell. Sign me up," said Scott. "I'll be right back to take the Red oath."

"Now that's what I expected to hear," said Cairn. "I *knew* you had it in you to turn traitor and betray the trust of those who depend on you. I know it better than anyone else, don't I?"

"I guess you've got it all figured out," said Scott, and then he opened the door and marched out of the cell without looking back.

CHAPTER 33

Cairn's confirmation was enough. After getting the word from Scott, Perseid contacted Command and gave them the news. Then, he initiated preparations for the *Sun Tzu* to meet the fleet at Tack. If cleanup on Oberon finished on schedule, the ship would depart in three hours.

As for Scott, he fell through the cracks. Normally, his duties would focus on working on his Battlenaut, repairing and prepping it for action...but with his Battlenaut gone, and no replacement available, he had no immediate assignment.

It was a situation that wouldn't last; he wouldn't let it. Even as he grabbed fresh coffee in the mess, he was thinking about what to do next. Engineering always needed manpower, but Scott could do without Azimuth...so maybe he'd work on other pilots' Battlenauts in the hangar. He had to do *something* to keep his mind off worrying about Bern.

First, though, he headed for the medicenter to check on Donna. He didn't care that she was probably still asleep; he just wanted to see her, even if only for a moment. He just wanted to take another look at the one truly good thing that had happened that day. If Donna could come back from the brink of death, maybe Bern could come back from being stolen away.

Sipping his coffee, Scott walked down the corridor, lost in thought. Before he got to the medicenter door, his reverie was interrupted by footsteps rushing up behind him.

Turning, he saw Private First Class Sharmaigne Clancy zipping up alongside him--the comm booth attendant. "Corporal Scott!" She sounded out of breath, and her freckled face was flushed to match her bright red hair. "I'm glad I caught you!"

Scott stopped walking. "Why's that?"

"There's a message for you," said Clancy. "It came in shortly after you went down to Oberon."

Scott frowned. "What kind of message?"

Clancy shrugged. "It came under top secret seal for your eyes only. Authorization Alpha-Alpha-Zero-Black."

A chill ran up Scott's back. It was the highest possible authorization in the Commonwealth Marine Corps, which could mean only one thing. "Holy flux." He dropped his coffee on the floor, and it splashed all over his and Clancy's shoes and pants-legs.

Clancy stepped away from him. "Is something wrong?"

"You didn't tell me this until *now*?" snapped Scott.

"Things have been insane!" said Clancy. "There were *tons* of encrypted communications going back and forth between Major Perseid and Command!"

"Let's go!" Scott whipped around and charged back down the corridor. "I need to see that message *immediately*."

Clancy fell in step behind him. "I'm sorry I didn't tell

you sooner! You were off comm on the planet's surface, and then the next time I tried to find you, you were in the brig!"

Scott didn't answer. His mind was hurtling ahead on a single track now. All he could think about was getting to the comm booth and viewing the message with the Alpha-Alpha-Zero-Black authorization...the message that could have come from only one person in the entire galaxy.

"Hi, Solly." Sure enough, when Scott opened and decrypted the message, a holographic image of Bern stared back at him from across the round black table in the comm booth.

He hadn't seen her in a while, but she seemed much the same as he'd expected--a compact woman in her early hundreds who looked more like she was in her late sixties. As always, her bright white hair was tied back in a tight bun from her round face...but the expression there was different, more grim than grandmotherly. There was no twinkle in the pale green eyes behind the big glasses, no dimple of a smile in the chubby cheeks.

The rest of her showed similar signs of distraction. Her loose-fitting black uniform with the white piping was creased and rumpled, not impeccably pressed as usual. Her posture and body language were nothing like those of a grandma talking to her beloved grandson. This time, Bern was weighed down with worry, and her call was all business.

"Hi, Grandma," said Scott, though he knew he was talking to a recording. It felt good, just for a moment, to pretend that Bern was free and speaking to him live from her office at Command.

"I got your message," said Bern. "Sorry I haven't gotten back to you until now, but things have been crazy."

"No problem." Scott was completely alone in the booth, cut off from everyone, including PFC Clancy. He'd had to implement a total lockdown protocol in order to access the sealed message.

"Even now, I don't really have time for this." Bern looked away--at a chronometer, perhaps?--then back. "But I don't have a choice. You've really stepped in it, Solly."

Frowning, Scott leaned forward, gripping the edges of the table. "Stepped in what?"

"I can't help being proud of you, though." A smile flickered across Bern's face. "Leave it to my grandson to uncover the biggest secret project in the history of the Commonwealth."

"Lethe." Scott said the word softly.

Bern's expression turned back to grim. "You're lucky all that happened to you was getting data-blocked by Military Intelligence. Poking around Project Lethe can lead to much, much worse."

Scott's frown deepened.

"Lucky for you, the Marine Commandant's your grandma," said Bern. "But that will only get you so far. After you've heard what I'm about to say, I'm afraid you're going to have to watch your own back more than ever."

Scott nodded.

"The road to Hell." Bern took a deep breath and let it out slowly. "They say it's paved with good intentions.

"Well, that's how Lethe started. With good intentions." Bern sighed and reached off-camera. Her hand came back with a steaming black mug of coffee. "Eighty years ago, someone had the bright idea to end post-traumatic stress disorder forever." Bern raised her mug for a sip of coffee, then lowered it again. "All those soldiers were coming back from the Pyrrhic Wars with memories full of horrors that they literally couldn't *live* with. There were epidemics of insanity and suicide. Somebody had to *do* something, didn't they?"

Scott nodded. He knew all about the Pyrrhic Wars and the alien hordes of the Whispering Ones; he'd studied the unspeakable atrocities they'd visited on the Commonwealth fringe worlds and the soldiers who had gotten in their way. Bern had earned her stripes in that war, though she'd never liked to talk about it much.

"What they did was this," continued Bern. "They figured out a way to inoculate against PTSD." She had another sip of coffee, then put the cup down off-camera. "The brain trust created a virus that alters the mind's response to violent stimuli. The virus re-routed perceptual input during memory formation, limiting the long-term mental trauma that typically results from exposure to acts of extreme violence.

"Test subjects could still form memories of violent acts," said Bern. "They did not see extreme violence in a positive light or feel encouraged to perpetuate it. But the virus diminished the lingering trauma that causes PTSD. It took the edge off.

"It was so effective that the Joint Chiefs approved it for general use among the armed forces...but they decided to keep it off the radar. They worried that some folks might object to having their memories tampered with. Some people might see it as a form of mind control. So everyone across all the services got the Lethe inoculations and thought they were nothing but flu shots. It worked out fine, and the incidence of PTSD faded away to almost zero." Bern paused and folded her hands in front of her so it looked like they were resting on the comm booth table. "But that wasn't enough, was it? Because *almost* zero isn't the same as *zero*.

"It turns out some people were immune to the virus. The shots weren't having any effect on them. So how could they get around this?" Bern looked down at her folded hands. "Well, someone figured out that giving it to *babies* would eliminate this problem, because their undeveloped immune systems wouldn't be able to resist the virus. It would take root and become a part of their internal microbiome before resistance could develop.

"*This* is how they ended up inoculating every citizen of the Commonwealth at birth." Bern looked up and shook her head. Her gaze seemed to connect with Scott's, though she was only present as a recorded image.

"They did a wonderful job of rationalizing it, too," said Bern. "After all, PTSD is universal. Even among a civilian population, it causes extensive human suffering. Wouldn't it be better to limit such suffering through universal inoculation?

"And look at all the conflicts we must fight to preserve our freedoms. Wouldn't it be a good thing to create a universally PTSD-resistant populace? Wouldn't it make us stronger if every man, woman, and child were a potential warrior unable to be mentally traumatized by violence? Of course it would.

"That was what they told themselves, anyway." Bern nodded. "Which is why, for the past 75 years, every single citizen of the Commonwealth has been secretly inoculated at birth. And only a few at the top..." She spread her arms and bowed her head. "...have ever known the truth. And we have carried the burden with us, never speaking of it even to our closest loved ones." Bern lowered her arms and raised her eyes to look at Scott. "Until now."

Scott shouldn't have been surprised. Bern was the

Commandant of the Commonwealth Marines; he'd always assumed she was carrying many dark secrets. But knowing she'd been hiding something of such vast scope left him reeling. It didn't seem possible that his beloved grandma had been at the heart of a massive conspiracy affecting every citizen of the Commonwealth.

Yet the proof of it was evident right there in front of him. He could see the weight she'd been carrying in every crease and hollow of her face, in the dark dullness of her eyes, in the slump of her shoulders.

For as long as Scott could remember, Bern had been his moral compass. Whenever he'd landed in a tough situation, he'd always asked himself what she would do and acted accordingly. But now, he found himself wondering if her moral compass was as certain as he'd always imagined it to be.

All he knew for sure was that he had to keep listening, and hope he didn't hear anything else to taint his image of Bern any further.

"So why am I telling you all this?" she asked. "Because I have come to believe that Lethe is a terrible thing. By creating a populace without true PTSD responses to traumatic violence, we have made our citizens less likely to find war abhorrent. Just look at the endless conflicts that have sprouted up over the past decades--one after another after another, right up to the current Civil War." Bern thumped her fist on the table. "I believe war has become more commonplace because of Lethe.

"I also believe that Lethe has left us defenseless against the greatest threat of all. I believe it has fallen under the control of the Reds.

"This explains how the Reds have made themselves

undetectable to Commonwealth forces," said Bern. "The same applies to the Rightfuls, who've only recently broken away from the Commonwealth and therefore have all been inoculated.

"Somehow, the Reds have figured out a way to use the Lethe virus against us...to use it to switch off our ability to process sensory input related to them. And if they can do that, God help us." Bern shook her head. "Because I think they can do much, much worse."

Something in her voice made the hairs stand up on the back of Scott's neck. He leaned farther forward, stretching his arms out on the table as if he expected to be able to touch her...as if that might somehow reassure him in spite of what she was saying.

But Bern did not reach back. She just kept talking, her expression growing more grave with each passing moment.

"If the Reds can control our perceptions, they can control our actions," said Bern. "There is nothing stopping them from setting us all at each other's throats, thinking we are killing the very Reds who control what we see and hear.

"Think of it." Bern steepled her fingers in front of her. "Commonwealth forces turning on each other, laying waste to the core worlds they are sworn to protect. Destroying their own homes, murdering their own *families*...believing, the whole time, that they are wiping out the enemy Reds." Narrowing her eyes, she leaned forward. "The whole Commonwealth, and the Rightfuls, too, would be gone in a fortnight, wiped out by our own creation.

"This is what you have stumbled upon," said Bern. "The ultimate power. The end of civilization as we know it. Everything we love and believe in swept away.

"And for all the resources I have at my disposal, damn

little hope." Bern shook her head and rubbed her eyes. "Command--myself included--has come around slowly--*too* slowly. The Civil War has blinded us to the true threat, and now it might be too late to deal with it.

"We took a chance and sent you out with the Diamondbacks because you're the only individual on record who can see the Reds. I think it could be something to do with the way you died and were brought back. An alteration of your brain chemistry or neural pathways. Maybe the resurrection procedure simply killed off all the Lethe in your system. I don't know." Bern shrugged. "But it's starting to look like your mission is too little, too late.

"I'm about to leave for a top-secret meeting with the Rightfuls, to propose we join forces against the Reds. But, honestly, if we can't *see* the Reds, I can't imagine we'll ever defeat them. And if they've ratcheted up their perceptual control as I suspect, they can make our closest allies appear to be our worst enemies."

Bern sighed heavily and closed her eyes. "Only one thing is clear to me. We are running out of time.

"Bellerophon Station, Lethe's center of operations, just went dark. This tells me the Reds are getting ready to make their final moves.

"I imagine this means it will all be over shortly," said Bern. "I'm just sorry that I have to be the one to break it to you." Leaning forward, she stretched her arms across the table; this time, her hands came to rest in the same space as Scott's, their insubstantial holographic forms merging with his own solid mass. "Though I'd have to say I'm much more sorry that I might not see you again by the time this mess is over."

Bern's eyes glistened with tears. "I love you, Solly," she

said, and then she looked off-camera at what might have been a chronometer. "And I just hope we can see each other again in the next life, if this one keeps going the way I think it will." Smiling bravely, she blew him a kiss. "Got to go now, grandson. Good luck with your own battle against the Reds, wherever it takes you."

She blew him one more kiss, then, and got up from the chair. He watched her march out from behind the table and disappear as she left the camera's field of vision.

As the recording ended and the room dimmed, he just sat there for a while, staring into space, thinking about what she'd said. Letting the story of Lethe and all its terrible implications sink in. Wondering what his next step should be.

Then, he left the comm booth and went to tell Perseid what he'd just learned.

CHAPTER 34

When Scott had finished his story, Perseid got up from behind the desk and paced his office, rubbing the scar on his left cheek.

Meanwhile, Scott kept standing by the door, hands clasped behind his back. "That's everything," he said. "The whole message."

Perseid shook his head. "It's hard to believe. Every Commonwealth citizen inoculated at birth with a mind-altering virus? And the news never leaked in 75 years?" He rubbed his scar harder. "If it was anyone other than Bern breaking the story, I wouldn't buy it for a second."

"So what now?" asked Scott. "This changes everything, doesn't it?"

"Does it?" Perseid flashed him a look. "We have confirmation of a strike against Tack, which might already be in motion. Does it matter how the strike's being directed? We still have to stop it."

"But what if the attack is by our own forces, controlled by Lethe?" said Scott. "Rushing to the defense of Tack would just add more firepower that can be turned against our own people."

"But we have the countermeasure virus, don't forget," said Perseid.

"Which, as far as we know, might not do anything but let our forces *see* the Reds."

"Or it might block all the effects of Lethe, preventing any warping of sensory input that makes friendlies look like hostiles." Perseid pointed a finger at Scott as he marched past. "In which case, you can bet we'll be ready for them. We've already transmitted the specs on the countermeasure virus to all Commonwealth forces, and replication and inoculation are underway."

"But it won't get to everyone in time," said Scott. "Not if the attacks have already been launched."

Perseid stopped pacing. "We'll get to enough, hopefully, to minimize the damage. What the hell else can we do?"

Scott narrowed his eyes. "We can stop Lethe at the source. We can cut off the Reds' signal and stop it from turning our forces against each other."

"Stop it where?" said Perseid. "Bellerophon Station?"

Scott nodded. "Bern said it went dark."

"Which could mean any number of things." Perseid resumed pacing. "There could have been a power blackout."

"Or the Reds could have taken it off the grid to launch their attack," said Scott. "Otherwise, it's an awfully big coincidence, don't you think? Lethe's secret center of operations goes dark just as the Reds are gearing up for a massive Lethe-based assault?"

"So you think we should divert assets to Bellerophon?"

Perseid blew out his breath. "What if you're wrong, and the Reds *aren't* directing their assault from that location? Tack is *eight hours* across the quadrant from there! We'll never make it to the front in time to push back the Reds."

"But we can't afford *not* to go to Bellerophon!" said Scott. "And we only need to divert *one* asset--the *Sun Tzu*. Roll out the rest of the fleet to the core worlds as planned, equipped with as much of the countermeasure virus as they can get their hands on. Hopefully, they can hold the line long enough for the *Sun Tzu* to shut down Lethe at Bellerophon."

Perseid paced in silence for a long moment, passing Scott five times before he spoke. "Bellerophon is too much of a longshot to risk keeping the *Sun Tzu* out of the action. We have confirmed intel, Solomon--*confirmed* intel of an assault on Tack. Everything else is *guesswork*."

Frustration bubbling up at Perseid's resistance, Scott stepped forward and smacked his fist in the palm of his hand. "I'll take the *guesswork* of Commandant Chalice over the *confirmed intel* of Cairn Barrie *any* day of the week."

Perseid stopped and fixed him in an icy stare. "But *you're* not in command here, are you, Corporal? You don't get to make the final call, and you won't have to *live with it* if you're *wrong*. So don't *tell* me what to do with *my* ship."

Scott started to say something, but Perseid cut him off. It was probably for the best, given the hotheaded nature of what he'd been about to say.

"*Here's* how it's going to be," said Perseid. "We're going to *Tack*, and here's why.

"If somebody tells me a building's on fire, I'm heading straight for the building...not another building across town where I think the guy who set the fire might be. I'm going to save whoever I can, not try to prevent other fires that might or might not happen.

"End of story!" Perseid jabbed Scott in the chest with an index finger. "Do we have an understanding?"

Scott stared down at the finger and stiffened. "Yes, sir."

Perseid held his gaze for a moment, then leaned back and withdrew his finger. "Your opinion is noted, but we don't have time for debate. We are leaving for Tack in two hours at best possible speed. Once we get there, we will join elements of the Commonwealth Defense Fleet in an all-out effort to protect the core worlds from the Reds." Perseid rubbed the scar across his throat. "Nothing--and I mean *nothing*--will persuade me to pursue another course. Understood?"

"Yes, sir." Scott nodded. "Understood, sir."

"Good." Perseid gestured at the door. "Then report to your duty station and help get this ship ready for the fight of her life."

"Aye, sir." Scott fired off a salute that was a little too crisp. "Reporting to my duty station, sir."

Then, he turned his back on Perseid and marched out the door.

The corridors of the ship were filled with activity as Scott drifted through them. Diamondbacks ran past in both directions, rushing to prepare the *Sun Tzu* for impending departure and battle. No one spared more than a fleeting glance at Scott, just enough to make sure they didn't collide with him.

Scott paid the same amount of attention to them. He was lost in thought, processing all that had happened in the last eventful hours, from Bern's message to Perseid's decision. So much had happened in a short amount of time; it was hard to wrap his head around it, let alone figure out how to deal with the fallout.

But he *had* to deal with it, and fast. In less than two hours, the *Sun Tzu* would be on its way to Tack with Scott aboard, irrevocably committed to the course of action Perseid had chosen.

It was a course of action that Scott believed was dead wrong. Every time he went over it again, he came to the same conclusion--and felt more strongly than ever in his heart that he was right.

Going to Tack would be a mistake. The only way to stop the Reds and save the Commonwealth was to go to Bellerophon Station.

The thought of it ate at him, because Tack was his homeworld. He badly wanted to rush to its defense in this dark hour, no matter the consequences.

But every time he tried to convince himself to go along with that plan, he hit a wall. An inner voice caught him and pulled him back, turning him again toward the plan he knew was right.

It was the same voice that had guided him all his life. It was *Bern's* voice.

What would *she* do in this situation? There was really no doubt in his mind, as much as he wished there would be...as much as he wished he could go the less arduous route, just this once.

He damn well knew exactly what he had to do.

Even without consciously making a decision, he found himself moving toward the Training Deck. Even without telling himself that he was definitely starting down a path, he entered the vast, deserted chamber and headed for a certain gate.

Only when he was standing before it with his hand on the opener did he pause and reconsider. He ran it all through his mind once more, weighing the alternatives and possible outcomes, second-guessing the inner voice and the dictates of his conscience.

And when he was done with all that, he realized he had three choices. He could go along to Tack and do his part to stop the Reds--or the friendlies who imagined he and his allies *were* the Reds. Or he could try to start a mutiny, convincing the *Sun Tzu*'s crew to place him in command in less than two hours...asking them, essentially, to turn their backs on Tack and put their faith in his gut instinct.

Or this. He could open the gate, and...this.

Taking a deep breath, he opened the gate. As it slid away, he found himself gazing up at a towering metal figure, plated in gleaming blue and silver armor.

It was Vic Fong's Mark VI Marine Corps Battlenaut, the one that was identical to Scott's old unit. It stood there silently in its bay, staring out at the darkened Training Deck as if thirsting for action. Even as other, newer Battlenauts were prepped for the fight, the Mark VI remained alone in its bay, held back from the very purpose for which it had been built.

But not for long.

CHAPTER 35

If the crew of the *Sun Tzu* had known what Scott was up to, somebody would have stopped him. But as it was, they were all too frantically busy to think twice about what he was doing. Not to mention, as he had proven himself in battle again and again, they had to come to trust him completely. He was the man with the Red-sight, the light in the darkness, the Commandant's grandson, not someone who would disobey direct orders on the brink of an epic battle to preserve the precious core world of Tack.

That was why he could move around so easily, doing exactly what was needed to set his plan in motion. That was why he had the time and privacy to override access codes on Fong's Mark VI and order its delivery by robotic hauler to the Hangar Deck.

It was also why Trane wasn't suspicious when Scott showed up unannounced at Lab Five.

"Hey there." Trane looked downcast as he packed gear

in a ruggedized black case. "All ready for the big hoedown, rookie?"

Scott shrugged and leaned against one of the metal workbenches, looking over the equipment scattered there. "Are you?"

"Are we going to Dornick VII, where the evidence is pointing?" Trane scowled.

"Nope."

"Then no." Trane tossed a double-pronged silver instrument in the case with a clang. "No, I am not jazzed big-time about this particular hoedown."

Scott was pleased. He'd expected Trane to react this way, since he'd also presented a target dismissed by Perseid. Now all Scott had to do was play him just right to get what he wanted. "Well, that makes two of us."

Trane snorted. "Not like we have any *say* in the matter. Almighty Perseid has spoken!" Puffing up his chest, he jabbed his finger in the air dramatically. "No mere *mortal* can hope to influence the *gods*."

"Well, I don't know about that." Scott rubbed the back of his neck. "There might be *something* we can do."

Instantly, Trane's attitude changed. "Oh, yeah?" He narrowed his eyes and folded his arms over his chest. "And what might that be?"

Scott pretended to think it over for a moment. "I'd like to make another run at Cairn Barrie," he said. "With the gloves off this time."

"To what end?" said Trane.

"I think he lied about Tack," said Scott. "I think he misled us on purpose."

Trane rubbed his chin. "What about the other prisoner? He named Tack, too, and he did it under extreme pressure.

Perseid and the boys *broke* him."

"I think he was conditioned to give that answer under pressure," said Scott. "Maybe all of them were, if they broke--but not Cairn. He's too tough, too much in control. He gave up Tack because he *wanted* to, and he had no motivation to tell the truth. No *pressure*." Scott raised his eyebrows. "But we can *apply* that pressure, can't we?"

Trane nodded slowly. "The bomb."

Scott shrugged. "It's worth a try, don't you think?"

Trane frowned. "But the Red bastard said he *wanted* to activate the bomb, didn't he? He wanted to take the *Sun Tzu* with him."

"Which I think was *also* a lie. I'd like to see how he reacts when I tell him he really *is* about to blow up."

"Hmm." Trane scrubbed his fingers through his white crewcut and stared at the floor. "You sure wouldn't have much time to get it out of him."

"Either it'll work or it won't," said Scott. "If he calls my bluff, oh well. If he gives us the actual target, we'll have something to take to Perseid."

Trane looked up and smirked. "You think I'd send you in that bastard's cell with the remote control for a weapon that could destroy the ship?"

"That's kind of the point, isn't it?" said Scott.

"Well, that isn't going to happen." Trane crossed the lab and punched numbers on a keypad mounted on the metal wall at eye level. "I'll tell you why." A rectangular panel of the wall slid aside, revealing a secure storage box. Trane reached in and drew out the exact device that Scott wanted--a gleaming silver oval mounted on a wrist strap. "Because I'll program this baby to respond only to your DNA. Right now, it's set for mine and Monique's, but it's a simple matter to add yours to the mix."

Scott nodded. "So Cairn won't be able to set off the bomb himself."

"That's right, rookie." Trane started tinkering with the device. "And then you can scare the truth out of that Red bastard, and we can talk Perseid into changing course for Dornick VII."

"Absolutely," said Scott, though his real intentions were quite different. "We'll save Commandant Chalice and stop the Reds from destroying the Commonwealth."

"And Perseid will probably *still* end up getting all the credit." Trane chuckled and walked back across the lab, holding out the device. "But what the hell, right? You and I will always know the truth about what happened."

"Oh, yeah." Scott extended his left arm, and Trane wrapped the band around his wrist. "Nobody can take the truth away from us."

When Trane had finished adjusting the bomb control, Scott headed straight for the medicenter.

His timing could not have been better. Donna was awake when he got there, and Beauchamp had just finished removing the casts from her left arm and right leg.

"Free at last!" Beaming, Donna turned her hand and wiggled her fingers. "I was starting to think they'd *never* come off."

"Nevertheless, you must still be gentle," said Beauchamp. "You still have some healing to do."

"May I take her for a spin down the hall, though?" asked Scott. "Just to get some fresh air and a change of scenery?"

Beauchamp pursed her lips and gave him a cautionary

look from the corner of her eye. "You may, but only if you promise to be very careful. I do not think she would be pleased if you bumped her into a wall and put her leg back into a cast for another week."

"She's right." Donna nodded emphatically. "I wouldn't be pleased at all."

"I'll take *good* care of her." Scott winked at Beauchamp. "You have absolutely nothing to worry about."

Nurse Tourmal brought over an antigrav chair and helped Donna get into it. With a last warning from Beauchamp to be careful, Scott pushed the chair and its occupant out of the medicenter, promising to bring them back soon.

But by soon, he meant not soon at all.

"You seem to be feeling better," he said as he and Donna moved slowly down the corridor.

"*Much* better," said Donna, and he could tell she meant it. She seemed much more energetic than the last time he'd seen her...and that was a damn good thing, considering the circumstances.

Considering she was one of the only two people on the whole ship he could trust to help him with what he was about to do. "How would you like to get a *real* change of scenery?" he asked.

Donna looked up and back at him, grinning. "Like a vacation, you mean? A real getaway?"

Scott kept pushing her down the corridor, heading in the direction of the Hangar Deck. "A getaway that could cost you your career," he said. "And maybe a lot more than that."

This time, when she looked up at him, she wasn't grinning anymore. "Tell me, Solomon. Tell me what you need me to do."

"It might be too much for you," said Scott. "It isn't even fair of me to *ask*, since you just woke up from a coma. So if you decide you can't do it, for any reason at all, I'll take you straight back to the medicenter. All I ask is that you don't report me until I've had time to make my move."

"Enough with the foreplay." Donna smirked up at him. "Tell me what you have in mind before I start to lose interest."

It was then that Scott knew he'd done the right thing by coming to Donna. But even as he found a secluded spot and told her his plan, his mind was racing ahead to the next stop he would make.

Because the next person he was going to approach could be the biggest challenge yet.

"I'm here to take the Red oath," said Scott as he barged into Cairn's cell in the brig, "as promised."

Cairn, who was sitting cross-legged on the cot, didn't bother to open his eyes. "Took you long enough," he said calmly. "What makes you think the offer's still open?"

"This." Scott held up his left wrist with the bomb remote control strapped to it.

Puffing out his breath, Cairn opened his eyes. When he got a look at the remote, he broke into a smile. "Oh, no! What will I do? Please don't blow me up and take your precious ship with me!"

"Now why would I do that?" This time, it was Scott's turn to smile. "Reds don't blow up fellow Reds, do they?"

Cairn's smile widened. "Now you've got me interested." Uncrossing his legs, he got up from the cot. "If you're not here to threaten me, then what *are* you going to do, pray tell?"

"Prove my loyalty to the cause," said Scott, "by breaking you out of here."

"Let me see if I've got this straight." Cairn narrowed his eyes as he crossed the room. "You're going to use the bomb in my head to break me out of the brig?"

"Nope." Scott shook his head. "To break you out of the whole damn *ship*."

Cairn stopped walking toward him and folded his arms over his chest. "Assuming you *could*, what makes you think I'd want you to? Hasn't it occurred to you that I might be exactly where I *want* to be right now?"

"I can't join the Reds without you, can I? They'd blow me to smithereens."

Cairn sneered. "And that would be a *bad* thing?"

Scott felt himself growing anxious and had to force down the feeling. Time was running out as Cairn played with him, but Cairn would just drag it out more if he knew it was making Scott nervous. "Maybe I want to pay you back for saving me from Vore all those years ago. Maybe I want to make things right between us."

"Oh, good." Cairn tipped his head to one side and tapped his lower lip with a fingertip. "Because for a minute there, I was worried you might be trying to use me to save your sweet little ol' granny."

"That's the icing on the cake," said Scott. "Making things right with you is the main course."

"As if that's even possible." Cairn laughed. "You crack me up, you know that? I went through hell for *years* because I saved you, because you never bothered to *look* for me, and now you think we can just wipe the slate clean?"

"Not wipe it clean." Scott clasped his hands together, then flung them apart to mimic an explosion. "Blow it up."

Cairn laughed again. "With the bomb in my head? How do you plan to pull *that* off?"

"You'll see." Scott walked to the door and typed on the keypad beside it. When the door swept away, he gestured for Cairn to follow him. "Come on."

Cairn hung back, looking suspicious. "How do I know you haven't lost your damn mind? Or that this whole 'breakout' isn't just a trick to get me killed?"

"Do you see my grandma standing here safe and sound?" Scott shook his head emphatically. "Neither do I." Patience exhausted, he gestured more forcefully. "So no trick. Now come on."

Cairn hesitated a moment more, then headed for the doorway. "What the hell. I'm guessing this won't be boring at least."

"Congratulations," said Scott as Cairn walked past him and peeked through the doorway. "You've guessed correctly."

"That's for sure." Cairn let out a low whistle as he looked around the brig anteroom. "Maybe you should go on without me, ol' buddy."

"Don't worry. I've got it covered." Stepping through the doorway, Scott raised his left arm with the remote control wrist device strapped to it. "Hey, guys. Remember this?"

The four guards in the anteroom kept their rifles aimed at Scott, but no one pulled a trigger. They were the same four who'd been joking with Scott not long ago about his trip to the medicenter--but they weren't in much of a joking mood now.

"Coming through." Scott started across the anteroom, keeping his left arm up and his right hand over the device. Three quick taps, and Cairn's bomb would blow, destroying the *Sun Tzu* and all hands aboard her.

The four guards never took their eyes off him, but they did make way. Scott walked between them, then realized Cairn wasn't following and stopped. Turning, he glared at Cairn and bobbed his head toward the anteroom exit.

Cairn took three slow steps, then rolled his eyes and rushed to catch up. "This is your great breakout plan? Am I the *escapee* or the *weapon*?"

"Both." Scott crossed the anteroom and stopped at the exit. Keeping one eye on the guards, he tapped the pass code on the keypad, and the door slid open. "This way."

The corridor outside the brig was lined with guards on both sides, stretching as far as Scott could see in both directions. Every one of them was aiming a rifle at Scott and Cairn.

"No one's going to shoot, huh?" said Cairn. "You sure about that?"

"Think of them as your honor guard." Scott swung right and marched briskly between the rows of men, women, and guns. "All part of your V.I.P. treatment."

"Why do I feel like I'm back on Penitent Peak all over again?" said Cairn. "Going through the grinder to save your sorry ass."

"Funny," said Scott. "It seems like the other way around to me."

Given the number of guards and guns along their route, Scott and Cairn's trip to the Hangar Deck was quick and painless. No one made a move to stop them or even said a word, just let them slip past as if they weren't the real targets at all.

But when Scott opened the Hangar Deck door, he saw

the trouble-free transit was over. There, between him and the jump-ship Donna had hotwired, stood Perseid and Rexis. They were both unarmed, with hands extended palm-up at their sides--but the glares on their faces could not have been any icier.

"What the flux, Scott?" said Perseid. "You switching sides on us?"

"Just doing what I have to." Scott raised the bomb remote control. "Now please don't make me use this. Both of you, step aside."

"Seriously?" snapped Rexis. "You're planning to fly off with an asset just as we're going into *battle*? And you've got your *girlfriend*, who just woke up from a *coma*, piloting it?"

"I've got my reasons," Scott said flatly, and then he looked at Perseid. "You're wrong about Tack."

"It's a confirmed target," said Perseid. "Confirmed by your Red buddy there."

"You trust *him*?" Scott laughed. "Don't be *ridiculous*."

"Hey!" Cairn sounded offended. "I'm standing *right here*!"

Scott ignored him. "Tack's the wrong call." He shook his head at Perseid. "It's like plugging one hole when the dam around it's about to explode."

"So *you're* going to save the day single-handedly?" Rexis snorted. "You're going to be the *hero* of the Commonwealth?"

"Something like that," said Scott.

"The hero of the Commandant, is more like it," said Perseid. "When it comes down to it, he just wants to save his grandma."

Scott took a step forward. He was running out of time--which, of course, was why Perseid wanted to keep him talking. "You can't tell me you wouldn't do the same in my situation."

Perseid didn't budge. "I made a mistake recruiting you. You were never Diamondback material."

"Never said I *was*." Scott kept walking toward him. "Now *move*."

Still, Perseid stood his ground. "I'll give you one more chance. Surrender now, and I'll recommend deferring your court-martial."

Scott shook his head. "*Move*." He tapped the remote control once, priming the mechanism. Two more taps, and Cairn's bomb would blow.

Perseid raised his hands in front of him. "You win." Never taking his eyes off Scott, he backed away to one side. "But just so you know, your military career ends here. Right now. It's over."

"I kind of figured." Scott looked back at Cairn, who wasn't moving, and bobbed his head toward the jump-ship. Cairn looked behind him at the armed guards crowding the doorway, then rolled his eyes and followed.

"I mean it," said Perseid as Scott walked past. "You're done. Go save grandma, go be the hero and save the whole Commonwealth if you want, but there's no coming back from this. You're a traitor. You're finished."

"So is Donna," added Rexis as she also let Scott pass. "What do you think she'll have to say about that?"

Scott shrugged. "I guess I'm about to find out."

"God help you, you selfish son of a bitch." Rexis hissed out the words.

"God help us all." Scott reached the shadow of the jump-ship. The open gangway was less than ten meters away, slanting down from the ship's belly.

"I should've called your bluff," said Perseid. "You'd

never have triggered the bomb and destroyed Commandant Chalice's only chance of being rescued."

Scott stopped at the gangway and gave Perseid and Rexis one last salute. "Good luck at Tack."

Rexis turned her back. Perseid returned the salute, albeit half-heartedly.

Then, Scott and Cairn ran up the gangway steps into the jump-ship.

The *Sun Tzu* could have easily blown up the jump-ship, the *Sun Bin*, as soon as she cleared the Hangar Deck. Donna took her out fast, but the *Sun Bin*--named after a Sun Tzu descendant and fellow military strategist--was still no match for the bigger ship.

Scott fully expected a fusillade of fire as soon as the *Sun Bin* got far enough away. There'd be no reason to hold back when Cairn's quantum bomb was distant enough to no longer be a threat.

Sure enough, the *Sun Tzu* threw shots--but they were all warning shots across the *Sun Bin*'s stern. Not one of them got close enough to singe the jump-ship's armor or bump her off course.

It was then that Scott knew the Diamondbacks were letting him go. For all Perseid's accusations about being a traitor, he'd deliberately let the *Sun Bin* escape without a scratch on her. Either he thought Scott might have a chance, or he just didn't want to kill him in cold blood--but he clearly didn't make any kind of effort to cut the fugitives' mission short.

Moments later, Donna kicked on the negative mass drive, and the *Sun Bin* darted away into the starry darkness, leaving the *Sun Tzu*, *Sam Nicholas*, *Augustus*, planet Oberon--and Frank, wherever the hell he was--in the distance.

Watching the light of Oberon's twin yellow suns recede and fade through the rear viewport, Scott finally relaxed...a little. He was aboard a stolen ship piloted by a recently comatose woman, heading for a suicide mission alongside a man who despised him, who had a quantum bomb in his head--but at least he had cleared the first hurdle. He had broken away from the *Sun Tzu* and committed himself to the choice that he felt in his gut was right.

And there was something liberating about that. There'd be no more self-doubt and second-guessing; the momentum of his decision would carry him forth like a wave, roaring across the light-years and crashing into the Reds at Bellerophon Station.

He felt like nothing could stop him.

"Now leaving the Sigma Zeta Gamma system," said Donna from the dashboard at the front of the *Sun Bin*'s control room. "Setting course for Bellerophon Station. ETA six hours."

"Great flying, Donna." Scott, who was standing behind her, gave her shoulders a squeeze. "That was one smooth getaway."

"Bellerophon Station." Cairn spoke up from the center of the room, where he'd slung himself over the command chair. "What the hell do you expect to find at Bellerophon Station?"

"The red carpet treatment." Scott turned and smirked at him. "From the Reds themselves. The ones I'm selling out the Commonwealth for." He felt Donna squirm when he said it, and he squeezed her shoulders reassuringly.

"What makes you think there are Reds at Bellerophon?"

asked Cairn. "It's nothing but a mining colony."

"A little bird told me," said Scott. "A canary in the coal mine."

"Must be a real bird-brain," said Cairn, "because I'm telling you, the Reds aren't there."

"Whatever you say." Scott bent down and kissed the top of Donna's head. "I guess we're on a wild goose chase, then."

"I guess so," said Cairn. "Story of your life."

"It's too bad, though." Scott let go of Donna's shoulders and turned to face Cairn. "You'd be a *hero* if you brought *me* in--the one man who's fought back with his Red vision when no one else could see them."

Cairn was sprawled over one arm of the command chair, with his legs draped over the other. "As if you'd ever defect, you goody-two-shoes." He pointed a finger at Scott and sneered. "I heard them say you just want to save your grandma and be the hero of the Commonwealth."

"Just running their mouths." Scott walked over and glared down at him. "They *think* they understand me, but they don't...just like *you*."

Cairn laughed at him. "I understand you better than *anyone*. Better than you understand *yourself*."

"Obviously, you don't," said Scott, "or you'd realize I'm the only friend you've *got*."

With that, he walked back over to Donna and picked up where he'd left off, rubbing her shoulders as she steered the little ship through interstellar space.

CHAPTER 36

As the *Sun Bin* rocketed toward Bellerophon Station, Scott spent most of his time in the ship's cargo bay, prepping his stolen Mark VI Battlenaut for action. Truth be told, he knew and loved the model so much, it was a pleasure to work on it...though having to listen to Cairn the whole time took some of the fun out of it.

"All I'm saying is, the Commonwealth is on its way out," Cairn said nonchalantly. "It's collapsing under the weight of its own corruption."

Scott sighed as he adjusted the servos in the Mark VI's right leg. He wished he didn't have to keep an eye on Cairn at all times--and listen to his ramblings--but the jump ship didn't have a brig or another secure place in which to lock him up. The only other alternative was to leave him in the control room with Donna--and access to the *Sun Bin*'s controls--which just wasn't going to happen.

Tossing Cairn out an airlock wasn't an option, either;

Scott knew he'd need him to infiltrate the Red facility at Bellerophon Station. So all he could do was keep Cairn close at hand and block him out as best he could...and, sometimes, change the subject to something other than the impending fall of civilization as they knew it.

"Ever pilot a CORE Battlenaut?" Scott said, interrupting Cairn's latest string of anti-Commonwealth invective.

Cairn switched gears without batting an eye. "Why? You got one armed and ready to go for me?"

"Yes and no." Scott finished adjusting the servos, wiped his forehead on the back of his right arm, and slid the tool he'd been using into a loop on his belt. "C'mon and give me a hand."

It was the first time Scott had asked for help, but Cairn didn't refuse. "What do you mean, 'yes and no?'" he said as he followed Scott across the cargo bay.

Scott stopped in front of a big black plastic shipping cube that was at least fifteen meters on a side. "Open 'er up." There was a keypad on the middle of the front panel, and he typed a pass code on it. The keypad rotated clockwise, retracting four metal bars from a set of latches along the rim. Next, Scott grabbed a handle on the top left corner and signaled for Cairn to do the same with the handle on the top right corner. Together, they pulled the panel free and lowered it to the deck, exposing the contents of the cube.

Inside was the gleaming black armor of a CORE Battlenaut, folded so its legs were in front, toes pointed toward each other, knees even with the top of its head.

"Yes, I've got one for you," said Scott. "Hot off the Hangar Deck of the *Sun Tzu.*"

"Nice." Cairn stood with his hands on his hips and gazed admiringly at the folded-up armor. "So what's the 'no' part?"

"No, it isn't armed." Scott reached into the cube and touched a pressure point under the Battlenaut's chin--then quickly backed away. Suddenly, the armor came to life, sliding out of the cube. "It's CORE civilian armor. Defensive capabilities only."

Cairn backed up out of its way, too. "You're *kidding* me. You're giving me a unit that isn't *loaded*?"

Scott looked at him with an innocent expression. "That won't be a *problem*, will it? After all, Bellerophon Station isn't a Red *outpost*. You said so yourself."

When Cairn didn't answer, Scott smiled. *Gotcha.*

As the two of them stood there and watched, the CORE Battlenaut automatically unfolded. With a series of whirs and clicks, it extended to its full seven-meter height, just three meters shorter than the Mark VI.

"You know, you're right," said Cairn. "So are we going to disarm *your* Battlenaut too, then?"

Scott turned and eyed the Mark VI at the other end of the cargo bay. "I don't see why not. What could possibly go wrong?"

Just as he started to turn back around, Cairn leaped at him from behind, throwing him forward. Cairn's momentum carried them both straight to the floor, slamming Scott down hard on his right side and knocking the wind out of his lungs.

Before Scott could buck him off, Cairn pressed his advantage, hitting him hard across the back of the head. Shaking off the shock of the blow, Scott quickly gathered his strength--only to take another hit to the head, this one harder than the last. Dazed, he slumped forward.

That was when Cairn scrambled off and flipped Scott over on his back. He grabbed Scott's right wrist in a viselike grip, did the same for his left, and jerked the two together.

Scott snapped out of his daze when he realized what was happening--but by then, it was almost too late. Cairn had already forced the fingers of Scott's right hand to tap the remote control device on his left wrist, shifting it into standby mode. He did it again, bumping the device into ready mode--one touch away from final activation.

Cairn was just about to make the final contact when Scott unleashed a surge of strength, wrenching his hand away from the device. Then, with another surge, he pitched off Cairn, sending him crashing to the deck.

Before Cairn could recover and bounce back at him, Scott sprang from the floor and pumped a fist into his face. He followed that with a left hook to the jaw, then a roundhouse square in the breadbasket. Cairn went down, twitching--but still managed to catch Scott in the side with his right knee.

A bolt of pain flashed up from the impact point, but it only pissed Scott off more. With an angry roar, he plowed another blow into Cairn's belly, then locked his fists together and swung a pile driver like a wrecking ball into the side of his head, shooting it from one side to the other.

This time, Cairn offered no retaliation. He just lay there on the floor, chest heaving, face bruised and bloody...utterly beaten.

Scott was heaving for breath, too, as he got to his feet and checked the remote control. The silver oval on the wristband was no longer swirling; the device had reverted to a dormant state. Thinking back, Scott remembered Trane saying it was set to deactivate if more than thirty seconds passed between any two contacts.

Looking down at the man on the floor, he shook his

head. Cairn must have realized the device had been keyed to Scott's DNA. Otherwise, how could Scott have stayed close to him, leaving the remote control within easy reach? After figuring that out, the solution was obvious--if blowing himself to bits was the solution he'd wanted.

"What the *flux*, Cairn?" said Scott. "I thought we were *past* this."

"You *would* think that, wouldn't you?" said Cairn. "You never *did* have a firm grip on *reality*."

"Who's the one losing his grip?" said Scott. "I mean, what good would it have done, blowing up one Marine, a pilot who just woke up from a coma, and an outdated Battlenaut unit? Why bother?"

Cairn shrugged. "Does it matter?"

"According to you, we're not even heading for a Red facility!" snapped Scott. "You would've died for *nothing*."

Cairn glared up at him with a flash of rage and hatred. "But I still would've *died*." Suddenly, he lunged up to a sitting position. "I would've been *free*."

"Free from what?" said Scott. "Me?"

Cairn shook his head and lay back down. "You're an idiot," he said. "You don't know anything."

"I was just thinking the same thing about you." Scott reached into a pocket and pulled out a white plastic zip tie he'd been carrying in case he needed to restrain Cairn. It was high time he used it; now that Cairn had tried to trigger the bomb once, he could try it again at any time.

So why did Scott hesitate? Binding Cairn's wrists was the only way Scott could be sure he wouldn't have another shot at tripping the remote.

But he couldn't *keep* him restrained. Scott planned to trick the Reds into thinking Cairn was in charge, so they'd let the *Sun Bin* land and allow the crew inside the facility. That wouldn't work if Cairn was in restraints.

It also wouldn't work if Cairn refused to cooperate. Getting him to play along would be tricky at best, but keeping him tied up would kill any chance of success. Cairn's bitter stubbornness would lock him into a path of most resistance.

Even if Scott somehow managed to get Cairn to cooperate, then got him off the ship and into the facility, how could he know Cairn wouldn't try some other strategy to wreck the mission? There would be a million ways for Cairn to ruin things or kill himself at Bellerophon, and Scott wouldn't be able to stop him.

Unfortunately, the only way Scott could hope to get through the mission and achieve his objectives was to trust Cairn. Keeping him in restraints would be counterproductive... and given the stakes involved, Scott couldn't afford to do anything that would make the already steep odds against success any steeper.

With a sigh, he stuffed the zip tie back in his pocket. For better or worse, he would take a chance on Cairn. He would try to win him over.

"Tell me something," said Scott. "If you're such a huge pain in my ass, why the hell do I keep trying to help you?"

"To lord it over me?" Cairn sniffed. "To make yourself feel superior?"

"No, seriously," said Scott. "All you've done since we picked you up on Shard is treat me like a dick. You've lied to me, insulted me, threatened me, and tried to kill yourself and take me with you."

"Don't forget, I got you drummed out of the Marine Corps for using me as a human shield." Cairn looked proud when he said it.

"So *why* do I keep reaching out to you?" asked Scott. "Why do I keep *fooling* myself that I can get through to you?"

"Guilt?" said Cairn. "You feel guilty because you were the one who got away back in Iridess Chasm?"

Scott shook his head. "What if it's because I'm still..." Frowning, he rubbed his chin. "That couldn't be it."

"Because you're still *what*?" said Cairn.

"Forget it." Scott turned and headed for the door, leaving him lying there. "Not important."

Cairn sat up and shouted after Scott. "Tell me! Tell me what you were going to say, so I can laugh my *ass* off."

The door slid open, but Scott didn't rush through it. Instead, he turned slowly and gave Cairn a troubled look, one that mingled confusion and deep disappointment. "What if it's because I never stopped being your friend?" he said. "What if that's what I was going to say?"

"Then I'd say I feel sorry for you," shot back Cairn. "I'd say I can't think of anything more pathetic."

"Then it's a good thing I can still be your friend," said Scott, "without giving a plang *what* you think."

With that, Scott left the cargo bay and heard the door sweep shut behind him. He was taking a risk leaving Cairn alone in there, though he was locked out of the Battlenauts and heavy equipment. Theoretically, Cairn could still do some limited damage with the tools at his disposal.

But Scott's gut told him to take the chance. He had a feeling that somehow, it was a smarter play than cuffing Cairn with zip ties until they got to Bellerophon.

Either that, or Cairn could never be trusted, and this was the mistake that would doom the mission and sign Grandma Bern's death warrant.

CHAPTER 37

Scott was starting to worry. Cairn had been alone in the cargo bay for over an hour without letting out a peep.

"Still nothing?" Donna kept her eyes trained on the viewport in front of her, where the disk of Bellerophon's solar system was quickly approaching.

Scott stood behind her, rubbing her shoulders. "I guess it was a dumb idea." He sighed. "The guy just tried to blow himself *up*, for crying out loud."

"I think it was worth a try," said Donna. "Sooner or later, you need him to cooperate."

"Which I can't *do* if he *strangled* himself with a coil of *cable*." Scott stopped massaging her and stepped away, heading for the door. "I'd better go check on him."

"Just watch out in case he's waiting to *ambush* you," said Donna.

Scott was about to say something when the door slid open, and he nearly collided with Cairn, who was coming through from the other side. Both of them stumbled a step to avoid bumping into each other.

"Watch where you're going!" snapped Cairn, who didn't exactly sound conciliatory.

"*You* watch!" Scott was relieved to see him but knew better than to show it. "Next time, I'll go right *through* you."

Cairn pushed forward, getting right in his face. "I'd like to see you *try*." He lingered for a moment, gaze locked with Scott's...and then, when Scott didn't flinch, he brushed past him and sprawled over the command chair as he'd done earlier.

Watching him, Scott wondered if his strategy had worked, or if Cairn was just playing along and picking his moment. At least he hadn't killed himself--but that might come later, at a much worse time.

"So how long till the big dance?" asked Cairn. "When do we get to your supposed nest of Reds?"

"One hour, forty-five minutes," said Donna. "That's a half-hour sooner than expected."

"Good," said Cairn. "I can't wait to see *that one's* face when he realizes he's come to the wrong place." Laughing, he hiked a thumb over his shoulder at Scott.

"*That* won't happen." Scott walked up and bumped Cairn's right leg off the armrest with his hip. "All you'll see is a big *smile* as we mow down those Reds."

Cairn shook his head and sneered. "Whatever you say, Boss."

"Good," said Scott. "That's what I like to hear."

"I just have one question for you," said Cairn. "What happens after we're done? What's your plan?"

Scott gazed at the viewport and shrugged. "Don't know. Haven't thought that far ahead."

"Typical." Cairn snorted. "You let me know when you figure it out, okay?"

"I'll be sure to keep you in the loop," said Scott.

"That's what friends are for, right?" Cairn said it sarcastically, then laughed and threw his leg back over the armrest.

Grinning, Scott knocked the leg off the armrest again. "Truer words were never spoken."

An hour and a half later, the *Sun Bin* closed in on Bellerophon Station--a sprawl of black domes on a tiny, airless moon orbiting a bigger moon in orbit around a gas giant. It was a low-profile outpost in a remote corner of Commonwealth space, the perfect location for a secret black ops facility turned conspiracy headquarters.

"They haven't hailed us yet." Donna's fingers danced over the dashboard. "There's no radio traffic at all. No outgoing signals of any kind."

"Oh, well. Nobody home," said Cairn, who was still draped over the command chair. "Guess we'd better turn around."

Scott ignored him and leaned over Donna's shoulder for a closer look at the viewport. "I don't see any activity down there. What about heat signatures?"

"Power's on under the domes," said Donna. "Beyond that, I can't be more specific."

"Life signs?" asked Scott.

"Hard to map." Donna frowned at a holographic chart hovering in front of her. "Something in the domes is interfering with sensors. Some kind of shielding." Her fingers flickered across the controls, and the holo chart changed. "There could be several dozen lifeforms in there or several hundred."

"Way to narrow it down," said Cairn.

"Weapons?" asked Scott.

"Six missile batteries installed around the complex," said Donna. "None currently powered up or targeted. No detectable weapons locked on us at this time."

Scott felt the hairs stand up on the back of his neck. "They're watching us. Waiting until we cross the line, wherever that is."

"Orrr...," said Cairn, "they're just a bunch of friendly *miners* who'd never *dream* of shooting at a Commonwealth ship."

"Keep going." Scott turned to Cairn. "All ready?"

"If you mean am I ready to die of *boredom*, then hell yes," said Cairn. "Sign me up."

"You'll need to talk our way in there," said Scott.

"What are you *smoking*?" snapped Cairn. "There aren't any *Reds* here. We've got the *run* of the place."

"Just get ready," said Scott. "Think of what you're going to say to them."

"Other than, 'Hey there, people who aren't Reds?'" Cairn laughed. "'What's it like, not using mind control to take over the quadrant?'"

"Ten kilometers and closing," said Donna. "Still no change."

"There will be." Scott ran through a mental checklist of the preparations he'd made. He remembered getting the Battlenauts ready to go and putting them in standby mode; every step was clear in his memory. He also recalled going over his plan with Donna, reviewing it three times from start to finish. As for Cairn, the less he knew, the less he'd be tempted to wreck it; Scott had sketched a few points and otherwise kept him in the dark about the details.

Scott, his people, and his gear were as ready as they were ever going to be. And go-time was coming any minute now; he could feel it in his bones like a storm approaching.

"Five kilometers," said Donna. "Still nothing."

"Bo-ring." Cairn yawned loudly. "I'm taking a nap. Wake me when you've set course for Tack."

As Bellerophon Station grew larger in the viewport, Scott could make out more details of the complex. A big, six-sided landing pad sprawled in the middle of the cluster of domes, occupied by three small ore haulers. The black domes themselves, which had looked smooth from a distance, were actually covered with grooves and studded with antennas and other instrumentation. The domes gave off a pale glow, a faint nimbus of dust, radiant energy, or refracted light.

Arranged in a circle around them, the six missile batteries pointed in the *Sun Bin*'s general direction. They were big enough to push out some serious megatonnage; the *Sun Bin*, a light jump-ship built for speed rather than combat, wouldn't stand a chance once they cut loose.

The question was, when would that happen?

"One kilometer and closing," said Donna. "Missile batteries remain powered down. No missile locks, no movement, no signals of any kind."

"I hate to say 'I told you so,'" said Cairn. "But..."

"Five hundred meters," said Donna.

Scott leaned down beside her, bracing himself on the dashboard. "That's right, dipshits," he said, talking to the Reds he imagined watching from below. "We're calling your bluff."

"Three hundred meters," said Donna. "Switching to

thrusters. I'll put her down on that landing pad in the middle of the compound."

Just then, a loud beeping noise erupted from the dashboard. A blinking yellow holo popped up over the middle of the viewport, displaying a column of statistics that told the tale.

Scott knew what it meant immediately. "They're hailing us."

"Audio only," said Donna. "And that's not all they're doing." Another holo appeared on the left side of the viewport, bright red this time. "Three missile batteries just powered up."

Scott's heart pounded. "Open the channel," he said, "and set thrusters to station-keeping. But be ready for evasive maneuvers."

Donna nodded as her fingers played the controls. "Already ahead of you, Solomon."

As Scott waited for the call to connect, he looked back over his shoulder--and saw Cairn standing behind him instead of sprawling in the command chair. Their eyes met, an unspoken message flashing from Scott to Cairn: *I told you so.* But Cairn just shrugged and turned to watch the viewport.

"Putting the call on speakers," said Donna. "Good luck."

She flicked one last switch, and a man's deep voice rolled into the control room. "Bellerophon Station to unknown vessel. Identify yourself."

"This is the jump-ship *Sun Bin*," said Scott, leaving out the part about it being a CORE spacecraft. "Request permission to land for emergency repairs."

There was a pause on the other end of the call. "What

repairs, specifically? Your ship appears to be in working order."

"Problems with the oxygen scrubbers," said Scott. "The ship flies fine, but none of us will live through the trip to our destination, which is thirty light-years away."

Another pause. "Request denied. Recommend you proceed to Warwick III, distance three light years from this location."

"You do realize we'll all be dead by the time we get there," said Scott.

"Suggest you administer cryogenic procedures to conserve life support," said the voice from Bellerophon.

"We don't *have* cryogenic equipment," snapped Scott.

"You have thirty seconds to alter course," said the voice.

Donna muted the call. "He's right. The three powered-up missile batteries have just targeted us."

Scott smiled grimly at Cairn. "Then I guess it's time for a word from the captain." Grabbing him by the arm, he pulled him forward. "Take it off mute, Donna."

Donna hit a button and gave him the thumbs-up.

"Bellerophon Station, please hold for the commander of this vessel." Scott nodded at Cairn and gave his shoulder a squeeze. "Captain Cairn Barrie."

For a long moment, Scott thought Cairn wasn't going to cooperate. He just stood there, glaring, with his jaws and fists clenched, saying nothing.

Scott nodded encouragingly, yet still Cairn kept his mouth shut. So much for the great plan; it looked like Scott was going to have to switch tracks and explain why "Captain" Barrie couldn't join the call after all.

But just as Scott gave up and opened his mouth to speak, Cairn finally took the leap. "This is Captain Cairn Barrie," he said. "Request permission to land, Bellerophon Station."

There was silence on the other end of the call.

Cairn cleared his throat and tried again. "I repeat, this is Captain Cairn Barrie requesting permission to land."

There was another moment of silence before the voice from Bellerophon replied. "Did you say 'Cairn Barrie?'"

"Affirmative," said Cairn.

Another pause from Bellerophon. "Verify your credentials immediately or be destroyed."

Cairn looked at Scott with an expression that slowly changed from angry resistance to disgusted resignation. He flipped up his right middle finger in an obscene gesture just for Scott, then looked away and spoke up once more.

"This is Cairn Barrie," he said. "I.D. number Alpha Bravo seven five niner whiskey victor six...red." When he said the last word, he showed Scott the obscene gesture again without looking at him.

"Challenge epsilon three," said Bellerophon. "Good ships are in short supply in this sector. How do you respond?"

Cairn hesitated, then sighed. "I know a dealer who can sell you one cheap."

There was another pause from Bellerophon Station, the longest yet. Scanning Donna's readouts, Scott could see that the three missile batteries were still charged and aiming at the *Sun Bin.*

Then, finally, the voice rolled out of the speakers again. "Permission to land granted, Captain Barrie. Please proceed."

"Affirmative," said Cairn.

"Bellerophon control out," said the voice, and then the speakers fell silent.

Everyone in the control room seemed to relax at once--

except for Cairn, who looked like something had crawled up his butt and died.

His lies had been exposed. It was clear now that Bellerophon Station was in Red hands, and he had known all about it, right down to the challenge and response code they needed to get through the front door.

Scott was glad for the confirmation that he'd come to the right place; finally, he could set aside his doubts and focus on the mission ahead. He was also glad he wouldn't have to listen to Cairn's denials anymore.

Part of him wanted to go up to Cairn and rub it in, put him in his place now that the truth was out--but Scott knew that wouldn't help the cause. The goal was continued cooperation, not increased animosity.

It was better to stay all business. "Great work, Cairn." Scott considered trying for a handshake, then settled for a nod instead. "Donna, take us down."

"Already on it, Solomon." Donna's fingers flew over the controls, and the *Sun Bin* started its descent.

Through the viewport, Scott could see the black domes of Bellerophon Station approaching. He could also see the missile batteries moving to keep the *Sun Bin* in the crosshairs.

"How long until landfall?" asked Scott.

"Twenty minutes, give or take," said Donna.

"Long enough to send Perseid a message," said Scott. "Tell him we were right about Bellerophon Station. Tell him we're going in."

"Roger that, Solomon," said Donna.

Scott leaned down and gave her a lingering kiss on the lips. Then he drew back, smiled, and did it again.

"How romantic," Cairn said sarcastically. "All we need's some violin music in the background."

This time, it was Scott's turn to flip a middle finger at Cairn.

Cairn snorted. "Let's get this cluster-flux over with," he said, and then he stomped toward the exit.

Scott pulled back from Donna. "Any last questions?"

Her eyes sparkled as she held his gaze. "Are you coming back to me?"

"Hell yes." He kissed her again. "I'd have to be a pretty big jerk *not* to."

"Damn right." Donna grinned. "Now get out of here. I'm sick of looking at your face."

One more kiss, and Scott left her at the controls. "Good luck!" he said as he ran for the door.

"You break a leg, too," said Donna. "And don't keep me waiting!"

"Wouldn't dream of it!" said Scott as he ran out of the control room. "How long can saving the Commandant and the Commonwealth possibly *take*?"

And then the door slid shut and he was gone.

CHAPTER 38

By the time the *Sun Bin* landed, Scott and Cairn were suited up and ready to go--Scott in the Mark VI Battlenaut, Cairn in the CORE civilian armor. They stood side by side in the middle of the cargo bay, waiting for the hatch to open at the far end so they could venture outside.

As they stood there, Scott wondered if Cairn's heart was pounding as fast as his--and if so, was it for the same reason? Scott was nervous about the mission because he wanted it to succeed; would Cairn be nervous because he wanted the opposite result?

Whatever his intentions, Cairn didn't *sound* nervous...just cranky. "You're sure I can't shut off this damn A.I.? If I needed another *brain* in my armor, I would've *brought* one."

"It'll grow on you." Scott left out the part about Frank going rogue back on Oberon. Why add fuel to Cairn's griping? "Isn't the voice activation nice, though?"

"If you don't mind delays every time you give a

command," said Cairn. "Are you sure this armor's *cutting edge*?"

"You're in a civilian unit with a defensive profile only," said Scott. "The fully loaded combat model's another story."

"Better than that antique you're wearing now?"

"Are you kidding?" said Scott, though he preferred the antique hands-down to the CORE models. He was glad he'd brought it for this critical mission, where everything was on the line. He felt at home in its tried-and-true cockpit, unencumbered by supposed improvements that had gotten in the way of instinctive combat...and ultimately almost killed him.

"So what the hell happened to it?" asked Cairn. "Your new model, that is. Why did you bring the antique?"

"I had my reasons." Just as Scott said it, red lights started flashing in the cargo bay, signaling that the hatch was about to open.

"You're sure this armor's spaceworthy?" said Cairn.

"Absolutely." Scott double-checked to be on the safe side, then nodded. The Mark VI was perfectly airtight, pressurized, and shielded from head to toe. Fong had taken great care of his baby; she was pristine all around.

"*Red* Battlenauts are *all* spaceworthy," said Cairn. "They're the greatest fighting machines ever *built*."

"That's what *you* say." Scott grabbed his interface helmet from a hook on the cockpit wall and lowered it onto his head. As soon as the padded halo fit down around his skull, the visor display lit up in front of him. The frontside camera feed appeared automatically, showing the cargo hold's rear hatch sliding open in the flashing red light. "But they're not so *tough* when people can actually *see* them, are they?"

"I bet you'll have another chance to find out," said

Cairn. "Or do you think they're going to just let us waltz in there on our own?"

"I thought you'd have more pull than that," said Scott, using the keypad on the left armrest to set up his weapons. Without the CORE Battlenaut's morphing capabilities, he was stuck with the standard complement of projectile weapons, lasers, sonics, and missiles--but that was enough for him. It was all he'd ever needed to win on the battlefield as a Commonwealth Marine, before the Diamondbacks had come along.

"Maybe they're wondering if--oh, I don't know--I'm being forced to do this against my *will?*" snapped Cairn. "There *is* that *possibility*."

Scott could see that the hatch was almost all the way open now. "You did a great job talking our way down here," he said. "Just do more of the same, and we'll be fine."

"No, we won't," said Cairn. "You don't *know* these people like I do."

"Good thing you're here, then." Scott worked the keypad on the right armrest of his couch, bringing up Cairn's telemetry on the far left side of his visor. Then, he locked it there so he could quickly refer to it at any time, instantly assessing Cairn's status. "I couldn't do this *without* you."

"What the hell can *I* do? I'm in armor without any *weapons*." Cairn made a snorting sound over the comm. "Not that I'd use them to *help* you if I *had* any."

"You'll do the right thing when the time comes," said Scott. "I believe in you."

"Then you're in for a rude awakening," Cairn said darkly.

The two Battlenauts stomped out of the cargo hold of

the *Sun Bin* and onto the landing pad pavement. Scott put Cairn in front to keep him visible and let him take the lead in dealing with the Reds. *How* he planned to deal with them, what exactly he would do when the time came, was impossible to know.

Cairn carried a lot of hate around with him, much of it aimed at Scott for what had happened at Iridess Chasm. Scott had tried to get him to switch it off, to understand that Scott had never meant to let him be hurt and would have saved him if he'd known he'd survived. But was any of that enough, after so many years, to earn them a second chance? Would Scott himself have been quick to forgive under the same circumstances, if he'd been the one spirited away by Larvis Vore and subjected to untold tortures for decades? He couldn't say.

But Cairn's redemption was his only hope. It seemed like a pathetically fragile frame on which to hang the survival of Bern and the Commonwealth...but it was all he had. Here at the end of the road, he couldn't depend on the Diamondbacks or the Marines or anyone else--just Donna Perihelion and Cairn Barrie. The woman who loved him and the man who despised him.

"Which way do we go?" Cairn stood and looked around at the black domes surrounding the landing pad.

"Beats me," said Scott. "Let's ask for directions."

After a pause, he heard Cairn's voice over the comm. "Come in, Bellerophon Station." Before leaving the *Sun Bin*, Scott had tweaked Cairn's armor so he could hear every call he made over the comm. Secretly contacting the Reds just wasn't going to happen. "This is Captain Cairn Barrie. Please direct us to the spacecraft repair facility."

No answer. The incoming comm channel remained

silent.

"Give it another try," said Scott.

"Right," said Cairn. "Because maybe they forgot we're *out* here." He took three steps forward and opened the channel again. "Come in, Bellerophon Station. Please direct us to the repair facility."

Still, there was no response.

"Maybe they stepped away," suggested Scott. "Or their radio equipment's malfunctioning."

Cairn tried again without being asked. "Bellerophon Station!" This time, he raised his voice. "Where's the damn repair facility?"

Again, no one answered.

After a long moment, Scott nudged the joystick and brought the Mark VI lumbering up to stand beside the CORE civilian armor. "Let's just pick a direction. I guess they don't want to be bothered with us."

"Wrong." Cairn raised his Battlenaut's arm and pointed at a gap between two of the black domes about half a kilometer distant. "They sent out a *welcoming committee*."

Scott looked where he was pointing, and there they were: two Red Battlenauts, striding out from between the domes in close formation. "An escort?" At first, he thought it was possible. After all, Cairn had established his Red credentials and requested assistance.

But no. While they were still half a klick out, the Reds started shooting. Both of them cut loose their golden energy beams at once, merging them into a single colossal stream rushing straight toward Scott and Cairn.

"Move!" Scott jammed the stick right, and his Battlenaut bolted that way, getting out of the line of fire just in time. The searing beam of energy blazed past without touching him; it struck one of the domes instead, splashing harmlessly off its protective surface.

Cairn, who'd darted left instead of right, was also in the clear. His black CORE armor wobbled a little from the sudden start and stop, then stabilized. "Hey!" He was shouting over the comm at Bellerophon Station. "You guys're shooting at one of your *own*!"

No answer came back over the comm channel. So much for being on the same side.

"I said *stand down*!" said Cairn. "I'm as Red as *you* are!"

The Reds' only reply was to fire another merged beam of golden energy. This time, it was heading straight for Cairn.

He dodged out of the way in time but stumbled and went down on his belly on the pavement. Scott heard him cry out when he hit, but according to telemetry, he wasn't hurt badly.

In which case, Scott realized, that was the best place for him--out of the action, out of the way. Instead of having to worry about the guy in the civilian armor, Scott could focus his attention on fighting the Reds.

Without a word to Cairn, Scott wrenched the stick forward and ran away from him.

The Reds were waiting. As the footfalls of the Mark VI pounded across the landing pad, the Reds opened fire with their energy beams again. This time, instead of mingling the beams, they kept them separate, catching Scott between them--then scissored them together.

Playing the right keypad and yanking the stick back, Scott leaped clear before the twin beams could slice into him. While airborne, he brought up the coordinate grid over the frontside feed on his visor. When he came back down, he quickly calculated a bearing on one of the Reds and punched it into the left keypad, then thumbed the firing button on the stick. A missile shot out of his shoulder-mounted launcher, streaking straight at the Red he'd targeted.

The firing solution was sound, but the target swatted away the missile at the last instant. In retaliation, the Red unleashed a stream of slugs in Scott's direction, and his partner did the same.

This time, the fire didn't miss. Both torrents of slugs slammed into Scott's armor with shuddering force, knocking him back but not off his feet.

Tapping the keys madly, Scott cooked up a new solution and launched another missile. That one had barely left the launcher when he pumped out another.

The missiles rocketed toward the Reds, covering three hundred meters of airless moon in milliseconds. Each missile looked like it was going to strike one of the Reds head-on--but then they both veered suddenly downward and blew apart the pavement at the Reds' feet instead.

The streams of slugs stopped battering Scott's armor as the Red Battlenauts went down. Debris moving fast enough to escape the low gravity shot into space, and the rest of it showered around them.

Determined to press his advantage, Scott charged toward the Reds. He knew from experience how tough their armor was and didn't expect them to stay down for good.

He wasn't sure he could beat them at all, in fact. The last time he'd taken on a Red Battlenaut while piloting a Mark VI, the Red had wrecked his ride, forcing him to eject.

Not that he was going to give up. He knew the Reds and their fighting style better this time. He'd just have to hope he could win by being trickier and more relentless.

Plus more determined because of the stakes. Were the Reds fighting to save a beloved grandmother? Were they single-handedly trying to save a planetary Commonwealth? No fluxing way.

As Scott raced the Mark VI toward the Reds, he cut loose an unholy bombardment of slugs, missiles, and lasers. It was back to basics without the exotic weapons of the CORE Battlenaut--the drone pods, biofilm, Dragon's Breath, etc.--but he didn't mind a bit. He couldn't reconfigure his armor into Missile Mode or make it beanstalk or turn into a Red Battlenaut...but that was okay, too. It felt more hands-on this way, more personal...just right for handing out payback.

The two Reds kept trying to get up, but the barrage wouldn't let them. It was one thing deflecting incoming ammo when the Reds were upright with good leverage and their strongest shields facing forward--but quite another to be floundering on the ground under constant attack.

The Mark VI kept pouring it on, too, as if seeking vengeance for the destruction of Scott's first Mark VI back on Chelong III. Rivers of slugs flowed from its guns, interspersed with crimson laser bolts. Smoke and debris rose in a cloud around the Reds, obscuring the sight of them.

Then, Scott's guns stilled for the briefest of moments. One Red got halfway up, using the other Red to climb off the pavement.

Just as the rising Red made it the rest of the way to his feet, Scott fired another missile, followed by two more. All three shells struck the standing Red in the chest, just as the twin cannons mounted there were seething with golden energy.

The bearing and timing were perfect. The exploding warheads triggered a chain reaction with the golden energy, ripping the Red apart in a cataclysmic burst. The force of the blast crumpled the other Red on the ground, caving in the cowling over its cockpit and snapping both its legs like kindling for a campfire.

Scott cheered and eased up on the stick, which he'd been white-knuckling. Even with an outgunned Battlenaut, the same model he'd piloted to destruction against the same enemy on Chelong III, he'd managed to put down the two attackers. It was a brief rush of victory, a small step along the way to his final objectives, but he let himself savor it.

Then, he felt the ground shake through his armor and jumped back to the task at hand. Throwing all five camera feeds on the visor at once, he quickly spotted the source of the tremors on the leftside feed.

Three more Red Battlenauts were stomping across the landing pad toward him, all charging their energy cannons at once.

Scott clenched his jaw and swung the Mark VI around. The odds were worse this time, but so what? He'd just taken down two Reds, and he'd take down three more if he had to. He'd do whatever it took to save Bern and the Commonwealth. He wouldn't let anything stop him.

Reading the grid overlaid on the frontside feed, Scott figured out bearings and targeted his weapons. Maybe the same trick would work twice: choke them with ordnance, then send in warheads to kick off a chain reaction.

"Here we go, plang-holes." He marched three steps toward them, planted his feet, and thumbed the firing button atop the stick.

At that exact moment, a heavy weight slammed into him from behind, blowing his focus. Glancing at the backside feed, he glimpsed a gleaming black figure pulling back and plowing forward--and then he felt another impact. This one pitched his Battlenaut forward, knocking it off balance.

It didn't take Scott more than an instant to realize what was hitting him--*who* was hitting him--back there. But that still didn't give him enough time to stop the next impact.

This time, the gleaming figure--the CORE civilian Battlenaut--slammed into him harder than ever. Scott's armor lunged forward and stumbled, barely staying on its feet.

Instead of pulling back to ram him again, the civilian unit stayed on top of him, driving the Mark VI down with all its weight. Meanwhile, the three Reds kept storming toward him, ready to unleash bolts of searing golden energy from their chest cannons.

"Cairn!" Scott tugged the stick back, fighting to hold the Mark VI upright. "Stop it! Get off me!"

Cairn's only answer was to keep pressing against him... and then he suddenly pulled away.

With the weight of Cairn's armor gone, the Mark VI stopped tipping forward and shot to an erect position. Scott wasted no time swinging around to open fire, hoping he could disable the CORE Battlenaut and move on to face the oncoming Reds.

But he never even squeezed off a shot. Cairn crashed into him with the greatest force yet, catching the Mark VI at a bad angle and sending it toppling toward the pavement.

Scott's armor crashed down hard on its right side, setting off an alarm klaxon in the cockpit. He shut it down fast, then worked the stick and keypads to try to roll forward and get back on his feet.

Not that Cairn was going to let that happen. Before Scott could start his roll, Cairn darted up and kicked him the other way. Instead of rolling onto his front, Scott found himself rolling onto his back.

He wrenched the stick around, but it was too late. His Battlenaut landed heavily on the pavement, facing up.

Determined to bounce back fast, Scott keyed commands and jimmied the stick, telling the Mark VI to sit up. The armor started to comply, but didn't get far before Cairn threw it back down with a kick to the head.

"*Stay* down!" Cairn said over the comm. "Don't make this any *harder*!"

At the sound of the double-crosser's voice, Scott glared and clenched his teeth. Adrenaline blazed through his bloodstream, giving him the burst of energy he needed to keep fighting.

Scott started to lurch up off the pavement, but it was a feint. He only came up far enough to draw Cairn in, then flung up a gauntlet to grab his ankle.

With a mighty swing, he hurled Cairn's Battlenaut down on the ground. Then, with the armored ankle still in his grip, he jolted up to a sitting position, ready to press the attack.

And came face to face with the three Reds who'd been charging across the landing pad. They stood at his feet, side by side, with their energy cannons aimed down at him. With all the crash-bang action going on between him and Cairn, he hadn't noticed their approach.

Scott let go of Cairn and wondered what to do next. His weapons were charged and ready to fire; he thought about blasting away and going down in flames...but what would that accomplish? He'd be signing not only his own death warrant, but those of Bern and the Commonwealth, too.

As much as he hated to admit it, he was responsible for them...and therefore had just one move left to make in the face of irresistible Red force.

Slowly, he tugged the stick back, lowering his Battlenaut's upper body to the pavement. Then, he powered down his weapons and waited, watching the glittering stars in the sky on the frontside feed.

A moment later, his Battlenaut's lower body lifted--each leg in the grip of a Red. Scott's view of the sky changed as they dragged him across the pavement on his back, carrying him off as their prisoner.

And the whole time, on his leftside camera, he saw the gleaming black feet of Cairn's CORE Battlenaut marching alongside him.

CHAPTER 39

The Reds dragged Scott's Battlenaut into one of the black domes, hauling him like a sack of garbage through a big gate. Watching his topside feed, which showed the view behind him, Scott saw the gate slam shut and seal. Then, according to the sensor readings on his visor, air was pumped into the room around him.

As soon as the air pressure stabilized, the Reds dropped his legs, letting them fall to the metal floor plates with a loud clang. Then, he heard Cairn's voice over the comm.

"Open the cockpit," he said. "Get out of your armor now."

Scott took a deep breath and let it out slowly. The second he stepped out of the Mark VI, he'd be defenseless.

Then again, they could have killed him by now if they'd wanted him dead. And if he wanted to accomplish his mission, what other choice did he have?

Unfortunately, as he knew all too well, there *was* another

choice. It was a choice of last resort, a sacrifice play...but maybe the time to use it had already come.

"I said *open up*." Cairn's voice was louder this time, followed by a knock on the cockpit cowling. "Unless you *want* us to kill your *grandma*."

Another deep breath; another slow release. With each passing second, it became more obvious to Scott that the time for last resorts was upon him.

Raising his left arm, he gazed at the remote control device on his wrist. The ultimate weapon, the quantum bomb in Cairn's head, was still within reach. According to Dr. Beauchamp, it might be powerful enough to destroy a fleet of ships. If that was the case, perhaps it was powerful enough to destroy Bellerophon Station, too.

In one fell swoop, he could take out the Project Lethe control center and save the Commonwealth. He'd be sacrificing himself and Bern in the bargain (and Donna, too), but the price would be worth it.

Wouldn't it?

"Last warning!" said Cairn. "Get out or Commandant Chalice dies!"

Someone pounded on the cockpit three times, then stopped. Then pounded three more times, more insistently.

And three more times after that.

Scott knew what he had to do. Lowering his arm, he tapped a sequence on the left keypad, then another on the right.

The cockpit seal hissed open, and the canopy raised on its hydraulic struts. The cold, metallic air of the chamber rushed in and washed over him.

Cairn, still in the black shell of the CORE Battlenaut, stared down at him. "All the way out. You heard me."

Scott unbuckled the safety harness on the couch and sat up, then drew his legs in and got to his feet. Bracing himself on the sides of the cockpit, he boosted himself up to sit on the edge and look around.

The three Red Battlenauts surrounded him, keeping their guns fixed on his position. Cairn's civilian unit stood next to the Mark VI's right shoulder, looking menacing in spite of its lack of weapons.

"Get away from there," barked Cairn. "You're finished as a Battlenaut jockey."

Scott felt an icy chill cut through him as he hung on the brink of his sacrifice play, hand hovering near the device on his wrist. This could be his only chance to save the Commonwealth, and he knew it. The Reds would never let him hold on to the remote control.

On the other hand, triggering the bomb would kill Bern and Donna. While they were all still alive, he had hope that he could save them...but the bomb would end all that. What if there was another way out, a wild card waiting to present itself if only he survived a little longer?

"Come on!" said Cairn. "Quit pissing around!"

All three Reds took a step toward him at once, guns gleaming.

What would Bern do? That was always the question Scott asked himself, the standard he lived by. And as he thought of it, he knew without hesitation exactly what the answer was, exactly what Bern would do.

And he knew he couldn't bring himself to do it. He couldn't kill her while there was still a chance he might find another solution.

Swinging his legs out of the cockpit, he climbed down the side of his Battlenaut and planted his feet on the floor.

Even then, there was still time to blow it all to kingdom come, and he reconsidered.

Bern would *want* to die; she'd do it in a heartbeat to save the Commonwealth. Donna would gladly do the same, if he asked her. No doubt in his mind about either of them.

Then there was Cairn. Scott knew he'd want to die, too, he'd have no qualms...but for different reasons than the others. He'd tried to kill himself sooner, for lower stakes, and why?

Because he'd rather be dead than alive. Because his life had been a horror show, and he wanted out. Because Scott had failed to save him before, in Iridess Chasm.

And now, Scott was thinking about giving up on him again. Giving up on him and Bern and Donna all at once, to save the Commonwealth.

Again, Scott came around to the same decision. It went against everything he believed, every oath he'd taken as a Marine, every battle he'd fought. Again and again, he'd thrown his own life on the line to protect the Commonwealth and its interests...but throwing down the lives of those he loved was another matter. So was throwing down the life of someone he owed a debt to, even if he'd never intentionally let him down. It wasn't as cut and dried as it had always seemed before, in the line of action as a Marine.

But he wasn't a Marine anymore, was he? He'd resigned from the Marine Corps when he'd fled the *Sun Tzu* against Perseid's orders. So the oaths and the life-and-death choices they spawned didn't seem quite so hard and fast at the moment.

What mattered most to him? The people he cared about...even the one who couldn't seem to accept it. Maybe, there would still be a way to save the Commonwealth without sacrificing all of them in the bargain.

"Okay then." Scott lowered his hand from the remote control and stepped away from the Mark VI. "What's next?"

Cairn stared down at him in silence for a long moment, as if he were waiting for something. Almost as if he'd expected him to set off the bomb.

When he spoke, he sounded less forceful than before. "Hand it over," he said, reaching out one Battlenaut gauntlet. "Give me the remote."

Scott loosened the wristband. "You won't be able to use it, you know. And it'll keep blocking you from using thought activation."

"Just give it to me." Cairn pushed the gauntlet closer. "We're not taking any chances that you'll set it off."

"I haven't yet, have I?" Scott pulled off the device and dropped it in Cairn's gauntlet. "Even though I *could* have."

"You probably *should* have. You won't get another chance." Cairn raised the gauntlet and tipped his Battlenaut's head down to stare at the remote control. "So why didn't you?"

"The truth? I couldn't bring myself to blow up a friend." Scott shrugged. "Even after he betrayed me."

Cairn stared at the remote a moment longer, then clenched it in his fist. "Get moving!" He raised his other hand to point at a gate on the far side of the chamber. "That way!"

As Scott started walking, he could feel the Reds' guns following his every step, keeping him locked in the crosshairs. "Sure. Where to?"

"Behind the curtain," said Cairn. "Where you'll finally find all the answers you've been searching for."

CHAPTER 40

Cairn and the Reds marched Scott down a dimly lit gray corridor ending in big double doors. Scott stood there a moment, staring at his reflection in the doors' silver surface... and then they slid open, shooting into the frame on either side.

For a moment, Scott stood there on the brink, taking in what he could see of the room on the other side. Even from the doorway, it looked vast.

"Go ahead." Cairn nudged Scott's back with the touch of a gauntlet's finger. "They're waiting for you."

"Keep your shirt on." Scott stepped through the doorway and found himself on a ledge without any railing, gazing into a cavernous chamber.

Instantly, he realized that he'd entered a nerve center of enormous proportions, a giant cylinder big enough to hold three ships the size of the *Sun Bin* laid end to end to end. Every wall was lined with instrumentation--control panels, monitors, gauges, scopes, and more--all tended by red-uniformed men and women floating in antigrav harnesses.

They weren't the only airborne figures in the chamber, though. A massive antenna array rotated in the middle of the place, running the length of the room from end to end. The array bristled with a filigree of silver branches twined and twisted around a pearlescent central shaft--all of it glowing with pulsing crimson energy.

From where Scott stood, on a ledge that circled the perimeter midway between floor and ceiling, the chamber spread out like a chasm ready to swallow him up. It looked the way the nerve center of a cosmic conspiracy ought to look, and sounded like one, too--constantly roaring with voices, the rattling hum of the giant array, the beeping/pinging/buzzing of equipment, and the cacophony of weapons fire from distant battles playing on video feeds, blaring through speakers.

"Pretty impressive, huh?" said Cairn, stomping up behind him on the ledge. "Welcome to Apocalypse Central."

Scott shrugged. "It's okay, I guess."

Cairn stepped up beside him and swept the arm of his Battlenaut around to encompass the vast chamber. "As you can see, the action's already underway. You never had a chance of stopping it."

"Actually, I think I did," said Scott. "Until you turned against me, that is."

Cairn let his arms fall at his sides. "It was for your own good, Sol. You'll thank me later."

"If you say so," said Scott.

They stood there silently for a moment before Cairn spoke again. "Why didn't you do it?" His voice was quieter than before. "Why didn't you trigger the bomb when you still had the chance?"

"Honestly?" Scott looked up at him. "Because as much as it *galls* me, I still *give* a flux about you." He shook his head and laughed. "Isn't that something? I kept thinking there had to be another way to stop this without blowing you up... especially after everything you've been through in your life."

Cairn didn't say anything for a moment. Then, he snorted. "Why don't you just admit the *real* reason you didn't do it? You didn't want to take the chance the explosion would kill Donna or Grandma...or *yourself*."

"You're only partly right," said Scott. "I'm expendable. I'll throw down my life as needed for the greater good. But I didn't want to kill the people I care about if I could help it." He shrugged. "That includes you."

Cairn laughed. "What a load of hoozehock."

"You're wrong." Scott shook his head and scuffed his toe on the ledge. "I've told you the truth."

Just then, one of the Red Battlenauts stepped up and pointed its guns squarely at Scott. "Move back from the edge!" snapped the pilot.

"Why?" said Scott. "Afraid I'll jump?"

The Red stepped closer, crowding him and Cairn. "I said *move back*. Do it *now*!"

"Jeez!" Scott backed up two steps. "Would it kill you to say *please* once in a while?"

"Cut it out, Sol," said Cairn, moving back with him. "Don't make this any worse for yourself."

Suddenly, Scott understood why the Red had told him to move. An antigrav platform shot up from below, loaded with armed men in red uniforms--two dozen of them, standing in a tight circle around the edge.

Like an elevator, the platform stopped climbing when

its deck met the ledge. All at once, the Red soldiers swung up their weapons and aimed them at Scott.

Just as Scott was wondering what he should do next, the men parted in the middle, opening a gap for someone to walk through. At first, Scott thought the gap was meant for him, that the men had come to take him away.

Then, he glimpsed movement behind the men and realized that someone was walking out through the gap instead.

Involuntarily, Scott held his breath. Whoever was back there, protected by all those armed guards, it couldn't be good news for him.

Or could it?

As Scott watched, a figure emerged from between the guards--and the breath he'd been holding rushed out of him in a sudden cry.

It was *her*. She was *alive* and apparently *unhurt*. And all he could think to do was run over and wrap his arms around her, if not for all the guns aimed point blank at him.

Then he decided that the guns didn't matter. Just as her feet stepped onto the ledge, he charged over and wrapped her in a hug.

"Thank God!" he said. "I was so *worried* about you!"

"Well, there's nothing to worry about anymore," said Grandma Bern, eyes twinkling as she beamed at him. "Everything's going to be all right from now on, I promise."

Scott broke the hug. "I'm so glad you're all right. I didn't know if I'd ever *see* you again."

"Well, *I* never had any doubts." Bern patted his back. "After all, you're *my* grandson, aren't you? You can do *anything*."

"So they haven't *hurt* you?" asked Scott.

"Not a bit, Solly," said Bern. "I'm perfectly fine."

Scott hugged her again and whispered into her ear. "Don't worry. I'm going to get you out of here."

"That's very sweet," she whispered back. "But I don't think we can leave right now." Leaning back, she smiled sadly and patted his cheek. "The head of this operation has other plans in store, apparently."

Scott frowned. "The head? Who's that?"

"Someone you know quite well, actually," said Bern.

Just then, a flicker of movement from the antigrav platform caught Scott's eye. Someone else was walking out from behind the Red troops.

Someone Scott knew quite well indeed.

He froze, gaping in horrified amazement at the new arrival. It wasn't possible, was it? After so many years, how could it be?

Yet there he was. Older and grayer, yet oh so familiar. Thin as a reed, as a weed in a pale blue jumpsuit, with a stretched-out face like a mashed banana, like a painting that had run in the rain. The mouth with a life of its own, his most striking feature, with teeth like tombstones with names etched into them and lips that had been tattooed black. It was a visage that Scott could never ever forget, no matter how hard he tried.

And the voice, when he spoke, was familiar, too--big and deep and friendly. "What have we here? A *family reunion*?"

Thirteen years fell away in a heartbeat. At the sight of that man, Scott felt like a child again, like a thirteen-year-old boy being dragged into Iridess Chasm.

A thirteen-year-old boy being dragged by that man walking toward him.

"My, how you've *grown*." said the man, lips spreading in

a lecherous grin that the years hadn't dimmed.

Scott didn't answer. He just stood there, dumbfounded, as Cairn did the heavy lifting and said the name so Scott wouldn't have to.

"Mr. Vore," said Cairn. "I followed your orders, sir. I'm ready for my next assignment."

CHAPTER 41

Larvis Vore, the man who'd abducted Scott and Cairn thirteen years ago on Tack, spread his arms wide. "Your next assignment? Get out of that damn *armor* and get over here for a nice group *hug* with Scotty and Uncle Larvis."

As Vore kept coming toward him, Scott backed away. His mind raced as he tried to make sense of what was happening. "What's he *doing* here?" he shouted at Cairn.

But Cairn didn't answer. He just stood there in his civilian armor and hung his head.

Meanwhile, Vore grinned at Scott. "Hey there, buddy." Vore said it with exaggerated sweetness in his rumbling bass voice. "Who's my favorite little boy in the whole, wild world?"

Scott felt like he was trapped in a nightmare. He shook his head hard, trying to clear it, but couldn't.

"Isn't this cool, you guys?" Vore bobbed his head at Scott, then Cairn. "The three musketeers, together again on this historic occasion?"

Scott ignored him and shouted at Cairn. "This can't be right!" How could it? How could Larvis Vore, the perverted child abductor and parent killer, have ended up *here*, in the heart of a conspiracy to reshape the quadrant? "He can't *possibly* be the *head* of all this!"

Still, Cairn was silent.

But Bern was not. "Because he *isn't*. The only thing he's the *head* of..." She pointed a finger at Cairn. "...is *him*."

Scott frowned. "I don't understand."

Bern was frowning, too. "He's Cairn's *handler*."

"*Owner* would be more accurate." Vore's grin became a sneer.

"But I thought..." Scott stared up at Cairn's Battlenaut. "I thought you got *away* from him."

Cairn's voice, as he finally spoke, was somber. "I never said I escaped."

"Oh my God," said Scott. "All this *time*? You've been with him all this *time*?"

"Remember when you asked me how long I was with him after Penitent Peak?" Cairn sighed. "I said 'forever,' and I meant it."

Scott took more steps back, then bumped into the leg of a Red Battlenaut and stopped. "He *owns* you? What the hell does that even *mean*?"

"It means he's my *slave*," snapped Vore, patting his bony chest through the pale blue jumpsuit. "Just like *you* would have been, if he hadn't *saved* your ass."

"He pushed you off Penitent Peak," said Scott. "I thought you were both dead."

Vore laughed. "He saved your ass more times than *that*. I had a *jones* for you, boy. But every time I tried to grab you *up*, he somehow got in the way." Looking up at Cairn's Battlenaut, he winked one sunken eye. "You jealous thing, you."

"Jealousy had nothing to do with it," said Cairn.

"But now that we're all together," said Vore, "and *everyone* is getting a fresh start, I don't see why we can't *join forces* the way we were *meant* to. Three is *never* a crowd in *my* world."

"Enough of this!" said Bern. "You *know* he's *off limits*."

"But things are changing." Vore gestured at the cavernous command center spread out before him. "No need to stick to the old rules, is there?"

Bern shook a finger at him. "You're *not* in charge here, scum."

"Then who is?" asked Scott. "Who *is* the head of this operation?"

Vore's eyes widened with delight. "You mean to tell me you don't *know*?" He let out a belly-laugh. "Oh, that is just too *rich*."

Scott's frown deepened. "Why? What's going on?"

"No wonder you still think there's *hope*!" Vore said through his laughter. "No wonder you still think you can pull this off!"

Anger replaced shock as Scott stormed toward him. "What's *that* supposed to mean?"

Suddenly, Cairn stepped in front of him. "It's her." He pointed one Battlenaut finger at Bern. "She's the head of all this."

Scott felt a wave of intense cold rush through him. It couldn't be right, there wasn't a chance of it. His beloved Bern, the solid rock of his life, could never be responsible for this. Cairn's accusation was just a trick designed to come between them.

"Flux you," he told Cairn. "You're full of plang."

"I'm sorry," said Cairn. "But it's true."

"Never," said Scott. "Never in a million years."

But when he said it, he looked her way. Full of rage and defiance and absolute denial, he met Bern's gaze, expecting to see equally strong defiance and denial in her eyes.

And he didn't see it.

In a look, in a flash, he felt everything inside him go up in smoke. He was instantly hollowed out, left with just a shell, an echo of the person he'd been a moment ago. And then, when her gaze hardened, became something he'd never seen before, he lost that, too.

There were no words for it. He just stood there and stared at her, mesmerized, unconscious of anything or anyone else around him.

His feet were on the ledge, but he felt like he was drifting, rolling, spinning--as if gravity had no hold on him anymore. As if nothing could fix him in place now that his link to the rational universe had been broken.

She kept staring back at him. "It's true," she said, but how could that possibly be her? His Bern would never say that. "I'm in charge here."

Her voice seemed to come from a hundred light years away. Her words sounded like a foreign language he could barely understand.

Was he standing or sitting? Awake or asleep? Dead or alive? He couldn't tell anymore.

She reached out, and he backed away. Somewhere, in another universe, Vore was laughing his ass off. Commonwealth ships and Battlenauts were shooting the hell out of each other on dozens of video screens.

It was then he came to a realization: the world wasn't in

the process of ending, as he'd feared.

For him, it was already over.

CHAPTER 42

"Solly, wait," said Grandma Bern. "Hear me out."

Scott closed his eyes and put his hands over his ears. Maybe, if he tried hard enough to make the nightmare go away, things would go back to the way they'd once been. Maybe, he could go back to having a grandma who wasn't trying to bring down the Commonwealth.

But that kind of happy ending was out of his reach. After a moment, he felt someone grabbing his wrists. When he opened his eyes, he saw that Bern was the one who was holding on, straining to wrench his hands from his ears.

"Listen to me, please!" Her voice was muffled but still made it through his hands. "In the name of everything we've *meant* to each other through the years, please let me *explain*."

Scott let up the pressure on his ears and slowly lowered his hands. He didn't want to hear what she had to say, didn't want her image to be tarnished any further--but he had a change of heart brought on by a feeling that was new to him.

He was *afraid* of her. Afraid of what she might do if he didn't play along.

"Thank you." She nodded grimly. "I know this is hard for you, but thank you for giving me a chance."

Scott didn't think he had a choice in the matter. He was completely unarmed and alone in a den of wolves. Glancing around, he saw that the Red Battlenauts and troops still had their weapons locked on him. Larvis Vore still stood nearby, practically licking his black-lipped chops as he stared at him. Then there was Cairn, who'd spit on his attempts at friendship and betrayed him.

Scott was hollowed-out, shocked, friendless, and trapped. He hated to think what might happen if he refused Bern anything she asked for.

So he listened.

"In the message I left you," said Bern, "I told you that because of Project Lethe, every man, woman, and child has been secretly injected with a virus that diminishes the impact of violent memories. As a result, war has become more commonplace."

Scott nodded.

"I'm afraid that was an understatement," said Bern. "Over the past five years, the number of conflicts within the Commonwealth has grown exponentially. There are so many hot spots cropping up every day, we have trouble tracking them all. And *most* aren't even related to the Civil War."

Bern shook her head gravely. "The theory is, generations of inoculation and mutation have made the virus more potent, amplifying its effects on humanity. We have become a species of war-mongers, always spoiling for a fight.

"This has fueled the rising tide of conflicts and put us on the road to destruction. If the number of conflicts continues to spread at the present rate, it will soon reach critical mass. The Commonwealth will be engulfed by a wave of warfare the likes of which humanity has never before experienced.

"The end result is inevitable. The fall of civilization as we know it within one year. The annihilation of all human life within one year after that. Absolute doomsday.

"Unless we take drastic measures." Bern gestured at the vast command center behind her. "Unless we *burn it out* first."

Scott stared at her and tried not to look horrified. Was she actually *saying* what he *thought* she was? It didn't seem possible.

But the more she said, the more her conviction became clear to him. "My team and I worked through endless simulations, considered endless scenarios." Bern nodded firmly. "*This* was the only one that stood a chance of success." She gestured at the command center again.

"A *controlled burn* can be used to contain a forest fire," she said. "Destroy the fuel around the fire, and it will burn itself out. It will have nowhere else to go.

"The same principle applies here. Destroy enough fuel--enough military assets and resources--and the wars will stop spreading. They will burn themselves out.

"To that end, our scientists developed a catalyst virus, quantum-entangled with the Lethe virus. The catalyst virus has a two-pronged effect on those infected with Lethe: it makes catalyst-coated personnel, equipment, and facilities invisible to them, and it enables us to plant sensory input in their minds. It lets us make allies see each other as enemies.

"That's where this transmitter comes in." She gestured at the giant array spanning the length of the command center. "We developed it in the facility you destroyed on

Shard. The special properties of the biometal found there amplify the signal from the catalyst virus, extending it far beyond its normal range. With this transmitter, we are able to boost the signal across the entirety of the Commonwealth and Rightful space, activating Lethe in every human mind--and setting everyone at each other's throats.

"When it's all over, the Commonwealth and Rightful worlds will be shattered. The surviving population will turn inward, spending the next century or two rebuilding...and ridding themselves of the virus. New inoculations will stop, and without them, we project that humankind will develop an immunity to the virus within three to five generations.

"When we rise up out of the ashes, we will be a stronger and more peace-loving species." Bern smiled. "Instead of extinction, humanity will find salvation. A brighter future instead of no future at all."

With that, she folded her hands at her waist and watched him expectantly. "Do you understand now?" she said. "Do you see why the success of this operation is so critical?"

Everyone on the ledge and antigrav platform was watching Scott. He could feel the pressure of all those eyes bearing down on him at once, making it hard to breathe and harder still to focus.

What should he say? For the first time in his life, he was at a complete loss; for the first time, he couldn't ask himself "What would Bern do?" and instantly come up with an answer that seemed right to him.

His grandmother was talking about killing millions, maybe billions, to create a "controlled burn" that would save humanity from extinction. It was something that felt wrong from the start; it was hard to believe Bern had even come up with the idea.

Or was it? She'd always said how important it was to do what was necessary, no matter the cost. Sacrifice for the greater good was part and parcel of her philosophy, and that of the Marines, as well.

With humanity's very survival at stake, would *any* sacrifice be asking too much? Wouldn't *any* action, no matter how extreme, be justifiable?

Then why did Bern's plan still seem so *wrong* to him? If everything she'd told him was true, he could understand why she'd come up with it. If she thought it was the only chance to prevent extinction, he could see why she was going through with it in spite of the staggering cost.

But understanding Bern's plan and agreeing with it were two different things. And agreeing with it, Scott found, was something he just couldn't do.

It went against too many of the principles he held dear: that killing should be used only as a last resort, and even then should be minimized; that the welfare of civilians must never be ignored, no matter what their allegiance; that it is the responsibility of a just man to resist orders for the commission of unjust acts; and that where there is life, there is hope.

Ironically, these were all things that Bern had taught him through the years. In effect, she had taught him to oppose her.

"Scott?" Bern sounded impatient. "I asked if you see why it's so critical that this operation succeeds."

Instead of answering, Scott asked a question of his own. "So you weren't abducted from Oberon?" His voice sounded small to him, like the voice of a stranger. "You arranged all that?"

Bern nodded gravely. "I needed to make myself look

innocent," she said. "Someone has to step in when the dust settles and begin guiding humanity through the new dark age. I wouldn't be able to do that if my role in this operation was exposed to the population at large."

Scott frowned. "So you ordered the attacks on the *Sam Nicholas* and *Augustus*? To make your capture look convincing?" Just saying it made him feel sick in the stomach.

"It was all for the greater good. I truly believe that." Her eyes darkened and turned downward. "Which isn't to say it was easy. Or that it won't haunt me for the rest of my life." She met his gaze and frowned. "I'd say the same thing about *all* of this. I wouldn't wish this terrible weight on *anyone*."

Scott believed she was telling the truth, that what she'd done had been hard on her...and that made it harder for him to hate her. That made it harder to consider what he knew in his heart would have to be done.

Looking around at the Reds, at Vore, at the mayhem on the screens, Scott wanted to be somewhere, *anywhere* else. He wished he'd never come to Bellerophon, never gotten Bern's message back on the *Sun Tzu*...and then the thought of all that made him realize something. "You *wanted* me here," he said. "The message about Lethe and Bellerophon--you *wanted* me here."

Bern smiled grimly. "Guilty as charged."

Scott shook his head as he did the mental math. "That's why you're working with *him*?" He jabbed a finger at Vore. "With the man who killed my *mother*...your own *daughter*?"

Bern nodded. "I knew, from military intelligence, that he had Cairn. And I knew Cairn would be the perfect bait... first, to distract you--the one person unaffected by Lethe--from interfering with our plan...and then to lure you here when the time was right." She looked at Vore with an expression of distaste. "As sick as it made me to deal with that despicable *scum*, I believed it was necessary to bringing you in without arousing suspicions."

"But *why*?" said Scott. "How many people have you condemned to death? Millions? Billions? Why bother with *one person* like *me*?"

"Because I love you, of course." Bern shrugged. "You're my grandson. How could I *not* try to save you?"

"*Save* me?" Scott turned away from her. "This is *saving*?"

"We have resources here, Solly," said Bern. "A *refuge* from the madness. And no one will think to *look* for us here. You can *survive*."

"Who *gives* a flux?" Scott spun back around to glare at her. "Who cares about *survival* when everything else is *ruined*?"

Bern looked disappointed. "I know this is hard for you, Solly. But I promise, you'll feel better once you get used to the idea."

"You want me to feel better?" Scott stormed to the rim of the ledge and jabbed a finger at the giant array down below. "Then switch off that transmitter. The one you're using to signal all the virus-infected human *minds* out there. Switch it off *now*."

Bern sighed. "We can't do that."

"Can't?" said Scott. "Or won't?"

"It would disrupt the entire process," said Bern. "It would throw all our projections out the window."

"That's better than throwing billions of *lives* away, isn't it?" Scott stepped toward her. "Or don't you *care* about them?"

"It's not that *simple*. I'm only doing what I *have* to for the greater good."

"So all those billions of people out there." Scott raised his hands, palms up, toward the ceiling, toward space. "You think they'd *thank* you for this? You think they'd *approve* of what you're doing?"

"Once I explained the reason for it..."

"They *still* wouldn't thank you!" Scott took two more steps toward her, coming close enough that two Red guards got nervous and jumped between them. "I'll tell you *exactly* what they'd say if they were standing here *right now*, Grandma. They'd say, '*Switch it off!*'"

Bern stared at him for a long moment, her eyes filled with sadness...and then they suddenly hardened. Whatever love and mercy she harbored for him, she pushed them down deep and brought out a steel he'd rarely seen there before.

"Take him." As soon as she said it, the guards slung their rifles over their backs and grabbed Scott's arms. "Put him away somewhere until this is all over."

"No!" Scott struggled against the guards, but their grips were iron. "You've got to *stop* this!"

Bern turned her back on him.

"Do you *want* to become the greatest *mass murderer* in history?" said Scott. "The biggest *monster* who ever lived?"

Without warning, Bern whipped around and charged at him. "How *dare* you!" Hauling back her hand, she slapped him hard across the face.

And in that moment, Scott's heart sank without a trace.

It had been bad enough seeing what she'd done, hearing her explain it--realizing how far over the edge she'd gone. But that blow had sealed the deal. She'd never hit him before, had rarely even raised her voice to him...and now, she'd let him have it with all the force of anger she could muster.

There was no coming back from something like that. The Bern he'd known and loved was gone forever.

So was the galaxy he'd known, the Commonwealth he'd sworn to protect. He was helpless, without weapon or friend, and the final battle was already well underway.

There was no coming back from any of it.

The rage that had filled him drained away. He slumped in the grip of the guards, surrendering to utter desolation.

All was lost. For the first time in his life, he wished without reservation that he were dead.

Then, suddenly, he heard stomping and a rustle of movement. As he turned toward it, his eyes shot wide with surprise. What he saw there was so totally unexpected, he had to wonder if he was hallucinating.

Cairn, still inside the CORE Battlenaut, was standing at the edge, dangling someone over the chasm...someone scrawny as a scarecrow threaded with bone, held aloft by one arm.

Vore. It was *Vore.*

Cairn was holding Larvis Vore over the chasm of the command center, and it sure looked like he was about to let go of him.

CHAPTER 43

"Did you ever have one of those days?" said Cairn. "One of those days when you've just finally had enough?"

Vore howled with terror as Cairn shook him over the great chasm of the command center.

"Well, *I* have," said Cairn. "Like thirteen *years* ago." He swung Vore back from the edge, then swung him out over the chasm again. "The first time I laid eyes on *this* mother-fluxer."

"Please stop!" Vore's voice wailed in an upper register now, spiking with sheer panic. "Don't *do* this! What about the *good times*?"

"Like when you had the *bomb* put in my head, you mean?" Cairn swung him up, then down. "Like all the times you *used* it to make me do whatever you *wanted*?"

"I would never let you *blow up*! We were meant to be together!" said Vore, and then he howled as Cairn swung him up and down again.

"You know what your biggest *mistake* was, though?" said Cairn. "Hiring me out to the *Reds* to bring in *Solomon Scott*. Using our past connection as your *prisoners* to *screw* with him and get him to come *here*.

"Do you know *why*?" Cairn stopped swinging Vore and held him up to face his Battlenaut's faceplate. "Do you know *why* that was such a big *mistake*?

"Because *he* put the past *behind* him a long *time* ago," said Cairn. "And I *realized* that if *that* sorry sack of plang could do it, then *I* sure as hell could, too."

With that, Cairn extended his arm. Vore thrashed like a snake on a hook, trying in vain to grab hold of something--anything, even Cairn's armor, that would let him hang on to his life a little longer.

But it was hopeless. And then it didn't matter anymore.

"How does a monster say *goodbye*?" said Cairn, misquoting one of Vore's favorite lines. "*Raarrhh!*"

Then, Cairn opened his Battlenaut's hand, and let go.

Screaming, Vore plunged down into the vast space of the command center.

"I guess you were right, Sol." Cairn turned and looked at Scott. "I did the right thing when the time came, didn't I?"

Scott wasn't sure what to say. Cairn *had* done the right thing, but what good would it do? They were still surrounded by heavily armed Reds, and the Apocalypse was still in full swing. The only thing that had changed was that the universe had one less lowlife to drag it down.

And Scott had one more friend to help him face the end. There was something to be said for that, he had to admit.

"Yeah, Cairn." Scott gave him a thumbs-up. "Nice job, man."

Before either of them could say another word, the Red

troops opened fire on Cairn. Those who had a clear shot at him--a dozen, at least--blasted him with slugs from their automatic rifles.

Cairn couldn't shoot back, he had no weapons, but he didn't go down, either. The pumped-up defensive capabilities of his civilian Battlenaut were enough to shrug off the concentrated attack.

Storming into the torrent of firepower, he swept two soldiers off the ledge with one swing of his arm. They flew down into the chasm and hit the array, their bodies dancing in fountains of crimson arcs and sparks over the twisted silver branches.

"Stop him!" shouted Bern. "Stop him now!"

The Red Battlenauts already had Cairn in their crosshairs and opened fire with slugs and lasers. Their guns, much more powerful than the troops', staggered him, driving him back just as he pushed three more men off the ledge.

The flurry of fire came close to Scott, who stood near the middle of the action. For an instant, he let it cascade around him, trying to make sense of the swirling chaos. He felt naked without his armor, beaten by Bern, uncertain what he could possibly do to change anything in the face of insurmountable odds.

In the past, he'd found inspiration by asking himself one question: What would Bern do? But that wouldn't work anymore. Maybe it was time for a *new* question, one that was still relevant in the face of this madness.

Maybe it was finally time to ask, "What would *Solomon Scott* do?"

When he thought about it, the answer was pretty damn obvious.

With a sudden surge of willpower, he shook himself

out of his daze. Whipping around, he charged a Red trooper who didn't see him until it was too late. One broken neck later, he kicked the trooper's body off the ledge and turned with the dead man's rifle in his hands.

And he let it sing.

Red troopers dropped like flies in a cloud of pesticide--one, two, three, four, five. They were all so focused on Cairn that Scott plowed through them unopposed...at first, anyway. Once he took out his seventh man, half the survivors turned on him and cut loose.

Firing behind him as he ran, Scott bolted around one of the Red Battlenauts, using it for cover. The Battlenaut was so involved lighting up Cairn's armor that either it didn't notice, or it didn't care.

Peering out from behind his cover, Scott saw that Cairn was taking some serious heat. The Reds were pounding the civilian Battlenaut with ridiculous amounts of ordnance, making it jump around like a puppet.

To the credit of the CORE engineers, Cairn's Battlenaut was holding together under conditions that would have smashed other Battlenauts like piñatas...but Scott knew it wouldn't last forever. At some point, the focused fire would exceed the armor's every tolerance and turn it into confetti.

Cairn needed help, and fast--but what the hell could Scott do? He had cover, but the troops were blasting away all around him, trying to pick him off every time he bobbed his head out. Two of the bastards were stealing pages from his playbook, using the other two Red Battlenauts as cover in a bid to outflank him.

It was starting to look like he and Cairn would go down in a blaze of glory...which, frankly, didn't bother him that much. Given the circumstances, he could think of worse fates--like spending the rest of his life with Bern-gone-bad as the rest of humanity clawed its way back from oblivion.

Maybe it was even appropriate, when he got right down to it. He and Cairn would come full circle, dying together the way they almost did thirteen years ago.

Leaning out from behind the Battlenaut's leg, Scott cranked off ten more rounds, nailing two more troopers... and then he pulled the trigger again, and nothing happened. Out of ammo.

He ducked back just as a hail of slugs poured his way. His knuckles whitened as he gripped the empty rifle, catching glimpses of Red troops moving in on both his flanks.

Stealing another look outside his cover, he saw Cairn's Battlenaut jittering madly in the maelstrom. He watched just long enough to see Cairn fall to one knee under the onslaught, going down slow.

Clenching his teeth, Scott got ready for what was left of his life. All he had to do was pick a direction and charge like a lunatic into the fire...push past the pain as the slugs punched into him and keep going. Take as many of the Reds down as he could with his rifle butt and bare hands. Do it in the name of Captain Rollins and the men and women of the *Sam Nicholas* and *Augustus* and all the millions and billions who were dying and about to die at the hands of his grandmother.

Die like a *Marine*, like a *Diamondback*, like a *man*. Because *that's* what fucking *Solomon Scott* would do.

Breathing fast, he turned the rifle in his grip, bracing the barrel against his side. *Count to three, just do it, count to three and then go.* He looked right, then left, sizing up the outflankers, trying to pick which one looked weaker.

And then he decided to run forward instead, straight

ahead at the biggest bunch of them. Because he had more possible kills that way, a bigger bang in the making...and anyway, why the hell *not*?

Closing his eyes, Scott took a deep breath, then let it out and had another. Not far away, he heard Cairn cry out from his battered Battlenaut. It wouldn't be long now until the end of it for him, too.

Scott opened his eyes and grinned like the world's biggest son of a bitch. Swinging the rifle butt in front of him, he stepped out from behind the Red Battlenaut.

Just as a missile hammered into the Red from behind and exploded.

Stunned by the blast, Scott stumbled but didn't fall. As debris showered around him, he looked back along the missile's path, hunting its source. When he saw it through the smoke, his son-of-a-bitch grin came back bigger than ever.

The towering figure was plated in blue and silver armor. Light flared from its shoulder-mounted launchers as they sent two more missiles streaking toward the Red Battlenaut.

Scott couldn't stop grinning as he ran toward it, away from the incoming missiles. Nothing had ever looked more welcoming to him than that oh-so-familiar war machine, that beautiful engine of destruction.

The Mark VI.

CHAPTER 44

The Red Battlenaut exploded behind Scott as the second and third missiles from the Mark VI slammed into it. The shockwave from the blast nearly knocked him off his feet, but somehow he kept running toward his armor.

His heart thundered as he raced up and banged his fists on one leg. He could think of only one person who could possibly be piloting the Battlenaut, and he badly needed to hear her voice.

"Donna!" He kept pounding his fists as he yelled up at the gleaming giant. "Donna, is that you?"

He was rewarded with the sound of her voice over the Battlenaut's speakers. "Yes and no."

The sound of gunfire distracted Scott. Looking back, he saw the Red troopers regrouping and popping off potshots in his direction. "What's that supposed to mean?"

"It *is* me." As she said it, the Mark VI lowered itself to its knees. The canopy slid open, revealing an empty cockpit.

"But I'm not inside the unit. You didn't *know* Fong tricked this baby out with *remote control*, didja?"

The shots from the troopers were getting closer. "I do *now*!" One nearly chipped off his earlobe, and he started scrambling up the hull toward the cockpit. "Mind if I take her for a spin?"

"Just don't scratch the paint job," said Donna.

Scott slid down into the cockpit and closed the canopy. "I love you, honey!"

"Oh my God!" said Donna. "That's the first time you've ever *said* that!"

"I was talking to the *Mark VI*, actually," said Scott.

"Solomon!"

"But what the hell." Scott strapped himself in, pulled on his helmet, and played the keypads, prepping his weapons. "As long as you don't mind *sharing*, we can work something out."

"Less talking, more fighting!" snapped Donna, and then she closed the comm channel with attitude.

"You read my mind," said Scott, just as he unleashed a storm of slugs and lasers at the Red troopers.

The men didn't stand a chance against the Battlenaut. Scott's barrage mowed them down in a flurry of flesh and blood, leaving a jumble of bodies and abandoned rifles.

Then, without hesitation, he swung around to see if he was too late to help Cairn.

At first, the massive Red Battlenauts blocked his view--but telemetry told him the CORE unit was still powered up and Cairn was still alive. For the moment, that was all he needed to know.

"Buckle up, assholes!" Scott's fingers danced over the keypads, setting up missile strikes. "It's judgment day!"

He jammed home the trigger button on the stick, releasing two missiles. Watching the forward feed, he saw them streak toward one of the Red Battlenauts like the spears of avenging angels, leaving smoky contrails to mark their passage.

They struck within centimeters of each other on the Red's upper back. When the warheads flashed, they erupted with enough force to throw the Red down hard, opening up the view for Scott.

As promised on telemetry, Cairn's Battlenaut was still in one piece...though it was down on its hands and knees, throwing off some wicked sparks. As long as Scott kept up his momentum, it wasn't too late to save Cairn.

Scott launched another missile at the downed Red for good measure, then swung around. The second Red was already throwing shots in his direction, blasting Scott's armor with torrents of slugs...and charging its chest cannons with rippling golden energy.

Scott hit him with sonics, then queued up two more missiles. Worst case scenario, they might not pierce the enemy's frontal shielding, but at least they might jolt the Red enough for Scott to make his next play.

He thumbed the firing button, and the missiles took off. Then, with a guttural battle cry, he punched the stick forward, charging through their contrails toward the Red.

As planned, the missiles rammed into the Red's chest, blowing out the cannons. The Red reeled from the impact, throwing out smoke instead of slugs--and Scott came in like a locomotive, plowing his shoulder into the charred flashpoint where the missiles had hit.

The Red stumbled backward, and Scott kept pushing, driving it past Cairn toward the edge. Firing its remaining guns wildly, the Red blew out hails of slugs and laser beams, rattling and scorching Scott's armor--but not enough to stop him. He kept shoving the Red further back, moving it toward the point of no return.

Near the brink, the Red found leverage and resisted. Scott pulled back enough to interrupt the pressure, breaking the Red's momentum and focus. Then, he thrust forward suddenly with overwhelming force and cast the Red off the ledge, leaning back hard on the stick to keep the Mark VI from falling in after it.

Looking over the edge, he saw the Red crash into the array far below. As the full weight of the Battlenaut hit, the array exploded--a huge blast at the impact site, then a chain of blasts, one after another, along the whole length of it. With each new roar and flash and shockwave, blazing silver shrapnel filled the air, broken bits of the array's shattered branches punching through control panels, monitors, and human bodies.

Scott smiled inside the Mark VI. He was pretty sure he'd just stopped Armageddon. Without signals from the array, the hallucinations turning allies against each other would surely stop. Even if he accomplished nothing else, at least he'd done that much.

Suddenly, he heard a shout from Cairn: "Incoming! Move!"

Scott jerked the stick back, and the Mark VI lurched to one side--not a second too soon. Just as he got out of the way, searing twin bolts of golden energy poured past, less than a meter from cooking him in his shell.

Checking the rightside feed, he saw the surviving Red Battlenaut, the one he'd knocked down with his first missile attack, back on its feet, aiming its energy cannons in his direction. The first shot wouldn't be its last; he could see a fresh charge building in the cannon apertures, getting ready to break free.

There was barely time to leap out of the line of fire, let alone crank off two missiles...but he did both. The latest energy bolts lanced through the air where he'd just been standing, then cut out as one of the missiles exploded against the Red's left knee.

The Red teetered, unsteady, and limped around to retarget Scott's Battlenaut. Scott sent in another missile, followed by a punishing barrage of slugs focused on the Red's damaged knee--but it still wasn't enough. The Red built a new charge in the cannons, kept them locked on the Mark VI, ready to belch out tongues of killer force...

...and then Cairn's CORE Battlenaut charged in and threw all its weight against that knee. The Red Battlenaut's leg buckled, and the whole unit toppled. On the way down, the cannons fired out of control, stabbing the far wall and ceiling with blistering beams.

Switching on the comm, Scott quickly tuned it to Cairn's frequency. "Thanks for the save!"

"Yeah, yeah." Cairn was breathing hard, his voice was strained, but he still managed to pull off a smartass tone. "That and ten credits'll buy me a cup of coffee."

Checking the feeds on his visor, Scott saw that for once, no new opponents were storming out of the woodwork. "Finally." He blew out his breath. "They've stopped coming."

"Too busy fighting fires and digging out from under the wreckage, I'll bet," said Cairn. "You've sure made a mess of this joint, Sol."

"*We* did." Just then, a flicker of movement on the

leftside feed caught Scott's eye. Playing the left keypad, he threw the feed on maximum mag--and identified the source.

It was Bern, picking her way through the corpses of the troopers. She was carrying a rifle that must have come from one of the dead men, heading in the direction of the exit.

As if he was actually going to let her get away.

"Hey!" Scott stomped toward her, lobbing out scattered warning shots. "Stop right there!"

When she kept moving--speeded up in fact--he brought the warning shots in tighter. Still, she kept moving, so he tagged her with the sonics on their lowest possible setting. It wasn't enough to do permanent damage, but it finally stopped her flight, making her stumble and cry out from the bombardment of concentrated sound waves.

Unfortunately, she didn't drop the gun. After a moment of disorientation, she swung it up and whirled to face Scott, pointing the barrel at the Mark VI.

Scott, on the other hand, lowered all his weapons. "Seriously? This is what it's *come* to?"

Bern kept the rifle rock-steady, sighted in on Scott's armor as if it could do even the slightest bit of damage to it. "You've just doomed *everyone*. You *know* that, don't you?"

"I think there must be a better way to *save* them than *slaughtering* them," said Scott.

"*Zero hope*," said Bern. "That's what you've *left* us. That's what you've left *everyone*. *Zero*! *Hope*!"

"We'll see," said Scott. "Maybe, when people know more about the situation, when they're aware of the danger, they'll be able to fight it."

Bern shook her head. "The Lethe virus is too powerful. Might as well try to fight God Himself."

"I'm feeling pretty froggy." As Scott said it, a series of

explosions rang out through the command center. "Maybe I'll take a leap."

"*Shame* on you," said Bern. "I wish I'd never *brought* you here."

"You and me both," said Scott. "Because then, I'd never have known the *truth* about what you tried to do."

Bern kept the gun aimed at him a moment longer, then slowly lowered it. "Someday, you'll understand. You'll look back on this day and curse yourself for stopping what I tried to do."

"I'm thinking it'll be the other way around," said Scott. "*You'll* be cursing *yourself*."

"Never."

"Really?" said Scott. "Then you *don't* care about humanity? You won't keep trying to stave off extinction?"

"I already took my best shot," said Bern. "The *only* shot."

"The Bern *I* used to know?" said Scott. "She wouldn't give up just because Plan A went down the toilet."

"Maybe you didn't know her as well as you *thought* you did."

"She made me the man I am today," said Scott. "Maybe that's how you can get in touch with who she *really* was. When in doubt, ask yourself what *I* would do...because I learned it all from *her*."

Bern fell silent. Tossing the gun aside, she walked to the edge and gazed down at the ruined command center.

Scott stomped up beside her and shared the view. On the monitor screens that hadn't been smashed, he saw no battles in progress--just ships floating in space and Battlenauts standing idle on planets' surfaces. Now that the array had stopped transmitting, and everyone saw each other for who they really were, the shooting and bombing and killing were over.

Would the situation stay that way when the current crisis passed? Not according to Bern. If her projections held true, it wouldn't be long until the Lethe virus ramped up the violence on its own, driving humankind into an intra-species war that would only end with complete annihilation.

But that was a problem for tomorrow. Today's struggle was done, leaving chaos, casualties, and unfinished business galore...but, also, at least for the moment, a kind of peace.

And absolute certainty in Scott's heart that he had done the right thing.

Switching on the comm, he opened a channel. "Care to help me rescue survivors?"

Cairn yawned. "Got nothing better to do at the moment. What about Granny Genocide?"

Scott played the comm over his speakers so Bern could hear him. "She's going to give us a hand, aren't you? Getting survivors to safety?"

Bern took one last look at the ruins and turned away. Scott saw her on his frontside feed, nodding defeatedly.

"That's great." Scott muted the speakers, hung up on Cairn, and opened a different channel. "Hey, Donna?"

Her sweet voice popped up instantly, clear as a chiming bell. "Yes, my love?"

Scott grinned. So what if the cat was out of the bag about how he felt? They hadn't exactly rushed things, had they? "Could you place a call for me? Could you get in touch with Command?"

"You know I can." Her voice was so melodic, she could have just as well been saying "I love you."

"Tell 'em to get some folks out here ASAP," said Scott.

"They've got their work cut out for them."

"Will do, Solomon."

"Oh, and Donna?" Scott smirked. "Tell them I asked for one ship in particular. You know the one."

Donna laughed. "The *Sun Tzu*, Solomon?"

"Got *that* right," said Scott. "And if Major Perseid doesn't like it?"

"He can go flux himself," said Donna.

"Damn skippy," said Scott, and then he snapped the channel shut like he was slamming a door.

CHAPTER 45

Four weeks later...

Scott marched down a dimly lit corridor with an M.P. at either shoulder, heading for the door at the end. He couldn't wait to walk through it and soak up the fresh air and freedom.

He hadn't had much of either one lately. After returning from Bellerophon Station, he'd gone straight into a detention center on Archibald--not exactly a prisoner, but not really a free man, either. The events of Redmageddon (that was what the media were calling it) had been so devastating and struck so deep into the Commonwealth's heart that Command had demanded interrogation of all the central figures.

Scott was about as central as they came, so he'd gotten the full treatment. For four weeks, he'd undergone a steady regimen of intense debriefings, questioning under truth serum, lie detection tests, and intimidation. The interrogators had come at him from every possible angle, stopping short of torture but just barely. The whole time, he'd never changed his story one iota. He'd clung to the truth like a shipwrecked mariner to a floating plank, and he'd ridden out the storm.

Now, finally, they seemed to be done with him. His release had come through, and he could get on with his life... whatever the hell it was going to be.

The M.P.s marched him to the end of the hall, and the one on the left smacked his hand against a glass panel on the wall. A bar of white light behind the panel flashed from top to bottom, then went dark. A loud buzzer rang out, and Scott heard the sound of heavy lock bolts unlatching.

Then, as he watched, the door slowly opened. Sunlight streamed in, making him squint--but he never looked away. He'd imagined this moment over and over for the past four weeks and had no intention of missing a bit of it.

When the door was all the way open, the M.P. at his right gestured for him to go. "Whenever you're ready."

Scott nodded. "Okay." Heart pounding, he walked through the doorway with steady, measured steps.

He stopped on the other side, blinking as he adjusted to the brightness. A light breeze flowed over him, sweet with the fragrance of spring flowers, and he breathed deeply.

He was standing on a paved lot with walls on two sides and lush greenery up ahead. Thirty meters away, where the two walls ended, leafy green trees and long-stemmed pink and white flowers swayed in the breeze, beckoning him. It was the best thing he'd seen in four weeks.

At least until Donna darted around the corner.

The door slammed shut behind him, and he ran toward her. It was the first time he'd seen her since entering the detention center. She'd been interred and questioned there, too, though the interrogators had always kept them apart.

That had only made him think of her all the more. Knowing she was in the same facility but kept from seeing him had driven him crazy; he'd never longed for someone so intensely in his entire life.

Now, finally, there she was, leaping into his arms.

"Solomon!" She kissed him passionately, clutching at his face and shoulders.

He kissed her back with all that passion and more. His fingers roamed like wild animals over her back and through her blonde hair, which had started growing out in detention. They strained together like it was the end of the world and this would be the last time they'd ever see each other alive.

Scott lost himself in the blaze of it, gave himself over to the all-consuming fire. It felt even better than he had imagined during all the lonely hours in his cell...like something out of a perfect, impossible dream.

When the first frenzied rush finally faded, Donna leaned back and beamed at him. "Oh my God, Solomon! I missed you so *much*!"

"I missed you, too." It was the biggest understatement he'd ever made. "I couldn't stop thinking about you." He went in for another lingering, ravenous kiss.

Neither of them spoke until Donna pulled away. "Someone else is here to see you, Solomon. They insisted."

Scott frowned. "Who?"

Her reply was to stick two fingers in her mouth, turn her head, and let out the shrillest whistle ever over her left shoulder.

A moment later, Perseid and Rexis marched around the corner and headed straight for them.

"Corporal Scott!" barked Perseid. "We meet again!"

Donna tried to move away, but Scott wouldn't let her.

Instinct made him want to salute, but he wouldn't let that happen, either. "I'm not a corporal anymore, remember?"

"Really?" Perseid reached for a handshake.

Scott returned it, though he had mixed emotions about seeing him. "I lost my commission, remember? Back when I disobeyed your order not to go to Bellerophon Station?"

Perseid's frown deepened. "I don't remember that."

"You called me a traitor. You said I was finished." Scott bobbed his head at Donna. "You said *her* career was over, too.

"Seriously?" Perseid scowled at Rexis. "Do you remember any of this, Captain?"

Rexis smirked. "Hell no, sir. Not a word of it."

"I guess it didn't happen, then." Perseid shrugged. "So you're ready to report for duty, Corporal Scott? Or do you need a few days' R&R to bounce back from detention?"

Just like that, Scott had a second chance. But he wondered if there was more to it than met the eye. "What's the catch?"

"Nothing happened, right?" said Perseid. "Ipso facto, no catch. You just pick up where you left off."

Scott narrowed his eyes. "You mean I just go right back to my old Marine unit and all is forgiven?"

"No, actually." Rexis shook her head. "You're not going back to your old unit."

"But I thought you said..."

Perseid interrupted. "You're not going back to your old unit because you're a *Diamondback* from now on."

Scott's eyes widened. Perseid's statement totally floored him. Of all the things he'd expected him to say, that hadn't been one of them. "A Diamondback?"

Perseid nodded. "You saved the Commonwealth, didn't

you? And untold billions of lives." Reaching into a hip pocket, he pulled out a silver Diamondback insignia and held it out in the palm of his hand. "I'd say you've earned it, Sergeant Scott."

Sergeant. So there was a promotion in it for him, too... and a pay bump, no doubt. Perseid was pulling out the stops when it came to rewards.

"Oh, and did I mention your *medal*?" Perseid reached into another hip pocket and fished out a gleaming gold medal with a sword and stars inlaid in silver. "The Order of Zedsemene, in recognition of extraordinary valor in the preservation of the Commonwealth and all it stands for."

Donna hugged Scott excitedly. The Order of Zedsemene was a huge deal, the highest honor a Marine could attain. They both knew full well how much it meant.

Why, then, wasn't Scott more excited himself? Why, instead of a rush of pride, did he just feel a wave of anxiety?

"Congratulations, Sergeant." Rexis grinned. "I guess it goes without saying that there'll be a hell of a blowout to celebrate all this."

"Right." Scott grinned back at her, but he wasn't feeling it. For some screwed-up reason, he wasn't feeling it even a little bit.

"Here." Perseid stepped closer and held up the medal. "Let me pin this on you."

Scott surprised even himself when he shot up a hand to stop him. "No."

Perseid looked startled. "Would you rather wait for a formal ceremony? There'll be one of those, too, but I thought you'd like to have this now if you could."

Without a word, Scott held out his hand. Perseid hesitated, then placed the medal in his palm.

As Scott gazed at the gleaming object, he knew he should be thrilled to receive it. It was more than he or any man or woman his age could realistically hope for--and it held the power to shape his future. Without fail, Zedsemene honorees went on to become generals, admirals, senators, even presidents. And commandants, too...just like Bern. She had been a member of the order herself, in fact, though her membership had been revoked when she was thrown into prison.

Was that why the medal and the perks that came with it made him anxious? Was he afraid he might somehow follow in her footsteps and make terrible errors in judgment that led to disaster?

Scott thought about it as he turned the medal over in his hand. It felt wrong, somehow...and the longer he held it, the more wrong it felt.

Was it because he didn't see the outcome at Bellerophon Station as a victory? Because hundreds of thousands of people had still died that day before he'd shut down the array? Because he'd still lost his beloved grandmother, seen her replaced by a delusional extremist in league with Larvis Vore? And then, in appreciation of his hard work, he'd been locked up for a month, interrogated like a terrorist?

Whatever the reason, the medal felt wrong to him; he didn't want it. But he realized there was something he *did* want, though he didn't understand exactly why.

In point of fact, it made no sense whatsoever. It seemed to contradict every logical, reasonable course he could take. It went against everything he'd been taught to aspire to.

But as soon as it came together in his mind, he felt sure of it. The anxious feelings faded away, replaced by confident certainty.

"No thanks." He handed the medal back to Perseid.

Perseid scowled. "You don't want the Order of Zedsemene?"

Scott shook his head. "I don't want any of it. The commission, the promotion, any of it."

"Solomon?" Donna looked up at him as if he were crazy.

Scott just kept shaking his head.

"Whoa." Perseid put his hands up in front of him, palms facing Scott. "Slow down there a minute, Sergeant."

"Not Sergeant," said Scott. "I'll settle for Solomon. Or Sol."

"You've just gone through a lot." Perseid lowered his hands. "Why don't you think it over for a while before giving us a flat-out 'no?'"

Scott shrugged. "Don't need to."

"But *we* need *you*," said Perseid. "We need all hands on deck to pick up the pieces from Redmageddon."

"And who knows when the Civil War will flare up again," added Rexis. "Our truce with the Rightfuls could go up in smoke at any time."

"You don't need me," said Scott.

"We *do*," said Perseid.

"You *don't*." Scott shook his head. "But *I* need *out*."

"Maybe it just *feels* that way right now," said Perseid. "Will you just please think it over? Consider it a favor to me. I'll keep these safe until then." Perseid slid the Zedsemene medal and the Diamondback insignia into one of his hip pockets.

"There's really no need, Major," said Scott.

"Call me Jack," said Perseid. "And just humor me, okay? The offers are open as long as you need them to be."

"I still don't understand," said Rexis. "Why would you turn down a promotion, a commission with the most elite fighting force in the quadrant, and the Order of Zedsemene? Are you fluxed in the *head*?"

"I don't know." The breeze picked up, and the swaying flowers caught Scott's eye. He watched them for a moment, bobbing in the morning sunlight, alive in a way he hadn't thought of for a very long time. "Maybe it's just time to move on. Time for a change."

"What about you?" Rexis asked Donna. "Are you buying into this?"

"We've got a medal and a promotion for you, too, you know," said Perseid.

Donna thought it over. "Can I take a rain check like Solomon?"

"Absolutely not," snapped Perseid. "It's now or never."

Donna looked stung. "Really?"

"Just kidding." Perseid laughed. "Take all the time you need."

Donna laughed, too. "In that case, I'm with Solomon."

"So what are the two of you going to do next?" asked Rexis.

"I don't know," said Scott. "Make it up as we go along, I guess."

Perseid nodded thoughtfully and rubbed the scar on his left cheek. "You said it's time for a change. A change of scenery, maybe?"

"Getting away from it all?" Scott grinned at Donna. "That sounds about right."

"Then maybe I can do something for you, after all." Perseid turned to Rexis. "I think these folks deserve a decent *ride*, don't you?"

Rexis pulled out her tablet and tapped away at the screen. "The *Sun Tzu* just got out of the shop."

"Maybe something a little smaller." Perseid laughed. "After all, there are only *two* of them."

Just then, the detention center door swung open, and Cairn stepped out, blinking and squinting.

"Make that *three*," said Scott.

"What do we have for *three* then?" asked Perseid.

"The *Sun Bin*'s out of the shop, too," said Rexis.

"Now you're talking." Perseid rubbed the scar around his throat. "Would you say they did all right with it the *first* time they took it out?"

"I guess so." Rexis shrugged. "If stopping Redmageddon and saving the Commonwealth from complete destruction count as 'all right.'"

"Then yeah." Perseid grinned. "Their track record with that one doesn't *totally* suck."

"Great." Rexis kept tapping the tablet. "Then I'll transfer control and have it moved off the *Sun Tzu*."

"She's all yours." Perseid squeezed Scott's shoulder and Donna's, too. "Go find that change of scenery and figure out what you're going to do next."

"We will." Impulsively, Scott reached out and squeezed Perseid's shoulder, too. "Thanks for the ship."

"You have a ship?" said Cairn as he ambled over, shading his eyes against the sun. "How about giving a guy a lift?"

Scott grinned. He hadn't seen Cairn once in the four weeks of his detention, and he was damn glad to finally see him now. "Which guy? And where to?"

"Come on." Cairn walked past and kept going, waving for them to follow. "It's a surprise."

CHAPTER 46

The Iridess Chasm on Tack was blazing hot, just as Scott remembered it from thirteen years ago. It took him and Cairn hours to cross, since they weren't running for their lives this time with Vore in hot pursuit.

Though, truth to tell, Scott couldn't help checking over his shoulder every so often to make sure Vore wasn't back there.

It was the first time Scott had returned to Iridess Chasm since his abduction and escape in the wilderness with Cairn. Scott had never had the desire to go back; he wouldn't have gone this time, either, if not for Cairn. He'd always secretly worried that somehow the place would grab hold of him again and never let go. He'd feared that he would die a second time and not be found and resuscitated.

But the fear wasn't with him this time. Maybe it was because of what he'd been through; maybe he'd conquered all the demons that had had their hooks in him for so long.

Whatever the reason, he felt like he was finally seeing the place for what it really was--a desolate land devoid of mind or malice, able to hurt him only as much as he would let it.

To a child fleeing a lunatic, Iridess had seemed like a living, malevolent thing. Now, the swirling dust devils and scampering red lizards seemed like natural phenomena and nothing more. The vulture-like scavengers circling overhead were instinct-driven parts of the food chain, not demons imbued with wicked sentience. Thorny bushes and stinging insects were nuisances, not magical menaces.

And Penitent Peak was just a rock formation, not a towering spire alive with dark power and a mind of its own.

As they approached that lofty crag, Cairn quickened his pace, racing toward it with single-minded intensity. Scott had to run to keep up--though he still wasn't sure why Cairn wanted to get there. Back on Archibald, he'd simply named the destination without explanation beyond saying it was for "old times' sake."

Even now, as Cairn reached the bottom of Penitent Peak, he offered no insight. He just kept moving, scrambling up the dusty slope. Scott did the same, still checking over his shoulder now and then.

As more time passed and the sun lowered in the sky, the two men continued to climb. Their footsteps from thirteen years ago were long gone, but they didn't need to see them to follow the same route they'd taken as children.

The crag steepened, slowing the climbers, but not stopping them. Hand over hand, foot after foot, they pulled and pushed themselves up the face of the peak, closing in on the destination they'd been seeking since they'd first stepped into the chasm that day.

Scott missed a foothold and slipped once, but clung

to the rockface and steadied himself. Cairn, a good ten meters above him, paused and looked down, then kept going, scuttling the rest of the way to the ledge they'd been aiming for all along. He swung himself up over the edge and disappeared, leaving Scott to cover the remaining distance on his own.

As he'd done thirteen years ago, Scott reached the ledge and boosted himself up onto it. Getting to his feet, he dusted himself off and took a look around.

The ledge was crescent-shaped, thirty meters across. Its widest section, in the middle, was ten meters from rockface to rim. That was where Cairn was sitting, legs dangling over the chasm, gazing into the sunset.

Scott started toward him, then felt a sharp pain in his chest and stopped. It passed quickly and left him wondering: was it the same as walking over his own grave? Because the spot on which he stood was the one where Vore had beaten him to death so long ago.

Another wave of pain flashed through him, and he gasped. The memory of the beating welled up in him, the echo of each blow landing with fresh and terrible immediacy.

He remembered Vore's black-lipped face howling over him like the visage of a god gone mad. He remembered what had seemed like dozens of fists pounding away at him, so fast and furious had been their rhythm. He remembered blackness rushing through him again and again, only to be driven away as Vore shook him by the throat.

He remembered it all with the obsessive clarity of a fanatic and sole survivor. For thirteen years, he had thought himself the only witness, the only one alive who knew the full truth of what had happened. He'd thought he was the only one who could look at Penitent Peak and see the bloodstains and terror that were invisible to everyone else.

But all along, though he hadn't known it, he had not been alone. There'd been someone else out there, hidden away, who shared the same vision.

Making his way across the ledge, Scott sat down beside him. For a while, they watched the sunset in silence, faces glowing with reflected light.

"Wow." Scott shook his head as the blazing orb of the sun sank through layers of scarlet, rose, and gold. "Who knew this place could be so beautiful?"

"People who weren't beaten to death here, I guess," said Cairn. "Or snatched away by a wicked freak."

"Just another reason to thank Vore." Scott cupped his hands around his mouth and shouted into the distance. "Way to spoil a *natural wonder* for us, asshole!"

Cairn smirked, but only a little. For once, he was the more low-key of the two.

"So what's up?" asked Scott. "Why are we here?"

"To get rid of this place," said Cairn. "Once and for all."

Scott managed a smirk of his own. "Blow it up, you mean?"

Cairn shot him a sidelong look. "Can we *do* that?"

"They should totally let us," said Scott. "We're *heroes*, aren't we?"

Cairn smiled. "I guess I'll settle for putting it behind me, then."

Scott looked at him, then went back to staring at the sunset. "Didn't you already do that? When you killed Vore on Bellerophon?" He elbowed Cairn in the side. "Which, by the way, nice work, man."

"You'd *think* that would do it, wouldn't you?" Cairn let

out a heavy sigh. "But I keep feeling like he still *has* me. Like I'll *never* get away."

"But he *doesn't*. And you *did*. You're *free*."

"Maybe I'll never be free, until I'm gone." Picking up a stone, Cairn flicked it into the chasm.

Scott swallowed hard. Was that why Cairn had wanted to come back to Penitent Peak? To end it all? To leap off the ledge the way he had thirteen years ago, but without Vore and his antigrav vest to pull him back into bondage?

"I didn't mind going over the side with Vore, you know," said Cairn. "It was actually a *relief*, until he stopped us from falling.

"After that, I just wanted to get away from him. I just wanted to go home. But then he put in the *bomb*." Cairn tapped the side of his head. "If I went anywhere near my family, anywhere near *anyone*, he said he would detonate it. So many people would *die*, all because of *me*.

"But after a while, that didn't matter so much. I *wanted* the bomb to go off. I *wanted* to die. *Anything* to *get away*." Cairn sniffed and turned his head so Scott couldn't see his face.

"I don't blame you. Nobody would." Scott's heart went out to him. He could hear the pain in his voice, the kind of pain you couldn't blow away with an army of Battlenauts. And he knew that it was up to him, as the only other person who'd been through the same gauntlet, to keep it from taking over. "I would've felt the same way."

"But guess what? It's *gone* now." Cairn turned back to face him and tapped the side of his head again. "No more *bomb*. The docs took it out in the detention center on Archibald. So I've got my *options* back, y'know?"

Scott knew exactly what he meant. "So what are you

going to do with them?"

Cairn shrugged. "I haven't really thought it through. Coming back here was as far as I got." Picking up another stone, he sent it spinning into the darkening sunset.

For a while, the two of them sat silently, watching the colors deepen and the sun disappear. Soon, all that was left of it was a pale glow fading into an indigo horizon.

Stars flickered into view all around them, like fistfuls of diamonds scattered over black velvet. Somehow, they looked just as breathtakingly crystal clear and lovely as they did when Scott was among them instead of under an atmosphere.

Soon enough, he would be up there again. Donna, who'd skipped the desert trek to visit family in Tisserie, would meet him at the ship and take him back into space. Free of Marines and Diamondbacks, done with duty and obligations, they'd be able to go anywhere they wanted. They'd be able to *do* anything they wanted.

So where did he want to go? What did he want to do? And what about Cairn?

They were questions Scott hadn't really considered until now. His goals had been more immediate: get out of detention, get off Archibald, get to Penitent Peak. But maybe now it was time to think more long-term, while all the options were still on the table.

"Are you ready to move on?" he said.

Cairn whipped another stone into the chasm. "How do you mean?"

"Move on," said Scott. "Start over."

"Start over?" Cairn tossed another stone.

"There couldn't be a better time," said Scott. "You're *free*. You can do anything you *want*. You can change your whole *life*."

"And do what? Who the hell's going to give someone like *me* a chance?"

Scott raised his hand.

Cairn shook his head and laughed sarcastically. "*You're* going to help me change my life? Have you seen your *own* life lately?"

"So help me *make* something of it. Help me turn it into something worthwhile."

"Good luck with that," said Cairn. "Your career's in the *crapper.* Your big-shot *grandma*, the most hated woman in the *universe*, is locked up *forever.* And if you think there aren't any more *Reds* out there, and they aren't *gunning* for you, think again."

Scott shrugged. "I've got a *ship*, don't I? And did you see what's tucked away in the hold, courtesy of Perseid?"

Cairn nodded. "Battlenauts."

"*Three* of them," said Scott. "A Mark VI, a CORE model, and a salvaged Red. Now what does that tell you?"

"You can make big bucks selling them?"

"What it *tells* us," said Scott, "is that we have everything we *need.* I've *seen* the way you handle a Battlenaut."

Cairn pitched another stone. "Vore forced me to learn. He rented me out as a mercenary."

"So we have three trained pilots." Scott held up three fingers on one hand. "We have three Battlenauts, one for each pilot's specialty: Red for you, Mark VI for me, CORE for Donna." He held up three fingers on the other hand. "And we have a ship." He pushed his hands together, interlocking the six fingers. "That's everything we need."

"For what?" said Cairn. "To become a team of mercenaries?"

"More like a strike force," said Scott, "but not for

hire. We'd help people with no one else to turn to. People victimized by the Vores of this galaxy. Doesn't that sound like something worthwhile? Like something that could make a difference?"

Cairn snorted. "Sounds more like a pipe dream. A real waste of time."

"So you're not in, then?"

"It's a *joke*," snapped Cairn. "People like Vore keep coming. You can never really make a difference."

"Are you saying you didn't make a difference on Bellerophon?" said Scott. "That *we* didn't make a difference?"

Cairn didn't answer.

"Maybe this is it," said Scott. "Maybe this is how you put it behind you. You stop it from happening to other people."

Still, Cairn remained silent. He reached for another stone, then held it in his hand instead of tossing it right away.

Scott looked up at the glittering stars. After everything he and Cairn had been through, they had come back to the same place. It was a place that had led them to tragedy before, but this time, Scott believed a better destiny awaited if he could convince Cairn to make the right move.

"Would you do it as a favor to a friend?" asked Scott. "Do you think you might give it a try?"

Cairn looked askance at him, then looked back down at the stone in his hand. He didn't say a word, but Scott thought he could sense the question between them: *Friend? You're my friend?*

Of course. That's how Scott would have answered if Cairn had asked the question aloud. *Of course I'm your friend.*

"So what do you say?" asked Scott. "Want to give it a shot?"

Cairn didn't answer, but he did close his hand around

the stone.

Scott sighed. "You're a tough nut to crack, you know that?"

"Shut the flux up," said Cairn. "I want to see the damn sunrise in peace."

"Sunrise?" Scott frowned. "That's seven hours away."

Cairn shrugged and tossed him the pebble. "You got something better to do?"

Scott smirked and leaned back, gazing up at the universe sprawling above him, resplendent in its glimmering vastness, filled with promise. There was so much potential out there, so many opportunities for a new and better life. At the thought of it, his heart pounded in his chest; he couldn't wait to get out there.

Tomorrow.

"Hell no." Scott grinned and lay back, folding his hands under his head. "Nothing better to do than this."

ABOUT THE AUTHOR

Robert Jeschonek is an award-winning writer whose fiction, comics, essays, articles, and podcasts have been published around the world. DC Comics, Simon & Schuster, and DAW have published his work. His young adult slipstream fantasy novel, *My Favorite Band Does Not Exist*, won the Forward National Literature Award and was named a Top Ten First Novel for Youth by *Booklist*. His cross-genre science fiction thriller, *Day 9*, is an International Book Award winner. He also won the Scribe Award for Best Original Novel from the International Association of Media Tie-in Writers for his alternate history, *Tannhäuser: Rising Sun, Falling Shadows*. He was nominated for the British Fantasy Award for his story, "Fear of Rain." Visit him online at www.robertjeschonek.com. You can also find him on Facebook and follow him as @TheFictioneer on Twitter.

NOW AVAILABLE FROM PIE PRESS:

BEWARE THE BLACK BATTLENAUT

BY ROBERT T. JESCHONEK

All-out war engulfs a distant quadrant of space. Hardcore warriors clash in high tech Battlenaut armor, pitting the ultimate fighting machines in epic struggles on a planetary scale. In the heart of this raging hell, the sleep-deprived Redeye squad fights harder than anyone. Pumped up on drugs, wired to the max, the Redeyes tear through enemy forces like berserk Vikings. But fatigue takes a toll, as the Redeyes start to see things that don't exist. And something that might exist after all--a terrible harbinger of doom, a legendary herald of the end of all things. Does the Black Battlenaut truly tower over the blood-soaked war zone? Is it a nightmare brought on by exhaustion, or an omen of infinite devastation? Either way, the Redeyes set out to stop it by any means necessary...even if their private war requires the ultimate sacrifice and more.

AND NOW, A SPECIAL PREVIEW OF BEWARE THE BLACK BATTLENAUT...

CHAPTER 1

"Looky there," said Swindle, the *leper*chaun on Grist Halcyon's shoulder. He pointed with a crumbling green finger at one of the Battlenaut's cockpit video screens, and Grist looked in that direction.

On the screen, Grist saw the barren, storm-swept surface of the rebel-held moon, Sangre. The latest flare of lightning revealed a towering black figure on the crest of the hill. At that instant, the very first instant he glimpsed it, Grist knew in his heart what it was even as he knew in his head it just wasn't possible.

The flare of light faded, and the black figure faded with it back into the night. When the next lightning struck a moment later, the hilltop was deserted.

"Begorra." One rotting nostril fell away from Swindle's leprous face. "It's *him*, ain't it, boyo?"

Grist blinked hard and shook his head. "Can't say." Just then, his arm burned as the automated hypodermic cuff strapped to his bicep shot a fresh jolt of go-juice into his system. A ring of lights around the forward viewport flashed in a pattern designed to reset his body's circadian rhythms.

Must've been about to nod off. Can't have that, can we? As the go-juice pumped through his arteries, Grist felt himself return to full alertness. The Battlenaut's sensors and computers had done their job again, intervening at just the right moment with just the right dose of meds to keep Grist awake and alert for yet another hour.

Grist licked his dry lips and checked the video monitor again. Lightning spiked nearby, revealing six soldiers in Battlenaut armor facing off on a rocky battlefield...but no sign of the dark figure from the hilltop.

Grist stabbed the comm button and spoke into his mic. "Hey, Freak. Ever hear of the Black Battlenaut?"

When he didn't get a reply, Grist looked at the button he'd just hit and realized it wasn't the comm at all. He was just about to punch the real comm button when the cockpit rocked from a powerful impact. It was enough to crack his helmeted skull against the headrest and snap him back to the reality from which he'd taken a brief vacation.

Fight. That's right. His hands flew back to the steering and weapons controls. *I'm in a firefight.*

I'm fighting a war here.

Sharon "Freak" Freemare laughed like a maniac as she cut loose her Battlenaut's main guns against the oncoming enemy. One slug hit home in a big way, punching through the enemy's armor and leaving a jagged, smoking hole at the top of one leg.

Still shrieking with laughter, Freak swung a laser around and opened up on the damage. Metal and plastic melted before the onslaught, and the enemy Battlenaut's leg gave way within seconds.

The damaged Battlenaut went down hard, flat on its face. The enemy soldier in its cockpit tried in vain to force the smashed war machine to get up and fight, but it was still lying in the mud when Freak marched her own Battlenaut over to meet it.

"Hey, traitor!" shouted Freak, though she knew the downed pilot couldn't hear her. "Special delivery from the *Redeyes* for ya!"

Freak used her lasers to disable the enemy Battlenaut's weapons systems. The whole time, the smell of baking bread was so strong in the cockpit that it made her stomach growl.

Why she smelled baking bread in the cockpit instead of the usual sweat and stink, she had no idea, but she didn't let it trouble her. Better just to soak it in like the smell of roses that had rushed over her moments earlier, or the incredible smooth feeling of silk that had rippled over her skin moments before that.

Better just to enjoy the ride.

Eyeballing the display on her visor, she located the other members of her squad. Lieutenants Grist and Pellucid formed two points of a triangle enclosing the battlefield, with Freak as the third point. Four enemy Battlenauts were trapped inside the triangle, three still standing plus the one she'd just brought down.

Freak cackled as she swung her Battlenaut toward a fresh target. *These bums are no match for the Redeyes.*

That was what Freak's squad called themselves: *Redeyes*, because they fought without rest. Computers monitored the alertness of this experimental squad and administered countermeasures, chemical and otherwise, to keep them awake and fighting. Such sleep deprivation techniques promised to limit downtime for deployed Commonwealth troops, giving them an edge in the ongoing civil war against the Rightfuls.

From Freak's point of view, the experiment was the biggest success of all time. She and the others had been awake for days on end, so long she'd lost count, and still they suffered no ill effects.

If anything, Freak felt better than ever. She'd never fought more fiercely or thought more clearly in her life.

Who knew insomnia could be so much fun?

ALSO BY ROBERT JESCHONEK

SCIFI MOTHERLODE

SIX SCIFI STORIES VOLUME 1

SIX SCIFI STORIES VOLUME 2

SIX SCIFI STORIES VOLUME 3

SIX SCIFI STORIES VOLUME 4

DAY 9

THE MASKED FAMILY

“Robert T. Jeschonek is a towering talent.” – Mike Resnick, Hugo and Nebula Award-winning author of the *Starship* series

"Robert Jeschonek is the literary love child of Tim Burton and Neil Gaiman—his fiction is cutting edge, original, and pulsing with dark and fantastical life." – Adrian Phoenix, critically acclaimed author of *The Maker's Song* series and *Black Dust Mambo*

www.ingramcontent.com/pod-product-compliance
Lightning Source LLC
LaVergne TN
LVHW040824090826
845145LV00001BA/82

9780692023358